THE CHILDREN OF NEVER

A War Priest of Andrak Saga

Christian Warren Freed

This is a work of fiction. Names, characters, businesses, places, events, locales, and incidents are either the products of the author's imagination or used in a fictitious manner. Any resemblance to actual persons, living or dead, or actual events is purely coincidental.
Copyright © 2020 by Christian Warren Freed

Cover design by Guisy
Cover copyright 2021 by Warfighter Books
Author Photograph by Anicie Freed

Warfighter Books supports the right to free expression and the value of copyright. The purpose of copyright is to encourage writers and artists to produce creative works that enrich our culture.

The scanning, uploading, and distribution of this book without permission is a theft of the author's intellectual property. If you would like permission to use material from the book (other than for review purposes), please contact warfighterbooks@gmail.com. Thank you for your support of the author's rights.

Warfighter Books
Holly Springs, North Carolina 27540
https://www.christianfreed

Second Edition: January 2021

Library of Congress Cataloging-in-Publication Data
Name: Freed, Christian Warren, 1973- author.
Title: The Children of Never/ Christian Warren Freed
Description: Second Edition | Holly Springs, NC: Warfighter Books, 2021.
Identifiers: LCCN 2021907712 | ISBN 9781734907513 (trade paperback)
ISBN: 9781736804407 (ebook)
Subjects: Epic fantasy | Fantasy | Paranormal Fantasy

Printed in the United States of America

10 9 8 7 6 5 4 3 2 1

ACCLAIM FOR CHRISTIAN WARREN FREED

HAMMERS IN THE WIND: BOOK I OF THE NORTHERN CRUSADE

"I love this book. This book hooked my attention on the first page and it was hard to put down. There is darkness in this book, you know something is going to happen so you keep reading to find out what. The author writes it so good, it's like you are there experiencing what the characters are. And I love it."

"I purchased this book to read to see if it would be suitable for my daughter to read. She is advanced in reading, but some books for kids older than her can be a little to much content wise. I think this one will work out great for her and she would enjoy it as much as I did. I'm glad I came across this book and can't wait to read the rest of the series."

WHERE HAVE ALL THE ELVES GONE?

"This story is fresh and a little tongue-in-cheek, a nice fantasy change of pace with twists here and there that make you have to keep on turning the pages."

"Christian Warren Freed is a very gifted, well-spoken author and his story took me in from page 1. His descriptions of situations, momentary happenings and his vivid characters of the world within the story made my fantasy run wild. As a reader, I felt like being part of the carefully woven net of this book."

THE DRAGON HUNTERS

"Excellently written. The author is able to really capture the stress, fear, and panic of life and death situations such as combat. Greatly looking forward to the next installment in the series!"

"Mr. Freed weaves the parts of this tale together smoothly, keeping the story moving at a good pace. He uses his own military background to paint powerful battle images and then he moves on. With only a little background, he makes the reader care about the members of the band - to worry about them and want them to do the 'right thing'. He adds depth to the characters through their actions and his dialogue is very realistic."

ARMIES OF THE SILVER MAGE

"Armies of the Silver Mage was a great read...any fan of Lord of the Rings or Game of Thrones will love this book. I'm looking forward to next book."

"The book is almost an homage to the great classics like Sword of Shanara and the Lord of the Rings. The author has cleverly used his past military and combat experience to make the battle scenes more realistic."

Other Books by Christian Warren Freed

The Northern Crusade
Hammers in the Wind
Tides of Blood and Steel
A Whisper After Midnight
Empire of Bones
The Madness of Gods and Kings
Even Gods Must Fall

The Histories of Malweir
Armies of the Silver Mage
The Dragon Hunters
Beyond the Edge of Dawn

Forgotten Gods
Dreams of Winter
The Madman on the Rocks
Anguish Once Possessed
Through Darkness Besieged*

Where Have All the Elves Gone?
Tomorrow's Demise: The Extinction Campaign*
Tomorrow's Demise: Salvation*
The Lazarus Men: A Lazarus Men Agenda
Coward's Truth: A Novel of the Heart Eternal*

A Long Way From Home: Memories and Observations From Iraq and Afghanistan

Immortality Shattered
Law of the Heretic
The Bitter War of Always
Land of Wicked Shadows
Storm Upon the Dawn

War Priests of Andrak Saga
The Children of Never

SO, You Want to Write a Book? +

*Forthcoming   + Nonfiction

For my fans. You know who you are.

ONE

Fent

Mist hovered over the near empty fields. Stands of cedar and black pine broke the monotony of what many considered the endless boredom of the grass plains. Pastures and farmlands stretched as far as a man might walk in a day and beyond. Folks here kept to themselves and preferred others to do the same.

Spring was just beginning, and the early bloom of wildflowers peppered the ground beneath the roiling mists. Tombstones and other crude burial markers filled the small field outside of the village of Fent. Generations were buried within the field's confines, though modernity demanded fresh bodies be burned atop a pyre so that their ashes might get to the next realm quicker than the slow rot the earth offered.

Still, the old ways, however antiquated, remained strong in many of the older generations still toiling. Their reward, that final rest, had yet to come, leaving them in the unenviable position of becoming the stewards of what once was. A gloomy task on the best of days. Not all the dead were given the flame. Many continued to be thrown into the long, cold sleep of the ground.

Dawn was breaking, the first thin tendrils of pale light stretched across the darkened skies. Roosters crowed. Farmers rose and readied for the long day. Had any been in the fields, they might have caught a glimpse of an old man, crooked and dressed in faded grey robes, stalking down the dirt road leading to the cemetery. He carried a small lantern that swung with every step. The Grey Wanderer some named him. Others simply chose a more apt name: The Soul Stealer.

Smiling as he went, the Grey Wanderer sniffed the air for the scent of those freshly dead. Some whispered he was once a king of men. Others suggested he had been a sorcerer of great power who'd made a deal with fell powers. Most didn't care; they avoided all mention of him. Wherever the Grey Wanderer went, bad things followed.

He paused at the cemetery gates and raised his lantern high. A wash of light fell over the tombstones, showing him what he'd come to find. Fresh earth cast over the recently deceased. His smile was thin and insidious. The Grey Wanderer began to whistle. It was a ghastly sound, unfit for mortal ears. A cry to the ones in the deep beyond whose very existence threatened the sanity of the masses.

Once he finished his task, the Grey Wanderer lowered his lantern and continued walking. He avoided passing through the sleepy village, choosing instead to disappear back into the mists of time and space. His work here was finished.

The ground shook at his passing. Fresh dirt slipped from the top of the mound. The tombstone, carelessly erected, toppled and broke. Hands, withered and clawed, punched free from their eternal tomb. They reached and dug, frantic to free their body. Rock and dirt cascaded away from the naked body as the once dead man pulled his head and arms from the ground.

Shoulder length hair the color of midnight had fallen over his face. Bits of wood and dirt fell away from his flesh. The once dead man held up his hands and blinked the grime away from his eyes. His flesh was riddled with damage where the worms and underground rodents had already begun their feasts. Bone glinted from numerous places in the fading dark. He stared at what he had become and cast his head back, uttering a primal scream.

Frantic, the once dead man shoved armfuls of dirt away, desperate to be free of his prison. His chest was covered in hair matted to his flesh. A red and black snake dropped from beneath his armpit. The once dead man worked furiously before being rewarded. He crawled and climbed free and collapsed beside the pieces of his tombstone. Memory lost, the once dead man peered to make out the name engraved upon the stone. Brogon Lord.

He had once been a man named Brogon Lord. That name, and the life associated with it, no longer held meaning, for he had died. This mockery of reanimated flesh was a far cry from the warmth of life. The panic subsided, and the once dead man began to think. Images born of random thoughts filled his mind. He watched events play out, an entire age born and died in a heartbeat. The once dead man knew what must be done. Who he once was no longer mattered. He once again had purpose.

Far off on the dying night, he heard whistling.

Barin and Covis ran through the back alleys. The two boys were determined not to be caught by the third of their group. Slipping between the lengthy strides of grumbling adults, they hurried away in an attempt at hiding that would ultimately end in failure. Fent wasn't an overly large village, often being confused by the duchy it was named for, and there were only so many prime hiding spots where one might feasibly be able to avoid detection.

Covis burst into laughs as he dashed beneath a stationary horse and kept running. Crates of fruit and vegetables lined the wall to his right.

"Stop laughing, Covis! That wasn't funny," Barin scolded as he took the extra effort of going around the horse.

Undaunted, the younger Covis kept running. He hadn't been discovered the last three times the boys on his street played. It was an claim of great pride for the young boy. No one had ever won four times consecutively. He kept running, knowing having Barin clinging to him would only hurt his odds. Covis liked Barin, but the thought of winning was all that was on his mind at this moment.

He ducked down a narrow side alley, barely three feet between buildings, and hid behind a pile of old garbage. The stench was raw, overpowering. Covis plugged his nose and mouth and tried not to throw up. Through watery eyes, he saw Barin rush past without looking. Covis broke into a wide grin and turned to continue down the alley.

A crow cawed from the nearest rooftop, startling the boy. Covis slowed, suddenly unnerved. Cold spread through the alley. He shivered as his flesh prickled. Worried, Covis decided to abandon his game. Let one of the others win. He was already a legend. There'd be other times to defend his title. Right now, he only wanted to go home to the safety of his mother's arms while the bad sensations faded into memory.

He was halfway down the alley when what he thought was a pile of trash rose and blocked the way. Covis skidded to a halt. His muscles refused to work, rebelling against the screams from his mind to turn and flee. Waves of energy funneled off the man, for what else could it be? Covis squinted and was rewarded with identifying a pair of eyes the color of ice glaring at him from behind a mask of coal black hair. An arm rose. Maggots dripped from the desiccated flesh. Covis gagged. A hand stretched forth to clasp around his throat. Covis knew only darkness.

Realizing he had wandered too far, Barin decided to turn back and head for more familiar parts of the village. Concerned for himself, it took the boy close to an hour before he remembered Covis. They couldn't both be lost. Could they?

"Covis! Where are you? I want to go home," he called.

The squeak in his voice echoed up and down the brick walls towering over him. Barin began to worry. It wasn't like any of the boys to disappear in the middle of their game for any longer than was necessary to win. He knew Covis was a master at this and wondered if his friend was secretly watching from the shadows.

"This isn't funny! Come out, Covis. The game is over," he called, a touch of anger lining his voice.

Random voices from the main avenue drowned out any other noise. Frustrated, Barin balled his fists and rounded the last alley. Shadows half-filled the passage, but he was able to make out small piles of old garbage and what looked like a boot. Barin swallowed his rising fear. The boot belonged to Covis.

"Covis?" he called.

He crept forward. There was no reason he could figure out that Covis would leave one of his boots. Close enough to touch it, Barin bent down. His eyes followed what looked like scuff marks dug into the dirt and stopped on three specks of a dark liquid. Blood. Alone and suddenly afraid, Barin backed out of the alley and ran for home.

Late spring nights were always cool to Lizette. A mother to a well-loved daughter, she stood on her porch with a blanket wrapped around her shoulders as she gazed at the stars. There was majesty up there. Another realm of possibility very few understood. She often wondered if those pinpricks of light were more than just that. Was there more in the night sky? A rumor circulated the lands, no doubt spread by the Collegium in the city of Beacon far to the west. Yet another place she'd only heard of.

Lizette had never left the duchy of Fent. In fact, she'd hardly been beyond the edges of the village of Fent. Twenty-seven long, hard years spent toiling away, first as a seamstress and now adding the duties of a mother. Life wasn't kind to people like her. People the nobility ignored and the powerful dominated. She often wondered who would notice if she was no longer around. Pointless to think about that, Lizette knew she was going nowhere until her daughter was a grown woman and on her own.

A smile warming her face at the thought of her daughter, Lizette turned from the stars and went to check on Tabith. She reminded her of her late husband. Her smile dimmed a bit. She walked softly through the quiet, dark house, stopping by the fireplace to swing the teapot over the flames. A mug of hot tea was the perfect remedy for the cool spring night.

Their cottage was meager by every consideration, but it boasted having three rooms. Few families enjoyed the luxury of having separate bedrooms for their children. Lizette made it a point of pride among her friends. The living room flowed into a small kitchen. They had an outhouse in the back yard, complete with wash basin. She kept it as clean as possible, no small feat, all things considered. Tabith did her best to ensure her mother had work every time she came home from her actual paying job on Merchant Row.

Lizette listened to the flames cackle, relishing the sound of what she attributed to peace, before going to check on Tabith. She took only two steps before jerking to a stop. It is said that mothers were more in tune with their surroundings when children entered their lives. Lizette knew every crevice and shadowed corner of their home, from the busted shutter on the kitchen window that slammed into the wall every time the wind gusted, to the creaking board three steps in from the front door. She also knew that Tabith was adamant about closing her door each and every night. A door that was now cracked an inch open.

Crossing swiftly, Lizette reached for the wooden knob and pushed. The door swung open slowly, allowing darkness to creep out. A niggling sensation crawled over her flesh. Lizette closed her eyes and took a deep, steadying breath. Her mind tried to rationalize her unease, that her worry was a figment of an overactive imagination born from the whispers of missing children around town.

Peasants were always starting baseless rumors when the need to alleviate boredom arose. Lizette paid no mind to any of that, until now. Heart hammering, she entered Tabith's room and crossed to the edge of the bed, whispering her daughter's name. She reached down and felt… nothing. The bed was empty. Tabith was gone.

Lizette's screams were heard across the whole village of Fent.

TWO

Fent

Baron Einos awoke to unfamiliar sensations. Cold, almost unbearable, filled his bedchambers. Winter was a memory and spring well underway. This southern duchy was well south of the northern ice flows and far enough east of the Barbacus River to avoid the heavy winds. A thick blanket and small fire in the hearth were more than sufficient for keeping Einos warm throughout the shortening nights.

The Baron wiped the crud from the corners of his eyes, yawned, and sat up. His bearskin blanket fell away, exposing his naked chest. Young for one of the ruling class, Einos was broad across the shoulders and slabbed with muscle. His sand colored hair draped across his shoulders. Bright green eyes scanned the chamber.

His wife, still sleeping, shifted beside him and exhaled deeply. Einos resisted the urge to rouse her, at least until he was satisfied nothing was amiss. Not finding anything of concern in the immediate area, he slipped from the bed and donned a thick robe that fell to the floor. The fire had gone out, leaving the chamber in darkness. Frowning, Einos reached for the short sword he kept beside the bed. Fent was a relatively peaceful duchy, but one does not rise to power without creating enemies capable of extreme violence.

He took a step, then a strange noise froze him in midstride. Einos gripped his sword tighter. "Who goes?"

The sound of sobbing returned. Einos frowned, certain he'd heard a child. There were numerous children in the keep, though none his own. Aneth, his wife of nearly a decade, was heavy with child and due by the end of spring. He suspected the draft coming through the cracks in the walls provided the strange sounds, but one could never be too cautious.

Einos fumbled for a match and lit the candle nearest his bed. Soft light turned his bedchamber into a shadowed realm. Einos remained still, listening against the dark. His efforts were rewarded by uncontrollable sobbing coming from the far corner. Sword in one hand, candle the other, the Baron of Fent took a step closer to the sound.

His exposed toes kicked the chamber pot, spilling old piss over his foot. Einos snarled a curse and kept going as the sobbing intensified. A wall of light crept across the stone floor until it reached the huddled figure of a young child. Einos cocked his head as he tried to get a clear view of the face. Knees drawn with arms wrapped around them, the child, a girl by the length of her hair, had her face buried.

"Child, why are you here? Who let you in?" he asked, his normally rough voice softened so as not to frighten her further.

The sobbing increased as the girl lowered a fist and began pounding on the floor.

Einos, concerned, set the candle on the nearest table and crouched. "There is no need for that. You are safe here. Tell me your name, child."

Curls fell over her shoulders as the young girl lifted her head and turned to face him. Einos tripped and fell backwards as he gazed upon what remained of her face. Both eyes were gone. Dried blood streaked down her cheeks.

She reached a hand for him and cried, "Why did I have to die?"

The girl screamed. The candle flickered, then went out, leaving the lord of Fent alone in the darkness. Einos scrambled back and managed to light the candle after several tries. When he cast the light into the corner, he found only stone. The girl, if she had ever been, was gone.

"I know what I saw, Kastus," Einos glared.

Fent's constable folded his arms and snaked a long finger up to scratch his chin. "Forgive me, Baron, but I do not seek to name you a liar. It is just …"

Einos raised a weary hand. "I know, this whole affair sounds strange. I would doubt it myself had I not been there."

"But an apparition?" Kastus asked.

"In my bedchamber. Kastus, I have never been one to give in to wild beliefs of the supernatural, but I know what I saw, and I tell you, it was a small girl missing her eyes." He shuddered as her screams returned to haunt him.

Kastus nodded thoughtfully. "If what you claim is true, and I will not be the fool to debate you further, we are left with a greater problem."

"That being?" Einos was reluctant to ask. He wasn't sure he could handle more problems, given the current situation.

The constable tapped his fingers on the polished wooden desk between them. "We've a killer in our midst."

Einos sighed, having already considered this. "Have your people scour the duchy. Every village and farm. The only way we are going to get to the bottom of this is by questioning everyone."

Kastus almost balked at the thought of speaking to the few thousand citizens belonging to Baron Einos. A daunting task on the best of days, an impossible one on any other. "Baron, we do not have the time for that and …"

He shut his mouth in midsentence and looked away. Einos resisted the urge to throttle his second in command.

"Speak, Kastus. You know how I feel about withholding information," Einos ordered.

Clearing his throat, Kastus began, "There have been reports of missing children over the last few days. Until now, I found no reason to take them seriously. Children often run away, intent on making a name for themselves for this reason or that. I recall doing so when I was a lad. It is a right of passage of sorts."

"Of sorts?" Einos questioned. His stomach twisted as his mind busily concocted links between murders and disappearances. Even beyond these suspicions, Fent was a land embroiled in dark mystery.

Kastus shifted uncomfortably. "Einos, you have my vow that I will see this matter through."

"I've no doubt, but we must also look at preventing further incidences. We cannot afford to let this duchy suffer further loss," the Baron cautioned.

Fent was a small duchy, nowhere near as prominent as the merchant center of Mistwell, a city floating high above the land in the mountains far to the west, nor as populated as Thorn, where the various rulers met in council annually. Einos had only a few hundred men at arms and their retainers under his command. Many of those knights were selected to help defend the lands at Castle Andrak during the Burning Season when the Omegri sought to reclaim the world.

If pressed, Einos figured he could arm another five hundred peasants. So far south of the Indolense Permital, he had no need to maintain a standing army. Arming the peasantry was a measure of last resort, perhaps enough to send his people into revolt. Three generations of his family had ruled Fent, each increasing the prosperity of the duchy, while developing strong ties with the people. A call to arms over his perceived inability to halt the sudden increase in deaths and missing persons would likely see him at the end of a short rope.

"Kastus, how many children have been reported missing?" he asked.

"Several. I am not sure. We did not take the reports seriously at first."

"Are we the only duchy being assailed?"

Kastus had no answer. "In truth, I've not thought on it."

"Dispatch men to the nearest cities. I want to know if this is more widespread than just Fent," Einos said.

"You're suggesting all of this is being conducted by more than one person?" Kastus asked. He felt uneasy with the direction the conversation was going.

"That's the problem," Einos threw his hands out. "I have no idea."

"There is another option," Kastus offered.

Einos shook his head, knowing what the Constable meant. "No, I will not summon them unless there is no other choice. We have more than enough resources to handle this situation. I want patrols increased in every village. There is no point in attempting to deceive the population, since they are the ones reporting each incident. Bring them in, get them on our side, and we'll drive out this killer."

"I'll draft the orders at once."

"Oh, and Kastus, I want to meet with some of the families. Hearing what happened from their mouths might provide us with additional information," Einos said.

Kastus rose, collected his jacket, and left. There was much to be done, and if his suspicions were correct, not long before the next incident.

The Baron of Fent watched his closest advisor and friend depart, waiting until the latch clicked before sinking back into his chair and curling his fingers around the small crystal glass half filled with amber liquor. *Ghosts. Disappearances. Murder. How much worse can it get?*

The cemetery outside of the village of Fent contained generations of the duchy's citizens. It was a place of comfort to remember those lost, just as much as a place of sadness for those unable to get over their grief. Caretakers meticulously groomed the lands, weeding between graves and ensuring no vandalism occurred, or if it did, was cleaned up before any family members returned for their next visit.

So it was, the reopened grave was discovered shortly after sunrise. Fresh dirt was strewn carelessly over the surrounding area, mixed with the remnants of the cheap pine coffin. Both men, aged enough to have seen a fair share of life, stared down into the hole.

"Grave robbers," Lex murmured. "Ain't seen this in a long while."

Bert rubbed the iron grey stubble covering his chin. "Nasty business, this. We should tell the Baron."

"Tell him what? That there's an empty grave?" Lex shook his head. "Not much point in ruffling his ire without any proof of wrongdoing."

"There's an empty grave. Of a freshly laid corpse, I might add. How much more proof do you need?" Bert all but shouted.

Lex spit, "More than this. We got no signs of the body and got no proof of who done it."

Sighing, Bert removed his worn cap and wiped his forehead. "There's been whispers of the Grey Wanderer moving about the countryside."

"Shhh, you damned fool! Do you want *his* attention?"

Bert glanced around. The Grey Wanderer was not a name to be thrown lightly around. Legend said he'd stalked the lands since the beginning of time. None knew his purpose or which side of the battle between light and dark he landed on. All they knew was that his presence brought turmoil, and he was an unwelcome visitor in the lands of men. If the Wanderer was responsible for digging up the grave, Bert didn't want to know.

The old man squinted at the broken tombstone. "Who do you suppose he was?"

Lex looked up from the grave. "Who?"

"This Brogon Lord. Must have been important for *him* to bring him back," Bert answered. "He's got a sword beneath his name. Makes him a knight of sorts, don't it?"

"Makes him someone else's problem, Bert. We go to the Baron. I want no part of this and I ain't coming back here until we get some security. There's ill all about us."

For once, Bert was inclined to agree. One man was already called from the grave. What was to say another wouldn't follow the next night? The caw of a lone crow in the branches of a white oak overlooking the cemetery chilled their flesh.

THREE

Fent

Lizette paced across the open assembly hall of the castle. Her hands were red from constant wringing while she waited. She'd never been to Castle Fent before, much less been summoned by the Baron. The shock of having armed guards banging on her door was almost enough to drag her from the depression of losing her daughter. Mother's grief threatened to render her useless, even as anger smoldered deep inside.

The desire to find Tabith and hold her once more was strong, as was the rising propensity toward lashing out indiscriminately. Lizette knew she was broken. Knew and seemed unable to do anything about. She barely ate. Slept only when her body couldn't keep going. She'd lost weight and hadn't bathed since that fateful night. What remained of her life was a shattered ruin of the promise of what once was.

Now she stood in the hall, surrounded by heraldry and banners representing generations of family leadership and past glories. Tapestries of rich fabrics collected from across the world decorated the high, arched walls. She scarcely glanced at suits of polished armor worn by the current Baron's forbearers or the various statues and busts of important figures in Fent's history situated around the room on alabaster stands.

The click-clack of boots striking the stone floor announced the presence of the constable. Lizette watched Kastus approach. Once she might have been impressed with all of this. Those days were gone. Life had lost all luster. All that she was had been tied to her precious daughter and that had been taken from her. Lizette tried to believe there was hope that Tabith lived. That she was alone and waiting for people to rescue her. The thought suddenly proved too much, and all Lizette's hope crashed into despair.

"The Baron will see you now," Kastus announced from halfway across the hall. His baritone voice rumbled like thunder, startling her.

Lizette didn't know whether to bow or nod. Confused, she mumbled a greeting and remained awkwardly in place.

Kastus had witnessed similar more times than he remembered. Being in the presence of royalty for the first time normally proved awkward for most citizens. He gestured for her to follow. There was a routine about odds facts and random snippets of information concerning the history of Fent he was supposed to give visitors, but Kastus felt this particular meeting did not call for conventional protocol. He wisely decided silence was prudent.

They found Baron Einos standing in front of his formal desk. A small fire cackled in the hearth to the right. Centered on the round pedestal in the middle of the room was a beaker filled with dark red wine and two goblets. Lizette took in the grandeur of the seat of power and felt something akin to awe. This one room held more wealth than her entire home.

"I am Baron Einos. It is a pleasure to meet you, lady," he began.

This time, Lizette remembered her manners and curtsied. "Baron, the honor is mine, though I wish different circumstances allowed for our meeting."

He gestured to the chair nearest her. "Please, sit. We have much to discuss and I wish to hear from you what has happened to your family."

Lizette pushed down the creases of her dress and fumbled uncomfortably under his gaze. "I ... I do not know where to begin."

Taking a seat across from her, Einos asked, "Perhaps you will allow me to begin. I awoke to a small girl crying in the corner of my bedchamber. When I reached for her, she turned and asked why she needed to die. Both of her eyes were missing."

She felt her throat constrict. Could it be? Tears brimming her eyes, Lizette asked, "What did she look like?"

"Small. Her brown hair went down her back. She was dressed in a flowered dress," he answered. The last detail felt oddly specific considering he'd barely glimpsed her before she vanished.

The walls broke and Lizette began crying. She pushed her hands against her eyes and released nights of pent-up emotion. Her body trembled as pain racked her. "Tabith ..."

The name came out as a wail.

Einos was unsure how to proceed. He'd seldom been forced to provide comfort during times of extreme duress. To have one of his people sitting before him, crying uncontrollably, left him unsure what to do.

"Where is she?" Lizette managed.

Einos jerked back. "Gone. She disappeared before my very eyes."

Lizette lifted her head. Tears streaked her cheeks and her eyes were red. "What do you mean? How could a child disappear?"

"I ... I do not know," Einos stammered. "One moment she was there and the next I was alone. Do you know her?"

She nodded. Golden hair swished over the fabric of her dress. "She was my daughter. Is my daughter. I have not seen her for days. Are you saying that Tabith is a ghost? That she ... she is dead?"

Einos held up his hands to calm her. "I cannot say why I saw her or why she disappeared. I can only tell you there was a little girl."

"How many children have gone missing, Kastus?" Einos asked.

"Seventeen," came the reply.

Einos winced. Seventeen innocent lives stolen, and perhaps ended. "How has this occurred without any of us knowing?"

"Baron, there is more at work here than we thought. The caretakers of the cemetery arrived a short time ago. They have something to report," Kastus informed.

"Why am I only now being made aware of this?" the Baron demanded.

Unused to his judgment being questioned, Kastus cleared his throat. "Your appointment with the lady Lizette took precedence."

"I am no lady," she corrected, a hint of anger mixing with the pain in her voice.

Einos gently asked, "Lizette, I would very much like to continue this conversation. Will you wait while I speak with the caretakers?"

"I will wait, Baron," her reply was terse. The overwhelming need to learn Tabith's fate compelled her to remain. Einos' confirmation, if what he said was true, of finding her ghost in the dark of night, intrigued Lizette as much as it horrified her.

Two timeworn men entered, covered with stains and dirt and looking out of place among the surroundings of Assembly Hall of the Castle of Fent. Lizette felt her knees trembling as she waited to hear what they would tell the Baron.

Einos wiped his brow and stared down into the pit of the empty grave. The rational part of his mind demanded a logical explanation. Wild animals, perhaps grave robbers trying to collect on an easy score before moving on. Einos wanted to believe there was no agent of the supernatural at work in his duchy. Signs were pointing to the contrary, yet the words refused to climb from his throat.

Lizette, overcoming her initial fear, knelt beside the grave, running her fingers over a sliver of coffin. "Every child grows up with stories. Tales inspired to maintain a healthy fear, but I never imagined them to hold truth. Has no one seen him?"

"Most likely not," Kastus answered. "The Wanderer isn't prone to allowing folk to spy on his business."

Einos cast a dubious look. The constable shrugged off. "Leastwise that's what I've been told. It makes sense, if you ask me. Any man who raises the dead is not likely to walk easily among the living."

There was no argument for that and neither Einos nor Lizette bothered. The caretakers leaned on the ends of their shovels, whispering. They had told their story and barring the return of the missing corpse, were ready to fill the hole in. Einos, while unconvinced of the shared versions of what might have happened, knew that filling the grave before villagers came by was the best thing for the duchy. Dealing with the parents of seventeen missing children was another matter. One he wasn't at all prepared to deal with.

As they each stood looking into the empty grave, Kastus blurted, "Do you suppose this Brogon Lord has anything to do with the missing children."

Lizette dropped the coffin sliver. "Absolutely. How long has this man been … removed?"

Bert and Lex suddenly grew uncomfortable. Lex opened his mouth but Bert gave him a sharp elbow.

Einos lost patience. "Enough of this. How long has Brogon Lord been missing?"

Lex dropped his head. "Bout four days, Baron. We wasn't sure what happened and didn't want to cause a panic. Getting the facts first, o'course."

"You mean to tell me that anyone and everyone could have walked by and seen this for the past four days?" Einos was furious. "Four days! The entire countryside from Fent to Calad Reach might know by now! I should have you both flogged."

"Please, Baron. We wasn't doing anything illegal or nothing. We just didn't know how to handle a man risen from the grave," Lex pleaded. "We just wanted to make sure is all."

Kastus moved between the Baron and the caretakers, unsure how Einos would react. He exhaled only after the Baron's shoulders sagged.

"Kastus, I want every parent with a missing child brought to me at once. Then find out about this Brogon Lord. Learn everything about him. Perhaps that will give us some clue as to what has happened," Einos ordered.

"I can help," Lizette offered.

Einos held up a hand. "You have helped enough, Lizette. Let us handle this."

Her fists were small but when placed on her hips, she presented a fierce figure. Even Einos flinched.

"Listen to me, Baron Einos. My daughter is one of the missing and if what you say is accurate, dead. I am just as much a part of this as any of you and I will not be denied the opportunity to avenge her."

Impressed and rebuked, Einos relented. "Very well, very well. Perhaps you can help with the families."

Lizette's face remained hard, etched in grief. She nodded her reply.

Einos glared at Bert and Lex. "You two, fill in this grave and fix the tombstone. I don't care if Lord is interred or not. The people need know no different. Am I clear?"

"Perfectly."

"Sire!"

Satisfied, Einos brushed off his hands. He, Kastus, and Lizette walked away from the empty grave, each lost in thought, none piecing the puzzle together. The sudden rash of missing children must have significance or else the culprit was a deviant with the taste for children. Einos did not recall the name Brogon Lord and that disturbed him. The location of the grave and the sword cut into the tombstone under his name suggested Lord had been of some importance. Perhaps even a knight. Why then didn't he know the name?

Einos reluctantly allowed his thoughts to consider Brogon having been mistakenly thought dead and buried. Ridiculous, but still. Einos feared the number of missing children might be enough to break his people. *If they are a sliver as disturbed by this as I am, recovery will be long in coming. I only hope Kastus solves this mystery before mass hysteria sets in.*

Einos knew that it all meant nothing if the Grey Wanderer was indeed more than myth. His mother once indulged his inquiries and explained that none knew the Wanderer's purpose. She said he was an instrument left over from a more violent time when gods roamed the world and myths grew around them. Magic was real, else how could the entire city of Mistwell float above the ground without fear of falling? A floating city he could deal with. The Grey Wanderer was an entirely different thing.

FOUR
Fent

The cave was dank, reminiscent of the eternal confines of the grave. Mold grew on the walls and in dark corners. The air was musty with the smell. Cobwebs sprawled across the rough stone surface, their creators long dead. Moss and windblown leaves carpeted a large part of the sloping floor. Bones from random creatures littered the area, remnants of meals past. The low hills south of the village of Fent were littered with hundreds of such places. Places for those who wanted to remain unseen.

Brogon Lord took comfort in the quasi-darkness. His unexpectedly short time spent in the cold forever of death inspired new appreciation for the merits of life, even in solitude. There, alone in his cave, beyond the mortal concerns governing the world, he closed his eyes in thought. Memories were blurred. He knew who he was, rather who he'd once been. What he was and what he'd been doing when death came for him, remained obscured. Not that either mattered. His time spent in the grave, where a deserved rest from his sins was assured, was ended.

Fragments of images struck between his eyes with a blinding pain. Brogon jerked back, his hand flying to his face to quell the agony. He watched a sword pierce thin leather armor and then there was an unstoppable flow of blood. Cold. Dark.

"I remember," he whispered.

Brogon dropped his hand to his side. Dirt coated fingertips traced the outline of the wound. *Why am I dead?* There was no answer. Death had come and taken him beyond. The greater mystery was who had returned him to the world above and for what purpose. He felt no mortal feelings, no hunger, no anger, no sorrow. He had no will of his own and no bodily needs. He occasionally snatched rodents or birds to eat, purely from forgotten instinct, rather than to fill a hungry stomach.

The darkness provided scant comfort from the ravages of his humiliation. Brogon dipped his fingers into the wound, oddly disturbed by the cold, necrotic feel of his flesh. He attempted to piece the past back together. Armor. He saw the boiled leather plate armor. Only soldiers wore this. Soldiers or sell swords. Brogon didn't know whether he had been an honorable man or not, but the armor suggested he made his way with a sword. Fitting he died by a sword.

Crouched under the low ceiling, Brogon made his way to the mouth of the cave. A slight breeze touched his face, prompting him to close his eyes in a moment of bliss. A forgotten pleasure? An indulging of fleshly delights? The burning began again. A now all too familiar itch buried deep in his nervous system. It was a song, a haunting sound driving him to perform foul deeds. The masters called, and he was helpless to resist. Pulled out of the cave by the sound, the creature that was once Brogon Lord began the hunt again. Dark had fallen. There was work to be done.

"You've barely touched your food."

Einos continued to stare out the ceiling high window to his right, his mind sorting through the confessions and examples of what could only be described as atrocities occurring within the borders of his duchy. How had this escape his attention for so long? That such evil would befall his people seemed inconceivable. More so, why now and to what purpose? Murderers were known to range across the lands. That much was no secret. He'd caught drippings of information mentioning such men and generally, their ultimate demise. But what was happening in Fent?

"Einos?"

The sound of his name jerked him back to reality. He glanced across the table at his wife. He had no doubt she knew some of what was happening. Aneth was a smart woman, perhaps smarter and wiser than he. Einos didn't know how much to tell her or where to begin. Events were picking up with surreal ferocity.

"My apologies, but my mind has been troubled for some time," he excused.

The arch of Aneth's eyebrow suggested a lack of surprise. "Truly? What purpose have I as Baroness of Fent, if my husband refuses to express his concerns to me? I am not an ornament to be worn on your arm in public, Einos."

"I know, my sweet, but this is … different," he said.

Einos would never know what compelled him to tell Aneth everything, but he did. He talked and she listened as they spent the rest of their evening in horror with no small amount of tears as he relayed every detail of what he knew. The roast pheasant cooled. The bread hardened, but the wine they drank, as each struggled to make sense of what he was describing. Aneth's arms wrapped protectively around her stomach holding their child.

Her questions went largely unanswered, for he had no answers. For how a man could rise from the grave to murder innocent children. Or how seventeen children had already disappeared. Einos confessed his feelings of failure, only to be scolded for what Aneth termed brash foolishness. He was the Baron of a small duchy and expected to act to the level of his station.

"I do not know what to do next," he admitted.

Aneth reached for his hand. She ran her fingertips over the silky hairs thoughtfully. "We are not equipped to combat the supernatural, Einos. There is little choice in my mind."

"Why should they concern themselves with our business? They spend their days warding the world from the Omegri. Our problems are our own, Aneth."

"Nonsense. What other purpose do they serve other than the protection of all people?" Aneth asked.

Einos sighed. He knew she was right. They were the only viable option, but it was his stubborn pride preventing him from admitting it. His failure to protect his people left him depressed.

"What does Kastus say?" Aneth asked.

Einos snorted a laugh. "He is against outside intervention. Lizette however urged me to send a messenger from the first."

"Perhaps our grieving mother is wiser than we give her credit for. Do it, Einos. Summon the war priests. They have magic and the necessary tools to stop the creatures of The Grey Wanderer," Aneth's voice turned cold at the mention of the old man, as if invoking his name was a summons.

Einos felt a cold draft creep down his nape, though whether from the wind or his rising imagination, he didn't know. His mind was locked in turmoil. Asking the war priests to come was admitting failure. Fent may be among the smaller duchies but he'd ruled with integrity, always looking to the needs of his people first. Without them, he was a mere figurehead in an aging castle.

However, if he did nothing and continued on the same course, the population would rebel. Not out of disloyalty but from fear. Seventeen children he presumed were dead and there was no foreseeable end. Unrest was already growing. Commerce slowed. Parents kept their children close by. Armed vigilantes roamed the streets against Kastus's orders. They were disbanded as quickly as the true soldiers discovered them. None of that made Einos' decision any easier.

"If I send for them, there is the very real possibility of them assuming command," he cautioned. "Are you prepared to live under their governance?"

Aneth laughed, a golden song bright and encouraging. "My love, the war priests are not concerned with the village of Fent. They have more important matters to attend."

The war priests were known the world over without actually being known. What occurred in their mystic keeps, segregated from the rest of the world, was kept secret from the public. Though the priests were often spotted roaming the countryside, very few of the everyday citizenry had any interaction with them. Many considered the Order dangerous, providing the basis of Einos' hesitancy.

"Perhaps, though I do not know if I have the courage to invite them in," Einos admitted. He felt embarrassment for the admission.

"Einos, what other choice is there?" Aneth asked. "We cannot continue losing our children. Send the messengers to Castle Andrak."

His head dropped. The last vestige of resistance crushed. Aneth patted his hand and said, "Now, husband, we must eat. There are difficult times ahead of us and we need out strength."

Kastus and Lizette entered the meeting chamber side by side. Einos no longer found it odd, for the pair was oddly inseparable. More, she walked with newfound purpose and an impressive confidence matched by few in his command. Eyes once filled with sorrow, now were filled with steel. He wondered if her loss had broken her. No person could deal with the knowledge that their child had been stolen from their home in the middle of the night by a man risen from the grave without breaking.

"Baron," Lizette said with a small curtsy.

"Please, be seated," Einos said.

Kastus remained standing as the Baron began.

"My lovely wife has helped clear the fog in my mind. Kastus, as much as it pains me to admit, we do lack the resources necessary to stop this evil menacing Fent. I have decided to summon the war priests."

His final words echoed across the stone walls. Einos watched his friend and Lizette, studying their reactions to his decision. Lizette straightened, her head rising slightly in approval. Kastus, predictably, remained apprehensive. Like Einos, he felt personal responsibility for events in Fent. Any failure on the Baron's part was inflated tenfold for the Constable.

"There must be another way," Kastus protested. He knew the rumors and they terrified him. Magic was thing for other races, not the frail hands of man.

Einos shook his head. "I have looked at this problem from every angle, and I fail to find a viable option. The coming of the Grey Wanderer changes much, my friend. We are not equipped to combat the supernatural."

"I agree with your decision, Baron," Lizette said. "Enough time has already been wasted, and if by calling on the war priests we are able to prevent another family from losing their child, I fail to see why we should delay."

Einos regarded her a moment longer than necessary. Timid and lost when she first entered his presence, Lizette was growing into a strong personality. Provided she continued her transitional development, Einos saw her assuming a permanent role among his core leadership.

"They are not to be trusted," Kastus reinforced his previous statement. "How many instances of these priests actually helping people are recorded? Yet, they demand subservience to fight faceless creatures none of us in this room have seen. We have enough men at arms to find this Brogon Lord and return him to the grave."

Einos wanted to slam his head into the table. "Kastus, finding Brogon and killing him–again–isn't the problem. We must learn the reason the Wanderer chose to come to Fent and we must find out what is being done with our children."

"The latter seems simple enough." Kastus remained defiant.

Unwilling to enter a debate, Einos winced and pinched the bridge of his nose. In a low voice he said, "Messengers will be dispatched today. In the meantime, I expect you to increase patrols throughout the duchy. Killing Brogon Lord is not your priority, Kastus. Protecting the children is."

Scowling, the Constable asked, "If my men happen across him?"

"I want him captured and brought to me," Einos ordered. Despite contrary evidence, he clung to hope that at least some of the missing children still drew breath. Vanity was ever the torment of good men, however.

Satisfied for the moment, Kastus softened his stance.

Lizette took advantage of the silence. "Baron, the first of today's families have arrived."

There had been a time, a mere week earlier, when his days consisted of relatively pointless meetings and unending boredom. Oh how he wished for those days to return.

FIVE
Castle Andrak

The alabaster walls of Castle Andrak stretched up from the depths of the world to touch the sky. They glowed with built in power. Built at the end of an all but forgotten peninsula on the far eastern coast, Andrak was not only a place of importance but one of constant battle and servitude. Men and women from across the duchies volunteered to stand the walls against the oppressing night. It was a thankless task, void of glory or reward. Life and death forever warred upon the ramparts.

Andrak was old. Almost as old as the world itself. Time had lost the truth of the original builders, though legends claimed golden godlings descended from the skies to construct the six sided wonder in a single night. More conventional theorists claimed it was built from the sweat of captured slaves over the course of a century. The one thing scholars agreed on was that Andrak was one of six castles built along the same lay line circling the globe. Their purpose was obvious; keep the Omegri from returning from the void and bringing the world to utter chaos and despair.

A massive tower loomed over the center of the courtyard. The current Lord General of the war priests occupied the very top where he could watch each day's battle unfold. Some said he was a necromancer, others a powerful sorcerer. Only the Lord General knew for sure and he was not a man given to prolonged conversation. War priests patrolled the outer wall, resplendent in their pale blue armor and snow-covered cloaks. Silver crosses decorated their chests, matched by larger versions on the alloy shields each war priest carried.

Guard towers built into each of the six corners housed spare weapons and armor. On the worst nights, the defenders could come in and get a hot cup of soup or coffee to ease the sufferings nature threw at them. There was, however, a curious lack of seating. None took their jobs more seriously than the war priests. They suffered so that others might enjoy.

Sky blue banners emblazoned with the mighty gryphon, a symbol of power and righteousness, waved proudly on the morning winds. Despite the proximity to danger, the war priests lived under the simple yet proud motto, "fear no darkness." A more fitting example of courage was not to be found.

Lord General Rosca had worn the blue for more decades than he remembered. A lifetime of service to the light, to the Purifying Flame buried deep within the hallowed walls. His body bore the scars of numerous battles and close calls. His face was lined and weathered. Life at Andrak was harsh in the best conditions. Time and age conspired to place more weight than he cared for around his waist and neck, without stealing any of his martial prowess. Rosca was the definition of a hard man.

He sat before the modest fire in his private quarters in his favorite chair, high backed and cushioned to relieve some of the day's stress. In his right hand was clenched an unrolled parchment. The messenger waited in the dining hall. The Burning Season was still some months away and Andrak was quieted by the lack of activity. Rosca reread the message for what felt like the tenth time before closing his eyes.

Rosca couldn't accept what he read. Couldn't believe that *they* were loose upon the world again. So much effort wasted, not to mention the number of lives spent trying to eradicate the disease. He hadn't felt a failure this great since his early days with the Order. Setting the parchment down, Rosca rubbed his aching temples. Sleep beckoned. Any decision made now would be born from passion, emotion. Two factors known to get men killed. Still, what choice did he have?

The gentle rap on his outer door dismissed any notion of rest. Scowling, Rosca rose, adjusted his armor, and crossed the wide room. His chambers were among the few with true hardwood flooring that were heated through the central furnace system. Indulgences were largely forbidden among the priests, but he saw no reason for unnecessary suffering when there was enough to be had for all on the ramparts each Burning Season.

He cracked the door and warned, "This had better be good or you'll be walking the walls for the next ten damned years."

A young novice swallowed his fear, eyes bulging at the threat. "Lord General, Brother Quinlan has arrived, as you ordered."

Rosca resisted the temptation to retort that he knew why the man had come. The novice was only doing his job and an unenviable one at that. "Send him in."

Grateful to have escaped further wrath, the novice bowed and tripped over his robes as he hurried away. Rosca almost chuckled, remembering his own days of awkwardness when he was first brought to Andrak. Like most priests, he began his career as a knight's squire. Every Burning Season, the knights arrived with delusions of grandeur and boasts of martial prowess. The Omegri tested and broke the vast majority well before the hundred days of service were ended.

Quinlan arrived without additional announcement, slipping into the chamber at Rosca's welcoming gesture. The younger priest was already a man of considerable experience. Enough for Rosca to consider him among the short list of qualified candidates to replace him when the time came.

"Lord General, I came as soon as Telas relayed your message," Quinlan began.

"That's his name? Telas?" Rosca grunted.

Quinlan concealed his smile. The old man appeared rough and surly but some of the priests knew he had a secret, a humorous side few ever witnessed.

"It is. He comes from a village near Mistwell."

The floating city of merchants was famed across the world for wealth and information, though the two were often interchangeable. Quinlan hadn't been there in years, not since he was last dispatched to discover the truth behind numerous missing sons and daughters of highborn nobles rumored to have been captured by the Witch Queen of Calad Reach.

"Dark times are approaching, Quinlan." Rosca wasted no time. His dour expression emphasized the lines scarring his face. "We received word from Fent of the Grey Wanderer."

Quinlan stiffened, suddenly uncomfortable. The priests often protected the lands from mystic creatures, but the Wanderer had not been witnessed in years. "Are they certain? That is not a name to be cast lightly."

"The Baron seems fairly positive in his missive. There is more," Rosca paused, allowing Quinlan's mind to finish tracing through potential outcomes and scenarios. "He also reports that since the initial sighting, nearly twenty children have gone missing and a man has risen from the grave."

"A F'talle? They are rumored to be extinct. Why would the Wanderer resurrect one now?" Quinlan asked.

"That is what I need you to find out," Rosca added. "Quinlan, you and I have seen incredible sights here on these walls and throughout the lands. Sights no person should have to endure, yet we accept each as truth and meet the challenge head on. If this man has indeed become a F'talle he must be found and dealt with accordingly."

"When do I leave?"

Rosca finally relaxed, thankful the task of convincing one of his finest priests was easier than he had thought. "As soon as you can and take your squire with you."

"Donal? His youth and inexperience may prove a liability," Quinlan said.

Rosca ran his index finger over the cushioned arm of the chair in a well-rehearsed move. Red felt gathered beneath the nail. "He's survived the Burning Season and is as close to priesthood as it is possible to be without actually being conferred. Unless you have reservations about your ability to train him properly…"

"Not at all, but he has not been exposed to the Grey Wanderer's manipulations," Quinlan refused to take the obvious bait. Donal Sawq was a fine young man and proving most capable. He would be a welcome addition to the Order once his training was complete.

"The situation may not be as bad as Baron Einos makes it seem," Rosca countered. "Initial reports are usually based on rumor and hearsay. It falls on you to discern the truth. Get to Fent and break this mystery. Regardless of whether the Wanderer tales are true, Einos is certain about the missing children."

"This could be related to the Witch Queen," Quinlan suggested. "She's been known to operate like this before."

"Possibly, but this feels different," Rosca said. "Make your preparations. Take what you need but leave soon. I fear time is not on our side."

Quinlan left the Lord General feeling more tense than before. There was evil afoot and the war priests might prove the only line of defense. Rosca couldn't shake the notion that the Burning Season would be upon them soon and that these incidents were related.

Towering a hundred feet over the scorched, dead earth rose the half completed structure. Tiny figures scurried about the base, hauling supplies and carrying old stone and wood away. Scaffoldings ringed the building. Hundreds of torches lit every inch of it, for the surrounding world was dark and empty. There was no warmth or natural light here, and the workers suffered. Hammers striking nail and rock echoed across the void. Bodies lay stacked in a small pile off to the side. Daily casualties were discarded and burned each night. Their desiccated flesh helped grow the monstrosity.

Shadows crowded around the workers. Each shadow, shapeless and indefinable, was a being alien to the world. Their existence threatened to undo the fabric of mortal life, while transforming the world in their horrid image. Brogon Lord stood among the shadows, wraiths he had come to call master. Confusion continued to plague him. Old memories remained just beyond his grasp, leaving him a shell of whatever he might have been.

Anger returned. Revenge didn't matter. He reckoned he would never learn who took his life or why. All that mattered was the whispering bells calling him here. Brogon gazed up at the structure, wondering its purpose.

Who or what the masters were remained a mystery. Shapeless, they communicated directly to his mind. Brogon found their intrusions debasing, yet he was powerless to resist. The masters controlled all in their realm with iron domination. He was merely a puppet, dancing on their strings. Their will was his reason for being, no matter that it disgusted any small dignity he retained.

Fidgeting at his side drew his attention away from construction. Brogon looked down at the small child standing beside him. Children. He'd lost count of how many he'd taken from the waking world. All he knew was the masters demanded more. More children to work the mechanisms within the heart of their construction. The confusion and anguish in the child's eyes touched him.

"Please, I want to go home," the child said with a high-pitched voice.

Brogon felt torn, just as he had the first twenty times he was forced to perform his task. Even if he wanted to, he had no ability to set the child free. Like himself, the boy was now trapped in eternal misery. Death would come quickly if the child were fortunate. Otherwise…

"There is nothing to be done. You belong to them now," Brogon said.

The boy froze as a pair of grotesquely disfigured people limped his way. Neither wore clothes but both suffered from numerous broken bones and abrasions. Cracked lips and broken skin decorated their emaciated bodies. Brogon thought they would be better off dead and in the ground, for this was no way to live.

The woman raised her skeletal arm and beckoned the child with crooked finger. Obeying without question, the child moved forward.

Brogon watched the child led away to become part of the nightmare steadily nearing completion. His task was finished for the day. Time now to return to the cave until he was summoned again.

SIX
Castle Andrak

Dawn crawled over the timeworn and battered walls of Andrak. The men and women within set about their daily affairs. Preparations were already underway to accept the incoming group of knights selected to defend the land from the Omegri. Though still weeks away, much needed to be done to refit the priests and their armories. Each Burning Season, the hundred day period when the Omegri sought to return to the world and lay claim, ended with massive loss of life and equipment. Replacing and repairing the damages occupied most of the time in between.

Quinlan balanced the sword Master Sergeant Cron offered, testing the weight and handling. All priests were renowned fighters versed in various weaponry and masters of martial skills. Quinlan preferred a two-handed sword, though he was skilled in the use of the short bow as well. Killing held no appeal for any of the priests. Rosca ensured that. The war priests were taught that all life was precious and killing was an act to be committed only when no other option remained.

"Fresh out the forge," Cron explained, approving the gleam in Quinlan's eyes as he swung the sword. "I'd claim it myself, but you seem to have more need at the moment."

Quinlan didn't argue. There was no way of knowing what he was going to find when he arrived in Fent. Danger was an ever present hound to many of the priests. Their lives were forfeit should agents of the Omegri catch them unaware. His fingers curled around the hilt with practiced ease.

"The weight is good. I like the way it sings when I cut," Quinlan said.

Cron nodded. The salt and pepper scruff on his face would be gone by the time the new group of knights arrived. It was the one luxury Cron allowed himself during downtime. He watched the younger Quinlan with measure. Many of the priests thought too much of themselves. Quinlan was different. Humble and modest, the man had fought more than his share of misdeeds and dark times.

"I had the smiths make it just for you," Cron lied. "Need an old hand to accompany you? I grow tired of being locked within these walls."

"The Lord General will never let one of his most valuable assets skulk about the countryside on what may well be a duck hunt," Quinlan countered.

Wind tousled his sand colored hair. Relatively young for an experienced priest, Quinlan was lightly muscled with piercing blue eyes. He sheathed the sword and sat atop a pile of hay bales stacked against the stable wall.

Cron snorted and spat. "Too much time here robs me of what I once was. Robs us all. Do you know how many cycles of knights I've tried to train? How many graves I helped fill?"

"We are given to a higher purpose, Cron."

"Don't try selling me on the recruiting nonsense," Cron replied with faux anger. "I've been here almost as long as you've drawn breath, whelp."

"Sounds like retirement is calling," Quinlan laughed.

Cron chuckled and sat beside his friend. "I wish you the best, my friend. The Grey Wanderer is naught to mess with. I don't envy what you're about to undertake."

"Neither do I, Cron. Neither do I."

He rose, extending his hand. They clasped forearms, each wondering if they'd gather for an ale once the mission was complete. A longstanding tradition among the Order was the return celebration. Glory was attributed to the individual, while the Order grew stronger. Cron knew these opportunities were rare, despite the number of occasions when he was forced to watch friends ride off into harm's way.

"The light protect you," he said.

Quinlan dipped his head. "Fear no darkness."

The war priests separated, Cron returning to his offices, with Quinlan entering the stables where Donal was already busied preparing their mounts. Saddlebags were filled and stacked against the first stall. Quinlan watched as Donal brushed his favored mount's mane. It was, Quinlan noted with bemusement, the same horse Donal had ridden on his initial journey to Andrak some two years ago. Understanding the emotional attachment, the war priest went to do the same.

"Brother Quinlan, all that remains is to saddle up," Donal reported.

His youthful face betrayed inexperience. Fighting the Omegri was one matter. Scouring the duchies for a resurrected man, far more complicated. Quinlan placed great faith in his novice. Donal had shown immense fortitude while taking the place of his former squire after the man was killed on the walls. It was through Donal's observations that the war priests were able to determine one of their own had succumb to the predations of the Omegri and tried to betray them by destroying the Purifying Flame.

"Very good, Donal. We should be going soon. I want to clear these lands before sundown," Quinlan instructed.

"Yes, sir," Donal bobbed his head. Giving his horse a final pat, the novice tucked his brush in a saddlebag and hurried about his tasks.

Quinlan regarded him a moment longer, ensuring the youth was sufficiently armed. The threat level he expected to find was substantially increased over the violent service Andrak offered. Donal wore a short sword strapped at the hip and a dagger tucked inside his left boot. Two quivers filled with arrows sat among their gear, along with a pair of bows for both hunting game and villains. The war priest didn't know if that would be enough to stop the evil manifesting in Fent.

Priest and novice were soon mounted and heading out of the gates. Castle Andrak was built at the end of a peninsula several leagues long. Mist and fog occluded vision after a few meters on either side. It was widely theorized that the castle wasn't part of the physical world, instead built in the in-between where the immaterial lurked. Quinlan didn't know for certain nor did he much care. He served the Order without question. What lurked in those quiet places unwitnessed by the waking world held limited power over a war priest.

Donal failed to share Quinlan's lack of concern. The young squire shivered as the mists curled around his ankles. Each sensation was a new experience, changing each time a priest entered or exited the peninsula. This was only Donal's third expedition outside of Andrak. Much of his previous life was forgotten, put aside to focus on the battle with the Omegri. His time spent as Sir Forlei's squire felt a lifetime ago. How many years had it been since Forlei enlisted to fight the Burning Season? How many seasons had passed since Donal watched Forlei fall atop the walls of Castle Andrak?

Time no longer held meaning. Donal abandoned the past, while devoting all he had to becoming one of the war priests. He spent hours each day practicing with sword and staff, bow and dagger. Additional hours were devoted to studying the art of war and the philosophers from ages long past. The last moments of daylight were spent in devotion to the Purifying Flame; that beacon of liberty and human individuality keeping the world safe. Each knight was expected to be the very best humanity offered, well versed in literature and weapons. Donal took pride in his studies.

"Are you ill, Donal?" Quinlan asked.

The fatherly tone seldom left his voice, for he knew no other way to be with the squire. Donal was his first charge and he still was not quite comfortable with the responsibility. War priests were solitary by nature. Their personalities best suited for handling issues without additional support. Not that having a squire was personally displeasing. Donal was a good young man, worthy of being a squire to a war priest. Quinlan decided the problem resided within him.

Donal felt warmth in the air as the mists were pushed back by Quinlan's raw power. "No, Brother Quinlan. I suffered a moment of weakness. It will not happen again."

"Weakness is to be embraced if one is expected to overcome it," Quinlan said. "Do not be ashamed of such feelings. One might argue they give cause to our actions, strengthening us for the horrors we must confront."

"How are we to defeat darkness when it surrounds everything?" Donal asked. Anything to take his mind off the myriad nightmares potentially lurking in the mists. Everywhere he looked off the road, he saw vague outlines, shapes of monsters trying to break into the real world. He knew fear.

Quinlan nodded approval at the question. "Darkness is perpetual, as is the light. One cannot be defeated without obliterating the other. Instead, we must strive to find balance, for only through balance can there exist peace. It is not the defeat of darkness we seek, Donal. It is the balance of power."

The mists thinned. They had come to the beginning of the peninsula.

The fire crackled, crisp against the easy chill of night. Quinlan had forgotten how much comfort he found in such a trivial noise. Hands behind his head, Quinlan leaned back against a fallen tree and for a moment relaxed. Danger here was minimal, though there were threats hiding in the forgotten places of the world. Threats more than willing to assault one of the war priests.

Trophy hunters and villains crawled through the duchies in search of the ultimate prize. Hunters of men for the right price, Quinlan thought disgustedly. He'd planned the best, fastest route down to Fent. They'd follow the road west for a day before entering the Scour, a wild forest both dense and mystical. Quinlan had never had a negative experience within the forest, despite the rumors circulated among new recruits and knights.

After leaving the Scour, Quinlan intended on taking the road south to the Indolense Permital. The chasm was a league wide and a third that deep. Several small villages were within, concealed in the forests and rock formations. Fent was a few days ride south from there. He hoped for an easy journey without incident. Hope and reality seldom crossed paths.

Donal returned with a final armload of firewood. He was tired and sore from spending the day in the saddle, an act living almost exclusively in the castle made unnecessary. But he also felt joy. He'd almost forgotten what life away from the mist shrouded castle was like. So many shades of green and brown stole his mind away from the alabaster and grey he'd grown accustomed to.

"Where are you from?" Quinlan asked. His eyes remained closed.

Donal swallowed his mouthful of water and recapped the canteen. "Far to the west, outside of Beacon."

"You live near the Hell Drop?"

"South of it. We are a small logging community. My father's business sells quality wood crafts to many of the dukes and barons across the land." Pride edged his words.

Quinlan nodded. "You miss it."

A pause long enough to tell Quinlan what he sought.

"At times, though those grow more infrequent the closer I get to becoming a war priest."

"Leaving home is no easy task," Quinlan agreed. "It takes strength to walk away from all we know in order to find enlightenment. Sorely, far too many fall short of that goal."

"Where are you from, Brother Quinlan?" Donal asked.

Soft snores answered him. Donal fought off disappointment and shook his head, a small smile on his face. Life on the road was hard for them all, fully ordained war priests as well. Donal snatched a blanket from his saddlebag and covered Quinlan. The night was still young, leaving Donal ample time to reflect on those precious, private moments from childhood that helped guide the course of his life. He drifted off to sleep with images of that last family supper before Sir Forlei took him away. Some events time could not diminish.

SEVEN
Fent

"We are not doing enough to protect our people!" Lizette raged, pounding her small fists on the tabletop amidst stains of ale and food from meals long past.

Kastus flinched, despite knowing the blow was coming. His time spent with the grieving mother assured him of two realities. The first was that they were indeed missing a key element necessary to stop Brogon Lord from stealing more children. The second, and in his opinion more severe, was that Lizette was teetering on losing herself to the madness of vengeance. Losing your only child would have that effect, he supposed. Not that he had any way of knowing. His wife had died many years ago to the pox and he refused to remarry. Nor had he sired any bastards during his occasional indiscretions.

He drank deeply from the pewter mug, twisting his face at the bitterness of the late winter ale. "We lack the resources required to canvas the entire duchy. Finding a walking dead man in the middle of such a large area is problematic. Anger won't solve anything, Lizette."

The wounded look flaring at him suggested he'd taken a step too far. "You have no idea what anger is, Kastus, though I would be more than happy to demonstrate for you right now."

He quickly surrendered. "There's no need for that. We are on the same side. Besides, I was just making a point. We're missing something and until we figure out what it is, we're going to be a step behind this monster."

Satisfied, Lizette lowered her gaze until she regained composure. Until the abduction and murder of her daughter, she had seldom raised her voice or allowed the slightest inkling of anger to overcome her carefully constructed façade. Like Kastus, she suffered from the loss of her spouse. Her husband had been serving as a caravan guard from Fent to Mistwell. A normal occupation for the peasantry and one he was quite good at. They were returning from the floating city, when a pack of Ig'lakelli ambushed and slaughtered every man, woman, and beast. The Ig'lakelli were monsters worthy of the name.

She shuddered at the thought of running into the bipedal lizards in the open areas of the world, where no one heard your screams.

Scholars claimed the race was left over from an ancient time when the world was young. Lizette didn't care. All that mattered was they murdered her husband and by some accounts, devoured him before his flesh cooled. Brogon Lord was a monster, too. He just took lives in a different way.

More than one night she awoke to rabid screams and cries of anguish. Lizette was horrified to learn they poured from her throat. Each time was the same. She saw her husband's torn and bleeding body in the morning light, while the monster Brogon Lord dashed off with her daughter, laughing with wicked intent until they disappeared in the mist. Each night provided livid moments of terror leaving her weakened and tormented.

Einos insisted she stay in the castle until the resurrected man was found and destroyed. He couldn't help but feel obligated, considering all she'd been forced to endure. Maids came to her room daily with fresh sheets and towels, knowing her bedding was drenched in sweat through the preceding night. Lizette turned down their offers to remake her bed and wash her linens. Stubborn pride clashed with embarrassment to prevent her from accepting charity. She slipped off to the laundry when she thought no one was paying attention and washed her own soiled linens.

"Are you well?" Kastus asked after too many uncomfortable moments of prolonged silence.

Trance broken, she offered a false smile and shook away the demons of the night prior. "Fine. I apologize for snapping. My emotions no longer seem within my control."

"I understand." Though he wondered if he did.

Satisfied he wasn't going to pry, Lizette changed the subject. "Has there been any word on the war priests?"

"None the baron has given. He may be keeping the information private until one or two arrive. There is no need to shock the countryside prematurely," he replied.

A thought sparked and Kastus hung his head. "Of course! The countryside."

"What do you mean?" she asked.

He grabbed his tattered leather jacket and said, "We need to find Einos."

"We've been focusing our search efforts in concentrated areas of population when we should have been sweeping the countryside with places for him to hide. No one has reported seeing him in daylight, which means Brogon Lord needs a lair to wait out the day," Kastus explained.

Einos scratched his chin in thought. "If he has a lair, we have a way of tracking him down."

"And putting the bastard back in the grave," Lizette finished.

Excitement rippled through the trio for the first time since combining forces. Every attempt at finding Brogon resulted in disappointment and another child missing. The Baron remained unconvinced the resurrected man was killing them, however, for no additional bodies had been found and his efforts produced no other ghostly sightings. His wife worried about him spending countless hours roaming the darkened halls in the hopes of confronting Lizette's daughter again.

"There is one problem, Kastus," Einos suggested. "We lack the manpower to search every meter of this duchy. And even if we had the resources, there is every chance Brogon would return to his lair after we'd swept through. Still, your conclusion has merit. Can you conscript any of the peasantry to assist your efforts?"

"It is possible, though I am not sure how many men are available. Most of the men would want to stay home to protect their children," Kastus replied.

"We could always secure the village first, thus ensuring their peace of mind," Lizette said.

Einos shook his head. "Would you accept having to go out in search of this monster while other, better armed men stay behind to protect your home? I can think of no quicker way to foment rebellion. Especially considering the losses we have sustained. No, deploying squads into the villages is fine, but our men will need to take the lead if we are to form adequate defenses."

"What if we trained the villagers? Basic defense measures. Give them limited weapons," Kastus suggested with hesitation.

An eyebrow arched. "Do you have any idea what you are asking?"

"What's wrong with ensuring your subjects are safe from predators?" Lizette demanded. Since arriving two weeks ago, she had grown accustomed to being around both Einos and his wife. The natural reluctance separating royalty and peasant was dissolving.

"I much prefer maintaining my office," Einos smiled weakly. "While I have no doubt my leadership is generally viewed positively, current events are no doubt driving my popularity down. How much more can our people take before they decide removing me is in their best interest? An armed revolt is not on my agenda, Lizette."

Rebuked, she sat back in her chair. Policies and strategic planning were beyond her scope, leaving her disadvantaged when speaking of the possible courses of action involving the future of Fent. Lizette lowered her eyes, studying the intricate patterns woven into the crimson rug covering most of the office floor. Rich blue and warm yellow blended with crimson and deep green in intricate designs, reminding her of the borders of the wall tapestries depicting scenes of those responsible for ensuring the security of the duchy in battles past. A far cry from her modest home.

Lizette groaned with self-chastisement. Her home was only an empty frame, bereft of the mirth once consuming it. Dreams died within with the loss of her husband and her beloved daughter. She refused to go home again. Not until they caught Brogon Lord and made him divulge what he had done with the missing children. Peasants and those working in the castle whispered about her. She was fast becoming a hero to the commoner.

The aroma of mint scented candles tickled her nose, allowing her to draw restorative breaths as the world continued to spin out of control around her. Lizette would never have been able to afford scented candles before joining forces with the Barony. Did she join or force her way into the inner circle she wondered? She no longer recalled, but she knew that this was what all her life had built up to. She was meant to make a difference.

"That still leaves us with the problem of deciding where to begin looking," Kastus said, interrupting her thoughts.

Einos stared at the map of his small kingdom. Fent was no larger than a few hundred square leagues, most of it open plains or lightly forested. Searching even that small area would take manpower and far too much time. Small dots marked the locations of the disappearances. Each was accompanied by a number underneath, showing him the progression of the crimes.

"We follow the numbers," he said after much thought. Einos continued after noticing the confusion on their faces. "Each of these children has been taken at roughly the same time of day and at least according to the way they are displayed on the map, in geographical progression. Look here."

He went to the hanging map and began tracing a line from the first to the last incident. "While not entirely in the same direction, this Brogon Lord seems to be operating in a linear pattern."

"Meaning we have a means of anticipating where he might strike again," Kastus finished.

"Precisely."

Lizette followed the line on the map. "What is to say he will continue this pattern? Surely he must know his actions have not gone unnoticed. Won't he expect us to come after him?"

Einos approved. She was clever and a fast learner. She might end up proving a valuable asset to his leadership once this matter concluded. "Weeks have passed since his reported resurrection. Weeks in which nothing has changed."

Kastus stepped closer to the map. "If what you suggest is true, there is still a lot of territory to cover. It is possible we will miss him."

Villages lay on either side of the current trajectory, substantiating Kastus's worry. Brogon's course often zigzagged without apparent reason, but always moved forward. His targets had been standalone farmsteads to small villages. Preparing the wrong target was far too viable and until Einos was able to find more information about Brogon, they needed to act with caution.

"We have enough men to screen the villages of Palis and Jul. Deploy roving patrols to cover the main and secondary roads," Einos said.

"Which leaves us with his lair. He may not be staying in the same place twice as his hunting ground changes," Kastus suggested. His revelation shattered his previous theory.

"Putting us right back where we began," Lizette finished. Her shoulders slumped in defeat.

Einos said, "Not necessarily. Kastus, take a hundred men north to secure those two villages. I will follow with another hundred, hopefully we'll flush Brogon out into the open."

"What of me?" Lizette asked. She refused to sit back and watch as others fought her personal battles.

"Lizette, I appreciate your fervor for aiding the duchy, but this is a matter best left to men at arms. What we will face out there is no place for a …"

"A what?" She rose, hands balled to fists. Her cheeks flushed crimson. "A woman?"

Einos quickly moved to defend himself. "I was going to say someone inexperienced in the ways of war. These are modern times. Trained women fight alongside men. Many serve in my defense forces. In fact, I …"

"Baron, you have defended your statement adequately, but I need to be part of this…."

Kastus snorted.

EIGHT
Fent

Dawn found a company of soldiers marching out of the village of Fent. They were heading north, on the trail of Brogon Lord and the dangers associated with him. Thus far, only children had been hurt. The once dead man was selective and elusive. Kastus prayed that the former remained so. Taking his responsibility more seriously than before, the Constable of Fent was determined to end the threat of Brogon Lord, thus eliminating the necessity of having a war priest snooping through the duchy.

Kastus, like so many across the lands, was raised to be leery of the mythic priests. They dealt with the unnatural, forcing them into self-imposed exile in their fortresses at the ends of the world. Kastus based his opinions off old stories and rampant rumors. Hand-me-downs from generations past. More often than not, the war priests created issues for the people left behind. He did not want Fent devolving into chaos. *Leastwise no more than this bastard knight is already creating.*

One hundred men marched at his back, a sizeable portion of Fent's defensive capabilities. It was a calculated risk, but with no active war anywhere close, one both he and the Baron were comfortable taking. The black and purple banners waved in the morning breeze, offering flickers of the royal standard, a gilded eagle, to those onlookers already going about their daily life.

Men and some women bowed their heads, casting their eyes downward as the soldiers marched off to the unknown. They knew, of that Kastus was certain. Word spread quickly in a small town. Even when the Baron insisted on operational security. He snorted at the irony of failed secrets. *How many of these people would insist on joining me, if for only a glimpse of their child again? Surely they must understand their children are never returning?*

"Sir?"

Jarred, Kastus glanced at the young captain on his left. Lightly bearded with youthful eyes, the captain looked out of place. Kastus doubted the man had any field experience, not that it was a bad thing. Going to war was an act of failed consequences. A last resort any responsible ruler sought to avoid. "Captain?"

"I asked to our destination," he asked.

A stain, no larger than a fingernail, drew Kastus's attention. "What is your name, Captain? It feels foolish referring to you by rank alone."

"Ah, Thep, sir. First Company."

A nod, clipped. "Captain Thep, we are heading for the village of Palis. What have you been briefed of our mission?"

"Not much, sir. Command suggested we were heading out to find this child stealer," Thep supplied.

Kastus quickened his step, forcing Thep to follow to get out of earshot of the front ranks. Soldiers talked. More than they should, in most instances. This close to Fent proper, Kastus required secrecy. "We are trying to secure the duchy, find this monster, and prevent the war priests from establishing a foothold. A most ambitious task, though one I suspect we are capable of executing."

Thep forced his jaw shut, lest he appear a drooling idiot in front of one of the senior-most men in Fent. "Sir, my men and I will do everything within our power to accomplish this."

"I've no doubt, Thep. No doubt. However, not a word of this to the rest of the men. Not until we are well underway and about to make our move."

Any reassurance meant by the deliberate subterfuge left Thep feeling cold. He turned back to the long road stretching away before him. His thoughts should have focused on developing plans to find Brogon Lord. Instead they centered on the war priests. *Are they as powerful as legend says?* He wasn't sure if he wanted to meet one or not.

Nightfall saw the column several leagues from the security of home. The soldiers marched at reasonable pace, stopping in accordance with active military regulations. Thep used his sergeants wisely, knowing their proclivity for exacting the most out of the men. Their growls and curses were the only sounds heard above the stomp of marching boots.

Nils watched the captain go by and dumped the dirt from his boot, scowling as the small pebble that had been giving him grief since leaving Fent dropped out. "Bout time!"

Across from him, Alfar got the most out of his yawn. "You are the unhappiest person I've ever met, Nils. What are you whining about this time?"

"Eh? Mind your business, pretty boy. This is grown folk talk over here," the dark-haired soldier scoffed and threw a rock at his peer.

The rock bounced from Alfar's chest armor. "You throw like my sister."

"You mean my daughter?" Nils countered. He broke into a toothy grin, the off-white of his teeth peeking from beneath a thick moustache.

Alfar brushed the dust from his chest. Golden hair on the backs of his hands reflected in the building firelight. "Where do you suppose we're headed? Not like the Capt'n to be closed up."

"Don't suppose it matters. He ain't been in a real scrape, so it can't be that. More like a presence patrol," Nils replied.

Alfar's blue eyes pinched. "A what?"

Nils rolled his eyes, forgetting his friend had less than half the time in service as him. "The Baron's been having trouble, right? With them missing kids and all. I figure we been sent out to reassure the towns and villages that it's gonna be fine."

"Oh. I'm hungry."

A second rock, thrown harder, missed his head.

"What are you lubbers quipping about?"

Nils winced. Alfar tensed, unsure whether to go to attention or not as Sergeant Sava stomped up to them. As wide as he was tall, his sun bronzed skin lent Sava natural menace. A fact not lost upon the men.

"We was just speculating about our mission, is all," Nils answered before Alfar managed to get them in trouble.

Sava rubbed his jaw and spat a mouthful of juice from the kaappa leaves he constantly shoved in his mouth. They'd long since stained his teeth red. "The Baron don't pay you to speculate, soldier. We go where the Captain orders. Do what he says. Anything less and it's treason."

Alfar opened his mouth to speak. This time the rock struck home. Nils quickly followed up, "Won't happen again, Sergeant. Me and Alfar will keep it quiet."

Satisfied, Sava spat again. "Good, and just to make sure you do, you both got first guard shift. Move out."

Nils waited until Sava was out of earshot before snarling, "See what your mouth got us into?"

"I was just…"

Nils pointed an angry finger. "You was just about to get us cracked by an angry sergeant. Come on. Collect up your gear. We got work to do."

His stomach growled angrier than before as the pair began their guard shift. It was going to be a long night.

Kastus lay looking up at the stars. He'd never been comfortable sleeping outside and the life of a soldier proved disagreeable with his finer senses. No dandy, he was a hardworking man with an iron rod down his spine. A compliment to the people of Fent. He just despised sleeping under the stars. The ground was always too hard, making it impossible to find a comfortable spot, and the nights grew cold enough to leave him covered in dew by morning. No. No soldier life for the Constable.

Stars winked as the heavens spun. He tried recalling what he'd been taught as child, but those memories eluded him. He liked to think they were reflections of sunlight, though a theory gaining popularity suggested each star was on track to strike the planet, killing everything on impact. Kastus held little stock in the naysayers. Without any verifiable way of knowing the truth in the stars, he was content to let them be wonders of light dancing across the midnight sky.

A sound stirred him. So faint he nearly missed it. Kastus rose to his elbows, looking to see if any of the soldiers nearby also heard it. Most were asleep. A few stared blankly into the campfires. There was no immediate danger in this part of Fent, though Thep was wise enough to place both stationary and roving guards around the perimeter. Thus far Brogon Lord had only gone after children, but there was nothing to say he wouldn't strike a grown target. Even if it was part of an armed column of soldiers.

The sound repeated. Kastus crawled from his sleeping roll, slipped into his cloak, and clutched the hilt of the short sword at his waist. Foul deeds were afoot and he wasn't about to succumb to complacency in the middle of the wild. Kastus decided against waking the others, though for reasons he failed to understand. Strange sounds came from the surrounding area, but he felt no threat.

Silent as possible, he crept through the mass of sleeping soldiers and their kit. He never understood how these men and women could sleep anywhere, without complaint. The hard soil and multitude of rocks jabbing into his flesh managed to keep him restless, and that after but half a night. Kastus almost longed for the comfort of his bed and hearth. Almost. Their quest was just beginning and he feared it would be long before he was able to return.

At last he emerged from the ring of bodies. Kastus searched the night for sign of the roving guards. There were none. Was it possible that all of them were asleep? His knowledge of the military was limited, but he knew enough that there should be soldiers awake at all times. Security was paramount and he discovered it lacking this night. He turned to find Thep and give him a proper dress down.

The sound began as a low whistle, the cry of the wind across the grass. Gradually it grew into an enchanting melody. Kastus's eyes fluttered, threatening to close. He clenched his fists, fighting the desire to return to sleep. There was magic at play, and for reasons he failed to understand, it left him unaffected. A blessing, or bane. Yet still he felt no threat. The song struck chords deep within his soul. He felt pulled forth.

Kastus edged across the open field and up a low rise. A bank of clouds concealed what moonlight there was, cascading the landscape into an ethereal place trapped between worlds. His heart lurched, for the possibility of encountering the Grey Wanderer chilled him. He scanned the area, absorbing every bush and shadow. There was no sign of a hooded figure bearing a lantern.

He had almost relaxed when movement to the right drew his attention. Kastus dropped to the ground and with some difficulty, drew his sword. The figure emerged from the night, walking with casual purpose on a course parallel to that of the soldiers. Kastus squinted to get a better look and gasped as the image cleared.

The figure was almost as tall as a man and had a mane of blackest hair. Kastus could just make out the flat, expressionless face. What stunned him most was realizing the figure had pale green flesh beneath a vest of woven bone. A shaman! One of the fabled Sclarem.

They were an enigmatic race, long thought to have become extinct. Wanderers of the world with magic infused in their essence. Neither good nor bad, the shamans were rumored to possess great insight in the ways of the races. Kastus had scoffed at them, thinking their kind no more than childhood foolishness. Seeing one this night offered him the opportunity to reexamine all he thought to be true.

The Sclarem walked north, uncaring of being spied upon. Kastus watched as the grass circled around thong clad calves in an almost loving manner. The shamans were one with the world. A living memory of all that once was. He did not know why, but his heart felt lighter upon seeing one. Tears welled in the corners of his eyes as the Sclarem faded back into the night. When he managed to return to his sleeping roll, Kastus found sleep ready for him. He did not awaken until the dawn.

NINE
Northern Fent

Sunlight had never felt so good. Freed from the strange world he'd stumbled into the previous night, Kastus rode with conflicting emotions. There was serenity to be found in his encounter with the shaman. A peacefulness he'd never known and doubted he would ever find again. Therein lay the illusion. Whatever arcane purpose the Sclarem was about, Kastus doubted it coincided with his. They belonged in separate worlds, disparate of relationship or bearing.

Digging beyond the scope of serenity, Kastus was troubled by the appearance. He wasn't a man prone to thoughts of grandeur. A simple man, the Constable performed his tasks with alacrity and professionalism that often collided with his genuine humble nature. So why had the Sclarem deigned to cross his path? Was this a warning from the other world? A chance for Kastus to take heed and reorganize his thoughts before encountering Brogon Lord? He wished he had answers, but Kastus feared they would remain elusive until too late. Fear of failing his Baron assailed him. Doubt was, he learned long ago, a crippling monster.

"Sir, you seem … disturbed this morning," Thep managed, after half the morning passed. He respected Kastus for his position but remained wary of where they stood in relation to the chain of command. The highest law enforcement in the duchy, Kastus was a separate entity from the meagre military Einos possessed.

Thankful for the disruption, Kastus feigned a smile. "Bad night's sleep. I fear the wild is no friend of mine."

"It does take some time getting used to," Thep confirmed his posh status.

Kastus suspected the young officer was one of the upper class. Perhaps the son of a wealthy merchant. Men like that seldom spent time in the ranks, moving immediately into the officer corps. This formed rifts between the rank and file and middle leadership, though Kastus was unaware of any animosity rippling through the army. Other duchies weren't as fortunate.

He decided not to make his counterpart any more uncomfortable. "Were there any issues with the guards last night?"

"The guards?" Thep was taken off-guard. "None that Sergeant Sava has informed of. Do you suspect something?"

A slight wave. "No, just curious to the mannerisms of the army. I've spent my lifetime in law enforcement. Military life lacked appeal for me."

"We share similar hardships. I doubt I would have made an adequate constable. My father certainly wouldn't have approved," Thep admitted. His cheeks flushed, fearing he'd said too much.

Kastus immediately noticed the discomfort. "Relax, Thep. I pass no judgment. Men are called to their individual strengths. We seldom choose our paths. Tell me, what does your father do?"

"Did, Sir. He passed some years ago. He ran a small merchanting house. It was never one of the more successful ones though."

"You were forced into the army," Kastus concluded.

A nod. No more needed saying. Constable and Captain came to an understanding. Both men respected the other and agreed to allow each the opportunity to do his job. Kastus was an accompaniment to the army. His task was to acquire and train volunteers from the northern villages to trap the once dead man. Thep and his men were meant to provide the hammer to end the threat once and for all. They were already deep into the afternoon when the thatch roofs of Palis edged into view.

"First platoon! Fall out and occupy this village," Sava bellowed. He appeared wider than usual with both meaty fists on his hips. "Second platoon! Cordon off the roads. I don't want anyone getting in or out until Cap'n says. Move it, dogs! We're burning daylight!"

Squad leaders peeled their men off from the main column and much to Kastus's amusement, undertook their assignments with remarkable precision. The army of Fent was barely one thousand men and that included the civilian reserves, but if these one hundred were any indication, Kastus feared for any invading force. He was impressed.

Orders had been given ahead of time that no one was to draw their weapons unless confronted. Palis was a loyal village in the duchy and not under any suspicion. Conveying this to the village leaders fell on his shoulders. Occupying the village would further reduce the Baron's effectiveness in maintaining control. An act they couldn't afford. This basic order conflicted with Kastus's mission of finding the child stealer.

Two men with white beards waggling down past their sternums and a rail thin woman with the most severe look he'd ever seen, stalked out of the town hall to meet them. Kastus took Thep with him, insisting the Captain walk a step behind so as not to imply this was a military takeover.

"Constable, welcome to Palis. I would say we were expecting you but …"

"Your intrusion is most unexpected and unwelcome," the woman interrupted. The rigidity of her stance left no doubt as to her position.

Kastus bowed his head in respect. "Lady, we are not here to complicate your lives. Rather, the Baron decreed we move north."

"My name is Deana. I am no lady," she remarked. "Has Einos reason to suspect duplicity?"

"This, ah, matter would be best discussed in private," Kastus choked.

Thep shifted uncomfortably behind.

"We have no secrets here. Palis is an open community," Deana replied.

Patience lost, Kastus drew up to his full height and fixed her with an equally glowering look. "Lady Deana, do not force me to have you placed under arrest for obstructing a royal investigation."

Lips pursed, Kastus mused at the venom building in her expression. "Very well. If this foolishness is to be conducted, let us adjourn indoors."

"A wise choice, *Lady*."

Several citizens came forth. Most were curious, for it had been almost a generation since the last time the Barony was forced to send soldiers. Others were enraged at the indignity. Kastus had no doubt Deana would fuel their fire the moment his back was turned. Clasping her in irons might be best for all. He and Thep followed the village elders into the largest structure in Palis. The reek of damp thatch twisted his nose. An old dog, blind in one milky eye, watched as they went by.

Deana whirled on Kastus the instant they were secured within, the doors shut. "There is no call for what you are doing, Constable. We are a loyal village with no ties to any other duchy. Remove your forces and allow us to return to our business."

"You are in no position to submit demands," Kastus replied. "We have not come to demean your citizenry. Baron Einos, as you may have heard, is beset with a most dire problem."

"How is this our concern?" Her flat tone suggested she knew the issue and was disinclined to implicate Palis any further than it already was by his being there.

Kastus clenched a fist, tapping it against his thigh. Arresting her proved more enticing the longer she spoke. "You are citizens of the Baron. It is not your place to question what he deems best, or right, for the duchy."

"How dare you …"

"Deana, shut up and let him speak. If there is a threat to our village, I would know of it," the eldest snarled. Not giving her the opportunity for rebuttal, he faced Kastus. "My apologies sir, but we are very fond of our way of life here. I am Elder Mugh. This is Elder Waern. What is this issue Baron Einos deems important?"

At last. We might be able to accomplish something. "The Grey Wanderer has been seen."

Gasps rippled through the elders, for the name was synonymous with doom.

"He has returned a man from the dead. A man we believe to be behind the abduction and possible murders of nearly twenty children."

"You suspect this man is here, in Palis?" Waern asked. His pale face grew ashen.

Kastus held up a hand, lest panic grip them all. "No, sir, but we have tracked the trail of reported abductions and plotted several eventualities. The once dead man is moving north, choosing victims at random in the main villages along his route of march. Palis and Jul are the two villages in his path. Our plan is to occupy your village until we either catch this fiend or deem enough time has passed that he is no longer a threat."

"A F'talle! Here in Palis! We are beset by great evil," Mugh wailed. His hands began to tremble.

Kastus studied them, curious to their mixed reactions. Mugh was visibly shaken. Deana managed to maintain a modicum of composure. It was Waern who drew his attention. There was coldness in his eyes, as if he'd been expecting such revelation. *What are you hiding, Elder? What demons occupy your mind?*

"We are ahead of him, and it is possible he may not come to Palis. We must be prepared in any event," Kastus continued. It took great effort to spread his focus to all three elders.

To his surprise, it was Deana who asked, "What do you require from us? Palis is a small village with limited resources."

"Allow us to establish a command post here, in this hall if possible, from which to operate. Gods willing, we should be able to stop him soon."

"You may use this hall for your base of operations but know that you are unwelcome here. No matter the circumstance," she insisted.

He'd encountered her type many times in the past. A powerful figure unwilling to relinquish a fraction of authority, despite being subservient to the Baron's authority. She knew Kastus could have her executed if matters became dire, but it stood an empty threat. He bore the people of Palis no ill will, even cantankerous ones in need of being put in their place. She was not the threat. Waern, on the other hand, bothered him for reasons he wasn't sure of.

"Where do you propose I garrison my men, if not in the village proper? We have not come with campaign equipment, Lady Deana," Thep stepped forward. "We are a judiciary punishment force."

"Who travels in haste, with improper equipment? I daresay Einos has acted rashly."

"It is not for you or I to say what the Baron does. Shall I order my men to occupy key homes, Constable?"

Kastus grew impressed with the inexperienced Captain. What he lacked in experience was compensated through quick wit. "That is their decision, Captain."

Mugh sputtered. "N ... now wait a moment! We are not the enemy. If this matter is as grave as you intone, we shall do all within our power to ensure not another child is stolen. Deana, relent and give the Captain access to whatever he requires."

Kastus almost felt sorry for the old man. Raw hatred spewed from her eyes. "Very well," she said with terse voice. "Your men shall utilize the hall for sleeping and eating. There are latrines in the rear. Conduct your soldierly business in as least offensive manner as possible, Captain. Find this monster and be gone lest you force me to reevaluate my decision."

Knowing there was little point in debating further, Kastus allowed her the illusion of superiority. There'd be time enough to see who was in charge once Brogon Lord was captured. He waited until he and Thep were alone before continuing. "Captain, I believe we have business to attend."

Thep's grin reminded him of a child getting away with doing wrong. "How do you think they will react when we tell them some of their people are being conscripted?"

"One battle at a time, Captain."

TEN

North of the Indolense Permital

Decades of service to the war priests robbed Quinlan of a life that could have been. What imagined occupations might have awaited him had he not dedicated his years to defending the world from utter darkness! Sadly, Quinlan was a child of violence. A bastion of hope, standing firm against the crushing tide of the Omegri in their eternal struggle to conquer the world. Few understood him. Fewer knew he existed. The war priests were never many.

His stoic eyes considered his apprentice. Donal Sawq was becoming a quality man, one whose worth was more than his weight in gems. Too few who survived the Burning Season decided to join the cause and become a war priest. Not that Quinlan blamed them. If was no easy task surviving one hundred days of pure horror. The majority of knights and squires, thrill seekers and sell swords fell to the Omegri, leaving shells of those survivors. Had matters gone differently, he might have shied away as well.

Lord General Rosca recognized Quinlan's potential early and began grooming him for increasing positions of authority. Rumor suggested he was going to appoint Quinlan his successor. Quinlan discounted such theories as nonsense. He'd come to Castle Andrak a broken man. The lone survivor of the now fallen Castle Bendris. More failure than saint. Wiser men would have shunned him as cursed.

Ghosts of fallen comrades haunted Quinlan on his travels south to Andrak. Of the six mighty castles designed to prevent the Omegri's return, only Andrak stood. Each castle was built upon a gateway to the ethereal plain. Passage between realms was only possible at these specific points, thus limiting the Omegri's influence among the population. They were the key to the defense of the world.

Rosca refused to turn the broken priest away. War was coming. He needed every priest he could get. Even ones with shattered confidence. Quinlan's passion for the Order spread through the ranks. He was one of the few who gained the Lord General's confidence, enough that Rosca admitted he was attempting to rebuild the Order and reclaim all five fallen castles.

While glorious, none of that mattered to Quinlan. His task to Fent was paramount to all else. The Burning Season was yet weeks away, ample time for him to complete his task and return to defend the walls. So far, his journey had taken him off the Andrak peninsula and beyond the haunted forests of the Scour. He and Donal spent a night in the village of Spindle before continuing southwest.

The Indolense Permital lay ahead. A mile-wide chasm half as deep. A massive forest sprawled across the floor, sprinkled with small villages of Majj. These warriors were rumored to have come from the elder races and bore animosity toward all that had come later. Whisper suggested the Majj constructed the six castles of the war priests. True or not, Quinlan had yet to see one of the red skinned creatures and wasn't sure he wanted to.

They were said to stand seven feet tall and had great shaggy manes. Claws and fangs. Many who survived an encounter, claimed the Majj appeared as great cat-like beings, as cunning and intelligent as they were vicious. The magic in Quinlan's shield was powerful enough to reply any attack, but he desired to avoid confrontation. There was enough fighting on the castle walls to last him a lifetime.

The air began to change as the duo drew closer. He felt the chill. Caught the aroma of dead leaves and humidity on the air. Quinlan tensed. Nightfall wasn't far off. They needed to find an adequate campsite before darkness crawled across the land. One defensible. Keeping his concern private, Quinlan directed Donal to seek out their resting spot for the night. It was almost dark by the time he was satisfied. Even then, Quinlan couldn't stop looking over his shoulder.

The Majj were said to remain in their hidden forests, not wanting to interact with the lesser races. That suited Quinlan fine, if it was true. Summer was beginning, meaning the nights in the wild were still prone to heavy chill. Loathe as he was to do so, Quinlan allowed Donal to light a small fire. There was no point in suffering just to avoid what might not be.

He chewed on the rabbit leg, deep in thought. Fent was yet days away and if what Baron Einos's emissary said was to be believed, it was imperative he and Donal arrive with all haste. A F'talle had not been encountered in many years, giving him pause to consider what game the Grey Wanderer played at. The world of men was disparate from that of the other life. Whatever the Wanderer once was, he was an agent of chaos, though neither good nor evil. Quinlan recognized the duality, while understanding that where the hooded man strode, bad things followed.

"Will we ride close enough to see it?" Donal asked. He tossed aside the leg bones he'd been gnawing on for some time. Not a scrap of meat remained.

Quinlan disliked being interrupted but couldn't blame Donal for his excitement. "I should think so. Close enough, but not within. Doing so would create too much delay and our services are needed."

Undeterred, Donal pressed. "Have you been within, Brother Quinlan?"

"Once. Long ago. I was … lost and needed to find myself," he admitted. That he was fleeing the ruins of Castle Bendris remained his private misery.

Donal's face turned to fancy. "It is one of the many places in this world that I wish to one day explore. My father often read to me of these things."

"All comes in time, young Donal. Do not be so quick to rush into things. The Permital is said to have lurking dangers we lack all knowledge of."

Donal took the warning as more of a scolding. He'd been reprimanded harsh and often as a child. His father was an ill-tempered man with little self-control. It was his way, all the time. Donal learned the hard way. How many nights had he cried himself to sleep, accompanied by the sting of a belt? For all his emotions, Donal grew up a disappointment. Every idea he held was cast down as foolish. Every dream thoughtless.

Rather than succumb to depression, Donal took the opposition and used it to become something sterner. He became determined to make a name. To eclipse the disapproving scowl of his father. That passion drove him to Andrak in the service of a brave knight.

"Is it true there are Majj villages below?" Donal asked.

"A great many mysteries haunt the world, Donal. As to the Majj, I have never seen one. Perhaps they are real. Perhaps they are figments of our imagination designed to explain ancient times," Quinlan theorized. He scowled, furious that he'd given in to foolish wastes of time. Quinlan was a man who dealt with what is, not what might be.

"Go to sleep, Donal. I shall take first watch."

Night passed uneventful. The war priests awoke refreshed, despite Quinlan's reservations, and broke camp. Donal poured a pitcher of water on the remains of their fire and was about to store it in his saddle bag when he froze in mid-stride. Three massive creatures stood among the trees, a handful of steps away, glaring back at him. Naked from the waist up, their almost crimson flesh was marred by black streaks in varying patterns. Wild manes crowded their necks and backs, presenting an untamed look. Donal's knees almost gave out.

The Majj rushed before he managed to alert Quinlan. Both men were tackled and tied without managing any defense. They were bound, hands behind their backs and heavy sacks placed over their heads. Quinlan caught one of the horses whinnying. To be eaten? Rough hands dragged him to his feet and shoved him forward.

How many hours passed before they halted, he did not know. The Majj were ruthless in their march down into the Permital. Both Quinlan and Donal stumbled and tripped numerous times during the descent, prompting threatening growls from their captors. At last the slope leveled out and they came to a stop. Exotic birds called and chirped from the canopy. The air was choked with aged vegetation. Primordial to his senses. It was as Quinlan recalled.

They were shoved to the ground, forced to sit while their captors decided what to do with them. That Quinlan wore the light blue of the war priests mattered not. They were trespassers, from what the priest gathered. The animalistic nature exhibited by the Majj prompted many dark thoughts and a dim vision of the future. Without his shield or weapons, there was little Quinlan could do to affect change. His head jerked back as the sack was whisked off.

Filtered sunlight tormented his suddenly sensitive eyes. Quinlan risked a glance to Donal, relieved to find his squire unharmed but for the shock of their experience. He counted more than a dozen Majj surrounding them. None appeared friendly. A bad sign for their continued journey. Donal coughed. A wet sound sparking concern in the older priest.

"Donal, are you well?" he dared ask.

"No speak," the largest Majj snarled. "Priest magic!"

So, they understand what I am. Not as primitive as I supposed. Quinlan found their intelligence accessible. All he needed to find was a common spark. He decided to press.

"Why have you taken us prisoner? You know I am a war priest."

The Majj drew back to strike him but stopped short. Strands of crimson hair fell from his fist. Quinlan became emboldened. These creatures were being prevented from assaulting them. "Who is in charge? I demand to know why you've captured us."

Other Majj straightened, ready to attack. They were unaccustomed to being challenged within their domain. Anger rippled through their muscles. Quinlan had no doubt any one of them was capable of tearing him apart and might do so if he continued his taunting.

A lone howl tore through the trees. Birds of white and green burst into flight. It was a sound long revered for bringing danger. The Majj settled, calmed by the sound. One by one, they parted to allow a much smaller figure through. Quinlan studied him, knowing that this was the being he needed to reason with if he and Donal were going to escape with their lives.

The figure, a male Majj, was tiny compared to the hulking creatures around him. His crimson fur was faded, dulled by time and age. Lines formed on the backs of weathered hands. His face drooped, longer than the others. He wore a hood to conceal all but the lower jaw. Chipped and stained fangs jut up. Leather panels draped down over his shoulders, scraping against his bone vest. He halted a step away from the prisoners.

Quinlan tensed as moments passed without a word spoken. Doubt crept in. Was this strange beast come to pass judgment? They hadn't the chance to defend themselves. The prospect of turning over a Majj spit soured his stomach.

"You should not be here," the figure warned.

Quinlan struggled to keep his sense of relief in check. "My apologies, but we had no intention of entering your territory. My colleague and I have been dispatched on a mission of grave importance by the Lord General. We are en route to the duchy of Fent. Forgive us for trespassing."

The elder creature waved his hand. Gnarled fingernails rested at the end of withered fingers. "This is not my concern. You have entered our kingdom unbidden. Judgment will be passed. Freedom awaits should you prove worthy."

"And if we fall short?"

"Death."

He and Donal were jerked up again and led down the dark and winding paths few humans had ever trod. What awaited at the end remained in doubt. The Majj howled and hurried on.

ELEVEN
Majj Village

Any indignity suffered during their forced march through the thick forests of the Indolense Permital was done in silence. Quinlan, grimacing as claws tightened around his biceps, allowed his captors to shove and drag him through dense vegetation. Thorns from a dozen species of vines and shrubs tore into his trousers, drawing blood on several occasions. Gasps from behind told him Donal shared his torments.

The elder Majj set a quick and steady pace, barreling down time-worn paths all but forgotten by the world above. Sunlight and shadow alternated on his face. Quinlan scuffed across the forest floor, kicking up dust and tripping over rocks and vines. The journey was unpleasant but he arrived unharmed. Aromas of roasting meats filled the air, reminding him of just how hungry he was.

Quinlan hit the ground hard after being shoved down. A corresponding huff from Donal was enough to calm the war priest, if only just. They were considered untouchable in regular society. Defenders of the world, paragons of virtue meant to inspire lesser men. The Majj suffered no such delusions. Quinlan considered their plight, wondering how many tribes were scattered across the continents. Hidden, secreted away from the slow crawl of human expansion. It was a sad dilemma, but one he could not effect.

"Now, perhaps we have a little chat."

Quinlan recognized the elder Majj's voice as his hood was ripped off. They were inside a grass hut with a dirt floor. It lacked the stench of habitation, suggesting the Majj used it sparsely. Quinlan doubted they received many visitors.

"You can speak now."

Quinlan licked his lips. "Our coming here is through no fault of our own. My people were led to believe the Majj lived within the Permital. It was never our intention to come down this far."

The Majj sneered, or perhaps it was his natural look. "Your people once hunted mine to the steps of extinction. We are no allies, you and I."

"Those I associate with have never harmed the Majj. We are peaceful men and women who stand on the edge of the darkness. Keeping the Omegri at bay is our only concern."

Quinlan winced inwardly. He wasn't accustomed to begging, nor was he adept at presenting meekness. A warrior from late youth, Quinlan lived humble, yet in a position of power. What little he knew of the Majj was enough to suggest they respected strength above all else. Quinlan changed tactics.

"Let us go. We have important business to attend," he demanded.

Eyes narrowed. The Majj seemed unsure whether to laugh or attack. Quinlan didn't know if that was a good sign.

At last the Majj tipped his head back and chuckled, a throaty growl vibrating the ground. "You have courage. Good. You die otherwise. Many warriors would gorge on you. You," he gestured toward Donal, "not so much."

Donal blanched. The thought of being devoured by hungry warriors sickened him.

Quinlan pressed. "Why abduct us at all? There is evil afoot and we have been sent to stop it. Surely you Majj understand the concept of evil?"

"Many lifetimes we fight. Evil is part of life. You know this, I think. These colors I have seen before. What is your name?"

"I am Quinlan. This is Donal, my squire. I am a war priest from Castle Andrak," he said.

The Majj tapped his chest. "I am Oonal Oonalak. Clan elder."

Progress. "You speak very well."

"I have learned many languages and mannerisms, from most races. It is part of my position," Oonal boasted. "Most Majj remain in the lower warrior caste."

"If you recognize who I am, why force us down here?" Quinlan asked. Curiosity got the best of him. There was duplicity among the Majj. Of that he was now certain.

Oonal made a show of looking around to ensure they were alone. "Great evil is stirring. War is coming. Which side we Majj join remains to be seen."

"What war?" The implications, if true, were staggering. Quinlan struggled to imagine a world at war.

Oonal waved him silent as two guards arrived. "We will continue this later. I have matters to attend." He leaned conspiratorially close. "Ware your tongue. All is not as it seems."

He left Quinlan untied and cornered. Even if Quinlan had his shield and weapons, he would not have been able to overpower the massive guards standing outside the door.

"Are you well, Donal?"

Rubbing his chaffed wrists, the young squire nodded. His glum mood reflected in his face. "Well enough, sir. I admit they frightened me at first."

"So, too, with me. I do not believe they mean us harm though. The Majj seem enigmatic, reclusive. I sense hesitancy in Oonal. It is almost as if he laments detaining us," Quinlan admitted. "Do not speak more on this. If what he said is true, we are most certainly being eavesdropped upon. Take rest. I suggest you meditate. Perhaps the solution to this problem will present itself." *And we can be on our way to Fent.*

Quinlan closed his eyes, mind racing through scenarios and possibilities, both absurd and terrifyingly plausible. Oonal's words sparked fear. War. It had been generations since the duchies last went to war with each other. The war priests had helped broker peace after years of unending slaughter. Only now was the land recovering to the point of prosperity.

The thought of war proved doubly concerning when Quinlan failed to recognize any meaningful threat aside from the Omegri, and they could only attempt to enter this world during the Burning Season. Who then? He'd originally come from Thalis, far to the west, but the continent was too far away for any major force to amount an invasion. Lacking information, he was resigned to stewing over what might be.

Dusk brought two bowls of water and roasted meat. Quinlan and Donal devoured each before settling back. They'd lost much energy and strength during the trek down into the Permital and then, in his estimation, halfway across the valley floor. The proximity to the center suggested Oonal's clan was one of immense power, perhaps overall in charge of their diminutive empire. If such were true, he should find treating with Oonal much easier the next time he arrived.

"What happens if they decide not to let us go?" Donal spoiled the mood. His youth and inexperience brought out harsh questions many others might not have asked.

Quinlan faked a smile. "We must have faith. Do not despair, for it leads to misery. The Majj will come around and we shall be free to resume our purpose."

"I wish I had your confidence," Donal admitted.

Is that what it appears? Do not be so quick to long for another's life. You might not like what you find. "All in due time, squire. The mastery of confidence does not come to all, though I deem you of higher quality than most. You will become a great priest, Donal. I sense it."

Beaming with pride, Donal yawned and stretched. Most of the soreness was gone. The minor scratches were closed, already healing. The food and water revived him, providing much needed strength. He found he could think clearly again. A small price for remaining captive. Donal stole glances at Quinlan. The older priest sat cross-legged with the backs of his hands resting on his knees. His eyes were now closed. Donal knew better than to interrupt when Quinlan was like this.

Scratching his jaw and surprised to find a rose ant attempting to bite into him, Donal listened to the sounds of the forest. It was alien. A foreign landscape he wasn't prepared to endure. Birds and insects sounded different, providing him with a feeling of terror inspired loneliness.

Night deepened. Many of the Majj passed off to sleep. Only a core handful remained around the fires. Donal wondered at them. Ancient, the Majj were said to be one of the first races. He found them frightening to behold. Monsters from a less civilized era. That entire continents were once filled with tribes of Majj left Donal uninspired, for their fall reflected all life. How long would it be before future historians said the same of humanity?

Sleep beckoned and Donal was ill fitted to refuse. He yawned again, this time fighting his drooping eyelids. Half asleep, he barely made out the sounds of bodies falling to the ground in boneless heaps. It was enough to rouse his fledgling warrior senses. Donal picked up rustling. The faintest scrape of bare feet across the carpet of grass. He looked to Quinlan, surprised to find the priest's eyes open and staring at the entrance.

Why aren't you doing anything? Donal felt panic. The Majj were coming to kill them. An anonymous demise in a forgotten part of the world. He searched the hut for anything he could use as a weapon, but Oonal had been clever. The hut was empty. Red feet came into view. Donal felt the iced fingers of death curl around his throat.

"We must hurry. There is no time," Oonal announced as he entered. His bright yellow eyes bore a pained expression.

Quinlan was on his feet and moving before the Majj finished talking. It felt to Donal as if he'd been expecting such a move. The duo followed Oonal outside, stepping over the pair of snoring guards as they made their way to the south end of the village. Oonal insisted on silence until they were well beyond the range of sight and sound. Donal felt as if they'd been walking for hours, though in truth it was less than one before they emerged from the thick forests and once again looked upon the walls of the cliff face.

"Your horses and weapons await you up there," Oonal gestured. "You must hurry."

"Thank you, Oonal. I shall not forget this," Quinlan affirmed.

The elder Majj regarded him, wild mane shifting as he cocked his head. "It might be better if you did. The Majj will be furious when they learn what I have done. It is possible I lose my status. We shall see."

Donal asked, "Why are you helping us?"

Good lad. Quinlan approved of his squire's curiosity. The order went far to develop initiate's critical thinking skills.

Oonal bobbed his head. "The Majj are split. Some believe all outsiders to be threats to our way of life. Others think that we should join forces, for the betterment of both species. I stand in the middle, forced to hear all complaints. There was a plot to kill you this night. I could not allow that to happen, for I have not yet made up my mind about you."

Donal's stomach lurched.

"There is ... something about you, war priest. A light most cannot see. I believe you are important to the coming days." Oonal shrugged. "As I said, war is coming. We must all choose sides."

He stalked off, leaving priest and squire to ponder his words while making the arduous climb free of the Indolense Permital. Donal's desire to explore the lost places of the world faded after his experience at the hands of the Majj. He was starting to think the world was more dangerous than his youthful mind entertained.

Hand over hand they climbed. Quinlan set the pace, knowing that at any moment their absence would be discovered and a pack of Majj would be after them. Gain the summit and they stood a chance of escape. He climbed faster, urging Donal on. They were halfway to the top when the first bloodcurdling howl broke the night still. They'd been discovered.

"Quickly, Donal! There is no time!" Quinlan urged.

The war priest took great strides, feeling his legs burn from the effort. Additional howls arose. The hunt was on. Quinlan wasn't a man prone to fear, but the primal demeanor the Majj exhibited told him all he needed to know of what would happen if they were caught. For every step up, the surface appeared farther away.

TWELVE
Village of Palis

Sergeant Sava was a cruel man out of necessity. Hardened as only a noncommissioned officer could be, he drilled his platoon relentlessly through day and night, regardless of the weather. Two days of drill brought most villagers out to witness the spectacle. Seldom had entire units of soldiers occupied Palis. They were in awe of the uniforms and polished steel.

Sava snarled with each miscue, though in truth, it was difficult to tell if he was angry or if this was his natural state of being. Puddles of crimson colored spit marked his passing. Every step taken rang across the cobblestones of the main avenue, for he made a show of stomping the iron ferrule tip of his walking stick. His soldiers knew too well that the stick had little to do with walking. All of them bore bruises from being cracked at one point for some infraction they weren't aware they'd committed. Sava laughed with each blow.

The sound grated on Nils. He bore his share of bruises over the last two years and liked to think he was evolved beyond the punishment. There was a time when he viewed Sava with abject hatred, but time proved a valuable teacher. Nils learned that, despite Sava's gruff appearance, the sergeant had only the best intentions for his platoon. He was a consummate professional, if angrier than most. The company benefited from his experience. They were the best of Fent's ten companies.

None of that mattered for the men and women grinding away in the sleepy village of Palis. Nils had never been this far north and after spending a pair of days here, didn't see much reason to return after their mission ended. The crack-crack of Sava's stick echoed somewhere behind him. Nils cringed at the thought of another soldier being knocked. Maybe he wasn't used to it after all.

"Does he ever stop?" Alfar asked. His voice was low to avoid being overheard.

Nils sighed, already tired of the conversation. They'd drawn the lucky straw and were assigned guard duty at the southern entrance. Thus far, not a single traveler had come calling, making for a pleasant afternoon.

"Have you ever heard that speaking about someone usually draws them near?" he asked.

Alfar blinked. Clearly not.

"Keep talking about the sergeant and he'll find a way to come over here," Nils warned. He almost hoped Sava arrived and knocked sense into Alfar. The boy was driving him mad with innocuous questions.

Alfar shrugged. "Too late."

Nils reluctantly looked down the road and watched as Sava stomped toward the guard post. *So much for a quiet afternoon.* Nils braced for the storm and ordered Alfar to tidy their area up. Anything to prevent Sava from erupting.

"Sergeant Sava," he acknowledged.

Sava spat. Thin ropes of red-brown saliva trailed down his chin. "Trooper. How goes it?"

"All quiet, Sergeant," Alfar chimed in.

Nils winced.

Sava turned his predatory glare on Alfar, withering the young soldier. "Wasn't speaking at you, soldier. You'd do well to remember your place in the future."

Alfar gulped.

Sava returned to Nils. "Not so bright, this one. Is he?"

Nils stood at a crossroads. He wouldn't mind seeing Alfar get cracked, but they were a team and he wasn't the sort to abandon a comrade when moments grew tense. "Sergeant, what can we do for you?"

The stick twitched.

"Captain wants all hands on full alert. He's leading a patrol out to scout those low rocky hills to the east. No sleeping till we come back. Understood?"

The realization that they were going to be trapped on guard duty for much longer than their original shift sank in. Nils was starting to think Alfar was a bad luck charm. *So much for a quiet day and a night off.* He watched Sava storm off. The man was in a perpetual hurry, as if some battle loomed just over the horizon. The crack-crack of his stick made Nils flinch.

Kastus paced the length of the mostly empty hall under the waiting gaze of Captain Thep. Close to half of the garrison was deployed on patrols in the surrounding countryside. Discourse was yet to develop among the citizenry and neither man anticipated problems. None of this caedlm the rising doubt in the back of Kastus's mind. The longer he spent in Palis, the more he suspected something sinister lurking beneath the friendly façade.

"Constable, you're going to wear a hole in the floor," Thep commented when the constant repetition started to annoy him.

Kastus scowled and kept walking. "Captain, why can't I shake the feeling that we are missing a vital component of this task?"

"Everything about this feels surreal," Thep answered. "We are dealing with the supernatural. If this Brogon Lord exists."

"It would be easier if you had seen the grave site," Kastus stopped. "Some matters are inexplicable. Unfortunately, it is not Brogon Lord that worries me."

"The elders," Thep concluded. They'd bothered him as well, enough to prompt his doubling of the guards and presence patrols.

Kastus nodded. "Yes."

Nerves getting the better of him, Thep began pacing. "Which one? I suspect Deana of hiding something. Her actions are too hostile. She poses a problem."

"She does, but Deana is typical of many of these small villages. A bitter hag by most accounts. I shouldn't worry too much about her. She is what I expected," Kastus admitted. "No, Thep. It is the others who worry me."

The other elders were already in the twilight of their lives. Time was catching them. Death but a step away. Thep thought Mugh already had a foot in the grave, whereas Waern was obstinate for the sake of. How progress was made in Palis was beyond his comprehension. Many of the villages he'd visited lacked the central infrastructure of the capital, despite established trade routes and government assistance. Thep figured that far too many people were content with the old ways when each village stood alone. That archaic form of self-governance had long since proven ineffective.

"How do you wish to proceed?" he asked. The prospect of interrogating his own people felt wrong, despite the growing necessity.

Kastus mused at the reflection Thep presented. *Interesting how one mimics the other.* "Divide and conquer. It would be easier if we got them alone. Together they are too conflicting to be useful. We question them one at a time and keep the other occupied so they cannot corroborate stories."

Thep agreed, deciding there was prudence in allowing Kastus to exercise judicial authority. Use of the military in this setting was fraught with peril. "We should be able to accomplish that with minimal effort and manpower. Who shall I summon first?"

The grin he showed was hollow. "Bring me Deana."

It had been a long time since he felt cowed in the presence of a woman. The last one to bring him to heel had been his mother. Memories Kastus neither appreciated nor enjoyed. The overly stern look Deana bore as she was escorted into the hall left little doubt as to whether he was going to enjoy what came next.

"Lady Deana, please do be seated," he gestured to the empty chair on the near side of the table.

Her look was one of disdain, as if the low-quality furniture were unworthy of her grace. She sat anyway. "What is the meaning of this, Constable? I grow weary of your presence, and only after two days. Perhaps it is time to conclude your investigation and move on."

The thought of slapping her smug look away was the only thing calming him. "We will leave once our business is finished. As of yet, there has been no sign of our quarry. I am pleased, however, to say that the villagers have proven most helpful."

They'd only been forced to detain one older man when Sava and a squad attempted to search his home. Other than that, the occupation was proceeding smoothly.

"Let us stop mincing words, Constable. What is your true purpose for being here?" she asked.

He thought he detected the slightest hint of caution in her tone. A good sign if true. "Very well. I have never been one to dance around the heart of the matter. The Grey Wanderer has risen a man from the dead. His name was Brogon Lord and we have tracked his movements in this direction. It is plausible that he may strike here at any moment."

"You mentioned this earlier," Deana was unimpressed.

Kastus nodded. "I did, but I did not understand the politics of what was transpiring here. There is something amiss with you elders. Captain Thep and I have concluded that one or more of you are possibly in league with the F'talle."

Her stunned silence was the reaction he'd hoped for but did not expect. "Who do you suspect?"

"That is what we are attempting to discover. If our belief is true, the once dead man will either be alerted to our presence or move up his schedule," Thep interjected.

"Is it you?" Kastus asked.

Her bottom lip quivered as she began to speak.

Stepping outside after several hours of interrogation was a welcome blessing. Kastus was good at his job. Baron Einos enjoyed the confidence of knowing any task would be performed to standard with Kastus in charge. That did little to assuage his gnawing doubts the deeper into this mystery he became entangled. He almost wished he smoked.

"That was ... difficult," Thep said after joining him.

The last of the elders was escorted away, leaving the pair with more questions than they had to begin with. The only certainty Kastus came away with was madness gripped half the kingdom, making his desire to catch Brogon Lord that much more powerful.

"I think we could get away with chaining them together and throwing them into the river. Obstinate fools the lot," Kastus agreed. "What was your impression?"

That it was time to depart Palis was his initial thought. Their leaders were ineffective and clearly harboring secrets none were meant to know.

"I am starting to think we are wasting time here," he said. "The elders aren't ready to break, though I suspect Deana will crack first. She seems to love power and will go to great lengths to preserve it."

"That was my thought as well. Mugh and Waern are more problematic. Of course, they are also bordering senility," Kastus chuckled. "We keep the pressure on Deana. One of these bastards will talk. Has there been any word on the patrols?"

A clouded look marred his face. "None. I admit that I am growing concerned. They should have reported in by now."

"What would your fearsome platoon sergeant have to say about that?" Kastus asked. There were very few men he could think of that inspired genuine fear. Sava was high on that list.

"He would have already sent another squad out. Losing people doesn't sit right with him," Thep said. "If it were bandits I might agree, but not against the supernatural."

"Agreed. Has there been any movement around the perimeter?" The words felt awkward rolling off his tongue. Kastus was no soldier and seldom had reason to use their language.

Thep shook his head. "All is quiet. Do you think our dead man decided to strike the other village?"

Kastus had considered the possibility. "He might have, but we should have received word by now if he had. The platoon in Jul is no less capable than the one we have here."

Discoloration on the horizon drew their attention. Near enough to spy, yet just far enough away to blur it

"What do you suppose that is?" Thep asked.

Thunder rolled across the grassy plains, yet no clouds filled the sky. Arcs of lightning followed by flashes of bright green light raged. Kastus suspected he knew but was loath to tell the young captain. After all, he still wasn't sure if he had seen the sclarem or whether it was but a dream. One mystery at a time. It was all he could handle.

THIRTEEN

The Once Dead Man

Resurrection awakened previously unknown desires. Brogon Lord once lived honorably. A true knight in every sense. His last thoughts, as he lay dying from a stab wound to his stomach, were only of having lived as well as possible. Death held no regrets. Awakening, trapped in his decaying body, vilified all he once stood for. Necrotic impulses spurred him. He was locked in a realm that shouldn't exist.

If his masters found irony in any of this, they failed to display it. Brogon never saw who controlled his strings. Never spoke with those in command. All orders were issued through the mouths of his children and he was powerless to disobey. Worse, he was discovering that he enjoyed stealing children. The world was such an awful place. They deserved better than to be trapped in a mundane existence until their bodies stopped working, or worse. Better to leave the land of the living behind and embrace a higher calling.

The clock tower was progressing on pace with his masters' wishes. He wasn't privileged to know what it was for. The masters never spoke of that. Only that they needed more children for the construction. Brogon wasn't the only child thief. Several others came and went, delivering fresh souls for the great labor. One day, his purpose would end. He knew that. What he didn't know was what the masters would do with him.

Northern Fent was unremarkable. Brogon stalked across the night landscape. Always at night, lest the living see his true persona. Muscles drooped from bones. Holes, created by an army of insects, pockmarked his body. Yellowed bones showed through. Brogon was disgusted with what he saw, yet marveled that he managed to function. And with greater strength than in life.

Remnants of clothing, once finery fit for a king's court, clung to him in tattered rags. His station had fallen. Brogon spared no thought for loved ones still among the living. They meant little. Paramount was the desire to accumulate more children. That desire fueled him in unimaginable ways. Some primal instinct he failed to understand sent him to the children's homes. He liked to think they felt no pain. Just a snap of the neck and they were free.

Why the masters chose Fent mattered not. One duchy was the same as the rest. The people were the same in every village. Oh how he imagined mothers wailed upon discovering that empty bed. Worried in the doorway when their child did not return home. He wished he could help them. Reassure them that their children were now safe and fulfilling a greater purpose. He might even take the parents with him, but the masters were adamant about him taking children only.

The moon had yet to rise, leaving the land blanketed in the haunting state trapped between light and dark. It had rained earlier in the day, leaving the ground cleansed and with a fresh smell. Did he ever take the time to enjoy the little things in life? He doubted it. Brogon was a warrior. His every thought was bent to the task of becoming better.

Brogon slogged through a small brook, where the water came up to his shins. Much of it seeped into the cracks in his flesh, adding unnecessary weight. He came up the slope on the opposite side and halted. Danger was nearby. An enemy he did not expect to confront.

"You should not walk this world."

Brogon stared up at the green skinned monster looming over him. He grinned, or would have, if he still had lips. It had been too long since his last true battle. Brogon Lord attacked.

Sava was born for walking. His people came from across the sea. They were ever on the move. Nomadic. The how or why was lost to time. All he knew was that a great diaspora occurred, forcing his parents to make the fraught-filled voyage to a distant land where assimilation was next to impossible. Sava didn't mind. He enjoyed roaming the world, for there was so much to see. The colossus of Apocalon was by far the most intriguing sight. A one hundred twenty foot statue of a forgotten warrior from lore. It inspired Sava, giving him hope that one day he, too, might become immortalized.

The mood among his platoon did not reflect his personal preference. Grumbling echoed through the ranks when they thought he was out of earshot. Sava was no fool. He knew his reputation among the men and did everything within his control to foster that illusion. Soldiers, in his estimation, needed to be hard. Softness was weakness that got people killed. He had no plans for dying anytime soon.

The squads branched off shortly after leaving view of Palis. Sava wasn't pleased by having half of his force outside of his operational control. These were his men and women. It was his duty to bring them all home, alive and in one piece. He watched them for as long as he could stand, as long as mission could broker a delay. Their squad sergeant was junior but had more experience than Captain Thep. Sava begrudgingly admitted they were in good hands and ordered his squad forward.

They swept leagues of land over the course of two days, searching caves and deep forests. Thus far, they'd found nothing to suggest their quarry was anywhere in the region, further disheartening the squad. Sava pushed them on. He'd left his walking stick behind, but managed to find a thicker, greener branch to utilize. Anything to keep his men comfortable.

Disappointment prompted Sava to push the patrol longer than it was meant to last. He couldn't return to Palis without results. Thep would be furious, but Sava learned long ago that it was better to ask forgiveness than permission. The hallmark of every good sergeant was the inherent ability to accomplish tasks with minimal supervision. Sava was considered one of the best in their army. A compliment he would take to the grave.

Dusk was settling in a slow crawl Sava found soothing. His calves burned from the endless marching. Blisters formed on his feet, but the curtain of night dropping eased his worries. It felt like the daily cleansing of his soul. He never spoke of it to anyone. How could they understand? Sava was the meanest man in the army. To learn he was soothed by nature would evoke unending laughter.

Undaunted, Sava enjoyed his moment. He ordered them to resume the movement only when he was satisfied the sun was well below the horizon. A chorus of groans echoed his orders. Sava left them to their complaining. Armies moved on gripes. They were far enough away from civilization that he wasn't worried about it.

"Sergeant Sava! I spotted movement ahead," Burgil, the youngest ranker started to shout before remembering his training.

Sava's right arm shot up, fist clenched. Those nearest stopped immediately and took a knee. A rippling effect followed until they were all crouched to reduce their silhouettes. The moon was still out of sight, forcing them to adjust to the semi-darkness. Sava scurried forward to where Burgil was pointing. This late in the evening, every tree or bush was a potential enemy waiting in ambush. They were also harmless and slowed operations to a crawl.

"Where?" he whispered. Sava wasn't one to take unnecessary chances.

Burgil eased forward another step and pointed to the right. "There, behind that stand of trees. Whatever I saw was large, bigger than a man."

"Are you sure?" Night played havoc on a soldier's mind.

"Enough," Burgil replied.

That was enough for Sava. He had the squad on line, in battle order. Crossbows flanked him. Long swords protected the ends. Satisfied all was in order, he led them forward. Rocks crunched underfoot. Boots sank into soft dirt and random spots of mud. Every sound was amplified, threatening to give their position away.

A twig snapped, forcing Sava to glare. About to dress the soldier down, Sava froze in place when an explosion of energies lit the night sky. Burgil was blown off his feet. Others staggered. Arrows flew.

"Ceasefire! What was that?" Sava bellowed.

A second explosion, this one bright green, shredded trees. Sava spied a man-sized figure flying back to crash into a boulder. Dust and stone billowed around him.

"Close ranks. Full circle!" Sava ordered.

Soldiers hurried into position. The jangle of armor shifting reassuring. They advanced in step. Whatever awaited was about to meet Fent steel. Sava swiveled into the point position. He was going to be the first to engage. A monstrosity emerged from the night, halting the circle in muted fright.

Taller, bulkier than any man, the creature was green with unkempt hair the color of blackest night. Sava caught the scent of warm urine from one of his men. He didn't blame him. There was no reason for this monster's existence. He was about to order the attack when a scarier image charged at the monster. It took a while for his eyes to adjust to the low light, but Sava could determine the second, smaller creature was a man. A decomposing man.

"Got you, bastard," he muttered. "That's our target! Ignore the green thing and take down that dead man! Attack!"

The soldiers of Fent roared and charged across the final twenty meters. Crossbows, already reloaded, thrummed. Both arrows struck Brogon, penetrating deep into desiccated flesh where they remained. Enraged, Brogon drew his sword and turned on the soldiers. Sava broke free, sword in both hands, and met the once dead man alone. Sparks showered over his gloved hands as swords clashed. Sava was bigger, stronger, but Brogon was faster. He blocked a blow aimed at his head and drove his elbow into Sava's face. Cartilage crunched and Sava reeled back with a broken nose.

Bolts of green-yellow energy blasted from the green monster and struck Brogon in the face and chest. The once dead man howled and leapt at the monster. A massive staff, easily the size of a man, swung out to catch him in midair. Velocity swept Brogon away from the battlefield.

The green monster looked down on the soldiers of Fent with blazing yellow eyes. "Go, this is not your battle."

His muscles bulged. They could see rivers of power running through his veins. A musky stench choked the air. Men and women gagged. The green monster clicked his tusks together and stormed after Brogon Lord. His message was delivered. Burgil and one other helped their dazed sergeant up and started the long retreat back to Palis. Sava grumbled for the first third of a league before relenting. He was forced to admit his squad was no match for the green monster.

They halted far from the battle. Flashes of green light continued to march across northern Fent. It was a sight Sava hoped to never see again. His vision swam. Blood caked his chin, staining his tunic and armor. Every time he tried to speak, jets of pain lance through his head.

"Sergeant Sava, what was that thing?" Gurri asked. Her sword lay across her right shoulder. Her chest heaved as she struggled to catch her breath.

"What just happened?"

"Will they come back?"

Sava shrugged off Burgil, and reaching deep into his trouser pocket, produced a pinch of kaapa leaves. He shoved them in the corner of his mouth and felt near instant satisfaction. Too many questions. Sava made a quick headcount, surprised to find all of them present.

"That was a nasty surprise if I ever seen one," he said, wincing with each syllable. "What you just saw was an impossible battle between our quarry, Brogon Lord, and one of the Sclarem. Remember this night, kiddies. Remember it and pray you never have another like it. The bowels of the underworld are alive and well in Fent."

As one, they stared off in the direction of the fading blasts of power.

FOURTEEN
Castle Fent

Einos found difficulty in believing in ghosts after a lifetime of disbelief. Folk tales belonged among the people, not among the ranks of leadership expected to guide them through the trials life offered. Weeks had gone by and the memory of seeing Tabith sitting in his bedroom continued to bother him. What could not exist, should not exist.

The confliction drove current policy. Einos spent hours mired in the examination of his beliefs, knowing the monster that was Brogon Lord was reaping a terrible toll across his small duchy. That similar incidents might be occurring throughout the lands never entered his thoughts. Grieving families petitioned him daily, forcing his waking hours to see to their comfort, such that he could offer, while hoping Kastus and the army found success in the field.

Faint streaks of light streamed through the bank of hazy clouds to strike his back. Einos felt no warmth, however, for he stood before the empty hearth staring down at where he saw the ghost. The Baron of Fent liked to think he was a practical man, void of the superstitious nonsense gripping his population. Hands clasped behind his back, Einos frowned. The red and gold of his robes were at odds with the drab grey floor.

"Husband, you worry yourself to no end," Aneth chided from behind.

He hadn't heard her glide into the room. Einos erased the look of consternation before turning. "Beloved, were these not such troubling times, I would have no reason to worry."

Her hands slid over his broad shoulders, burrowing into the softness of the fabric. "Do you truly suppose you saw Lizette's daughter?"

"I don't know what I saw. A vision perhaps. A glimpse into the future or even the past? I do not pretend to know all that happens in the natural world."

"There was nothing natural about what you saw," Aneth said. "The wall between realms must be thin for children to return."

He grunted, unwilling to commit further answer.

Sensing his mounting frustration, Aneth placed her head on his back. "We will get through this."

Einos reached a hand up to cover hers. "I know, though I fear how much more we will lose before the end."

They stood like that for a time. Affairs of state robbed him of much quality time with his wife. Time he should have given to developing his family. Such was the burden of leadership. Einos sighed, feeling some of the weight slip away. He wished for simpler times, but wishes were akin to the supernatural. Neither was meant to reach fruition.

"What news of the war priests? Has the Lord General dispatched anyone?" Aneth asked after a time.

"I can only assume," Einos slipped from her embrace to face her. "Rosca is not known for his endearing personality. There is every chance he has deployed one of his priests, but no way of knowing unless he sent a messenger bird."

"Or the priest arrives," she finished.

He nodded. A faraway look clouded his eyes. First the appearance of ghosts and a F'talle ranging his lands. Now comes the war priests and their unnatural ways. Ways he believed the world would be better off without. Einos snorted after realizing his views were close to Kastus's. The man was a boon companion and quality leader, but his distrust of the war priests was borderline hatred. Obsession came to mind.

"Lizette is waiting downstairs," Aneth mentioned. They'd become friends over the past few weeks. It was a friendship born of mutual loss.

Einos closed his eyes.

"I can meet with her if you like," she suggested.

His posture told her Einos wasn't up to entertaining his newest staff member. *Self-appointed staff member. Forceful woman. Still, I suppose there is much to be said for having strength around me.*

"That would be a welcome kindness," Einos admitted. "Thank you."

She edged up on her toes to kiss his cheek. "Of course, husband."

She was almost at the door when he called, "Aneth, I love you."

Aneth flashed a grin. "I know."

Lizette felt like she was losing her grip on reality. Sanity threatened to abandon her the more she studied the map marking all the abductions. She snorted. Murders. None of the children had been seen again, save for the spike in ghost sightings. Any hope of seeing Tabith again was lost. Shattered upon the stone. Lizette was finally alone in the world. A listless woman with no future and only a fragmented past. At least until she found solace in comforting other families who had endured similar loss.

Fent was much smaller than most of the other duchies, providing an intimate community where everyone knew each other. Lizette imagined life was somewhat different here in the capital, but the smaller villages and communities clung together. She liked that. The notion that all were one, felt right. She now had the opportunity to unite others, to make a difference.

Einos had different views, or so she assumed. The Baron was polite and tolerated her more than she expected, but there was a limit to his generosity. Paramount to his designs was finding and stopping Brogon Lord. The once dead man was a plague upon the duchy. Fent lingered on the edge of panic. The people were scared. Revolutions began from less.

"I thought to find you here."

Lizette struggled to suppress her sigh. She hadn't wished to be disturbed. "Good morning, Baroness."

Aneth waved off the formality. "Hush. It is only the two of us. Let us leave titles for my husband. We can be ladies here. Friends."

To a woman like Lizette, who had only seen the Baron from a distance before her plight, speaking with royalty on equal terms was astounding. She was a commoner. A face in the crowd. "Old habits are hard to break."

"They are. As we are all discovering," Aneth slid forward to grab Lizette by the arm and guided her away. "I am pleased to see you settling into your new role. This castle needs more strong women. Too many men spoil matters and the conversation is drool."

"Where are we heading, Aneth?" Lizette forced the name out.

The Baroness smiled in return. Genuine, warm. "I wish to show you my favorite part of the castle. All know of it, yet none are permitted to enter unless my permission is given."

Visions of being cast into the deepest dungeon flashed past, leaving Lizette confused.

"Problems?" Aneth asked.

Embarrassment flushed her face. "No, I fear I am still finding difficulty in this transition."

Truthfully, she endured long hours in the darkest night lamenting her losses. Staff often whispered of hearing a woman's sobs. Lizette was trapped in an impossible duality. Broken internally, she presented a fierce, determined stance in front of others. The pain continued to lessen, if only just.

They continued walking in silence. Aneth was at a loss for words. She had no comparable experience, other than the knowledge of too many families suffering similar fates. It was her hope that she might alleviate some of that pain this morning by showing Lizette her secret place. She lurched suddenly, bracing a hand against the wall to keep from falling.

"Aneth! Are you all right?" Lizette almost shouted.

The Baroness nodded, eyes filled with amazement. "The baby. I felt it move!"

Lizette became lost in the moment. She reached out to touch Aneth's stomach. "That is wonderful!"

For a moment, thoughts of hardship and sorrow dissipated. They were two women celebrating life.

Midmorning was always Einos's favorite time. The sun was up and warming the world, yet not hot enough to prove uncomfortable. Today, however, there was no joy. He stood over the empty grave, peering down as if to make Brogon Lord's body magically reappear. The matter had drawn on long enough and was now threatening to stall progress.

Two others accompanied him. One was old, borderline decrepit. His robes were in tatters and stained from too many years without a proper cleaning. Grime caked under unhealthy nails. Lines trailed out from the corners of his eyes. Eyes showing remarkable clarity. Rail thin, the man stood with hunched shoulders.

"Tender Cannandal, are you ready to begin?" Einos asked.

His distaste for the tender of the dead was plain on his face. Speaking to the dead twisted a man, rendering him incapable of interacting with others in a normal fashion. Einos made sure to stand away from the man. He would have like to have said it was out of respect, but the truth was much darker. Tenders were to be feared.

Cannandal waved. "Yes, yes! Begin now is best. Ill powers linger here."

The second man stepped back. His hawkish glare diminished when confronted by the insanity the Tender presented. In contrast, his clothing was of the finest material. He presented a well-kept, manicured appearance. Coal black hair tapered down the back of his neck, ending in a neat line at the collar. A thin cape, as was the fashion in the larger duchies, hung limp in the windless morning.

"Baron, is this necessary?" his voice was deep, grinding on the ears.

"I would have us do all that is possible before the war priests arrive, Merchant Giles." Einos wasn't certain which one he liked less. One helped the dead move, on while the other busied fleecing pockets in the name of social advancements. He'd never felt more trapped.

"This man offends me," Giles insisted.

If Cannandal was offended in return, he failed to show it.

Einos glared. "Begin if you please, Tender."

Cannandal nodded, his focus on the grave. The elderly man knelt and placed his hands on the grave's edge. His finger burrowed into the soft earth. Moments passed without anything happening. Einos grew concerned. Then it began. Minor vibrations in the ground. Hairs standing on end. Einos felt the urge to urinate as his innards shook and twisted. Eldritch magic.

Giles turned and retched as the Tender continued. Smoke drifted up from his collar. His flesh sizzled from unnatural heat. The world blurred. Einos thought he heard moans, supernatural wailing coming from the depths of the earth. Ethereal hands reached up, desperate to gain purchase in the realm of the living where they were no longer welcome. And then it was over. Cannandal withdrew his hands. Blood seeped from his fingertips.

"Were you successful?" Einos asked. His vision swam, threatening to nauseate him.

The Tender kept his gaze to the ground. The shame of failure preventing him from speaking. It was that moment Einos knew the once dead man was not vanquished. That he yet walked the world in search of fresh souls and that Fent was not going to find succor until the war priests arrived. If they arrived.

"This was all for nothing," Giles spat, hands on his knees. "I invested a lot of money in this endeavor, Baron. I expect to be compensated."

Heartless prick. Einos could have censured the man, claiming the funds as his due for the greater good of the duchy. Doing so would spark riots between the state and merchant guild. Fent was already small, engaging in a war with the most powerful faction in the land would ruin him, condemning future generations to poverty, or worse.

"You will be, Merchant Giles. All in due course," Einos ground out. Were he a lesser man, he might have cast Giles into the dungeons. Instead, the merchant was a demon he was forced to endure. Some battles weren't worth the effort.

"Baron Einos! A rider has returned from Palis!" the herald shouted as he ran up the dirt lane.

Einos jerked his head, eyes ablaze with hope. "Show me."

He prayed that this would be the end of the once dead man and the ills plaguing his duchy.

FIFTEEN

North of Fent

Mild as the brutality they'd endured at the hands of the Majj was, neither Quinlan nor Donal felt like speaking for the remainder of the day. Not that either had been afforded the opportunity. Packs of Majj warriors continued hounding them long past the boundaries of the Permital, suggesting they were about to expand their realm. Quinlan viewed this as a bad sign as he forced his steed to go faster. There was an urgent warning hidden in Oonal's words. One with potential implications for the war priests. It wasn't what the Majj chieftain said, but what he didn't. Quinlan couldn't shake the ominous sensations crawling over his flesh.

They rode hard, evading the Majj throughout the remainder of the day and stopping only when he was certain the warriors had given up and retreated back to their secluded villages. Quinlan guided them to a small copse of red firs standing alone beside a quiet stream. Open plains surrounded them, stripping would-be attackers of camouflage. The prospect of danger was still real, forcing the war priest to abandon thoughts of a fire. Donal groaned inwardly at the prospect of cold travel rations once again.

They settled down in silence as the curtain of night began to drape across the land. Quinlan finished his meal of hard biscuits and dried meat, washing it down with water from the stream. Having their horses waiting for them where they escaped from the Permital was a blessing, but one that came with fresh suspicions. What game was the Majj chief playing at? His actions suggested he was seeking allies for the coming war he hinted at.

There were many strange events occurring across the world, most going unnoticed. The war priests were a force to stand against the uncanny, ready to defend the people from nightmares both real and imagined. Brush wars were a constant source of irritation, for it seemed that mankind had no interest in living in harmony. Quinlan fumed at the ignorance of it. The Omegri threatened to erase humanity from existence, yet still the duchies squabbled and spilled blood in the vain pursuit of dominance.

"Is everything all right?" Donal asked. He covered his burp with the back of his hand, wincing at the stale flavors reentering his mouth. "Aside from the food, that is."

Quinlan forced a smile. He enjoyed his conversations with young Donal, but there were times when solitude was required. "No, Donal. I am plagued by many concerns, none of them need worry you. Yet. Give me some time to process what we have been through. I am troubled but know not why."

Donal responded with a nod. He learned long ago to allow his superiors room when they asked for it. Sir Forlei wasn't a cruel master, but he expected his demands met without question. Snatching up both canteens, Donal stalked off to the stream. The night was crisp and cool. A telltale sign that summer was drawing to a close.

Night insects began their symphony, a roaring chorus of chirps and whistles that once irritated him. Donal had never been one to enjoy the hard comforts of the wild, not when a soft bed awaited. Life among the war priests changed that opinion. He'd entered Castle Andrak a boy. One Burning Season transformed him into a man, complete with the cynical view many of the priests shared.

Life wasn't meant to be lived this way, Donal reflected as he dipped the first canteen into the cold waters. Forlei didn't deserve his fate. Perhaps none of them did. That was not a factor the Omegri considered, however. They killed with impunity, unfeeling masters of a world that shouldn't exist. Donal shuddered. He'd given up wondering what life would have been like had he remained at home. Those days were forever lost to him. It was the colors of the war priests now. Or death on Andrak's walls.

A splash got his attention. His hand crept to his sword. Eyes scanned the semi-darkness for a threat. The insects fell quiet, leaving him locked in indecision. Donal crouched down and tried to steady his heartrate, while clearing his mind. A confused mind led to defeat, or the wrong decision. A new sound drew his gaze. Water trickled down into the stream. From what? He tracked the sound and was rewarded by a sight he couldn't have expected.

"What is your name?" a golden voice asked.

He swallowed. The nymph stood on the opposite shore five meters away. Water dripped from her naked form. Donal struggled with modesty. Moss and smooth bark stretched across her body where flesh should have been. Her hair was dark green, reminding him of simpler times on endless fields. Leaves and twigs jut out from various places, lending her the appearance of being more elemental than flesh.

She cocked her head. "Did I not say that right?"

"N … no. You caught me unawares," Donal stammered.

Her laugh was gilded, like the morning sun. He felt warmth in her tone. Quiet warning rose from the back of his mind. Subtle voices begging him to beware. Donal's hand slipped from his sword.

"Why are you here? This is not a place for men such as you," she asked.

"What do you mean?" he asked.

She glided into the water, edging closer. Her pose was provocative, lowering his guard as she inched ahead to stand in the middle of the stream. "You should not be here. These are dangerous times. Are you a good man?"

"Donal," he uttered. "My name is Donal."

"Silly Donal," she giggled.

He was amazed how she failed to make a sound as she kept approaching. Donal found her beauty mesmerizing. He couldn't take his eyes from her. She was within arm's reach when a brilliant golden light flooded the area. Donal's arm rose to protect his eyes. An inhuman shriek was followed by a loud splash.

"These are not safe places, Donal. You should remain aware at all times," Quinlan admonished as the golden light retreated back into the cross emblazoned on his armor.

Blinking away the spots in his eyes, Donal asked, "What was that?"

"An elemental," Quinlan replied. "They are not wholly dangerous but must be treated with caution. This one was but a step away from you when I arrived."

Donal glanced around, able to see again as his night vision slowly returned. "Elemental. I thought they were friendly. Like the one we encountered on the way to Calad Reach."

"Donal, there are many forces in this world. Many that we do not yet understand," Quinlan explained with a sigh. "I cannot confirm this nymph's intentions, but I suspect she meant you harm."

"I am sorry, Brother Quinlan," Donal bowed his head. Shame echoed in his words.

"Raise your head, young Donal. There is nothing to be ashamed of," Quinlan said. "We must each learn our way in this world. You have the potential to become great, should you live long enough."

He clapped his novice on the shoulder and stalked back to their campsite. Quinlan stretched out the soreness from riding all day and settled in for a long night. Thoughts of the nymph returning, or something far worse, stayed with him as he drifted off to sleep.

They were leagues southwest of their camp before either man felt like talking. Quinlan continued his private deliberations on the Majj's words, while Donal was replaying his encounter with the nymph. Both suffered their individual torments, lost in moments already fading to memory. It was no easy thing to wear the sky blue of the war priests.

The landscape started to change around midday. Plush, rolling plains of vibrant greens were replaced by gentle hills covered sparsely in yellowed vegetation. Jagged boulders littered the ground for as far as they could see, stretching to the far horizon. Thin clouds scattered across the sky, blocking the sun just enough to leave the land in a chill.

"Donal, we have entered the duchy of Fent. Whatever dangers prompted the Baron to summon our aid must not be taken for granted," Quinlan advised. "Do not speak our mission unless it is to the Baron or his appointed representative. There is a good chance the local population does not know what evil has befallen their lands."

He understood. "Brother Quinlan, what are we facing? I have not heard of this creature before the Lord General dispatched us."

Quinlan cocked his head, approving of the question. Donal's foresight served him well, further proving Quinlan's belief that the youth would make a fine war priest. "The F'talle are rarities in this world. Some scholars claim they come from the Other Realm. Born of nightmares best forgotten, they are creatures of great violence, as well as intelligence. Others believe the F'talle are naught but thieves from childhood fancy. We must be open to anything. Regardless of opinion, the F'talle are demons."

"Have you encountered one before?" Donal asked.

"Thankfully no. They are very rare," Quinlan answered. "Making them more dangerous than perhaps the Omegri."

Donal failed to see how any creature, living or dead, could be worse than the monstrosities of the Omegri. The Other Realm nightmares threatened the world with the promise of unending torments. What more could a F'talle threaten with? During his time in Castle Andrak, Donal had witnessed a monster born from smoke. Lizards with animal heads. Savage giants with skin of diamond. All trying to breach the walls and extinguish the Purifying Flame deep within the castle's bowels. Kill the light and darkness won.

"We should have come across a village by now," Quinlan thought aloud.

Gone were the great herds roaming the plains. This land wasn't conducive to maintaining their size. Quinlan was reminded of the northern continent, where he'd once served the light. Smaller mammals popped up from holes, jerking and twisting their heads to watch the riders. Large winged birds burst from outcroppings to land in the thin trees with wide canopies. The air smelled dry, arid.

Donal glanced at the dust clouds kicked up by their horses. "Why would anyone choose to live here? This is the closest to a desert I have seen."

"Not everyone has the ability to choose where they live, Donal. Others are not as fortunate as the upper class."

Unsure if he was being rebuked, Donal asked, "There are inherent freedoms granted to each man and woman."

"God given," Quinlan agreed. "But there are rulers who only know strength through force. They keep their people subservient so that they may continue to serve their masters. Humanity is not as unified as it should be."

"If they only knew of the dangers of the Omegri, they wouldn't be as obstinate," Donal offered.

"True, but many do not wish to know of the dangers lurking beyond the edge of vision."

"Why would anyone wish to remain ignorant of the truth?" Donal failed to understand. "I saw much of the world come through my father's shop. How many of them knew what awaited? Would their lives change if they knew of the Omegri?"

"You have keen foresight, Donal, but do not let that drag into circles of confusion," Quinlan said. "There is something to be said for self-imposed ignorance. How would a person react if they discovered they weren't the top of the food chain? That monsters do exist and they are coming to kill us all? Do not be so quick to judge. Were I not a war priest, I do not believe I would want to learn of the Omegri."

They kept riding, eager to end their travels and be about their purpose. Donal spied the approaching riders first. The war priests halted upon seeing the black and purple armor of Fent. Six men, each armed with lances and swords, hurried up the slope to where the priests waited.

Quinlan thought it best to avoid confrontation with the people they'd come to assist.

"Keep your hands where we can see them," their leader said, as he drew near. "Don't touch those weapons either. What is your business in Fent?"

Hands on his saddle pommel, Quinlan leaned forward and said, "I am Brother Quinlan of Castle Andrak. This is my novice, Donal Sawq. We come at the behest of your liege, Baron Einos."

"A war priest," a second man uttered.

Quinlan gave a curt nod. "Indeed, but that is irrelevant until I speak with the Baron. We are more than capable of riding to the castle on our own, but it would be faster should you detail a man to guide us. We are, after all, strangers in this land."

The sergeant stared aghast. War priests were people of legend, not mortal beings walking the hills and fields of his home. "My apologies, Priest. You shall have an escort for as long as you desire. Welcome to Fent."

Quinlan thanked him and followed the young guard assigned to him. The village of Fent lay ahead, and with it, the mysteries of the F'talle and the Grey Wanderer. Quinlan's mood improved the deeper into the duchy they rode. The clouds parted and the sun streamed down. He knew it was an illusion, however, for dark things often lurked just beyond the edge of sunlight, waiting for the unsuspecting to lower their guard. Quinlan couldn't help but wonder what dark nightmares awaited him.

SIXTEEN
Fent

"Baron Einos, the war priest has arrived."

Einos glanced up from the reports recently arrived from Palis. Anger flashed across his face before he gained control and turned to the page. Nothing Kastus reported was good, leaving Einos in a soured mood. Each day he failed to discover Brogon Lord meant another that his people were forced to live under the blanket of fear. Already traffic in the city had fallen off. Parents refused to allow their children outside, often keeping them under armed guard in what was supposed to be the security of their own homes. Fear gripped the duchy as word of the missing children continued to spread. Hands tied by circumstance, Einos knew that nothing short of stopping Lord would restore order to his duchy.

"Where is he?"

The page stiffened, as if worried he faced reprimand. "Baron, he is being escorted to the castle as we speak."

A grunt. "Keep me informed of his arrival. I will meet him in my parlor."

The page bowed, turned and left. His slippered feet barely made a sound. Einos had grown up in the castle, destined to assume the burdens of leadership after his father passed, but he had never grown accustomed to being served by so many. Freedom was a curious thing, he mused. No time for delay, he hurried to his private chambers and slipped out of his informal robes. No doubt the war priest was expecting crown and scepter.

Doubts suddenly gripped him. Einos wasn't sure he was doing the right thing. If word of his troubles got out into the other duchies, there was the potential for catastrophic damages to his people. Trade would be cut off. Embargoes on caravans and craftsmen enacted. Fent would be severed from the rest of the continent, with no one to turn to for help. He slammed a balled fist into his palm. Damn Kastus for not reporting back with positive results.

"Aneth!" he shouted as he entered his wardrobe. "It is time. The war priest is here."

No answer. Confused, he searched the complex of rooms for her, not stopping until he discovered she was still in bed.

"Did you not hear me call?" he asked, his voice softer, gentler. "The war priest has arrived."

Aneth smiled. A strained act. "Forgive me, husband, but my body is not agreeing with my mind this day. I think I will remain here and rest."

Einos accepted that the baby came first, though it chaffed him to know that he was going to face the most powerful order on the continent alone.

As if sensing his dilemma, Aneth added, "Summon Lizette. She is more than adequate to handle this situation."

"That woman is becoming a burden on my conscience," he grumbled.

The longer Lizette remained in the castle, the more she inserted herself into daily affairs. Not that she wasn't capable. Einos found her brilliant in many matters. Perhaps it was guilt that gave him pause. Guilt that he hadn't been able to find her daughter. Guilt that he was forced to look into her searching eyes every day and feel the pain of loss reflecting back. Yet another reminder that he wasn't up to the task at hand.

"She is becoming the one woman who can run this castle, and the duchy, and you know it," Aneth chided. "Lizette must have time to grieve, on her terms. Allow her some time, love. She may prove more useful than all of your advisors combined."

He leaned down and kissed her forehead. "You don't know how true that sentiment is. I'll have food sent up once I finish meeting this defender of the world."

Aneth's face darkened. "Remember, you were the one who summoned him."

He forced a grin. "Where would I be without you?"

"I can only imagine. Now go. Best not keep our guest waiting."

Einos watched the two men cross the short hall and enter his parlor. Neither was impressive to look upon. They wore simple riding clothes, with no sign of their station. *Curious. One would assume the war priests would flaunt their tokens so as to keep the population in awe as they went about their business.* The elements of their legend combined to form impossible ideations. What strode into his presence was anything but the haughty, powerful priests of his imagination.

They walked with humble steps. Each man well aware of their lot in life and what that represented to others. There was no avoiding the reasons for their arrival, yet they showed nothing of the arrogance Einos thought them filled with. No matter how long he lived, or what sights he was granted, he'd come to understand that the world was not what he once thought.

"Baron Einos," the priest said with a clipped bow. "I am Brother Quinlan. This is my novice, Donal. Lord General Rosca dispatched us to assist with your dilemma."

"Welcome to Fent," Einos said. The words felt wrong, like sand scraping flesh.

His reservations were rooted deep, the product of years of belief. Einos struggled to maintain decorum, for tension thickened the air. For their part, the war priests stood with hands folded before them. Neither assuming or aggressive. They had been summoned and had come with all haste to help solve a problem no one in Fent was capable of. That he was forced to seek outside assistance continued to sit ill. Now that the war priests had arrived, he found he wished they hadn't come.

They stood, staring blankly for a time in silence. Einos broke first, unable to match the intensity of the awkwardness. "Gentlemen, please sit."

They did. Quinlan placed his hands on his thighs and leaned back into the cushioned chair. It felt good to be out of the saddle and among civilization again, despite the unspoken hostility filling the parlor.

"The Lord General tells me you have experienced a F'talle," he began.

Einos ground his teeth. Images of the empty grave, mothers crying, and his own encounter with the apparition in his bedchambers swirled to collide with his disturbed emotions. He was a man lost, unsure which way to turn or what the proper decision was.

"That was but the beginning of our troubles," he said. "Fent is largely innocuous. We are small enough to remain insignificant among the Council of Lords. We have no standing army of note due to our location and the bond we've forged with our neighbors. This duchy is as peaceful as you can imagine. Until now."

He stalked to the empty chair opposite the priests and sank down. Einos cracked his knuckles, the sound crisp and echoing. "Rumors of the Grey Wanderer have been circulating for the last few weeks. I point out that there have been no confirmed sightings, just whispers on the fringes."

"What do you believe?" Quinlan interrupted.

"Me? That we are cursed. The day after the Wanderer shows up, we are mired in reports of missing children and a man risen from the grave. I tell you I have no desire to have a once dead man roaming my lands," Einos snarled. "The people are panicked. Many have bolted their doors, refusing to come out until the matter is solved. My duchy is slowly transforming into a dark land where nightmares are the currency."

"We have encountered these types of events before, Baron," Quinlan reassured him. "Have faith, we shall rid your lands of this once dead man and any spawn the Grey Wanderer has left behind."

Einos went from Quinlan to Donal and then back. "How? I already have a hundred of my best soldiers deployed to the countryside. Armed patrols have tripled since the first reported incident and *still* children are coming up missing. What can the fabled war priests of Andrak do that my men have not?"

Quinlan shifted his lower jaw, careful not to betray his ire. "We are well versed in handling nightmares, Baron. The Burning Season finds us besieged by the creatures of the Omegri, and the Other Realm."

"I lack your confidence," Einos replied, rising to begin pacing. "Between the Wanderer, the once dead man, and the ghosts, I fear there is no clear direction in which to begin."

"Ghosts?" Donal uncharacteristically spoke.

Amused, Einos said, "The squire has a tongue, eh? Yes, lad. Ghosts. I saw one in my very bedchamber. A little girl with no eyes."

"There must be some relation between these events," Quinlan passed Donal a frown. "Have others witnessed the apparitions?"

"Several, I believe," Einos said after some thought. He poured three glasses of honeyed liquor from the decanter on the table in the corner of the room and offered one to each of them. "The ghosts are the least of my concerns. They haven't harmed anyone, not like Brogon Lord. Find him and you end this mystery."

Quinlan concealed his wince as the harsh liquid bit the back of his throat. Brogon Lord. Now he had a name. a starting point. "I would like to begin at once. May we meet with your records keeper?"

The Baron of Fent nodded and downed his glass. He had a feeling it was going to be a long day.

Donal stifled his yawn as dust crawled up his nose. His eyes burned from the strain. Night had fallen and they were mired with obscure records and documents pertaining to every aspect of life in Fent.

Not the thrills of standing the walls during the Burning Season. He was bored, and tired. Almost willing to trade this tedium for life back in the saddle. On the other hand, the food was good and there was plenty to drink. Baron Einos might not appreciate them being in his duchy, but he was sparing no expense for quality.

Disappointed with yet another book filled with the theories of architectural design by the men who built the main castle, Donal shoved the manuscript back into the pile and sighed. His gaze lingered on the growing stack of scrolls and books that had nothing to do with their quest. Now decidedly larger than the stack of unread books, Donal wondered how record keepers lived with themselves. Alcohol was his answer. Nothing else made sense.

"Have you found anything, Brother Quinlan?" he asked.

Quinlan raised a finger and continued reading. He flipped the page, sending a puff of dust across the ancient wooden table. The center of the table sagged, threatening to snap at any moment. That didn't surprise Donal. Everything about Fent felt as if it was too old for the modern world. Finished, Quinlan closed the book and leaned back. His chair creaked.

"What did you ask, Donal?"

"If you had found any clues to help us," he replied.

Quinlan pursed his lips. "Nothing. There has never been a similar event in Fent's past, making this a remarkable situation."

Remarkable? Donal would have chosen another word, one with more import than that. They were facing an undead man and the world's greatest supernatural entity and all Quinlan could theorize was that it was remarkable. Donal learned long ago not to vouch for others, but he was fairly certain Quinlan was as frightened as he was. The only difference being the older priest would never let it be known.

"I think we are done here," Quinlan said and rose to stretch. His muscles ached from so many days in the saddle, a sad reminder that he'd been kept inside Andrak too long.

Donal praised the words, hoping that their next task was to find the kitchens. His stomach growled from neglect. They hadn't eaten in the time it took a candle to burn down. Loath as he was to ask, Donal did the right thing. "Where should we look next?"

"That, Donal, is a good question," Quinlan answered. "I think it is time for nourishment. Maybe we can think better on full stomachs."

Those were the best words Donal had heard since arriving in Fent.

A slender woman interrupted their meal well before either had the chance to dig in. She bore a severe look, much too harsh for one so young. Quinlan stood as she approached, prompting a sulking Donal to do the same. With no one else in the kitchens, there was little doubt who she had come to see. Rather than smile or stand on ceremony, she took a seat and waited for them to follow.

"You are the war priests," she said. Blunt, matter-of-factly.

"Brother Quinlan."

She nodded. "Good. I am Lizette."

"You are one of the children's mothers," he grasped.

Another nod. "One of the first. Indeed, the first to bring it to the Baron's attention."

Quinlan wiped his mouth. "We grieve for your loss, but what brings you here? To us?"

"Einos has appointed me one of his special liaisons with the community. I send my days in meetings with parents of missing children and helping coordinate search efforts across the duchy."

"A worthy title," Quinlan said.

"It is, but I want more," she replied. "All is not as it appears in Fent. There are strange goings on that none can explain. It is all well and fine to place blame on the Grey Wanderer, but none have witnessed him."

"You suspect something more sinister," Quinlan ventured.

"I do, and I am hoping the two of you are up to the task of discovering what, or who." Lizette snatched a sliver of roast venison from his plate. "The Baron is a good man, as are most of his people, but I refuse to believe this once dead man capable of creating so much mischief without help."

Quinlan wasn't ready to explore the possibility that Brogon Lord was working in conjunction with men and women in Fent. Her suggestion led them toward a dark train of thought. "Why have you come to me, Lizette? There is but limited jurisdiction for the Order. Einos should be told of your suspicions."

She leaned conspiratorially close and said, "I am here because the Baron has made me the go between for you. Anything you need to help your investigation."

Quinlan couldn't believe his ears. She wasn't a spy, per say, but was close enough to open every locked door in Fent. His task just became easier, thanks to the fury of a mother scorned. "What do you propose?"

He and Donal finished their meals as Lizette described every detail she had in mind. The way forward was not going to be easy, leaving Quinlan with doubts as to what their next move should be. The situation in Fent just became complicated.

SEVENTEEN
Palis

"Ouch! Watch what you're doing, you daft bastard," Sava growled.

The company surgeon ignored him and continued to shift his nose and face around in his quest to find broken bones. Sava glared the entire time. The embarrassment of his failure, in front of his men no less, against the once dead man fueled the wells of his rage. He wanted to rearm and head back in search of Brogon Lord with all haste. Unfortunately, none of his commanders felt the same.

They'd been confined to Palis and the surrounding area, a swath of land little wider than a river, to conduct presence patrols. He was under strict orders to avoid confrontation. Sava didn't think Thep was a coward, but the captain wasn't showing the spine necessary for the occasion. His frustrations compounded every time he passed one of the squad who'd been there. Sava hadn't heard even the slightest snicker, but he *knew* they whispered about him behind his back. As if his lengthy career was naught but a laughingstock.

The surgeon stepped away and wiped his hands on a soiled rag. "We are done, Sergeant. Please do us both the favor of getting out of my sight. I've had my fill of you today."

"With pleasure," Sava growled.

Strapping his weapon belt on, the sergeant stalked out of the tent and into the village of Palis. They'd been here for little over a week and he already despised the place. Not only was there nothing to do, but they were also forbidden from drinking. Take away a soldier's entertainment and the option to drink away their pains, and you were left with a recipe for trouble.

It started small. A disagreement between friends that led to fists. An enraged father protesting to Captain Thep over one of the lad's coming on to his daughter. Sava snorted at that. He'd grown up in a farming community and knew the innocent reputation farmer's daughters tended to cluster behind. He'd be upset, too, but what did the leadership expect? These men and women were stationed near the Baron's castle and all the excitement life brought. Throwing them to the obscurity of the countryside was the worst possible outcome. It was only going to get worse.

Soldiers greeted him in passing but none remained to speak with him. Sava's reputation as a hard case was well deserved. The army, any army, was meant to be rigid. Soldiers weren't supposed to be nice. After all, how could any man or woman go willingly into battle, knowing they were going to kill or die, without transforming into a hard shell? He'd done his share of fighting but had only killed seven men. That lack of severity wasn't shameful. Sava attributed it to the professionalism and reputation of his army. Fent was one of the most secure duchies in the land. A mark of pride he hung his career on.

Consumed with the past, Sava stumbled upon his two favorite soldiers. "Both of you! Over here, now."

Nils and Alfar hurried over, neither pleased with being caught unawares. The last time Sava snagged them, they wound up on guard duty from dusk til dawn. Sava glared at them, noting their disheveled appearance and filthy boots. Neither looked to have shaved in days. Grimacing at the lack of standards, Sava grumbled under his breath, prompting both to straighten their backs, hands clasped behind.

"What are you miscreants doing?" Sava snapped. He reached into a pocket, in a well-rehearsed move, produced a pouch of fresh kaappa leaves, and stuff a pinch into his lower lip. The red juice trickled down his lip. "I asked a question."

Alfar closed his mouth after Nils shot him a withering glare from the corner of his eye. "We wasn't up to anything, Sergeant. Just waiting for dinner chow."

"That's a long time away," Sava grew suspicious. "What game are you playing at?"

"No game, Sergeant. Honest."

Sava took a step closer. "I don't like games. Games are for children, not soldiers in the Baron's service."

Alfar broke. "We met a girl. Pretty lass with flowing gol…"

"A girl!" Sava roared. Several nearby soldiers scurried away lest they, too, get swallowed by his rage. "This isn't a time to meet a girl! Especially not one of these villagers. I ought to have you both hung for dereliction of duty! Get your gear and report back here before I count to fifty, or I'll skin your hides and feed you to the pigs. Move!"

Later that night, during their twelfth rotation around the village, Nils punched Alfar in the shoulder. "You just had to open your mouth. *We met a girl*. Idiot."

The younger soldier kept his mouth shut and kept marching, never mind the pebble in the bottom of his right boot. He'd deal with the pain later.

Kastus emptied his mug of water and stared at the wall they'd converted into a map. Several charcoal marks scored the wall, each an indicator of Brogon Lord sightings. There was no discernable pattern, nothing to suggest the once dead man was moving in a logical manner. Frustrated, Kastus walked away.

Making matter worse, there'd been no sign of their quarry since the encounter with the sclarem, if that report were to be taken as truth. Kastus still doubted one of the mythical shamans was roaming the Fent wilderness, though, he reluctantly admitted, all manner of strange creatures were at play in his duchy.

"Coffee, Constable?"

Kastus accepted the mug from Thep with a tight grin. He was too disturbed to give thanks.

"Have any new reports come in while I was gone?" the captain asked.

"No. It is as if Brogon Lord has disappeared again," Kastus replied. *Leaving us standing with our trousers around our ankles. I can't go back to the Baron like this.* "We remain too far behind our prey. Unless something changes we will be forced to return to the Baron in defeat."

"It is still early," Thep said. "Some good may come of this. I've discovered a little more on our potential traitor on the council."

Kastus perked up. It was the first bit of good news he'd heard in days. "Which one?"

"Not the one we initially thought. Rumors of Waern dealing with other duchies has reached me. It seems our esteemed councilman is operating outside of his jurisdiction and possibly against the best interests of Fent."

"Are you certain? What proof is there?" Kastus demanded. His eternal quest for justice assumed control. Brogon Lord could wait, for the time being. Any subversive actions against the Baron must be dealt with immediately.

Thep glanced around. Night had fallen, but there were still enough people wandering the main street to prompt caution. They went inside, where he told Kastus all he knew.

"I'm not sure this amounts to treason," Kastus theorized after processing the information.

If what Thep said was true, the councilman was lining his pockets by selling grain and other food stores to the city of Forge. It was a violation of trade policies, in addition to being a criminal act against the throne. Robbery by any form was still illegal.

"We need proof before we can act," he continued.

Thep finished his coffee. "I can have a team dispatched to look into financial records. The soldiers are growing restless from not finding Lord."

"We cannot turn this village upside down, Captain. Regardless of our suspicions, these are still loyal citizens of Fent and must be treated accordingly. And with respect."

"What do you propose?" Thep asked.

Kastus groaned. "I need to speak with the one person I could do without seeing again. Fetch me Deana."

Thep snorted his amusement. He was already making plans to be elsewhere when the meeting took place.

The wait was longer than he assumed, despite knowing Deana would be enraged at the summons. Kastus thought taking her down a few steps was good for her demeanor, even while knowing it was a battle he wasn't prepared to fight. Time passed, until he began to think she wasn't coming. He'd just sat down when the door opened and in she walked.

"Lady Deana, thank you for coming," he said with a leopard's grin.

Haughty as ever, she strode with a stiff back and temperamental disposition etched on her face. "I was given the illusion that I lacked the option of declining."

"Indeed you did. Sit, please."

"I shall stand, thank you. What is this about, Kastus? You have no jurisdiction here," Deana accused.

"Perhaps, but I am qualified to exact the Baron's justice wherever I find it needed. And make no mistake, the village of Palis is sorely lacking," Kastus replied. He sat, placing his palms flat on the table.

A glint of something, fear perhaps, lingered in her eyes. "What do you mean? We have done nothing to garner false accusations. This village is as loyal to the Baron as any other."

"Is it?" he demanded. "We have begun an investigation into several odd goings-on here. You can thank the once dead man for that."

She snorted. "You suggest *we* had something to do with this F'talle? Preposterous."

"If only that were true, my task might be easier and we would be gone already," Kastus said. "No, Deana. I am on to a mortal prey. One of your council is in league with outside influences that have been deemed detrimental to the crown, but I suppose you know nothing about that."

"I know everything that happens in Palis. To suggest otherwise implies I am incapable of performing my duties," she stiffened, unsure what he was getting at.

He flashed a predatory grin. Good. Then you shouldn't take issue with us arresting the council and detaining them until the guilty confess."

"Unacceptable! This is a loyal, peaceful village. We neither harbor enemies nor broker with outside influences contradictory to the law," she fumed.

"Yes, so you keep reminding me. That does not excuse the actions of your council," Kastus replied. His face had returned to a blank mask. A move long practiced. "Tell me what I want to know and this ends before it starts. My soldiers are already preparing to place Palis under martial law, and when we do, it will be on your heads."

Deana remained defiant, though the flint in her tone weakened. "What proof have you? False accusations are akin to treason if I am not mistaken."

Kastus produced a handful of scrolls, all rolled and tied. "Here is the proof. There is enough damning evidence in these scrolls to see you all hung without trial. Feel free to examine them. Perhaps you can confirm which crimes you are guilty of."

Crimson flushed up her cheeks. Her shoulder sagged, showing the weight of her years. Eyes lingering on the scrolls, Deana accepted the offer to sit. She wasn't sure she'd be able to remain standing otherwise. "What do you wish to know?"

"I want to know everything you know. Dates, times, places. Who is conducting business against the crown and why. Give this to me, and if you are found innocent, you will be left out of the madness that follows." Kastus drummed his fingertips for added effect.

She stopped biting her upper lip long enough to tell him everything. Kastus dismissed her once he was sure she had nothing left worth telling. Only when the door closed behind her did he blow out the pent up breath he'd been holding. Thep entered after Deana left, an amused look on his face.

"What is so funny, Captain?" Kastus frowned.

He shrugged, offering a nonchalant smile. "I was wondering if she was going to call your bluff. Looks like you were right."

Kastus glanced at the scrolls, thankful Deana hadn't demanded to see them. He imagined what her surprise would have been to find the scrolls were blank.

"What's our next move?" Thep asked.

"Has there been word on Lord?"

"Nothing. He might have gone on to another duchy," Thep suggested.

Kastus shook his head. "Doubtful. My instincts tell me his purpose is here, though why, I do not know. Increase the range of our patrols. It was a mistake constricting our sphere of influence. We cannot return to the Baron empty handed."

"I'll have the soldiers moving at once. One way or another, we'll catch this bastard and make him pay for the children he's stolen," Thep vowed.

Kastus admired his audacity, while secretly knowing it was never going to be an easy task. The F'talle might prove the undoing of Fent.

EIGHTEEN

Castle Fent

A gust of chill woke Donal. It was the middle of the night. The candles in his chamber were burned out. Not cool enough for a fire, the bedchambers were left to heat and cool with the sun. Exhausted from their efforts in the records room, Donal closed his eyes, rolled over, and tried to fall back to sleep. He lay that way for a time, unable to find the sweet embrace of slumber. When he couldn't take it anymore, he slipped from the blankets and decided to use the privy. Unlike Castle Andrak, Fent had dedicated chambers for private use.

The door swung open with a groan. Aged wood and slightly rusting iron straps were feeling their age. Yawning, Donal scratched his cheek as he stumbled down the hallway. Dimmed oil lamps provided just enough light for him to avoid stubbing a toe. He walked halfway down the hall and placed a palm on the privy door, when a flicker of movement, the briefest hint of another presence, caught his attention.

Squinting, he tracked the path of movement, but found nothing. Donal grew suspicious. While there were many who lived in the castle, this floor was reserved for the baron and his family and the highest guests. Donal reached for the cold comfort of his sword, only to curse when he realized he'd left it. Unarmed, the novice stalked down the hall in pursuit of his quarry. Each time he thought he'd caught the shadow, it moved. Impossibly fast to track, Donal felt overmatched. He lacked experience in dealings with the Other Realm.

Shadows coalesced at the end of the hall, leading Donal to suspect his target was just ahead. A large part of novice training involved hand to hand combat. Thus, he had confidence if it came to facing this perceived enemy. Donal braced and made ready to cover the last few meters. A figure emerged before he could move.

Small, no taller than a child. The figure's edges were blurred, ill-defined. Donal's mouth dried. The closer the figure came, the more he was convinced he had discovered one of the missing children. Short, with mussed dark brown hair, the boy stood in threadbare clothes. His chest heaved from sobs. Donal tried to get a better look at his face, but again, each time he looked close, reality distorted.

"What are you doing here, little one?" Donal asked. The words stuck in his throat, as if a silent warning screamed in the back of his mind. "Are you lost?"

The child came closer yet managed to stay on the border of light and dark.

Hairs rose in waves, running from Donal's knuckles up his arms. He felt a charge in the air. This, he decided, was not right. Instincts kicked in and he held his ground. Donal knew that any attempt to flee would end badly. Instead, he crouched to present a low silhouette.

"These are the Baron's private floors. You should not be here," Donal whispered. "Tell me your name. I can help you find your parents."

A handful of steps away, the child halted. Blood trickled from empty eye sockets. The child pointed a finger at him and asked, "Why did you take me? Where are my parents?"

"I do not know your name, child," Donal replied. His heart beat faster. *Where are your eyes?* "Tell me your name."

The child's mouth distended impossibly large, showing rows of fangs. "You killed me! AHHHHH!"

Donal threw an arm up and twisted aside to protect his face and head as the child launched into the air at him, fingers curled into claws and aimed for his throat. A gust of wind blew past. Only when he realized that there was no impact did he open his eyes again. The hallway was empty, without so much as a footprint to show the child had been there. Shaken, Donal rose and hurried back to his chamber to dress and arm.

"Tell me again, from the beginning."

Quinlan studied Donal as the novice recounted his tale of the night prior. Frightened and confused, Donal told the truth insofar as Quinlan could determine. An unfortunate circumstance. Standing the walls of Andrak, and Bendris before, Quinlan bore witness to countless events that should never have existed. Monstrosities from beyond imagination driven by the unrelenting desire to eradicate all life. That such entities managed to trickle to faraway Fent was an ill portent.

He rubbed his hands together, eager to remove the film of sweat produced by Donal's tale. Quinlan supposed it was inevitable. He'd held out against hope that this was all a concocted dream, a nightmare of individual choosing, meant to inspire fear. The reality was much harsher. The Grey Wanderer. A F'talle. Even the Majj whispering of a coming war. Too many random events, all coalescing on Fent. *What have you awakened here, Baron?*

There was no other reasonable explanation. A member of the duchy must have made a deal with the dark powers. Quinlan paced. His thoughts outran him.

"Can you describe this boy?" he asked.

"No more than ten. Dark brown hair." Donal closed his eyes and thought hard. "He bore a small scar on his right temple. As if he'd been struck by a stone."

Lizette, who'd sat quietly in the corner until now, perked up. "A scar? Was it fresh or old?"

Donal's head cocked. "Old, I believe. It had grey-white flesh over it."

"I know that boy," she confirmed. Rising, Lizette hurried to the table containing all of the scrolls containing images of the missing children and rifled through them until she found the correct one. "Here. Valen. His parents were among the latest to report him missing."

"Are you certain?" Quinlan asked. The war priest refused to trust to memory, for it was a canny trickster.

"Positive," she said. Lizette held up the scroll for Donal. "Is this him?"

The novice swallowed hard, reliving the incident. "Yes."

"We should find his parents. Perhaps they know something we have overlooked," Lizette offered.

Quinlan was impressed. He hadn't wanted to believe in ghosts or F'talle but couldn't deny the connection after his novice had borne witness. "I think that is a good place to start. After we finish, I would like to see the F'talle's grave."

"The Baron already had a Tender examine it," Lizette replied.

His eyebrow arched. This was news. "Was there anything to report?"

"I don't believe so. Tender Cannandal is an old man. Somewhat of a recluse. If he shared his thoughts, they were not made known to the investigation."

Priest and novice shared a knowing look. "Is this Cannandal in the village?"

"He should be."

Quinlan nodded. "Good. I wish to speak with him as well."

Lizette narrowed her gaze, studying the war priest for signs. Only when she found none, she said, "You think you've discovered a link to all of this."

"The veil is thinning," he said after thought. "There are too many coincidences going on here to be chance."

There shouldn't have been surprise in the statement. Five of the six war priest fortresses had been overrun, leaving Andrak as the sole defense against the Omegri.

"The Omegri?" Donal asked.

"Possibly, but there are other dark forces at work in the world. Some we have yet to encounter," Quinlan said. "Come, haste is required."

Lizette grabbed Donal by the arm, holding him back as Quinlan headed down the hall. "Is he always like this?"

"Brother Quinlan is one of the more experienced priests. He has stood the wall many times," Donal confided. "The Burning Season changes you. Each experience you become a little less of who you once were."

He left Lizette wondering what sort of people it took to fight against an enemy most of the population didn't believe existed.

The once busy streets of Fent were empty. Scarcely a stray cat or wild dog could be seen. Quinlan noticed the shuttered windows. The barred doors of establishments that should be open. The smells of roasting meat and fresh baked breads were replaced by those of refuse and offal. Fent was being consumed from the inside. A rancorous wound no salve could treat.

They passed an armed patrol, yet even the defenders of Fent bore downcast looks. How much did the people know, and what measure of that burden was truth? Quinlan suspected the rumors were rampant, spinning an impossible weave with but portions of truth. He'd grown up in a village similar to Fent and knew life seldom changed. But now, all manner of nightmarish creatures had manifested among the population, paralyzing the otherwise sleepy duchy. The malaise was one only stopping the F'talle could remove.

Lizette knocked on the door once they reached the house. A bitter man whose face was partially concealed behind an unkempt beard answered. His stern glare warned he didn't wish to be bothered. This was a time of grief.

"Go away. We've already spoken with the Baron's constable," he said. His voice terse.

Quinlan cleared his throat and introduced himself. "Forgive me, but I am from Castle Andrak. I would have a word with you regarding your son. There has been an ... incident."

"You found him? Is he alive?" False hope brightened his granite face.

"This would be a conversation best had indoors," Quinlan reinforced. He should have expected such a reaction but wasn't thinking clearly. There was a cloud over Fent preventing him from seeing matters for what they were.

The father's shoulders trembled. Weeks of pent up hope and frustration colliding. His knees weakened and Quinlan rushed to catch him before he fell. Donal slid to the other side and they helped him back inside. A nagging sensation stopped Lizette as she was about to cross the threshold. She looked over her shoulder, unsure if she'd caught the slip of movement across the street.

Inside, Lizette crossed the small house to pour the man a mug of water from the pitcher on the table. The house wore the same disheveled look as the father. Both parents had abandoned normalcy with their loss. Her heart wept for them, for she, too, knew the agony. Yet where they had given up, Lizette found new purpose and forced the Baron to give her a task worthy of her need. Not that she'd gotten over her beloved Tabith. Quite the opposite. She'd merely replaced her bitterness with purpose.

"Here, drink this." Her voice softened, losing some of the severity with which she'd met Quinlan.

"We did not mean to mislead you," Quinlan said as the man drank deep.

"You should not have come. Not like this."

Quinlan agreed, but was left with little choice. He needed to find the truth of what Donal saw. "These are difficult times and I would not have disturbed you, if it wasn't for what my novice saw last night."

The man blinked, suddenly becoming aware that there was another man with Quinlan. "Who are you? Why did you bring me news my heart cannot bear? For my son is surely dead, else you would not have come."

"I am Brother Quinlan of Castle Andrak. This is Donal and Lizette."

The man balked. A war priest! In his home! "I have always dreamed of seeing a war priest, though never could I imagine it would be in this circumstance. My son is dead."

Lizette's hand was warm, comforting on his shoulder. "As is my daughter. These are trying times, but we must remain strong. For our children."

A single tear escaped, running down his face and into his beard. "I am Bael. Varen was a good lad. Full of life and vigor. He did not deserve his fate and I would gladly give my own life so that he could return."

"I believe you," Quinlan said. He alone caught Lizette clutch her breast as she choked back her emotions. "But we must look past our losses if justice is to be done."

"Is it true?" Bael asked. "Was he taken by the Grey Wanderer?"

"We have not been able to confirm this, but there is suspicion of a F'talle loose in the duchy." Quinlan slid into the nearest chair. "Bael, we have come to you because Donal believes he saw the ghost of your son last night."

Bael snapped his head up, fixing Donal with an uncomfortable stare. "You saw my son?"

"I did. He was wandering the castle. I stopped him and asked where he was going and he attacked me. I am sorry, but he seemed angry," Donal cut his statement short, knowing better than to speak what Valen's ghost accused.

Bael was silent in thought for some time. When he spoke, it was void of emotion, "What has this to do with me?"

Lizette's glance to Quinlan betrayed the suspicion in her eyes. "We are not accusing you of anything, Bael. We only wish to know the circumstances of how Valen became missing."

The father grunted and tugged on his beard. "The boy was always playing down by the water. He and his friends. They knew to come home at dark. Only, one night he didn't come. Me and my wife went looking. We found one of his boots on the bank and man-sized footprints coming out of the bushes. Never saw our boy again and now you come to tell me he is dead. It is true what they say. War priests are the bane of happiness."

They left Bael to his misery. Whatever slight comforts in knowing the truth of Valen's fate would come eventually. But not this night. Tonight belonged to the mournful wails of pain and the helplessness of failure that only a parent who'd lost a child would know. Quinlan's heart wept for the man.

"Will he be all right?" Donal asked, once they were on their way.

Lizette, back straight and chin out, said, "He will endure. As must we all. Where do we go from here?"

"This water Bael spoke of. Where is it?" Quinlan asked.

"Not far. There is a stream crisscrossing the village. I believe it runs out beyond the graveyard," she replied.

"Can you take us there?"

Brogon Lord felt used. His muscles deteriorated daily, a reality not even his new powers could prevent. Snippets of memory winked out, leaving gaping holes in who he'd been. Not that it mattered. His life ended at the end of a sword. It was his resurrection that disturbed him, for nobody should be woken from the depths of death. Each time he slunk back from his task, back to the cold indifference of his masters, he was less than when he began. Soon there would be nothing left.

His return to the Other Realm was not welcomed as before. The encounter with the shaman left him burned and beaten. Defeat forced him back to the cave where he could recover lost energies. The masters would respond by bestowing a wealth of power upon him so that he might not find defeat again. For his part, he did not desire to cross paths with the shaman again.

The great tower rose higher than the last time he was summoned. Tinkering hammers echoed across the surrounding emptiness. Brogon gave little thought to what the children were making. It didn't matter. The masters said they were necessary and that only children could accomplish this task, for their innocence was singular across the world. He looked up, surprised to find what looked like a giant face being shaped toward the top.

"You have failed us, Brogon Lord."

He turned and bowed, fearful of meeting their hollow gaze. Despite lacking physical definition, Brogon recognized the voice of the woman who'd commanded him earlier. He learned quickly not to cross her, having witnessed another once dead man obliterated by the pointing of a finger.

"I encountered … unexpected circumstances," he said.

"The sclarem should not have been in Palis," she replied. "That does not forgive you for your failures, Brogon Lord."

"Forgiveness. I did not know what to do," he explained. "I fought against the shaman and a squad of human soldiers. Their combined might was too great for me."

"Perhaps it is time to shift focus back to the main village," a second voice said.

A third added, "Yes, where the bounty is better. Time is running out. We must complete the tower before the Burning Season begins."

"There is another problem. One of the war priests has arrived. He may hinder our operations," the second said.

Brogon listened to them, unsure of what they spoke. He vaguely recalled hearing of the war priests but knew nothing about them. Clearly they were a powerful force. Strong enough to threaten his masters. Could this mean freedom? A chance to return to the grave and travel on to the next world? A sliver of hope dawned.

"The priest is a hindrance, nothing else," she decided.

The third snickered. "Do you forget what they do to our kind each year? He will find us and kills us."

"He is but one man! Alone and removed from the powers of the Flame. He is vulnerable," she said. "We can deal with him when the time comes."

"Time is too short. The war priest complicates our efforts. Should he learn of the tower, we will fail," the second countered.

"I know what must be done. Do not assume to command me," she snapped. "Brogon Lord, you are to return to Fent. Kill this priest and bring us more children! We must not fail."

Rebuked, the once dead man bowed again and backed away. He'd been given renewed purpose and aimed to please his masters. The alternative was not an option.

NINETEEN
Castle Fent

Quinlan knelt along the bank, examining the different footprints. A child and the decidedly large tracks of a grown man dragging one foot. Suspicions aroused, the war priest removed one of his gloves and touched his fingertips in the depression. The tracks lead away from the stream, into the bushes where they ended. They didn't disappear. They simply stopped. Quinlan had little doubts whose they were. Even after the ten days since Valen was reported missing, the hollow prints, faded and distorted, showed the truth.

"There was a struggle," he said after catching the meter long swipe running parallel to the tracks. As if the child refused to go along. "Valen did not know his abductor."

"You suspect this F'talle? Brogon Lord?" Lizette asked. Her arms were folded, fingers bled white from clutching her blouse tightly.

"I do. It is the only theory that makes sense. Add to that how the trail ends abruptly, and we must conclude that Lord was here," Quinlan confirmed.

Donal took in the scene with pause. He was reminded of the time when the Witch Queen of Calad Reach was stealing first born sons, but this had a much more sinister feel. "Where does that leave us if we cannot follow this Lord back to his lair?"

Unsure himself, Quinlan tugged his glove back on. He moved to the end of the tracks and studied the surroundings. Burn marks scored a handful of trees and bushes along his front, suggesting the F'talle slipped into the Other Realm. Why take the children there? What purpose could a once dead man have with living children in a realm where space and time were obscurities? Quinlan found too many questions without answers. A sliver of his mind screamed in warning. Go back before it was too late. Go back before he uncovered more than he was willing to accept. Fractured realities awaited, should he stumble.

"We must find a way into the Other Realm," Quinlan said.

"Are you mad?" Lizette bleated. "That is not a place for mortals. How could such be possible? A land of demons and nightmares is said to lurk beyond the veil."

"What choice have we? Unless we manage to lure Brogon Lord into a trap, we are powerless to keep him from striking again," Quinlan answered.

"That isn't reassuring," she said.

"It wasn't meant to be. We are facing a very real threat we might not be able to combat."

Donal wanted nothing to do with the F'talle. His experiences with the Omegri already threatened to break his mind. At least they'd been trying to kill him. This once dead man was intent on abduction, and worse. He was the monster mothers warned their children of. The creature under the bed.

"I thought the Baron had soldiers in the north searching for him?" he asked.

Lizette cocked her head. "Near the village of Palis, yes, but I have not heard any word from them yet. It is possible they have found nothing."

"Why go north?" Quinlan asked.

Still unsure of where the war priest's loyalties lay, Lizette debated telling him their intimate secrets, even at the expense of the children of Fent. Alas, Quinlan provided their best opportunity of success. She relented. "Einos and Kastus agreed that the pattern of abductions showed Lord moving north, out into the surrounding villages. Palis and Jut were the next two in geographical order. Sending soldiers to each was an attempt at getting ahead of the problem."

Quinlan processed the information and agreed. "That makes sense. Striking too often here would prompt increased security measures, making Lord's task too difficult in comparison to the reward. There is no guarantee that the F'talle will move in accordance with mortal constrictions."

"Which is why the constable hasn't reported anything of worth," she added.

"Leading me back to my previous point."

Lizette snorted. "The Other Realm. You priests are filled with a death wish."

"We are all that stands between the veil. Be glad you do not know the horrors that await should we fail," he replied. "There is nothing more to learn here. I wish to speak with the local Tender."

"Cannandal? He is an old man, Quinlan. Some whisper he is not in his right mind. Of course, they do so behind his back. His title earns him respect for the time being."

"What better way to learn the secrets of the veil than from one who minds the spirits of the dead?" Quinlan forced a grin.

They were too late. Donal was the first to find the Tender, calling the others into the room. Cannandal sat in his chair, head tilted back. His face was locked in a rictus of horror. The flesh was pulled back, tight against the bone. Bloodshot eyes stared into nothing. Whatever his last vision was, none could guess.

Quinlan circled the small desk, taking in each detail. A stack of parchments was half pushed off, trailing away across the floor. Small vials containing various colored liquids were knocked over. He leaned forward, catching the scratches etched into the chair's arms, trails of dried blood stretched down to the floor. Wood slivers popped most of Cannandal's fingernails up.

"Who would do this to an old man?" Lizette gasped, her hand covering her mouth. "Cannandal never hurt anyone. He was here to help us."

"The murderer is a man with secrets from the dead," Quinlan guessed.

Donal whispered a prayer. "What killed him?"

Quinlan wished he had more definitive answers, but whatever killed the Tender remained shrouded. "I do not know, but it is clear he died from fright. Look at his eyes."

Wide open, his gaze remained locked in the nightmares of his last sight. Librarians in Andrak recorded incidents of a great many terrible beings roaming the dark places of the world, many of which were capable of killing a man with a look. Quinlan suspected evil, but this felt wrong. He wasn't sure that Cannandal's killer was inhuman.

"Why is he still sitting in his chair?" he asked, more thinking aloud than expecting an answer.

Lizette overcame her shock, taking a moment to study the Tender. "He was caught off guard. What else could it be?"

"No, I believe there is more," Quinlan said. "Look at how his fingers dug into the chair. How his desk was scattered. Any man, regardless of age, would have put up a struggle upon being confronted, especially in the security of his own home."

Donal didn't follow. "What else could it have been? There are no signs of struggle aside from his desk."

"Precisely," Quinlan said. "I believe whoever killed this man was known to him."

"You're saying a friend did this?" Lizette asked. The idea that a killer was loose in Fent disturbed her. She'd just come to accept the actions of the F'talle.

"Not a friend, but a person he knew," Quinlan corrected.

"But why?"

Why indeed? Quinlan felt the answers were just out of reach. Answers he wasn't prepared to accept. Far too many events were conspiring in Fent to be coincidence. That thought had become too familiar. He was behind the enemy at every turn. Unless he managed to turn the odds against the F'talle, Quinlan feared for what the future held.

"Tenders are people of great influence. You said he had just assisted Einos. It is possible he was killed for what he knew," Quinlan theorized. "To prevent word from getting out."

"Quinlan," Lizette squared on him. "If what you are saying is true, someone is in league with the once dead man. A mortal agent!"

"No other explanation makes sense," Quinlan nodded.

His stomach twisted. Accusations without proof amounted to little more than hearsay. Einos would come to accept his word, for he wore the colors of Andrak. A war priest's integrity was beyond reproach. But would the rest of the duchy follow? Riots might ensue, or worse. Tensions continued to rise as the investigation had the appearance of getting nothing accomplished. Quinlan doubted it would take much to ignite the duchy in anarchy.

"We must take this to the Baron," Lizette said. Her demeanor changed. Gone was the doubt, the slightest hesitation. In its stead was a hardened resolve to find not only her daughter's killer, but that of Tender Cannandal. "The people must be warned."

"I agree," Quinlan said.

She paused, taken off guard. Lizette had expected more of a fight from the priest. Quinlan was proud, borderline arrogant, enough she believed, there was no way he was going to Einos without exhausting all possibilities first. Was he being duplicitous? The thought terrified her. It was possible the war priests had their own agenda in Fent, contradictory to what she was trying to accomplish. Trust, she decided, needed to be extended if any solution was coming.

They walked back to the castle side by side.

Einos pinched the bridge of his nose, head pounding. Each day the news worsened, placing him deeper into a position he could find no exit from. Lines had formed in the creases of his eyes, stretching across his cheeks, only to be outdone by the dark bags clinging. He felt older. As if the world conspired to torment him into ruin. He couldn't remember the last time he had a full night's sleep.

"You're telling me that one of my citizens has committed murder?" His words were flat, stretched.

Quinlan sympathized with him. Einos was a good man, perhaps even a good leader. Everywhere the war priest went, people spoke with respect. Many duchies could not say the same. Some leaders were tyrants, would-be usurpers of power. Others were weak, incapable of showing spine in the face of adversity. In his estimation, Einos had the best interests of his people at heart. A man worthy of the title.

"I understand this is not an easy concept, Baron," Quinlan began, "But we owe it to those lives lost to explore all possibilities. This has an ill feel to it. One I cannot fathom as of yet."

"Is there no other option?" Einos asked. "Why would anyone commit such a crime in the middle of what we already have going on?"

"Perhaps because they thought they could get away with it. Perhaps to keep us distracted," Quinlan ventured. "A more important question is what did Tender Cannandal know about the F'talle?"

"I fear that question is one that will not be answered," Einos said with dryness.

Quinlan saw the exhaustion in his eyes, lingering just behind the normally hawk-like gaze. He pitied the man. There was no greater burden than leadership. Quinlan saw it in Lord General Rosca each time he walked the walls of Andrak. Proud men carrying too much upon their backs. They walked with slumped shoulders, despite the strength of their conviction. It was inevitable.

Einos licked his lips. "Cannandal inspected the grave and was ... out of sorts after. I could tell it affected him negatively, but he refused to explain. I took it as part of his burden for speaking with the souls of the dead. Now, I'm not so sure there wasn't more."

"What more could there possibly be?" Lizette asked. "Aren't Tenders supposed to ensure the dead move on to the next life?"

"That and more," Quinlan supplied. "Tenders are a special breed. A dying one if I am correct in recalling my studies. They care for the soul until it is ready to move on. Each has a special bond with the Other Realm. They can see what most of us cannot. A gift, some say. Others, a curse. The more I think on it, the more I am convinced Cannandal discovered something he wasn't meant to."

"My military might is insignificant compared to many of the duchies. A heavy portion is already deployed north with Kastus. What little I have remaining is perhaps enough to impose martial law in the main villages," Einos offered.

"Doing so might turn your people against you, which would be precisely what our enemies wish," Quinlan denounced the idea. "I suggest increased presence patrols. Do not call up the levees but have a plan to enact such. Anything to prevent the danger I feel approaching from gaining a foothold in Fent."

"Do you think it will come to open conflict?" Einos asked.

"Wariness is our best hope until we discover the killer's identity. There is another possibility you must accept," Quinlan suggested.

"That being?"

"The killer is not alone. An entire cabal might be operating in the shadows. It is my experience that these sorts cluster together where we least expect it."

Einos sagged in his chair. More weight he wasn't sure he could handle.

"Why is he a baron, if this is a duchy?" Donal asked once they were back in their chambers for the night.

"Fent is an old land," Quinlan began after some thought. "Older than most of the other duchies. Rather than melt into obscurity with the rest of the ruling class, the original founders settled on calling themselves barons. The reasons are unimportant. Prestige perhaps. I doubt even Einos knows the origins with clarity."

"It feels odd, almost wrong."

Each moment like this proved Quinlan's instincts by insisting the Lord General accept Donal into the initiate program. Not only had Donal proven his martial worth standing the wall for the bulk of the Burning Season after his knight was killed, but he was a fast learner with a good mind for critical thinking. It was going to be a proud day, for master and apprentice, when Donal donned the sky blue colors of the Order.

"True, but who are we to dictate how others live? Our path in life is to protect, not rule," Quinlan reminded. "Remember your training. It will serve you well in the trials to come."

Donal resisted the urge to hang his head. Another long day contributed to his growing fatigue. "I feel, at times, that I am out of my depth. Every time I believe I've gotten my mind to accept what is something worse changes. How can we be expected to defeat the Omegri, if we can never get ahead of them?"

In truth, Quinlan doubted the Order was ever meant to defeat the Omegri. Contain and prevent from invading this world, but not defeat. To do so would require vast amounts of military might going into the Other Realm. They would be outnumbered and outmatched at every turn. Failure was all but certain. No. Best the war priests stay here, protecting the Purifying Flame.

"Many of life's questions aren't meant to be answered," Quinlan supposed. "The hour is late. I fear tomorrow will be more of the same. We are on to a conspiracy, Donal. The F'talle is but a player in a much greater game. Once we discover who controls the strings, we shall be able to unravel their plans. Good night. Oh and Donal, take a weapon with you should you need to visit the privy again."

Chuckling, he watched his novice close the door on his way out.

Some matters are meant for the dark of night. Betrayal. Treason. Murder. Until recently, Giles would have never considered any of that. He'd been an honorable man in charge of a small trading company. Life wasn't glamorous, but it was good and he had little need for want. Far from rich, Giles spent years developing a web of suppliers, while offering his specific services. Ones many of the other merchants refused to offer.

It was Fent's insignificance across the continent that led him down roads less desired. Giles reached out to the surrounding duchies. Their dukes and duchesses were more than happy to increase their flow of revenue by using his caravans. All under Einos's watch. The Baron still hadn't caught on or chose to ignore it if he had. Coffers of gold, silver, and jewels from across the continent soon prompted him to dig deep under his trading house. Secure rooms were constructed and filled with his newfound wealth.

None of that brought the happiness he once assumed. Loneliness crept in, haunting him with lullabies of prolonged misery. Single and without heirs, Giles realized that his legacy would be lost like flotsam in the river. All he'd done and strived for threatened to be forgotten in the moment of his death. That cold reality robbed him of many nights. His health declined. He began to question who he was, why.

Answers not forthcoming, Giles turned to the night with prayers. He was answered by a pair of mortal agents of the Omegri. Their overbearing desire to reclaim the world of the life drew many less than desirables to their name. Giles wasn't inherently wicked, but the opportunity to salvage his life's work demanded he take action. All he needed to do was reach forth his hand and the future was secured.

It was a deal with the damned. Giles felt slivers of his soul peeling away each time he was forced to deal with the shadow agents of the Other Realm. Thus he sat. Deep in the seclusion of his treasure rooms, with blood stained hands. Giles stared at the scars the Tender left across his hands and forearms. Regret twisted his aged features. The Tender wasn't a foul man. In fact, Giles often found him pleasant. What he was, was an impediment.

"What have I done?" he asked the dark, flashes of the old man dying taunting him.

"What you were expected to do," a thin voice, little more than a rasp, said from the shadows by the door.

A second voice added, "Have you regrets?"

"Perhaps we have chosen the wrong agent."

"There must have been another way," Giles defended. His anger at being disturbed, here where he thought the most secure, rose.

The first voice, an unpleasant woman with flesh so pale, it hadn't seen the sun in a generation, replied, "Tenders speak with the dead. It would not have been long before he learned of our operations in Fent. What do you suppose will become of you should the Baron discover your duplicity?"

Death no doubt. It took little imagination to seeing the executioner's blade swing down for his neck. "Why was I forced to be part of that … filth? I am no killer."

"A lesson in the true power our master's hold," the second, a portly man with a foul odor snorted. "We each have our part to play. Yours has but begun."

"And if I refuse?" Giles dared.

Darkness swelled, drowning the tiny light thrown off by the candles. Sharp pains, like stabbing fingers plunged into his chest. Giles clutched at his chest. His eyes rolled back.

"S… stop. Enough!" he begged.

Normalcy returned. The woman stepped forward, showing him the full horror of her face. Under another circumstance, Giles might have thought her pretty once. But time and service to the dark stripped her of her looks, as well as her humanity. She was little better than a ghoul.

"The once dead man is returning. He will contact you when he does. You are to do what he says," she ordered. "There is no leeway in this, Merchant. Fulfill your purpose and you shall be richly rewarded."

"Disappoint us again, and I will take great pleasure in stretching your suffering across centuries," the man added.

"I understand," Giles whispered. Closing his eyes, he hung his head in defeat.

He was alone when he reopened them. The message had been delivered.

TWENTY

Jut, Northern Fent

Nils wiped the sweat from his brow before replacing his helmet. "This is pointless. We've been bouncing back and forth between villages so much I can't feel the bottom of my feet!"

"What else is we supposed to do?" Alfar blinked.

Frustrated, Nils snapped. "One of these days I'm going to cut that stupid tongue out of your stupid mouth! This ain't what we signed on for. And you know it!"

"The Captain said this was for securing the duchy," Alfar reasoned. "How can that be wrong when we're keeping that dead fella from stealing more children?"

Defeated by an imbecile. What's this army coming to? Nils stomped off, leaving the younger soldier lost in thought. The patrol was executing their sixth rotation between Palis and Jut. If any of the soldiers were unaffected by the constant marching in full gear, they refused to show it in front of Sava. The sergeant was on a personal vendetta to hunt down and kill the once dead man. A ridiculous notion, Nils thought. After all, how does one kill a man who is already dead?

Their first night in the field was spent with him trying to figure that riddle out. Nils failed, and it bothered him since. Brogon Lord. The name had become a boogeyman. A shadow ever out of reach. The squad tired, weakening, whereas Lord remained unchanged. Nils figured a dead man didn't need to sleep, or eat, or use the privy, or well, anything. For all they knew, Brogon Lord might already be halfway across the continent by now.

Sergeant Sava neither cared nor was he interested in anyone's opinion but his own. His private humiliation was enough to invigorate the old man. Time may have slowed him down, for he wasn't the man he was when he'd first joined, but it made his mind sharper. Each time they stopped for a quick break, he snatched a trooper and went through a series of sword drills. The squad was slowing, breaking down from fatigue, but he wasn't about to let that be an excuse for a second failure. Sava intended to be ready when he and Lord next met.

The village of Jut, if it could be called so, was barely larger than an extended family compound. They had a well and a place to worship the light, but little else. The squad was forced to pitch tents and sleep in one of the surrounding farmer's fields whenever they wound up spending the night. Nils had been here three times already and failed to see any benefit from returning.

Less than a hundred villagers lived in Jut and many of them were grey beards. Children were scarce, leaving Nils to ponder why they kept coming back. There seemed little chance the once dead man would target Jut, even if it was on his way. Nils shook his head. He'd never met the constable before and didn't have a high opinion of Captain Thep, but their ideas felt odd. Anyone could see that a man trying to steal children would be better off in a bigger community.

"What are you staring at, Trooper?" Sava's voice growled from behind.

Nils winced at the sound of that damned stick slapping Sava's leg. "Nothing, Sergeant."

"Nothing eh? Good. Grab your sword. It's your turn."

Shit.

They passed a grinning Alfar, who hurriedly looked down to his gear and began cleaning his sword.

"Nothing. Six days with no results. I fear we are wasting our time," Kastus admitted.

He echoed the frustrations exhibited by the squad, though he was sure none of them thought they were being watched. Not only had there been no sign of Lord, they hadn't been able to dig any deeper on the crooked councilor. Deana's report was long overdue, leading him to believe she was either complicit or the guilty party.

Thep finished swallowing the last of his food, if army field rations could be called such. "We are ensuring the people that the Baron has their best interests and is concerned with their safety."

Kastus waggled a gloved finger. "Don't give me the motivation speech you give your soldiers, Thep. You and I both know the issues at hand, and what is at stake. Failure is not an option, but it seems that is all we are capable of."

"We haven't been recalled," Thep countered.

Kastus started pacing. "What are we missing?"

"There's nothing significant in Jut. We are wasting precious time here when we could be gathering leads in the south."

"Not until we solve the issue in Palis," Kastus said. He wasn't sure why, but his feeling that the misdealing of the council was related to Brogon Lord. Proving it was problematic.

The clash of blades drew his attention, relaxing only when he recognized it was Sava with yet another soldier. How many did that make in the last week? They must be exhausted from his constant harping. Kastus remained in the dark as to why anyone would take up arms for a ruler they might never meet. Working for Einos was different, at least insofar as he was concerned. The constable was responsible for the security of the duchy and in constant contact with the Baron. He wore a sword but used it only on occasion.

"Perhaps it is time to abandon this strategy," he said after more thought. Jut was a dead end. There was no point in trying to pretend that wasn't the case.

"Should we leave a presence here, just in case?" Thep asked. He was grateful for the decision and knew the soldiers would be as well. No one hated constant marching more than an infantryman.

Kastus bit back a laugh. "I don't see a need. There's barely a child here, or in the surrounding area. Best we consolidate our power and subdue Palis."

"Using too much force might cement their treachery," Thep countered. "An uprising is the last thing we need."

"True, but I believe applying the proper amount of pressure will break those guilty parties and ensure compliance with their potential replacements," Kastus said.

He found both advantages and disadvantages in having a triumvirate of leadership in a modest village like Palis. Regardless of what happened, he intended on transforming Palis into the most loyal- and possibly rewarded- village in Fent.

"Excuse me, sir. Are you busy?" a female private, Gemma, if Kastus remembered correctly, interrupted.

"Not if it is important," he replied.

Gemma nodded. "There is a man from the village wishing to speak with you."

Kastus and Thep exchanged hopeful looks. "Where is he?"

Neither could see any but their soldiers in the immediate area.

"In a shed by the creek," she replied. "He refuses to come out with the other villagers around. Something about being worried of the repercussions."

"Lead the way," Kastus ordered before Thep could ask the question burning the tip of his tongue. *This had better be worth it. Or she'll march back to Palis barefoot.*

They found the man partially hidden behind a stack of early season hay. He was old beyond count. Lines competed for space across his face and hands. A thin beard hung down past the top of his tunic, stark white and fading. Spots coated his exposed flesh. Signs of the merciless advance of time and age. Kastus would have discounted him as just another old man if not for the clarity in his eyes. This was a man with burdensome secrets.

"My name is Kastus. I am Constable of Fent. This is Captain Thep of the Baron's army. I am told you have information for us."

"Depends on if you can protect me or not," the old man said, with a voice stronger than his fragile body should have.

Kastus knew better than to waste time asking his name. He was jittery enough, suggesting the information he had was important. "Any manner of protection would depend on what you have to say. We are not in the habit of trading services. Not when the security of the duchy is at stake. Tell us what you know and if it warrants, we will ensure you remain unharmed."

Seeing there was no way around the barrier Kastus erected, the old man sighed. "Rumor is you are looking into corruption on the Palis council. I can help. There's been shady dealings with Palis for the better part of the last year. Strange people coming and going. Shipments of grain and wheat being diverted to different lands after being scrubbed from the books."

"Do you know which councilor is responsible?" Kastus asked. His heart quickened.

Tugging his beard, the old man said, "If what they say is true. I've been in charge of commerce here for decades. Only started turning sour of late."

"Why has no one mentioned this?" Thep asked.

"Folks around here want to live their lives in peace. Don't think anyone is looking for trouble, leastwise not from the authorities."

"Yet here you are," Kastus mused.

"I'm tired of holding my tongue," he replied. "There's dark tides in Fent, Constable. The council in Palis isn't working alone either. There's a merchant from the big village coordinating it all. Some say he's making a fortune on the Baron's ignorance."

"I need names," Kastus demanded. His voice was harsher than he intended. "There is more at play than your quiet village."

"Huh, has to do with those missing children," he guessed.

Thep grew wary. This man knew too much where no one else did. "What makes you say that? No children have been reported missing in this part of the duchy."

"Common knowledge. Word got here before your soldiers did. Fine looking men and women, but I hear tell there's a once dead man doing the kidnapping," he said. "Hard to beat one of them. I seen a few during my time. Always moving with a purpose. As if their last grasp at life came with specific designs."

"Have you seen this once dead man?" Kastus pressed.

"No, and I don't want to either," he said. "There's enough trouble going on. Why would I want to get involved with one of them, when I'm worried about being knifed by someone I know?"

The Constable found the entire testimony unsettling and embellished somewhat. He knew old timers who spent long days in taverns, waiting for younger patrons to listen to their stories. The thing about stories was they tended to get more incredulous with each telling.

"What leads you to think they would do so?" he asked.

A shrug. "I don't know who's in league with this merchant. Could be any of them."

Thep asked, "Do you know who on the council?"

"Not by name, but I can pick him out of a crowd without any problem." His reply was borderline boastful. "Take me with you and I'll lay him at your feet."

Him. Kastus frowned. He'd secretly hoped to place Deana in shackles. Anyone that haughty deserved to be taken down a notch or two. Humility was a wonderful condition. The potential of being misdirected remained, but Kastus felt the risk was worth it.

He looked at Thep. "Captain, I believe it's time to return to Palis and put an end to this nonsense."

Nils collapsed beside his gear. He was soaked with sweat and could barely lift his arms. Whatever grudge Sava held against Lord, the squad was being punished for it. He reached for his canteen and had unscrewed the cap when a harsh voice rang out.

"On your feet, kiddies! We're heading back to Palis."

Groans circulated the squad. Nils wanted to cry.

Waern sat alone in his private study. A half empty glass of brandy sat at the edge of his desk. The fire crackled behind him, warming his old bones. He was tired. Stacks of unread reports waited, but he lacked interest. Mornings were best for trivial work. Waern leaned back into the crimson leather chair and closed his eyes.

"We have to talk."

"I have nothing to say to you." His eyes remained closed.

Footsteps marching across the floor. "Then shut up and listen."

"What is this about? I am in no mood for games, Deana."

His eyes shot open, surprised to find she had taken the liberty of sitting on his guest couch. Rigid, her right leg crossed over the left, where she placed both hands on her knee. She wore that look suggesting he wasn't about to like what she had to say.

"Well? You're here and I have brandy to drink," he said.

Nonplussed, Deana idly picked at a loose string along the stitching of her sleeve. "What have you told Kastus?"

"About what? I don't have time for this."

"They are ready to cart the three of us back to Einos's jail," she pressed. "We are all going to suffer unless whoever it is they are looking for comes forward."

He leaned forward. "Are you accusing me of something?"

"Not at all, but I have no desire to spend my final years rotting in a cell."

"You worry too much. Word has reached me that they haven't found anything amiss. I suspect they will return to Einos with full reprimand," Waern suggested.

She wasn't impressed. "This is not a laughing matter. Kastus is an insufferable man. He won't stop until he has a prisoner."

"Perhaps a sacrifice is in order. There are plenty of rivals who would love nothing more than to see you or I carted away," he offered.

"A sacrifice? Give them one of our citizens to make them go away? What would stop them from returning once they got to the bottom of their investigation?" she asked. The idea soured her stomach. Stern, unforgiving, Deana still cared for the people in Palis. Delivering one to the executioner's axe was wrong.

Waern spread his hands. "Have you a better idea? Baron Einos's watchdogs won't be satisfied until they place guilt on someone. It is the only way to get them to leave."

Infuriated, Deana struggled to retain composure. "I will not sit idle while you throw one of our citizens to the wolves, Waern. This is unacceptable."

"Give me another solution." His deadpan expression challenged her.

"No, Councilor. It is you who need to present a more suitable answer to the dilemma you caused," she snapped and stormed out.

"I should have killed you long ago," he said to her back after she left.

TWENTY-ONE
Castle Fent

Time was running out. Every moment wasted in debate hastened the end. Lizette couldn't confirm this, for it was a feeling brewing deep in her gut. She watched and listened as Einos made plans and wished for the best, all the while knowing that it wasn't going to be enough. The once dead man always seemed a step ahead. The war priest and his novice hadn't proved much advantage either. Lizette continued to sink into loneliness.

She wanted to lash out. To find the F'talle and exact vengeance for her daughter. Why couldn't anyone see that they were falling too far behind? Lizette reasoned it was partly due to the fact that no additional children had been abducted. Security lagged in typical human reaction. Frustrated, she paced the length of her rooms. *Think, damn it. There must be something I can do to get them to understand.*

There was always the Baroness. Lizette had formed a close bond with Aneth during her time in the castle, but her pregnancy was moving along and would soon confine her to the bed until their child was born. Memories flashed. She closed her eyes and smiled at clips of the past showing her holding Tabith for the first time.

"That's it!" she blurted aloud.

Embarrassed, despite being alone, Lizette knew the angle she needed to approach Einos with. It was a desperate gamble that might not work, but it was all she had left for options. Tensions rose across the duchy, turning friends against each other as suspicions of collusion grew. Chaos threatened to tear the land apart. But there was a way to prevent such from happening. A way to prove to Einos that the way ahead wasn't as secluded as he assumed. If only she could help change his mind, they might have a chance.

Gathering her robes and taking a moment to run a comb through her hair—and frowning upon discovering the first strands of silver peeking through—Lizette went to find Quinlan. She was going to need allies before confronting an already fatigued Einos. The grin etched upon her face was both fierce and confident. Servants and low level functionaries moved out of her way, avoiding eye contact as she swept by.

Autumn winds swept down the narrow canyons of Fent, preceded by a wave of multi-colored leaves. Winter was coming, faster than any anticipated or wanted. Life, however, seldom cared for the wants of mortals. A sad fact Quinlan learned as a young boy. It had been a dark evening in early spring. He and his best friend ignored their parent's orders to return home by sundown in favor of playing a little longer. What child could resist the urge to keep playing after the snows melted?

Wooden wands for swords, they pretended to harry and chase monsters away from their stone castle. Quinlan got turned around as the sky darkened so fast. One moment it was bright. The next it was the darkest night. He halted, calling his friend's name for what felt like hours. Only the wind echoed back. Darkness fled almost as quickly as it arrived, leaving him stunned and in awe. Village elders claimed foul portents when the skies rebelled against convention. He didn't know anything about that. All that mattered was finding his friend.

Knowing they were going to be in grave trouble when they returned home, Quinlan started to run. His shouts grew frantic, fearful that something dark and twisted had happened. Searching without pause, he checked all their favorite places. Secret hiding spots among rock and tree. Nothing. His friend was gone. Alone, and afraid, young Quinlan stood along the riverbank wondering what happened to his friend and how he was going to break the news to his parents.

The answer awaited him. His mother smothered him with hugs, fiercely tight as if she were afraid to let go. When he asked why, they told him his friend's body was found downstream. The entire village was affected, brought together by the tragedy. Quinlan spent years lamenting his role, always wondering what he might have done different. That desire eventually took him to the walls of Castle Bendris, and the War Priests.

Pulling his pale blue cloak tighter around the neck, he and Donal continued down the street. Life threatened to return to normal now that there hadn't been any reported abductions in weeks. Quinlan found it disturbing how easily one forgot. A great evil stalked these lands, yet the human mind was conditioned to put harsh times behind and carry on. Would it be their undoing? He hoped not. Hoped that the authority he brought to Fent was enough to end the nightmare. Often, hope was enough.

"Are you hungry, Donal?" he asked.

Taken off guard, the novice pulled his gaze from the empty street. "I feels like I always am, leastwise since I encountered that spirit."

"This cold has a way of sapping a man's strength. Let us find a vendor." Quinlan empathized with him. The supernatural had a way of creeping into the soul, threatening to rob it of all it was, should one become unfocused.

They headed for the marketplace, mouths watering as the smells of roasting meats and fowl filled their nostrils. Stomachs growling in anticipation, they purchased skewers of venison and thanked the vendor with a pair of silvers.

Quinlan leaned back against the nearest wall and savored the juices as he bit into the meat. These were the moments where he missed simpler times. Not that he had much to complain about. They were a long way from the drear of Andrak and the all-consuming threat of the Omegri.

"What brought you to Castle Andrak?" he asked Donal.

Volunteering a lifetime of service to the Purifying Flame was no easy task, especially for one so young.

"I wanted more than what I had," Donal said after some thought. "Truthfully, I seldom think on it. Sir Forlei was a good man. Harsh when necessary, but he always had my best in mind. I tried to serve him as well as any squire. When he said he was going to fight in the Burning Season I was nervous but knew that he would survive. Little could I have known."

"The Burning Season is a war unlike any on this world," Quinlan said with a nod, remembering his first time standing the wall. "Only the best survive, and for that, the world gets to live another year. You never thought of following in your father's shadow?"

"I did, for a time. He loves what he does, but I realized far too soon that it was not the life for me. I wanted more."

"Just not what," Quinlan added.

Donal shook his head, finishing the last bite. "I feel like there is something more for me, waiting just beyond reach. Only, I don't know how to find it."

"Life is strange that way. I don't believe we are meant to know what comes next," he theorized. "Perhaps one day, when we are old and grey, there will come a time when we may both ride out from Castle Andrak and put this chapter of our lives behind. Perhaps one day."

Donal resisted the temptation to look decades ahead. He had yet to earn the title of war priest. Trying to imagine what retirement looked like seemed wrong. Most of his life, not that it was overly long, was spent in pursuit of other, better options. He'd never dreamed of becoming a priest until Forlei took him to stand the wall. Now it was his focus. His every desire was bent toward it. All else was secondary.

"It is time we return to the castle," Quinlan said, after enjoying the last mouthful. He wiped the juice from his lower jaw. "We must discuss alternative strategies for drawing out the F'talle. I fear it is the only way we are going to find him."

They walked side by side. Those few still in the streets gave them a wide berth. War priests were both feared and revered across the duchies, though a great many refused to believe they existed out of some antiquated superstition. Quinlan cared little for any of it. He'd been mocked, spit on, lavished with gifts, and ignored during his time in the Order. It was part of the role he assumed upon donning the colors.

Mired in reflection, Quinlan barely caught the glimpse of a man crossing the street before them. Out of the corner of his eye he saw the man, featureless and vague, stop in the middle of the street and wave before continuing on. There was an odd familiarity about him, as if Quinlan knew the man. He blinked and when his eyes opened after a split-second, the man was gone.

Quinlan held his hand out, the back striking Donal in the chest. "Did you see that?"

"What?" Donal asked. His hand dropped to his sword, ready for trouble.

Quinlan squinted, confused. "There was a man in front of us. He stopped here and waved at me."

Buildings lined the street, preventing anyone from disappearing. Donal glanced behind them but found nothing out of the ordinary. "Brother Quinlan, there is no one around us. What did this man look like?"

He began to suspect another apparition. Was the Other Realm attempting to contact them?

"He wore a faded grey uniform. A stripe ran down his trousers and his boots were coated in mud. I ... I could not see his face. He stopped and waved before disappearing."

"This sounds like the child I saw," Donal whispered.

Disturbed, Quinlan found no other rational explanation. The dead were walking the streets of Fent, harrying the war priests. They investigated the area thoroughly but produced no results. Whatever had shown itself to Quinlan achieved its purpose and departed. Flesh crawling, Quinlan made the rest of the journey in silence.

"A ghost. Walking my streets in daylight. You'll understand if I am reserved over this," Einos said.

His nerves were frayed. Each new event heightened the dangers his people faced and he was powerless to stop it. Ghosts of dead children in his bedchambers were bad enough, but if what Quinlan said was true, ghosts now roamed his lands at will. *Am I to rule a kingdom of the dead?*

"Would that I had a better answer," Quinlan replied. He'd come to terms with what he saw, though it left him unsettled. He went on to describe the uniform, all while failing to produce an image of the ghost's face.

"I know that uniform," Einos told them. He glanced up as Lizette flowed into the room. There was an air of power surrounding her. His shoulders sagged. Yet another matter he could do without. "It is from my grandfather's day, though it hasn't been used in decades. Are you certain?"

"I am," Quinlan's answer left no doubt.

Left without answers, Baron and Priest pondered the meaning behind the vision. "Could it have been Brogon Lord?"

"Not unless he's been dead for a very long time," Quinlan replied.

"No. He was buried not long ago," Einos rubbed his chin. Compounding his frustration, there was no record of a soldier, a knight, from Fent in the Baron's service. He might have been a mercenary, thus earning him the right to be buried with full honors, but Einos felt he would have remembered any such funeral. His records keepers failed to produce anything worth noting on Lord, deepening the mystery.

"Baron, I wish to speak with you," Lizette announced after the conversation paused. "Brother Quinlan. Donal."

Wishing for a decanter of wine, Einos closed his eyes and gestured for her to continue. There was no other way of dealing with her and now that his wife was taking a less active role in running the duchy, Lizette stepped forward to fill her position. *As if I need two wives.*

"I have been doing much thinking of late," she started. "Just because abductions aren't being reported, doesn't mean the threat is removed. All children remain at risk. To treat the situation otherwise not only places them in jeopardy, but also those who are yet unborn."

The word struck the intended chord. Einos's eyes snapped open and he fixed her with a sad look. Thinking of his unborn child being ripped away was sobering. "What more can I do? Kastus has yet to return from the north. My patrols here produce no results. Brogon Lord hasn't been spotted in over a week. Our efforts to find his lair have failed, and there has been no movement on finding Tender Cannandal's murderer. I am stuck, Lizette. I cannot move forward, nor go back."

Quinlan felt sorry for the man. There were many nobles and rulers who were less worthy of the title. Einos ruled as best he could. Always with the people in mind. He didn't deserve this nightmare.

"There must be something we haven't tried!" Lizette all but begged. "Baron, these are our children. Families suffer endlessly."

"I know this, woman!" he snapped. "Do you not think I stay awake at night wondering what I might do better? How I can halt this monster and restore order to Fent? Do not make the mistake of thinking that because I am not personally affected, I do not care."

"Perhaps there is another way," Quinlan offered, though he was loath to do so.

Argument ended, they turned to him. "I am listening, War Priest."

Quinlan detailed his plan. When he finished, Donal's mouth was ajar.

The next morning found them in the castle's kitchens, devouring as much as they could. Quinlan knew he was going to need as much strength as possible if there was any chance of success. Fresh baked breads, boiled eggs, leftover ham from the night before, and chunks of white and yellow cheese were accompanied by a pitcher of ale. Quinlan ate with abandon, while Donal picked at his food.

"Are you certain there is no other way?" Donal asked. He liked the idea of Quinlan exposing himself less and less as the morning wore on.

Crumbs spilled from Quinlan's mouth. "None that I can see. Baron Einos has tried everything within his power, to no avail. Lizette is correct. We must draw out the F'talle. Force the confrontation on our terms."

"But if you use your magic to draw him here, you'll be exposed," Donal protested.

"Precisely why I have you, Donal. Your sword will guard me until I can refocus."

Donal's nerves toyed with him. His hands already trembled from the thought of locking swords with a dead knight. "I'm no trained warrior."

"No, yet you stood the wall for longer than many who were better," Quinlan reasoned. "I cannot do this without you. This is what you have trained for."

"I know," he replied. *But I don't have to like it.*

TWENTY-TWO
Brogon Lord's Grave

The morning was crisp. Blue skies stretched as far as one could see, beckoning with the tranquility of distant horizons forever beyond reach. Wisps of clouds, so thin as to appear transparent, swept by. Any other circumstance and it might have been pleasant, just another autumn day. The pounding beat of horses rumbled deep within the earth. Birds leapt from perches. Deer and smaller animals fled across fields to whatever protections they could find. Six riders swept in behind.

They came from the castle with grave intent. An illness gripped the land of Fent. One that refused to relinquish its hold, while threatening to strangle the land into submission. Baron Einos refused to surrender, knowing that he forfeited the lives of every citizen by doing so. Left without choice, he insisted on accompanying the war priests. Two guards rode behind him. One hand on the reins, the other on their swords. Aneth wished for more, but Brother Quinlan's insistence that too many present would dilute his abilities. He and Donal followed. Lizette, grieving mother and advocate for the citizenry, was at their side, for she refused to be left behind.

The six represented Fent's best chance for peace. Einos rode with grave doubt, for he failed to see how any power was great enough to counteract that of the F'talle. A messenger arrived shortly after dawn with word from Kastus. The constable had discovered a conspiracy related to Brogon Lord and the missing children. One with the potential to unravel a great many mysteries. Kastus would return soon but needed more time to finish in Palis. With the rest of the duchy doing their part, how could Einos remain in his castle?

They arrived at the once quiet graveyard to find it deserted. Both groundskeepers were warned away, an order they were too willing to obey. They'd no stomach for the dead rising from the grave. Quinlan dismounted and followed Einos to Lord's grave. It hadn't been disturbed since Cannandal attempted to reach out to the once dead man's soul.

Quinlan knelt, pulling off his glove and gingerly touching his palm to the cold dirt. Flashes of light exploded in his mind and he jerked his hand away. "This does not feel right."

"You saw something," Einos whispered.

Quinlan nodded, unsure exactly what. "This area is infused with strange magic. It is almost as if … no. That cannot be."

"Damn it man, what? Speak plainly," Einos demanded. He forced a calming breath, frustrated with his inability to do more than stand idle.

"I feel the taint of the Omegri," Quinlan said.

"How is that possible?" Donal asked. His heart thumped harder. "The Omegri cannot enter our world outside of the crossing points."

Six crossing points. Six gates preventing the Other Realm from spilling into this one. Five had fallen, destroyed. Only Andrak remained.

"I do not know, but their taint is weak." Frowning, Quinlan considered what this meant.

The Omegri were insubstantial. Reduced to shadows in this realm. It was long rumored that the F'talle were connected to the great enemy, but there was never any proof. Quinlan suspected that, if the Omegri were indeed behind Brogon Lord and the abductions, they were attempting to bridge the space between realms at a place and time of their choosing. His task became more urgent.

"Clear a space for me. I do not want anyone getting close," Quinlan ordered.

The guards glanced about, hesitant.

"You heard him, fall back," Einos barked. "But be ready to attack if necessary."

He drew his sword for effect.

"Donal, listen to me. I want you standing at the grave marker. If I am successful, the F'talle will appear here. Do not hesitate to strike. It may be our only chance of defeating him," Quinlan said in rushed tones.

Donal could only nod. The words caught in his throat.

"What if you fail?" Lizette asked. Her fierce demeanor was gone, replaced by the pallid glow of raw terror. Not even the prospect of confronting Tabith's killer comforted her.

His smile was weak, almost helpless. "Then I wish you all the best of fortune."

The time for words was ended. Quinlan climbed down into the shallow grave. The ground was soft, almost welcoming. What little remained of the coffin was but slivers. A knight Brogon Lord might have been, but one unworthy of grand ceremony. Quinlan shed his cloak, exposing his armor for the first time since arriving in Fent. The symbol of the war priests, a mighty griffon, was emblazoned on his chest, right above the giant cross stretching across. He drew his sword and breathed deep to calm his nerves and control his heart rate.

Quinlan closed his eyes and plunged his sword deep into the earth. White light bubbled up from the ground. Worms and maggots writhed and tried to escape, only to be burned to cinders. Quinlan chanted. His words an ancient tongue unheard in this land for generations. The light grew.

Donal watched in awe as what he knew to be the essence of the Purifying Flame was channeled through his master. Raw power vibrated all around, reaching up his legs into his very core. The light brightened, forcing him to shield his eyes, lest he go blind. A tremor nearly toppled him. Unable to see, Donal cringed at the gut wrenching cry sweeping over the graveyard.

He forced a look. A figure took shape beside the grave. A man. Dead. Decomposing. A man in such agony that he could not take it. Brogon Lord. The once dead man was summoned. Donal stood in shock. Chasing a name was unlike confronting him. He watched as Lord solidified into a waste of flesh and bones. The urge to wretch gripped him, for never had he gazed upon a being so fell. Donal clutched his sword tightly and prayed his strength stayed with him.

Brogon Lord screamed at the top of his lungs. Dirt and clusters of hair fell from him. Confusion twisted his face. Specks of yellow poked through holes in his cheeks. A charred strip of flesh hung from his right cheek. Brogon glared through the light, attempting to discover who had brought him—unwillingly—back into the realm of the living. His gaze fell on the exposed priest kneeling in his grave. Brogon attacked.

A sharp cry from behind drew his attention, too late to stop the blade from catching in his neck. Infuriated, the once dead man spun and struck his attacker with a backhand to the side of the head. Donal tumbled away, sword skittering to the ground. Brogon waited until he was certain the man wasn't getting back up.

He turned and found two more swordsmen attacking. Death presented alternative strategies. No longer was he concerned with getting cut or wounded. He was already dead. There was little mortal blades could do. Brogon leapt from the grave and charged into them. Both swords struck glancing blows to his arms and chest. He laughed.

The guards circled, striking only when they found advantage. He let them. Overconfident, one guard tripped too close. Brogon snatched him by the throat and squeezed. Face turning purple, the guard desperately tried to peel Brogon's fingers from his throat. A final squeeze crushed his windpipe. Brogon cast the body aside and gestured to the now horrified second guard. Unwilling to wait, Brogon burst forward and plunged his fist deep into the guard's exposed throat, twisting and ripping it back out.

"Why have you summoned me? Why can't you let me die!" he bellowed to the priest.

Brogon stalked closer, the other still seemingly unaware of him. Head down, bathed in pale light already fading, the priest looked spent. Brogon snorted, disappointed with the ease of the kill. A boot sank into the dirt of the grave, followed by the other. Brogon crouched before the priest and lifted his head. He wished to look into the priest's eyes before robbing the life from them.

"No!" Donal shouted and crawled forward. His ribs ached.

Brogon ignored him, for he had already proved his worth. Advancing boots came from behind. Focused on his prize, Brogon stared deep into the priest's eyes. Was there a chance this was the one? He doubted it, all while holding on to hope. As if in response, the priest's eyes flashed open.

"Fear no darkness," he whispered and placed his palm on Brogon's chest.

Blazing white light erupted from contact. The once dead man flew through the air, crashing through headstones and grave markers to land at Lizette's feet. She screamed and jumped back, but not fast enough. Brogon, sensing he lacked the strength to defeat the war priest, snatched the woman around her waist.

Both priests were on their feet now and closing in. The third man stood nearby with sword drawn. Brogon recognized the danger. He began retreating, step by painful step until he was at the edge of the graveyard. He'd sorely underestimated his foes. These priests were keepers of the Flame, an undying tribute to the holy light of creation. Without sufficient strength to defeat them, Brogon was left with little choice. He must retreat, back to the Other Realm where the pain would fade.

Clutching the woman tighter, he uttered a single word and flashed from the world of the living. Quinlan struggled to remain afoot. He could only stare at the space where Brogon and Lizette had just occupied. Tiny flames sprout up in a loose circle. The ground was charred, leaving no visible trace of either. They were gone.

"Lizette," Quinlan whispered. "What have I done?"

TWENTY-THREE
Palis

Kastus winced each time Sava slapped his stick on his thigh. "Do you suppose he feels what he's doing?"

"Sava?" Thep asked with a wry grin. "I doubt it. He's been smacking himself with that stick for as long as I can remember. I suppose that's better than the alternative."

A far cry from being a soldier, Kastus failed to understand the point in striking oneself. There was no motivational factor involved. Just the sharp sting and a possible bruise. Fascinating as that was, he studied the soldier's reactions. Men and women, veterans and fresh faced recruits alike, snapped to whenever Sava came around. He doubted it was entirely out of respect. Kastus noticed a healthy fear ran in undercurrents among the lower ranks. That was good, for morale and discipline.

"What's the alternative?" he asked, even as the answer came to him.

"No one wants to get caught by that stick more than once," Thep explained.

"Seems excessive, even for a sergeant."

"Sava is one of the best I know. I'd put him up against anyone else in the duchies."

Impressed, Kastus couldn't help but wonder what had invigorated Sava since arriving in Palis. Aside from one minor skirmish, their time had been ill spent. "The only problem is we haven't found anyone to put him up against. He grows harsher as the days progress. Should we speak with him?"

Thep gave him a look suggesting that he could if he wanted to. "Constable, Sava is a proud man. Getting beaten by the once dead man in the manner he did is beyond insulting. All he wants is another crack at the beast. I have no qualms of his training methods, so long as they reinforce the soldiers. We cannot be caught unawares again."

Deciding he would never understand the mentality of a soldier, Kastus changed the subject. "Do you think the old man will be good for his word?"

They were less than a league away from Palis, returning from an otherwise wasted trip to nearby Jut. Despite the bold predictions of the old man, it still rankled Kastus that the man refused to give his name, inferred there was something off about the situation. He'd served as Constable for many years now and had developed a talent for sniffing out a rat.

"We shall see," was all Thep had to offer. His experiences were far different, normally ending with the flash of the blade.

Kastus yawned. Days of constant riding and searching left him more tired than he liked. His mental acuity was slipping, and that aggravated him the most. He needed that sharpness, especially now that he was plucking apart the strands of conspiracy.

"I don't trust him," Kastus continued. He glanced sidelong to the old man.

"You suspect a trap?"

"Not per se. I believe he is duplicitous. Why else would he come forward, claiming to fear retribution should he be identified, and then offer to show us the guilty party? It feels wrong, Thep."

The young captain turned to study the old man who remained oblivious to their scrutiny. "He doesn't look out of the ordinary. Just a plain villager who's had a tough life. I never understood farmers. So much work, only to give away most of their labor."

Kastus concealed his grin. "Not everyone is adept at a blade, Thep. We each serve a purpose. I only wonder what purpose he holds."

"I'll have Sava detail some soldiers to watch him," Thep offered. "For his security, of course. Are we going straight to the Elders when we arrive?"

"I think that best," Kastus said without thought. "Might as well get this over with and head back to the Baron. I've a feeling our quarry has fled back south."

That was fine with Thep. He was growing tired of being confined to the general hospitality of Palis. Soldiers were meant for tougher conditions. Too much longer being catered to and there was bound to be trouble.

The old man fidgeted in his chair in the corner of the room. Excessive flesh bunched up across the back of his hands as he wrung them repeatedly. Alfar watched, impressed and slightly revolted, with the way his flesh manipulated with each motion. He'd been hungry before Sergeant Sava assigned him and Nils this detail.

"Why are we here?" he whispered to Nils.

The older soldier scowled, believing his being here was pinned squarely on Alfar's inexperience. How he ever got saddled with the recruit was beyond comprehension. "Not supposed to talk on guard duty."

The last thing they needed was Sava circling back.

"There's no one here, Nils. What's the harm in it?" Alfar asked.

"Your stupidity continues to amaze me," Nils snapped back. "Haven't you learned nothing since we got here? Sergeant Sava is a …"

The door opened. Swift. Sure.

"Is a what?" Sava asked. "I'd very much like to hear what I am."

Nils swallowed the sudden ball in his throat. "Sergeant, we was just …"

"Answer my question, soldier." Each syllable came out a slow growl.

Deflated, Nils swallowed again. "Yes, Sergeant. Alfar, Sergeant Sava is a god. He's always around, even when you think he's not."

A bead of sweat popped out of Nils's hairline. He stiffened, looking straight ahead.

Sava's laugh made the old man flinch. "A god, am I? That's the funniest thing I've heard. Most folks call me a bastard. Guess I been promoted, eh, boys?"

Alfar made the mistake of breaking into a grin. Youthful, inexperienced. It was a fatal mistake. Sava crossed the floor faster than young Alfar could blink. He grabbed the soldier by his collar, twisted enough to choke him and lifted.

"You listen to me and you listen good. I'm no damned god. I am your sergeant. You do as you're told, when you're told, and how you're told. Understood? When I say no talking on guard duty, I mean no talking on guard duty. The next time I hear either of you utter a single noise, I don't care if it's a burp, I will personally relieve you of several teeth. Am I clear?"

Alfar struggled to nod. Sava's glare shifted to Nils. "I expect better out of you."

He released Alfar and stepped back, making a show of snapping his stick to his thigh. Alfar, to his credit, remained standing, though he struggled to breathe.

"Are we missing anything, Sergeant?" Thep asked as he and Kastus entered.

"Nothing at all, Captain. Just educating these two on proper guard procedures," Sava beamed.

"What's this about guards?" the old man asked. "Am I your prisoner?"

"Not at all," Kastus answered. "I have requested Captain Thep detail two of his finest soldiers to protect you during our time here in Palis."

"I doubt protection is necessary," the old man said, too slowly to avoid suspicion.

Kastus smiled. "Surely you understand that if the matter is as grave as you suggested to us in Jut, there is the potential for counter actions. These soldiers are here to keep trouble from coming to you. At least until we manage to escort you home again."

The old man swallowed. A simple gesture Kastus had witnessed many times before. A tell. One suggesting there was more to this tale than he was willing to divulge. Different possibilities came to life. Kastus imagined it might be as simple as a rival merchant, though he suspected the truth was much more severe.

"The Elders are arriving, gentlemen," Sava interrupted from his new position by the door.

Two squads flanked either side, waiting outside for the order to move in. A half squad was detailed to escort the Elders, lest one of them should decide it was not in his or her best interest to attend. Thep motioned for Sava to send them in and rested his hand on his sword. Kastus placed his hands behind his back. He wore his official tunic of office, the black raven proud upon purple background.

Deana entered first, dour and proud as ever. Waern came next. If he suspected anything, he didn't show it. *Remind me not to gamble against him.* Last came Mugh, a man of inconsequence in the Constable's opinion. Nothing Kastus found during his investigation suggested the man had interests in anything, despite exhibiting an overbearing presence.

"Welcome, lords and ladies!" he announced after Mugh crossed the threshold. "Please, be seated. This will not take long."

"What is the meaning of this, Constable? We are busy people. Once again you interfere with our daily business," Deana accused.

"Your business is also the Baron's, Lady Deana," his smile was anything but pleasant. Still, he begrudgingly admitted she had cooled somewhat since he forced her into a corner. Maybe she wasn't so bad after all. That and she seemed to embrace her role in his little scheme. If it worked, she stood to gain the most.

Waern cast a sidelong glance, barely a moment, at his counterpart. *I've got you*. Kastus caught the movement and knew he held the advantage. "Does anyone else object to being delayed on this fine autumn day?"

"Get on with it. I have little tolerance for theatrics today," Mugh snorted and took a seat at the large table dominating the center of the room.

Kastus wasn't sure where it came from, but he was assured by Sava that there was no wrongdoing involved. The other Elders followed suit, delivering the floor to him.

"I would like to inform you that we are preparing to leave. There is no evidence of the once dead man in Palis and after careful investigation, I don't believe there is any threat. A small garrison will be left behind, naturally, in the event that we are wrong." Kastus paused to absorb the varying degrees of anger flashing across their faces. "While there is no reason to think your village is in danger, we did uncover … other aspects both Captain Thep and I found disturbing."

"Go on, what is this nonsense?" Mugh demanded. "You and I both know the Baron doesn't know the first thing about Palis. What could he possibly find uncomfortable enough to leave soldiers?"

Kastus folded his hands in front of his waist. "I have learned of an illegal trade operation originating here. Not only does this contradict every law we have in Fent, but it is suspected that the guilty are in collusion with the once dead man."

Waern tapped his fingertip on the table. "Utter nonsense. What benefit would come from partnering with a dead man? One who steals children no less."

"The destabilization of the duchy. There is no doubt that a great evil is at work in our land. Why or how remains inconclusive, but it is clear that Palis bears much of the weight. You, Elders, have a rot in your village," Kastus announced.

Deana shifted, uncomfortable. She'd known this was inevitable, but hearing the accusations aloud inspired true fear. The suggested crimes were punishable by death.

"Palis is a loyal community," she said. "We have no reason to betray the duchy. What proof do you have, Constable?"

He gestured to Thep and the old man was brought forward. Kastus watched the Elders, eager to find displays of recognition. Deana's face relaxed as the man came closer. Her lack of reaction told Kastus she wasn't complicit in Waern's treachery. Mugh stared at the man, wondering why an outsider should be brought before him. Nothing to worry about there either. It was Waern who offered all the proof Kastus needed. Waern, who made an extra effort to appear disinterested. Waern who presented the calmest demeanor. Guilty.

"Tell them what you told me," Kastus gestured to the old man.

He looked around the room as if unsure of his course of action now that the time had come. His eyes finally settled on Waern and he licked his lips. "This man is working with other Dukes to undermine the Baron and rob his duchy."

Waern leapt to his feet. "Lies! I am no traitor! Kastus, who is this man, this outsider you bring before us? I'll not stand a moment longer in this charade. Open the door. I am leaving."

"Stop!" Kastus bellowed in his most commanding tone. "Take one step toward that door and the consequences will be more severe. If you are as innocent as you claim, there is nothing wrong with hearing him out. Is there, Elder Waern?"

Sava burst through the door, his cheeks red and eyes alight. "Captain, you need to come quick. There's a fire in the village's storage building."

Thep hurried away. Kastus pointed at Nils and Alfar. "Do not let anyone leave this room until we return."

Nils looked at his charges and felt comfortable for the first time since arriving in Palis. After all, how much trouble could four old people be?

TWENTY-FOUR
Castle Fent

Quinlan sat on the edge of his bed wondering what happened. How his efforts could go so terribly wrong. No answers were forthcoming, despite hours of self-induced misery. He replayed every moment, trying to find his error. The F'talle was strong, but the magic infused in Quinlan's armor should have been sufficient to stop him. Instead, all he did was lose yet another member of his team, while nearly dying in the process. What went wrong?

Inevitably, thoughts of his time in Castle Bedris during the fall surfaced. He'd been young, barely a decade of service when the Omegri overran the defenses and forced the war priests into full retreat. Quinlan couldn't confirm, but he long suspected he was the only survivor. That loss, combined with the futility of his initial attempt to destroy the F'talle, sent his mind reeling down empty corridors without exit.

He refused food and drink for the better part of the night and the following day, even then only quenching his thirst. Trips to the privy were equally infrequent. Quinlan hadn't lost heart, or the will to carry on, but his confidence was shaken. Perhaps irreparably. Sleep teased but didn't come near enough to grasp. Life had taken on the cold, emotionless aspects of the castle's grey walls. So it was he spent the day.

His isolation was not to be, however, for Baron Einos could stand it no longer. Along with Donal, he stormed into Quinlan's quarters shortly after midday. Einos was neither angry nor disturbed. He just wanted answers. Seeing the war priest frozen in misery rattled him somewhat, for the Order was renowned for their ability to stare down the dark things lurking just out of sight.

"Brother Quinlan, how much longer will you remain secluded in this room?" Einos asked. His tone was firm, yet considerate. "Good gods, man, there is a monster out there and now he has Lizette."

Quinlan didn't stir. His head hung low, hands wringing in frustration.

Einos sighed. He hadn't expected this to be easy, but always believed a war priest to be made of sterner stuff. "We must conceive a plan to get her back and end this threat. Fent needs you. I need you."

"I was not worthy of the task," Quinlan whispered. "Lizette is gone because of my arrogance. Hubris is a foul companion."

"This world would have fallen long ago without the hubris of men and women like you. There is no shame in your actions, Quinlan. We all fail from time to time."

At that Quinlan raised his head. "At what cost? How many more innocents need to die to satisfy my, or your, conscience?"

"Failure is how we grow. This conversation is pointless," Einos grew frustrated. "You do not know that Lizette is dead. There is still hope."

"Hope is a fragile construct," Quinlan replied.

Einos remained stiff backed. "Hope is what we have left."

Quinlan acknowledged the comment for truth but failed to find a way through his misery. It wasn't until he looked into Donal's eyes that Quinlan found renewed strength. Doubt still lurked, but the knowledge that he was not alone, that there was yet hope for tomorrow, offered fresh inspiration.

"I ask your forgiveness, Donal," he said. His voice was flat, yet sincere.

Donal jerked back. "For what, Brother? I failed you. I was unable to kill the F'talle when you were exposed. None of this would have happened if not for me."

Rising, Quinlan placed his hand on Donal's shoulder. "No, my friend. You are brave and loyal as any priest. The F'talle was stronger than either of us anticipated. It will take much more to finish it before Fent is secure."

Satisfied that positive movement was occurring, Einos relaxed his stance. He'd come expecting a fight, for it was always a challenge to get a man to rise after being knocked down. "What direction do you suggest we take this quest?"

"My gut tells me we are getting closer to unraveling this mystery. The F'talle was caught unawares. He will not be so again," Quinlan explained. "I fear the only way to get Lizette, and the children back, if they still live, is by going into the Other Realm. Whatever evil is at work is almost entirely there."

"Has anyone survived a journey to that foul place?" Einos asked. His concern deepened.

Quinlan had no answer. To his knowledge, no one had, but that didn't mean it wasn't possible. The Order dedicated lifetimes of research, always seeking to stop the Omegri from invading. Taking the war to another dimension was theoretical, if not practical. That Brogon Lord was able to make the crossing at will left him puzzled.

"The Other Realm is an unknown place," he answered after his thoughts ran into a dead end. "In theory, there is a crossing point not far from here."

"The grave?" Einos guessed.

"Possible, but we cannot know for sure. The spell I enacted was created for that specific point, without regards to the governing laws of the Other Realm. I am not qualified to give deeper analysis, however," Quinlan said. "Others at Castle Andrak are steeped in lore."

"I cannot afford to waste time sending for another priest," Einos shook his head. "Events are escalating. This matter needs to be solved now."

"Donal and I will do our best," Quinlan reassured.

His confidence returned, somewhat, and he was already thinking ahead. Losing Tender Cannandal was a major blow, for there the possibility of speaking to the dead was now lost to them. Quinlan was forced to search the depths of memory for any skills that might defeat the F'talle and restore order to Fent.

"You shan't do it alone," Einos reinforced. "I have received word that Kastus and the company of soldiers I deployed north will be returning within the next few days. He knows this village in and out. If anyone can help you find Brogon Lord and end his tyranny, it is him."

"His assistance will be most appreciated," Quinlan said in thanks.

"In the meantime, I don't see why you shouldn't be able to take the rest of the day to recover. I, for one, am still unsure of what I witnessed at the grave," Einos admitted. Losing two of his best house guards stung, enough that he hadn't come to terms with their deaths or telling Aneth. Though, he wasn't sure she needed the additional trauma, given her current condition.

"A respite would be most appreciated," Quinlan agreed.

Satisfied that they were back on the right path, Einos left the war priests to whatever it was they did when not fighting the Omegri.

It was then Quinlan realized he was hungry. He liked Einos, possibly enough to call friend if they each had different callings. Ally was the closest he could manage. Men like Einos were rare, offering solid glimpses into a brighter future. Quinlan found hope in that. He looked to his novice, now understanding how he had undervalued Donal for too long. Another mistake aimed to correct.

"You performed admirably in the graveyard, Donal. It has been my pleasure to train you thus far," Quinlan admitted. "There are many dark times ahead of us, and I am grateful to have you to ward my back."

"It is a privilege. I spent years not knowing which direction I wanted to go in life. The Order gave that to me, and more," Donal replied. His face was sincere. "You have done more for me than almost anyone. There is no way I can repay that."

"There is. Become a better man than I. My life is one of regret and mistakes. All I ask from you is that you rise above my failures and blaze a path on your own merits."

Donal was left speechless, for he had never viewed his mentor in any other light than perfection.

Breaking into a smile, Quinlan added, "Come, that fight took more out of me than I expected. If my stomach growls any louder, I'm afraid it may devour itself!"

The moment of crisis passed, and the war priests managed to relax. Brogon Lord remained at large, and with Lizette as his prisoner, but that could wait at least long enough for Quinlan to sate his hunger and think of a new plan.

"Calm down, love. You are beginning to worry me."

Aneth's concerns prompted Einos to exhale a deep, pensive breath. "What else can I be? Every move I have made thus far has turned out to be wrong. Kastus found nothing, or so he claims. The war priests led to Lizette being taken. I feel it all slipping away from me, Aneth. Slipping away and there is nothing I can do."

Her hand was warm in his. "There are always other options. We just haven't discovered the right one. Give it time."

Einos knew time was a luxury he didn't have. He was a man used to decisive, quick action, yet the once dead man robbed him of initiative. Unless he managed to learn why Brogon Lord was stealing children, he would forever be stuck behind. It was a game he could ill afford to play. Not with so many lives at stake.

"Perhaps I'll feel better once Kastus returns. Obstinate as he is, the old buzzard is a voice of strength, as well as reason. I need him," Einos admitted more to himself than her.

She grinned as his thoughts became transparent. *He will make a fine father. I could not have married a better man.* Aneth was disturbed when she noticed him giving her a queer look. "What?"

"You looked lost for a moment," he answered.

"I was thinking of happier times to come."

The brightness of her smile was enough to beat back the wall of darkness closing in, for a time. With her at his side, Einos felt empowered. He'd never understood why she said yes to marrying him but spent each day since more grateful than the last. Love, he decided, was much better than the alternative.

Placing his hand on her stomach, Einos closed his eyes and tried to imagine being a father. "We will come through this, won't we?"

"We must. Our child will have need of a strong father," she replied.

That was enough for him. Satisfied, Einos kissed her forehead and excused himself. Now that they'd escaped the encounter with Lord, it was time to settle in and prepare for the battle to come. This time, he intended on being prepared.

TWENTY-FIVE

The Fent Countryside

What little warmth remaining in the late afternoon sunlight bathed his face. Hidden valleys of flesh lost among the many lines and creases upon his weathered face remained cold, untouched. He didn't mind. It was a constant reminder of his time in this land. Several human lifetimes came and went, and he still roamed the plains and mountains. Some claimed it a curse, others a blessing from the gods. He decided long ago that it was neither. It just was.

Once lustrous black hair was streaked with grey. His bones, while strong, felt more brittle than a decade ago. Reluctant to admit, he was tired. His time was drawing to a close. And when he was gone, part of the world would weep. From a fading breed, he was caught in a life of perpetual loneliness. The promise of rejoining those others who'd gone on before him enticed him as he prepared for his greatest challenge.

He hadn't known what drew him to Fent until his encounter with the F'talle. They were an ancient enemy he'd long thought extinct. Disappointed, the sclarem scratched a long nail across his cheek. White streaks slowly faded in his dull green skin. The Grey Wanderer was at play again and where he went, foul things followed. Known only as Dalem, the sclarem crouched in the ankle high grasses and scooped a handful of dirt.

Soft winds blew the dirt away to form images in the air. Dalem watched as the F'talle appeared and disappeared. Children, young and frightened, working to build a great construct in the Other Realm. Each piece helped form an intricate puzzle. Dalem cocked his head, studying the vague figures without shape or definition before they fell to the ground in a whisper of dust. The true source of corruption in the land. But who were they? No power he recalled encountering over the course of many centuries. Could this new threat be in league with the Omegri? Or a replacement for their terrible evil?

Left with more questions than answers, Dalem decided there was but one course of action available. It was with great reluctance he rose, stretched, and began the long journey to the center of Fent. Destiny awaited.

Kastus was beyond furious. His hand lingered threateningly on his sword. A lesser man would have given in and taken heads for the crimes committed. Waern's warehouses were unsalvageable. By the time he arrived, the fires were already too hot and burning too fast to do much more than ensure the surrounding buildings were unaffected. Kastus knew this was no accident, nor did he have any doubts that all Waern's records were within. Most likely the source of the fire.

He faced the gathered crowd, for most of Palis had come out to watch. "Did anyone see who did this?"

That no one came forward wasn't surprising. He'd seen enough during his time as Constable to know information was seldom freely given in large forums. Kastus was left in a difficult situation. A crime had been committed, in his opinion, and it was his oath bound duty to find the culprits. Regardless of his personal opinion that Waern was behind the convenient blaze, he was in a position to appear to take action. Justice must be served.

"Captain Thep, no one leaves here until they are questioned," he ordered.

Thep was sworn to obey, for the Constable took precedence. "Sergeant Sava, you heard the man."

"Sir!" Sava barked. "I want everyone to form two lines. Keep it simple and let's make this quick so you can go about your business."

Some of the villagers grumbled until they spotted armed soldiers moving to hem them in.

Only one made the mistake of protesting aloud. "You can't keep us like that! We have rights as free citizens."

Each step was deliberate, heavy and intimidating. Sava cracked his stick against his thigh. The man, middle aged and balding, jerked back. "We can discuss this further if you really think that's a good idea?"

Muted, the man submitted and went into line.

Sava glared at the rest of the crowd. "Right. Anyone else?"

Kastus couldn't deny the effectiveness a man like Sava brought, though his methods often appeared harsh or unorthodox. No doubt Einos would disapprove. That was a concern Kastus didn't have. The Baron was far away and he needed answers now. Satisfied the crowd was in line, he hurried to Thep.

"I want Waern arrested immediately," he said, so only the Captain heard. "This is all the proof we need."

"He might not come quietly. You saw the resistance he already showed. The man is as defiant as they come. More so than Deana."

"And what a pleasure it was seeing her finally crack," Kastus admitted. "Sava has this under control. Let's go."

"What of the fire?" Thep asked.

Without looking back, Kastus answered. "Let it burn to the ground. I don't want a trace of his taint left. Just ensure none of the other buildings suffer from it. We'll never explain to the Baron how we allowed an entire village to burn down."

They slipped through the crowds, back to the building the Elders were sequestered in. Odd, the door was cracked open and no guards were present. Kastus and Thep drew their swords before cautiously entering. Deana was kneeling beside a wounded Nils. She dabbed an old cloth at the blood trickling down the right side of his face. Mugh paced, arms folded with one hand reaching up to his jaw. The worry on his face was evident. Alfar, the lone remaining guard lay on the floor. Kastus hoped he was merely unconscious. Waern was gone.

"Where is he?" Kastus ground out through clenched teeth.

Deana looked up, fright in her eyes. "Gone. Not long after you left a few armed men swarmed in. They overwhelmed your guards and escorted Waern away. We were warned not to follow or sound the alarm."

"Where are my guards? I had two men posted outside." Thep was furious, but like any good commander, more concerned with his soldiers than the missing Elder.

"I don't know," Deana said, shaking her head.

"Dead for all we know," Mugh puffed. "That or they helped him escape."

Kastus wondered if that was true. They'd been in Palis long enough to establish relationships. It was no stretch to imagine any of the low paid soldiers turning with the lure of extra gold. A quick headshake from Thep dismissed the thought. Loyalty was not a questionable matter.

"We need to find him. He couldn't have gotten far," Kastus said.

"Captain Thep! We spotted six riders heading south in a hurry," a soldier announced upon entering. She was red faced and out of breath from running back.

"Waern."

"It has to be," Kastus seconded. *Why is the bastard heading deeper into Fent? Surely he must realize his life is forfeit when he's caught.* The Constable didn't like the development, for it suggested

Waern was getting help from someone powerful and potentially close to the Baron. "I suggest we move up the timetable. We need to return to the castle now."

"I have a platoon of soldiers, on foot. There is no way we arrive before him, if that is his destination," Thep protested.

Another dilemma Kastus didn't need. Fortunately, Deana had come to her senses, abandoning the stern demeanor she'd worn during their first encounter. "I have horses in my private stables. Not enough for all of you, but perhaps to mount a squad."

"Thank you, Deana. Your horses will be returned and you will be repaid for them after our task is finished," Kastus swore. "Thep, pick your best. They ride with me."

"We're taking an awful chance on this," Thep cautioned. He knew that Waern might be going south as a ruse, shooting off in another direction once he was positive chase had been given. If he did so, he would never be seen in Fent again.

"What choice do we have? I want that man in my jail," Kastus said. "His guilt is clear. This charade has gone on long enough."

"What of the rest of us?" Mugh demanded. "We've done nothing wrong."

"Unfortunately, I don't have time to debate the merits of your ignorance, Elder Mugh. Take comfort in knowing that Waern will pay for his crimes, as will any others he reveals during his questioning. Pray your name stays off his lips."

Deana rose, the bloody rag crumpled in her tiny fist. "I will ensure any who gave Waern aid will be rooted out. That man is a poison Palis does not need. You have my word, Constable."

For once, Kastus didn't know what to say. He bowed out of respect and hurried out. They had a villain to catch.

Elder Waern was in denial of a great many things. His life had been uncomplicated until Giles approached him one dark evening at the beginning of summer. The man spoke with a golden tongue, presenting an offer too rich to pass up. Waern had never been wealthy, toiling under his mediocre life for too long. It didn't take much to entice him to abandon his principles and help Giles, however he asked.

That's where it went wrong. Waern had no way of knowing a F'talle was at work in the duchy. No way of knowing he was loosely connected to a scheme big enough to topple the entire world. He played along as any good servant would. Then Kastus and that irascible army company arrived. They destroyed his careful plans in less than a week, casting his life into ruin and misery.

He'd known it was but a matter of time before the Constable's investigation turned in his direction. His crimes demanded execution, and he very much wanted to live. So Waern concocted a diversion. Paid men took his transaction records and burned them, along with the warehouse full of illegal goods Giles funneled into other duchies. The merchant's wrath would be severe, but Waern was willing to face that over a short rope.

He and his handful of loyal servants now hurried south, deeper into a land in which he would soon be labelled an outlaw. Waern guessed none would suspect him of moving closer to the Baron, not when his crimes demanded he retreat to another duchy. It was the only play he had. He judged the time it took for Kastus to correctly guess his plans was more than adequate to report back to Giles and slip away to the east where he remembered distant cousins lived.

None of that reduced the fear building with every passing stride. The horses couldn't run fast enough. He needed to put distance between them and Palis. Kastus was the relentless sort. A dedicated professional who took great pride in his job. He wouldn't stop until Waern was in chains, or dead along the road.

The road.

"Bartus! We need to get off the road," he shouted. "They'll find our tracks and be upon us in no time."

"That will slow us down. We can't take the risk."

Waern jabbed an unsteady finger at his captain. "Do as I say. They'll hang you as well. Don't forget that. Off the road, now."

Murder lingering in his dark eyes, Bartus whistled and led them across country, into the rough brush. It was going to be a long ride.

TWENTY-SIX
The Other Realm

Darkness. Pure. Unadulterated. A frigid landscape of nothing. The yawning emptiness threatened to devour all she was. Lizette had never experienced such horror and prayed she never did again. If she survived. How she arrived here, in the center of a vast nothingness, was a blur. One moment she was watching Quinlan battle the F'talle. She vaguely remembered being grabbed, then a searing pain rippling through her entire body. The translation felt like hours but was less than a heartbeat.

On her knees, Lizette was wracked with pain and coughing. Her lungs burned from the faint acidic aroma lingering on the stagnant air. It was humid. Overwhelming. Soreness forced her eyes shut. They felt strained, as if staring to long into the sun. Fear kept her from moving. A quiet whisper in the back of her mind suggested death was a better alternative.

"Get up."

She refused to move, knowing the pain would increase if she did.

"Get up."

Reluctantly, she pried an eye open. Lizette was shocked by what she saw. Instead of the pitch black emptiness she feared, the landscape was cast in pales shades of black and grey. Once her eyes adjusted, she was able to see almost as far as in the real world. Scrub brush and broken rocks stretched across an endless plain. There were scattered clumps of dead trees, but little else. No wind blew. No clouds filled the barren sky, yet ash fell sporadically.

Shuffling. Lizette turned toward the sound of the voice. Threadbare boots stood before her. Torn and battered trousers stretched up gaunt legs. Her captor. Brogon Lord. The once dead man who'd murdered her beloved Tabith. Her fists balled, even while knowing she lacked the strength to do much in her weakened condition. Defiance surged and she remembered who she was. The once dead man needed to pay for his sins.

"Get up or I will drag you."

Both eyes open, Lizette glared at her captor. "Get away from me, monster."

Brogon cocked his head, trying to understand. "You think I asked for this? That I wanted to spend eternity a slave?"

"You killed my daughter!"

The accusation stung, despite his knowing it was a falsehood. He stepped back. "I killed no one. That is not what I was created to do."

"My daughter is dead because of you," Lizette's voice turned dark.

Brogon hung his head. The stiffness in his back and shoulders vanished. "She is dead."

His admission stunned her. Unsure how to proceed, Lizette rocked back on her knees and placed her head in her dirt-stained hands. Here she was, at last granted the opportunity to confront the monster responsible for ending Tabith's light, and she was just as lost as before. Confronting him didn't inspire the retribution that had burned in her heart.

Lizette looked up through her tears and saw the creature before her. He was broken. A twisted shell of what once was. Curious, she felt no malice pulsing from him. Could it be he told the truth?

"What are you?" she whispered.

The faintest hint of emotion entered his eyes. "What you say I am. A monster. They created me to steal children for them."

"Who? Who created you?" she asked. The prospect of a new, stronger enemy filled her heart with dread.

"I do not know."

A bell chimed in the unseen distance.

Brogon's head snapped around. Strands of coal black hair whipping across his shoulders. "Get up. We must go. Now."

"Go where, Brogon?" she took a chance on using his name, hoping it might inspire some semblance of humanity hidden within the recesses of his past.

"The masters call."

He said no more. Brogon Lord turned toward the sound of the chime and marched off. Abandoned and bereft of hope, Lizette struggled to her feet and followed.

How long they walked, she didn't know. Fresh aches ran up her legs and into her lower back. More than once she thought of halting and turning back. Only, there was nowhere to go back to. She was trapped in what Quinlan called the Other Realm, destined for whatever nightmarish torments the once dead man had in store.

Sometime later, they crested a slow ridge and she was granted sight of an impossible world. A low basin stretched out before them. Flashes of lantern light, faint as the crack of dawn, illuminated the center. A massive tower reached up into the sky. So large it avoided common dimension. Lizette had difficulty focusing. The tower shimmered, flickering in and out of time and space. She wanted to ask questions, refraining only after remembering Brogon was disinclined to answer.

They kept walking. Each step made the tower larger. She eventually made out individual shapes moving about the base and climbing the sides. The sound of tinkering carried over the stale air. Workers. Builders. They seemed so small, even from this distance. It was to her horror she realized they were children. Hundreds of children dedicated to building the tower.

"You bastard!" she hissed. "You brought my daughter here. As a slave!"

If her words had effect, he didn't show it. "We must hurry. Punishment is severe."

Lizette surged forward to grab him by the arm. Loose flesh moved in her grip. "What are they building? Why children?"

Brogon stood. Mute. No answer forthcoming, Lizette decided it was past time to take control. She gathered her now filthy skirts in a hand and stormed down into the basin. Those responsible would pay for their crimes. The once dead man stood on the downward slope, watching her for a time. She presented both challenges and a potential salvation. He so desperately wanted to die. To return to the earth and on to the next world. If, if she managed to gain the upper hand, that demise might finally be achievable.

The once dead man followed her down.

Whatever she thought she saw on the ridge was dwarfed by the reality of the situation. Hundreds of children toiled away on the tower. The base stretched almost one hundred paces. How high it rose, she didn't know. Piles of wood and stone littered the surrounding area. Greasy smoke rose from a small burning fire not far away. The stench of roasted flesh tickled her nostrils.

Brogon stopped her from investigating further. "Not there. You do not want to see the pit."

Tears welled. Lizette knew what burned and it pained her heart unlike anything she'd ever experienced. Now that she was here, she knew her daughter suffered a fate worse than she deserved, toiling away until she died and then burned unceremoniously. No child deserved such. Strength fled, leaving her a shell of a woman.

"What is this?" a female voice asked.

Lizette refused to speak. Brogon slipped before her. In defense? "She is an unfortunate occurrence. I did not intend to bring here with me, but I had no choice."

"Yet here she stands. Kill her."

No one moved. Lizette, doing her best to appear strong, struggled to remain standing. Her fury was extinguished. Knowing Tabith's fate robbed her of all she'd clung to. She wanted to die. But not like this.

"No."

Brogon's defiance offered fresh inspiration when Lizette needed it the most. Perhaps he wasn't as evil as she first reckoned.

Three figures appeared, each dark as night and shifting. Like the tower, Lizette found trouble focusing. Each hovered above the ground. Where two were smaller, less menacing, the third was tall and firm. Clearly the leader. And the one who was addressing them.

"You are defying us?" she hissed. "That you walk is thanks to us. Our grace has given you purpose. All that you are has been bestowed by my will. Without us, you are nothing."

"I have died once. There is no fear of doing so again," Brogon opened his palms, inviting the end. What little conscience remained, gnawed at him constantly.

"You dare!"

The shadow bulked, growing to terrifying proportions. Brogon stood fast. Fear died the moment his heart stopped beating. He knew the masters were capable of inflicting unending torments upon him from now until the breaking of the world. It was worth the suffering if he never had to steal a child again.

"All I was has been compromised by your filth," he said. "What more can you do?"

"There are fates worse than death," she snarled. Blue-green flames lit from the ends of her fingers.

"Stop this!" Lizette shouted.

Weeks of pent up rage and frustration returned to collide in the far recesses of her mind. A once quiet woman with little regard for the rest of the world, she'd transformed into a strong, determined woman with purpose. Brogon Lord wasn't as bad as the people of Fent thought. Yes, he stole children, but there was such agony in him, she almost wept.

He was just as much a prisoner as the children he stole. The true monsters hovered before her.

"You threaten without having the courage to show your faces. What gives you the right to steal our youth and bring men back from the dead? Show yourself!"

The flames winked out. The shadow shrunk and a woman laughed. Lizette reeled back as shadows swirled around all three figures, collapsing in tight circles until they vanished. What remained made her gasp. Two men and one woman, or so she thought, stood before her. Their robes were poor, tattered and ruined. Hairless, their skin was mummified and stained dark brown from age. Lines filled their face and hands, forming endless canyons. Only their eyes held signs of life. Wicked. Malevolent.

"Is this what you wanted to see, little one?" the female asked. "Are you satisfied? I would very much like to kill you now. Perhaps you will perform Brogon's task better."

"I … I will not be responsible for the deaths of these children," Lizette stammered.

"We do not want them dead. What use would they be?" the smaller male said.

"But that pit …"

"Is the result of their labor," the second male replied. "We need them to work. The task must be complete!"

"What task? Why children?" Lizette demanded. She felt the more answers she got, the easier it would be to escape. If such was possible.

The female slipped to the ground and walked closer on bare feet. Puffs of ash dusted up in her wake. "These are the children of never. Their great work is important to our purpose. They build a great clock that, once complete, will allow us to stop time and invade your world."

"Time must be stopped," the others echoed.

Lizette shook her head, confusion worsening. "You cannot stop time."

"We can. We shall. There is much you do not know of the universe," the female said. "We have been here before your kind crawled from the mud. We shall be here long after naught but dust remains of your bones."

"Our task hastens your demise. The world belongs to us," the larger male said.

"Time must be stopped."

Lizette stood defiant. "You didn't answer my question. Why children?"

"Because of their innocence. They are capable of withstanding this realm much longer than an adult. Children built the clock."

"What will you do with them once they finish?" She didn't want to ask, fearing the answer was evident before her.

The female cocked her head. "They will share your same fate. Brogon Lord, take this woman to the pens."

"She is not to be harmed," Brogon insisted.

"No. I have a fate much worse than pain in store for our interloper." Gesturing, the female and her companions disappeared beneath a wall of shadows.

"What happens now?" Lizette dared ask.

Brogon cast a baleful look. "I do not know. Come."

TWENTY-SEVEN
Castle Andrak

Lord General Rosca stood gazing into the impenetrable wall of mist perpetually surrounding Castle Andrak. There'd been a time when he was consumed with learning why. How such a thing could be possible. Time and the constant assault by the Omegri reduced his curiosity until nothing remained. The mist was. He accepted that and turned to use it to his advantage.

The Burning Season was approaching. Soon, streams of knights and mercenaries would flock to Andrak to be tested to earn the right to stand the wall. Many failed and were dismissed before they unpacked a saddlebag. Those one hundred found acceptable would stand the wall for one hundred days. History showed only a handful survived each year. A small price to keep the Omegri from extinguishing the Purifying Flame and overrunning the world.

Here he stood, a daily ritual leading up to the storm. Rosca was a troubled man. His instincts warned that a storm was approaching. One the war priests might not be able to weather. Sayers studied the trends of recent attacks, developing potential futures, and how the Omegri adapted their movements. All of it pointed to foul times looming just beyond the horizon. Rosca understood the changing of tactics, but until he was able to either invade the Other Realm or restore the other five castles, there was little in his control.

Castle Andrak was alone against the storm.

Winds whistled across the ramparts, forcing him to pull his bearskin cloak tighter. Light rain began to fall. It was always raining. Enough to drive a man mad. Rosca liked to think he was immune to the weather. If not the rain, it was the recent events in Fent that left him restless in the middle of the night. Any F'talle sighting was rare, and for good reason. The Omegri could only extend a small amount of influence outside of the Burning Season. To do so invoked great power.

Doing so now suggested a major offensive was beginning. Only what? He needed real-time intelligence from Quinlan so that he could make the best decision on how to proceed. Frustrated with being cut off, Rosca returned to his state offices high atop the tallest tower. From here he could view the world, or that much the mists allowed. It was no mistake Andrak was built on the tip of a peninsula where worlds collided.

"Lord General, a messenger bird has arrived from Fent," Brother Inverness announced upon Rosca's return.

Inverness was old, ancient in most regards. How he maintained a full head of stark white hair was a wonder to the balding Rosca. "Quinlan?"

"So it appears. Perhaps matters aren't as dire as you believe."

Rosca stared at his confidant and scribe, wondering when he mentioned his innermost thoughts. Like in most matters, Inverness knew more than he should. He'd been the conscience of Andrak for years, serving at the pleasure of the Lord General. There wasn't a living soul Rosca trusted more.

"I'll take the message in my study. Have a raven prepared to reply," he said.

Inverness bowed and said, "I am already working on it."

Rosca smiled. "Where would I be without you, Inverness?"

The old man chuckled and stomped away. His wooden leg echoed far down the hallway.

There was a time when the war priest network stretched to the farthest reaches of the world. An intricate web of associates, spies, and allies coming together with the intent of ensuring freedom and peace reigned. The ever present threat of the Omegri forced kingdoms to work together. It was a grand age. An age meant to last an eternity. Failure was swift and harsh.

No one knew who betrayed the priests of Castle Manlius. Protection wards were removed during the middle of the night, allowing the Omegri to slip in and kill the garrison. Once the priests were dead, the Omegri extinguished the aspect of the Purifying Flame concealed deep within the castle. It was but the beginning of the end. Each of the remaining castles fell in subsequent Burning Seasons. The world was rendered defenseless. Chaos and war ensued, for man's inherent nature was one of violence.

Now only Andrak remained. The last bastion against a faceless horde of unlimited size. One small garrison barring the way from the world being overrun. It was a task well received among the lands. Fresh lines of veterans surged into Andrak in preparation of each Burning Season. The crème of fighting men and women. That most fell was testament to their courage. Wars were never for the faint of heart.

Rosca stood with one of his castle's mainstays, Master Sergeant Cron. Bitter and a veteran of perhaps too many campaigns, Cron was the straight voice Rosca needed in times of crisis. Next to Cron was a rising commander among the priests, Arella. Her golden hair seemed out of place beneath the gloom. Rosca took pride in watching her develop. She was already one of the best he knew with a sword and a more than capable magic conduit. It didn't take much imagination to see her wearing the mantle of Lord General one day.

"Are you certain, Lord General? Quinlan is a proud man. He will not take intrusion well," Arella said. Her demeanor was straightforward. She was a professional. Time was important. Almost as much as life.

Rosca appreciated her tone. She was often the voice of reason where he needed it most.

"Quinlan knows what's good for him," Cron answered. "He's been that way since I first met him. If he says they need help, we should send it."

Rosca agreed but knew there was the potential for the war priests being perceived as weak. The damage such a reputation might do was frightening. Volunteers for the wall would dwindle, for his priests to fight harder and spend their energies against the creations swarming the walls rather than combating the true threat. It was a delicate situation he was forced to balance.

"Quinlan is one of the best, but even he has never encountered a F'talle. Curse the Grey Wanderer! Were it not for his meddling …"

"We cannot control the whims of the supernatural," Arella reminded. "I will take my novice and go. Two war priests should be more than enough to end the F'talle threat."

"Are you certain?" Rosca asked. Already wagon trains of fresh supplies, weapons, and armor were starting to roll in. "The Burning Season is not far off."

She flashed an uncharacteristic smile. "We shall be back in time, Lord General."

He hoped she was right. Arella saluted and hurried away.

Cron spit a mouthful of kaappa juice. "That is one person I never want to cross blades with. Do you think she can do it?"

"For all our sakes, I hope so. We will need her on the wall," Rosca said. "Ensure the quartermasters square away the supplies. I am going to the Flame to pray."

TWENTY-EIGHT

Fent

An autumn storm rolled in, seemingly out of nowhere. It wreaked havoc across Fent and the neighboring duchies. Doors and windows were shuttered and barred. No one stepped outside. Already high winds stripped trees of dying leaves. Many large maples and pines toppled over, their roots freed by the loose soil after hours of heavy rains.

Quinlan stared at the dismal day with veiled eyes. He'd overcome his doubts and the nagging suspicion he wasn't strong enough for the task, only to become trapped inside. Helpless. He needed to continue the hunt. The only way to get Lizette back, in his estimation, was by drawing Brogon Lord back to Fent and forcing a negotiation. How to deal with a dead man presented intimate troubles of its own.

He and Donal struggled with finding ways to invoke the F'talle without risking increased casualties. Too many of Einos's men paid the ultimate price for his failure. He vowed not to repeat the mistake. But how? No way he came up with could be done without placing others in grave danger. His purpose was to save lives.

The bodies of the guards horribly slain during Quinlan's mishap had been interred, but without a Tender, remained at risk of being reanimated. Einos had sent for one from their academy to the north, but it might be weeks yet before one arrived. Guards were stationed at the graveyard in the event the Grey Wanderer was seen again, though what they could do about it was largely inconsequential. As Lord proved, killing the supernatural was next to impossible.

"Brother Quinlan, I feel this is pointless," Donal blew his frustration out.

He wasn't wrong. Every time they rummaged through the pile of antiquated scrolls and manuscripts from generations long past, they felt further away from the solution. So far, there was nothing to connecting Fent to the Other Realm.

Quinlan appraised his novice. The young man continued to grow, developing into a potent war priest and a fine man. He couldn't ask for a better assistant in this trying time. "It is in the darkest hours where we often prove ourselves. The way ahead will become clear. We must have calm minds and steady hearts."

"But after what the F'talle did …"

"Trouble yourself no more over it. The matter is done. We were caught unprepared and paid for it," Quinlan said. "Einos continues to give us his support and we must not disappoint. Brogon Lord is our sole focus and I believe there is a way to defeat him. We just haven't discovered it yet."

Donal snorted. "How can you be so sure?"

"Because lad, the Flame seldom creates imbalance. Look about. Everything has an opposite. Night and day. The seasons. Time itself is mirrored."

"Good and evil."

"Exactly!" Quinlan praised. "There is always a way ahead. Finding it might take longer than we anticipate, but it will happen."

A knock disturbed them. Wind curled under the bottom of the door, flickering the candlelight.

"Enter," Quinlan said.

A page entered. Young. Nervous. He shook from being in the presence of such high ranking nobles. Never in his days did he imagine bearing witness to a war priest. Much less service notice to him.

"My lords, Baron Einos requests your presence at once," he said.

The tremor in his voice was born from awe.

"Thank you, lad. Inform the Baron we are on our way."

Grinning to one another, the war priests left the records chamber.

"Quinlan, good you're here," Einos said upon seeing them stride into his study.

"We came as soon as your summons arrived," he replied. "What is it?"

"News from the north. Kastus appears to have uncovered a plot that might lead back to the F'talle, though he remains cautious in his accusation," Einos said.

Quinlan nodded. He looked forward to meeting with the constable and learning what was discovered during the expedition to Palis. "I assume there hasn't been any sightings of our prey?"

"One, but his missive was clipped. Kastus is on his way back as we speak, in pursuit of the man responsible. We must be prepared."

Quinlan was confused. "Baron, our job is to stop the Other Realm from breaching this world. Your duchy is yours to rule. It does not fall under war priest jurisdiction in that manner."

"Not even when the suspect is accused of collaborating with the enemy?" Einos countered. "Kastus is seldom wrong in these matters. I fail to see how the war priests are able to enter the duchies at will to conduct operations in the name of humanity yet refuse to lend assistance for internal crimes. That is a remarkable double standard."

"I did not say I wasn't going to help," Quinlan countered. "Only that it is most unusual. Our rules are strict. The Lord General would admonish me for acting against orders."

"But?" Einos asked, hopefully.

"The Lord General is not here."

"Good. We must move fast. Fent is not overly large, but there are many ways to get into this village. No matter how tight the net we cast, there is the possibility he evades it and makes contact with his people. This is a dangerous game we play. One I can ill afford."

Einos began to pace. "Brogon Lord has not been spotted since the … incident in the graveyard. Tender Cannandal is dead. Slain by who knows. I can't help but feel my eyes are being stripped away. Quinlan, I am blind against the growing darkness."

"There is yet hope. I have struggled with what we've seen and done. Enough that I sent for aid from Castle Andrak," Quinlan admitted.

"Additional war priests?" Einos, like most, was under the impression the priests operated alone outside of their precious walls. "Is that orthodox?"

"Not per se, but these are unorthodox times," Quinlan said. "It is my hope that the priest dispatched will be better educated against the threat we face. I was caught wanting during my first encounter with the F'talle. I will not be so again."

"That is enough for me." He hoped it would be enough for Lizette as well. If she still lived.

The nights since the incident were spent restless and laden with foul dreams. Aneth cried more than once, for she'd grown close to the woman. The loss would be felt for a long time to come. Of that he had no doubt. He prayed for her safe return, while steeling his resolve with the unproven knowledge that she was dead and gone.

"What do you require of me?" Quinlan asked. He watched the confusion play out behind Einos's eyes but knew better than to inquire. A man with that much weight on his shoulders was already stretched thin. How much more could he stand before he snapped? Best to tread cautiously.

Einos licked his lips, suddenly unsure of his plan. "It is rumored that the magic imbued in your armor has the ability to force a man to tell the truth."

"It is an aspect of the Purifying Flame," Quinlan confirmed.

"Use it on this Waern. We can get to the bottom of the entire affair and end it before it gets worse. That Lord hasn't returned for more children is not a sign that we are safe."

"My task remains incomplete until the F'talle is destroyed and the children are returned," Quinlan said. He wasn't sure where Einos was going. That he knew about the war priest's magic was unsettling.

"Naturally," Einos seconded. "I also believe that capturing this village Elder will hasten our objectives. There is a plot at work here, Quinlan. Of that I am certain. Help me. I cannot do this without you."

Faced with conflicting interests, Quinlan's mind was already set. It would take time for the assistance from Andrak to arrive. Perhaps enough to complete the Baron's task. That was enough for him. Sitting idle wasn't productive. He already feared he was sinking farther behind the F'talle. This might be enough to shift the tide.

"I will accompany you, but I wish Donal to continue searching for anything we can use to combat the F'talle," Quinlan told them.

"Let us hunt our enemies and restore order to my duchy," Einos roared with confidence he hadn't felt in weeks.

Donal rolled his eyes at the prospect of spending another day trapped in the dusty confines of ancient histories. Life was downright cruel at times.

The thunder of hooves vibrated deep in the ground. Dust kicked up with each stride. Horses and riders stormed across the fields. Hundreds of soldiers marched behind, spread out in five meter intervals. Spears and pikes lowered. Dogs brayed, sniffing the grass and dirt for signs of their quarry.

It had been decades since the soldiers of Fent last deployed in such a manner. All for the sake of one man. A coward and a traitor to the crown. This was as close to war as they'd come, minor border skirmishes with outlaws and bandits aside. A grand event that drew throngs of citizens to bear witness.

The passing of the storm left a trail of devastation across the countryside. Downed trees and washed out roads slowed progress for much of the western approaches. Einos frowned at the delays as wagons became mired and soldiers were forced to find alternative paths through the countryside. Irritating, there was no way around it.

Three similar units were deployed across western Fent in the hopes of finding and catching Waern. Einos believed Kastus and his soldiers were in fast pursuit and hopefully, forcing Waern down roads of their choosing. Hope wasn't enough. He needed actionable intelligence if he was going to succeed.

Sometime midafternoon Einos called a halt. It was well received by one and all, himself included. Swirling water around in his mouth and spitting, the Baron took a moment to rise up in his saddle. He'd forgotten how sore it left him.

"There isn't much daylight left," Quinlan remarked. He left off mentioning the odds of missing Waern in the dark.

"We will find him."

Quinlan wasn't sure if Einos was actually that confident or if he was playing it up for the sake of the soldiers within earshot. What was clear was Einos had a different perspective since receiving word from his constable. There was a growing atmosphere of hope. Despite the setbacks suffered. The war priest was reluctant to join in, for he had seen too many wrong turns during his misadventures in the world.

A horn bleat to the north. Heads snapped up. A dog barked. Horses snickered. Einos nearly dropped his canteen. There. A second horn blast.

"That's it!" he roared. "Our foe has been spotted! Mount up. Form ranks. We head north!"

His army rallied, cheering as they obeyed orders.

Einos, filled with pride, broke into a wide grin. "Brother Quinlan, it appears our fears are delayed for another day."

They headed north as fast as they could manage. The beginning of the end was at hand. Einos and his soldiers readied to reap vengeance for the sake of all the missing children. And for Lizette.

Vengeance for their losses.

Quinlan gathered his reins and pondered the impetuousness of Einos. The Baron waited for no man. The war priest rode north.

TWENTY-NINE
Fent

Waern failed to think of a time when he'd been more afraid than now. All his carefully wrought plans were collapsing and he was trapped in the open. Baron Einos's men were slowly drawing the circle to a close. The noose threatened. He'd made it almost all the way from Palis without detection. The capital village was in sight. The tallest spires of Castle Fent poking up into the skyline.

Any illusions of escape dwindled the moment a patrol surprised them. Infantry swarmed out of a thicket of tall grasses along a stream where Waern and his men paused to rest and relieve themselves before continuing south. Neither group expected to find the other. A skirmish ensued, resulting in one of his men being wounded before they managed to withdraw and escape. Decades of experience told Waern it was but a matter of time before the Baron's forces picked up the trail and renewed the hunt.

He'd argued for keeping their current course, suggesting to move at speed to avoid further entanglements. The others resented that but kept their tongues. For now. Gold was a powerful motivator. They crossed a wide gully and entered a thin forest of tall pines. Enough to distort their silhouettes but nowhere near what they needed to screen them from searching eyes. The village was still just under a league away, and on flat terrain.

Waern called for a slow trot, knowing they'd escaped the present threat. He calculated the odds of reaching the village intact. They weren't in his favor. Surprising the patrol was happenstance and he assumed the noose would grow tighter the closer he got. The Elder cursed his luck, as well as his lack of foresight. He should have expected Kastus to send word back to Einos. Expected resistance upon his arrival.

Woe be unto the fool who didn't prepare. Waern was caught in a trap. He couldn't go back to Palis. Einos's dogs had the village under control. Nor could he continue forward without drastic changes. There was but one course of action that didn't result in him losing his head immediately.

"Bartus, we must split up," he said, after glancing about the forest.

The bigger man snorted and placing a finger over one nostril, blew his nose before wiping it with the back of his sleeve. "Split up. Why not order us to turn around and lead a suicide charge? I'm beginning to think you don't know what you're doing."

"Einos is clearly hunting me. We cannot reach Fent without help." He chose to ignore the comment. Alone, and in the wild, there was no help for him should his handsomely paid henchmen decide they weren't happy.

Bartus knew he held the upper hand. "Sure. We can split up. Only, I'm not going with you. There's not enough gold in the duchy for that. Hask, Thirl, you're with our esteemed village Elder. See that his pretty little head reaches Giles *and* get paid for it."

Disgruntled, they nodded acceptance and moved their horses beside Waern.

"Thank you," Waern said.

Bartus waved him off. "Don't waste your breath, Waern. I expect to be paid for this endeavor and when it's done, I don't ever want to see your face again."

The Elder grit his teeth. Should he reach Giles, he planned on contracting a hit on Bartus and his men. After all, there could be no loose ends if he hoped to escape.

"Move out," Bartus barked.

His group peeled away and headed north. Their part was done. Waern was on his own.

"We're getting closer."

Kastus gave Thep a skeptical look. He hadn't seen any indications of such. Then again, he admitted he wasn't a tracker. Any telltale signs might have easily gone unnoticed to his untrained eye.

"I wish I shared your confidence, Captain," he said.

The soldier grinned. A look of satisfaction. "Constable, if Sergeant Sava says we are close, we are close."

Ignoring the subtle differences between confidence and arrogance, Kastus took Thep's word. The race continued. Half a day later, they came upon the same infantry patrol Waern crossed. Greetings were exchanged before Kastus, growing increasingly impatient, decided to cut to the point. He feared Waern might disappear once he reached Fent and whatever network of villains awaited.

"You're certain he continued toward the city?" Kastus asked the ranking sergeant.

The Children of Never

"Positive, Constable. We even wounded one."

"That means a blood trail," Thep said. "Sergeant Sava! Search the area for blood. We've got wounded."

Kastus would recall the savage look Sava gave for the rest of his days. Never before had he known true fear and he prayed he never found so again. Raw emotions were surfacing, and Sava was a man Kastus never wanted to cross. He had no doubt the sergeant would rip Waern's head free should he reach him first.

Death was too rich a reward for a traitor like Waern. Besides, Kastus needed him alive if he was going to expose the network. "Can we catch him before he gets inside the city?"

"If I have anything to say about it, yes," Thep replied.

They thanked the patrol and passed a message along for the rest of Einos's forces spread out across the northwestern part of the duchy. Most of Fent's terrain was flat. A featureless landscape suited for crops and farmland. Opportunities for hiding were scarce, leaving Waern with few options. Kastus felt his blood warm. The hunt was on and it was but a matter of time before he captured his quarry.

The squad raced ahead, knowing the end was approaching. At their front was Sava and who had become his two favorite soldiers: Nils and Alfar. Both continued to lick their wounds, embarrassed by being caught off guard. Never one to miss an opportunity, Sava snatched them by the necks and pushed them forward. After all, the best way to get over a thrashing was by catching the bastards responsible.

Brother Quinlan rode alongside Baron Einos. He was silent. His mind lost in events years in the past. Was it ten? Twenty? He'd lost count. Enough that the grey hairs peeking through his head weren't imaginable. Memory was a tricky creature, for the edges blurred with time and events became confused. Quinlan longed for this memory to fade but knew it wouldn't. There were times in life when fear was that strong.

He was an apprentice the last time he knew true fear. Gripping his soul and nearly rendering him helpless. He and Brother Garan, his master, were trapped by a pack of stone wolves. Vicious creatures the size of ponies, with scales and fangs as long as his hands. Garan sent Quinlan in first, eager to see how his novice would perform.

Terror gripped him once the stench hit. Rotting flesh and feces, mixed with urine. Quinlan retched. A mistake. The wolves circled on him with the intent to kill. That moment of hesitation was enough. Young

Quinlan watched death stalk near. He forgot the incantations for his armor. His one protection against the creatures of darkness. Garan stormed in, saving him by driving the wolves away.

"Always keep your mind. Fear is a powerful foe but can be defeated through the strength in your heart. There is darkness. There is evil. We, as war priests, do not have the luxury of suffering their trespasses. Remember, Quinlan, fear no darkness."

Fear no darkness.

The mantra of the war priests. A lesson he learned long ago and it had stuck with him ever since.

"Are you listening?"

Jarred back to reality, Quinlan covered his embarrassment. "I was thinking of how to defeat the F'talle."

Unconvinced, Einos grunted but said nothing on the remark. Brogon Lord was a high priority but capturing Elder Waern took precedence at the moment. "I was saying we should be on him before long, if the scouts were accurate."

"Do you believe this Elder will have answers?" Quinlan asked.

He hadn't crossed half the continent to become embroiled in local political issues. Each duchy was responsible for policing its own matters. The war priests were above that jurisdiction and designed to operate outside of modern constraints.

"It's possible. Whatever he knows, I'll have it ripped from his tongue before I'm finished. There are too many irregularities going on in my duchy. The sooner this affair is finished, the better," Einos admitted.

"We are living in strange times indeed," Quinlan added.

Einos cast a queer look at the priest. Despite working side by side for weeks now, he still hadn't gotten a clear feeling about the man. They were odd by nature, the war priests. He supposed it was due to the nature of their mission. Why anyone would willing dedicate a lifetime of service to an order cut off from the rest of civilization and faced with death at all times was beyond his ability to comprehend.

Inbound riders barreling up the road ended the conversation. Einos stiffened, his anticipation rising. The urge to wrap his hands around Waern's throat forced its way to the front of his thoughts. Fighting the urge, Einos retained his demeanor and reined in to await their report. It wasn't long.

"What is it, soldier?" he asked, as a trio of red faced scouts halted before him.

Soldiers and commanders crowded around, making no small show of straining to hear what was said.

"Baron, we have a group of armed men surrounded. We suspect they were part of the group from Palis," the lead scout said. His voice was elevated just enough that those nearby could hear. "Contact has also been made with Constable Kastus and Captain Thep. They are heading southeast with a squad."

Good news on both fronts. Einos began to hope that he was at last going to end the nightmare gripping Fent. "Where are these men?"

"About a league to the north, Baron. We can lead you to them."

Einos looked to Quinlan, silently asking his opinion.

"These men might have the information necessary to learn Waern's plans," Quinlan guessed. Kastus and the others were capable enough, requiring little or no aid from the main army.

Einos agreed. He was about to order the army forward when a secondary thought occurred. "Soldier, where is Kastus going?"

"To prevent Waern from reaching the city."

"Deploy a company back to Fent. I want the city cut off before that scum can hide," Einos ordered.

"Yes, Baron."

The nearest captain saluted and took his company back to Fent. The thrill of the hunt was on and he wanted the prize. Satisfied with recent developments, Einos gestured for the scouts to lead the rest of the army north. The time had come for answers.

His first look at the men known to be associated with Waern was one of utter disappointment. Their haggard appearance was little better than that of vagabonds. Einos was no fool. He knew not everyone in the duchy lived under the same standards. Poverty was real across the lands, despite all his policies to alleviate their hardships. These men, surrounded yet defiant, were painful reminders of his inability to eradicate the issue.

Einos and Quinlan, flanked by a score of heavily armed guards, pushed their way to the front of the circle. "Who commands here?"

"I do. Name's Bartus."

Einos admired the man's bravado but was angered by the lack of respect. "Do you know who you are addressing, Bartus?"

"Don't really give a damn. I know enough that you have my men surrounded and can kill us at will. Doesn't mean we won't fight back. I'll take your pretty head if it comes to that," Bartus boasted.

"He's bluffing," Quinlan whispered. "Hoping to make the best of the situation."

Einos's eyes narrowed to slivers. "You may try, though how you will accomplish that stuck with arrows, remains to be seen. Or perhaps you would like to meet Brother Quinlan, from Castle Andrak."

The fire of defiance extinguished. Bartus knew he was no match for the war priest and valuing his neck over a bag of gold, dropped his weapons to surrender. Others followed suit. Einos had won his first battle without having to shed blood.

"Place the rest in irons and escort them back to the jail," Einos commanded. He turned to Bartus, an air of unmistakable authority surrounding him. "Now, Bartus, tell me everything about Elder Waern."

THIRTY
Fent

Dalem whistled. It was the most simplistic thing he did. An old tune his mother once hummed when his people were still plentiful. Before the blight. Dalem had been alone for more years than he remembered. The agony of knowing most of his people were dead did little to slow his quest. He had purpose. A singular task in life to accomplish before his time dwindled and the dust of the world reclaimed him.

He knew how humans viewed him. Mystic. Enchanted. The remaining sclarem had become one of the great powers in the world. How sad they would be to learn the truth. Gifted with abilities other races lacked, Dalem and those few sclarem roaming the lands sought out cruelties and eradicated them. Not their original purpose, but one filled with honor.

Dalem didn't mind. He needed purpose to reduce the sting of loss. Encountering the F'talle came as a shock. He hadn't heard of one haunting the lands for generations. That one should so stalk the duchy of Fent was alarming. The signs pointed to a dire event approaching. One he wasn't sure humanity could survive.

Regardless of what happened between now and his final encounter, Dalem understood the severity of his actions. He'd never battled a F'talle. The prospect of doing so filled him with anticipation. Confident in his ability, Dalem continued whistling as he walked. The short stalks of dried grass rubbed across his ankles, tickling him.

Yes. The world was vast and filled with terrors undreamed of. Yet it was also vibrant and stronger than the forces of darkness believed. He was but an instrument to deliver the end. The day grew shorter and Dalem drew nearer to his destination.

"Nothing."

Kastus's scowl cause deep lines across his forehead. There'd been no sign of Waern for some time, leading the constable to think the old man had escaped. Faced with the increasing possibility of failure, Kastus struggled with the urge to lash out. He fumed until a dark energy surrounded him, prompting the others to shy away.

"Where do you suppose a village elder managed to get her hands on so many horses?" Alfar asked, trying to avoid the wrath inspired glare beaming off Kastus.

Nils closed his eyes and exhaled. "What?"

"These horses. Palis seems poor. Nothing special leastwise. Where did that lady get all these horses from?" Alfar reiterated.

"Horses. We're hunting a traitor and all you can think of are stupid horses?" Nils growled. Easy as it was to grow angry with the junior Alfar, Nils decided he might be on to something. Anything was better than getting caught between Sergeant Sava and that Constable.

Alfar shrugged, oblivious to Nils's growing ire. "I grew up on a farm. Cows and goats were cheap enough. Chickens more so, but horses? We couldn't afford one, much less ten."

"What are you getting at?" Nils asked, suddenly suspicious.

"Maybe that lady had a bigger part in all this than we thought," Alfar said. He couldn't believe he was the only one who'd arrived at that conclusion.

Swatting the mosquito on his cheek, Nils thought hard. Inferno aside, the way events wrapped up in Palis was almost too easy. Both Kastus and the Captain were in a hurry to break south to catch Waern, leaving the remainder of the company without concise leadership. Or a sustained presence.

Fleeting images scrolled by when he closed his eyes. Snippets of memory from those final few moments. Three men bursting through the door. Being struck on the side of the head. A woman shouting *no* right before he blacked out. No. Why would she say that? Unless she knew the attackers. Nils thought hard.

He'd been suspicious of the old man from Jut from the beginning. There wasn't any reason for a nobody to fear for his life. Especially not when he was from a different village and faced no repercussions for his testimony. Unless he was in on the whole thing. But that would mean Deana was complicit as well. Nils's mouth fell open as the image of Deana and the old man exchanging a look focused.

"Sergeant Sava! We have an issue!"

Kastus listened as Nils explained everything, or at least tried to. Trained to follow clues, he hadn't spotted anything to suggest Deana was part of the conspiracy. The possibility she'd covered her tracks was there, however.

"I understand what you are saying, but there is no proof, soldier," he said, mind straying down impossible paths.

"Constable, you were focused on questioning that Waern," Nils insisted. "I know what I saw. They were all in on it."

Thep raised an eyebrow. "That would mean the entire elder council needs to be removed."

"Not that sour one," Alfar chimed in.

Nils winced, expecting Sava to snap.

"Come again?" Thep asked.

Alfar swallowed the lump rising in his throat. "That tall one that was always angry. He seemed genuine. I don't think he was part of it."

"If … if this conspiracy goes deep enough, there is no way Mugh would be innocent. Not unless he was purposefully kept out due to his defiance," Kastus theorized.

"Seems to me like we need to find Waern and beat the truth out of him," Sava offered.

They looked to see if he was joking. He wasn't.

"I agree," Kastus said. "Finding Waern is our priority. Though beating him might not prove the best course of action."

Sava gave a *whatever works* look and climbed back in the saddle. "What are your orders, Captain?"

"Find Waern and squeeze him for information. We deal with the rest of Palis after," Thep said without pause. He was tired of being misled and ready for this task to end. The expedition north was a waste of time, in his opinion. Soldiers were best used in battle, not policing.

The tiny group hurried on. Destiny awaited.

The sun was dropping over the western skies when they found signs of Waern's passing. The Elder wasn't far ahead, though he'd shed much of the excess amount of his initial group. Kastus insisted they follow the main tracks leading back to Fent. Whoever turned aside was meant to be a diversion, nothing more. Only Waern was important.

His eyes burned from lack of sleep. Every stride his horse carried him blurred into one continuous motion. Events from the past few weeks seemed almost surreal. He'd gone north to find and kill Brogon Lord. A mission that evolved into a hunt for traitors undermining the duchy. Nothing, he realized, turned out like he and Einos intended.

Dazed, Kastus snapped awake as he stepped into a hellish scene. Fires scoured the countryside. Smoke choked the air. Acrid smell filled his nostrils. Confused, he searched for the others. He was alone. Kastus raised a gloved hand, surprised to find the weight of armor weighing him down. *What?*

He didn't recognize the landscape, nor the dark armor encasing him from head to toe. Large, dark birds swarmed overhead in silence. A partially burned building sat off to the right, collapsed under its own weight. Kastus peered through his helmet visor and saw the bleached bones of a corpse. *Where am I?*

His right hand clutched a wooden staff. Flames whipped through the nearby treeline. Glancing up, Kastus saw the pennant atop his staff aflame. He couldn't make out the figure slowly turning to ash in the center. Was this a scene from the past? Or a vision of the future? Did Fent promise to become a burned wasteland if they failed to stop Brogon Lord? He was afraid of the answers.

Another step and the vision blurred back to reality. He jerked to a stop, forcing the others to turn aside lest they collide. Kastus held up a hand. An empty hand free of a burning pennant or blackened armor. There were no flames. No ruined buildings. No skeletons lurking in the grass. He was back in the forest with Thep and the squad.

"Constable, are you well?"

Jarred, Kastus wasn't sure how to answer. "I … I don't know, Captain."

"We can rest if you need to. It has been a long hunt and the horses could use the break."

"Perhaps that is best," Kastus agreed.

They pulled off the trail and established a small camp. Thep didn't plan on staying long, only enough to water and feed the horses while the soldiers had the opportunity to relieve themselves. Fent was near, and with it the end of their quest. Once he was sure the others were taken care of, Thep pulled Kastus aside.

"Care to tell me what's going on?" he almost whispered to avoid being overheard.

The Constable wished he knew. He tried explaining his vision, for that was the only thing it could have been. But how could any man explain a thought that had been so real? He tasted the lingering effects of smoke. Felt the grit of ash on his tongue and between his teeth. Everything felt real.

Thep listened with practiced patience only a commander of soldiers understood. He'd heard every story, every excuse during his time as a company commander. Soldiers never failed to surprise him with their ingenuity. This was a different matter. He'd never encountered anything comparable, and that left him worried.

"What do you suppose it means?" he asked. What else could he ask?

Kastus was left without an answer. "Does it matter? I didn't recognize the armor or the pennant. None of it was familiar."

"Sounds like you should speak with that war priest when we link up with the Baron," Thep offered.

Kastus had been thinking the same. If anyone in Fent was capable of deciphering his vision, it should be one of the vaunted war priests of Castle Andrak. He drank deeply from his canteen, relishing the cool sensation running down his throat. Odd that he continued feeling the aftereffects of the flames in the real world.

A cursory glance at the sky showed there were no alien birds circling. Yet the sense of foreboding remained. Kastus felt shivers course through his body. His flesh prickled. About to comment, he caught the first glimpse of a strange figure stalking toward them. Green skinned with coal black hair.

"Sergeant Sava! Come here please," he called.

The figure kept coming.

"Constable?" the sergeant asked, hesitant when Kastus didn't immediately reply. Experience told him to follow the constable's gaze. What he saw was unexpected.

"I'll be damned. That's that green fellow who saved my ass from the once dead man," he uttered.

"The sclarem?" Thep asked. "Are you certain?"

"How many of them can there be in the duchy?" Sava replied.

Thep felt his day getting worse. It was all spiraling out of his control. "What do you suppose he wants?"

"Looks like we are about to find out," Sava said. "I'll let the others know to stand down. I figure most of them will want to thank him as well."

Apart from the main squad, Nils and Alfar watched as the sclarem approached. They'd only caught hasty glimpses of him during the battle with the once dead man. Enough to confirm their kind still existed but not enough to become familiar with him.

Alfar whistled under his breath. "Well, I guess wonders never cease."

"No. I don't suppose they do." Nils wasn't sure about that and found the prospect of having a sclarem among them dire. *What are we getting into?*

THIRTY-ONE
The Other Realm

The endless cacophony of screams, of cries for help and mothers lost, were the hardest part of being ripped away from the world she knew. Lizette spent her days plagued with the knowledge there was little she could do to end their suffering. She was as much of a prisoner as them. Her pain stemmed from her inability to help. Accustomed to misery, thanks to the suffering of loss, Lizette dedicated her time to providing what comfort she could.

Many of the children she tried to console never returned from their work on the great clock tower. The energies of their lives spent under the wrathful gaze of the dark masters. Lizette wept in private for each life, whispering old prayers as their corpses were thrown into the pit, discarded like rotten meat. Each loss stabbed deep into her heart, for she knew that Tabith lay somewhere among the bodies.

Her daughter. Her only child. The last memory of all her husband had been. Whatever legacy she once thought to achieve was gone. Erased like so many dreams before. Lizette wept until grooves lined her face. Her body ached from constant sobbing. Was she destined for misery? It felt that way. Here, as far from home as possible, she was forced to confront her personal demons that had haunted her for years.

Lizette felt the breaking point rushing toward her. She'd been through so much, but nothing like the storm approaching. What might have been days passed. Or it could have been hours. Time mattered little in the Other Realm. Ironic, she decided, considering what the Omegri intended. Something in her mind snapped. There was only so much misery she could stand before she became numb. Vowing to prevent that from happening, Lizette turned her focus to the children. Even if it hurt.

Time. All of this was reduced to time. An abstract concept few bothered to consider. People rose with the sun and rested with the night. There was little point in worrying over such a thing when nothing could be done to alter it. She failed to understand why the servants of the Omegri thought stopping time would bring about the change they needed to conquer the world. The great enemy spent millennia attempting to destroy the world of men. Endless centuries dedicated to a singular cause.

Their failure to achieve results surely prompted them to enact new, more drastic measures. Lizette knew little of the Burning Season, or what the war priests did in their isolated fortresses. They served humanity, as well as the other races threatened by the Omegri. To her, stopping time meant nothing.

Frustrated and emotionally spent, Lizette sat at the edge of a ravine, feet dangling over the edge. Oddly, she felt no fear for the monsters responsible for imprisonment. They could kill her, or not. Her life, she'd come to realize, meant little in the grand scheme of the world. That knowledge was empowering. She ate what they fed her. Slept when she couldn't stay awake any longer. And helped the children the rest of the time.

Only now did she turn her thoughts toward escape. Not an impossible venture, but one that required far more than she had to give. Lizette rubbed the back of her foot against the grey dirt as she searched the area for Brogon Lord. He was the answer. The same murderer responsible for ripping Tabith out of her life.

She'd detected the defiance in him. The desire to break free from the creatures ruling this land. Turning him to her cause would not be easy. She had no idea how to begin. Not after dedicating weeks to hunting him down. He had become the bane of her existence and now she needed him. Life was cruel.

Brogon stood near the base of the clock tower. His arms folded across his chest. She felt his sorrow as he stared upon the great work. The endless ting of hammers striking was a symphony of despair that chilled her soul. What effect did it have on him? A once dead man. Did he still have a soul or was he a hollow animation of what once was? She feared the answer, while hoping it was the latter.

Brogon Lord. His name stained her lips. Gave her nightmares. Now here she was, hoping to turn him to her cause. Lizette gave up trying to figure life out. There were too many twists for her to keep up. So, she sat on the edge of the ravine and plotted. And waited. Time, after all, was the answer to all things.

Lizette walked along the edge of the prisoner's tents. Her heart strained at the sounds of children weeping or crying in their dreams. Several children sat, staring into the abyss of greys and blacks, without seeing. Their fragile minds incapable of comprehending what had transpired. Lizette wished she could do more, but there was only so much one woman was capable of.

She stopped beside a small girl with a filth covered blond mop strewn across her head. Dirt covered the girl's face, caked under her nails. The puffiness of her cheeks remained, indicating she was one of the newer prisoners. Lizette offered her brightest grin and sat beside her.

"Hello. I am Lizette. What's your name?" she said.

Confused, the child looked up. Everything about this place was wrong.

"Where am I?" the girl asked.

Lizette saw little point in lying. There was all likelihood that they were both going to die here. Every child deserved to know the truth. "You are in the Other Realm. Do you remember how you got here?"

Blond curls swung back and forth. "I went to sleep and woke up here. I'm scared."

Aren't we all? Lizette forced a smile. "I'm here to take care of you, as much as I can. Will you tell me your name now?"

"Emrys."

"Emrys. That is a beautiful name for a beautiful girl. What village are you from?" Lizette pressed.

The knowledge was unimportant, but it helped calm the new arrivals. Anything to keep that mummified horror from taking notice. There were, she'd come to find out, worse creatures lurking in the gloom. Terrible things who forced the children to work. Things with appetites for human flesh.

"Halm," came the reply.

A village Lizette had never heard of. Not in all her research in the castle was she apprised of any village of similar name either. The possibility of Brogon moving into different duchies for his prey dawned on her. Until now, this had been a problem for Fent. Lizette knew where every child had been stolen from. Emrys presented a new set of problems.

The workforce was either dwindling due to untimely demise, or because time was almost up. She glanced up at the tower. The frame for the giant clock face was almost finished. Soon it would be filled with machinery. A chill filled her soul as she imagined the gong of the clock, resonating and frightening, sounding for the first time. Only, the clock was being constructed to stop time. She professed no understanding of how that would work, or why.

The Other Realm was a place of mystery lacking human understanding. What should make sense didn't. Lizette felt adrift, but she was wise enough to know when a threat was serious. She had no doubts Brogon Lord's masters meant what they said.

Emrys began crying. "Why am I here? I miss my momma."

Her heart crying, Lizette pulled the child close and hugged her. "I know, Emrys. This is not a place for children. Would you believe me if I said I am doing everything I can to get you home to your mother and father?"

The child nodded.

"Good."

Emrys nestled deeper into the embrace. "Lizette, I'm scared."

Lizette felt her heart break. "I know, child. I know. I am, too."

Brogon Lord watched the exchange from behind a nearby tent. Head cocked to the side, the once dead man listened to the endearing words. Surely Lizette knew them to be lies? There was no escape from the masters, or this wretched realm. He'd tried and was punished for daring. The masters tolerated no disrespect.

Still, there was something different about this woman. He didn't know why he took her, other than to keep the priest from lashing out a second time. Brogon was hurt badly from the assault. Brought back from the dead, he was no match for the power imbued in their magic. Taking Lizette seemed his one course of action.

She didn't belong here. He knew that, but it was too late to change what he'd done. The masters would never let her go. Once, when he had emotions, he would have sympathized with her. Brogon was never a bad man, nor was he exceptionally good. He was ... a man. Filled with faults and strengths in equal measure.

Death robbed many of his memories, leaving him twisted and broken. He no longer remembered why he took up a life as a swordsman. Didn't know if he had a family. Flashes of battles and duels remained, providing just enough knowledge to confirm he was dangerous. How he died was how he lived. By the sword. Brogon remembered the blade driving into his gut. How the pain, so intense, spread through his torso—white hot.

Life hadn't been kind to Brogon Lord. Nor was death. Reduced to a child stealer, he was a ghoul who preyed on the unsuspecting. It sickened him. Trapped in an existence there was no escape from, the once dead man stumbled through the days, dreaming of a time when he could at last lay his head to rest.

He stared at the woman, wondering if there was any hope of finding peace at her hands. She went to great lengths to comfort the children. Even knowing they were meant to die here once the clock was finished. Could she do the same for him? He needed to know. Needed to discover if there was a path back to death. Brogon was so very tired.

Hatred for the masters kept him going, even as they forced him to betray the last vestiges of his conscience. Could there be a way to kill them and free himself? Brogon needed to know. Doing so meant one thing. He needed to speak with the woman.

The once dead man stepped from behind the tent, exposing his decaying corpse to both woman and child.

"Lizette."

Her head jerked up. Horror laced her eyes.

THIRTY-TWO
Fent

The trek to Fent was fraught and filled with peril, despite there being no legitimate natural predators in the duchy. None that is, but one. Man. Waern had never been a particularly strong man. He endured a childhood of shame and embarrassment. All those petty experiences shaped him into the thoughtful man he was now. One who twisted men to his bidding, while succumbing to temptations far too easily.

Rising to village Elder was no small task, but he dedicated his life to the pursuit. Waern craved power, knowing it to be the means with which he would extract vengeance upon all who wronged him. When Merchant Giles approached him with an offer, Waern couldn't refuse. He saw an opportunity to become wealthy beyond measure, while destroying his enemies in the process. For his greed, he fled for his life.

Kastus's hunters pursued him across the duchy until he was certain a blade was close behind. Separating from Bartus and the others, all of whom had proved worthless, was the best move he could have made. Let Kastus hunt those men down, while he inched closer to Fent. All his plans were in jeopardy of being exposed. No doubt that bitch Deana betrayed him, casting him to the wolves to save her own neck.

He didn't care. The castle loomed, filling the skyline. He was almost safe. Giles would know what to do. The merchant had a vast network of smugglers, spies, and informants to utilize. For a price, naturally. Nothing came cheap in the world Waern forced his way into. Men like Giles were vipers, capable of killing unnoticed. It was a delicate game the Elder was confident he could play well.

"What if the streets are being watched?" Hask asked.

Annoyed, Waern dismissed the sell sword. Neither were important. Losing one or the other did little to hinder his quest. The Elder had thought it through and determined Hask and Thirl were liabilities. He counted on filling their pockets to buy their silence once they delivered him safely to Giles. They were so close.

Waern frowned. "Einos will have his forces searching the countryside. Confident he can stop me, he won't think of garrisoning his own streets. We keep moving."

Thirl spat. "These horses will give us away. Need to ditch them as soon as we can."

He had a point. Horses didn't belong in the streets, not when Einos knew he was riding. "There are stables on the outskirts. You take the horses, while Hask and I continue on."

Thirl grew suspicious. "What about me? I never been to Fent before. Where am I supposed to go?"

I don't care. Waern debated ordering the man back to Palis, to catch up with Bartus and be gone from his life. Not that he expected the others to reach home uncontested. Fent's army was small, but they held a ferocious reputation. From what he'd seen of Thep and his company, Waern suspected the rest of the army was more than capable of capturing Bartus long before he reached Palis.

Which presented another problem. Bartus was loyal, but only for a price. How much would it take before Einos twisted him to do his bidding? Waern scolded himself for not taking better precautions. Then again, he never expected to be caught. A mistake he hoped did not prove fatal.

"Wait at the stables. I shouldn't be long," Waern finally said.

"Hold on! I'm not going to wait in the horse dung while you and Hask enjoy drink and food," Thirl snapped.

"You work for me, don't forget that," Waern fired back. "Once I get to where I need to be, I will send Hask back for you. The sooner we are all off the streets, the better."

Thirl pointed a finger at Waern. "Don't mess me over."

Waern ignored him and kept riding.

They shuffled through near empty streets, amazed at how a village so large could have so little pedestrian traffic. Waern grew concerned, wondering if martial law had been ordered. He'd been to Fent once, when Einos assumed his role. A grand fete was held for three days. Every village elder or duchy statesman was invited. Waern found the affair lavish and immediately decided that was what he wanted out of life. Oh the irony of his current position.

"This way," he gestured down a tight alley.

Merchant Giles had several properties dotted across the duchy, including a modest home here to accompany his warehouses and offices. Anticipating any of his network might need to find him without attracting unwanted attention, he developed a maze. Only those who knew what to look for could find their way into his private safehouse. Which was where Waern headed.

Waern halted at a black iron door. His protectors flanking him, the Elder struck the knocker three quick times. Nothing happened. Waern began to fear he was at the wrong location. That Giles had been arrested and his schemes were finished. Footsteps on the other side of the door drew his attention. He tensed, fully expecting Einos's guards to rush out and arrest him. The door cracked. Faint light cascaded into the alley.

"What?" a stern voice demanded.

Waern licked his lips. "I have come to see Giles."

An eye appeared, dark and suspicious. "Piss off."

Waern fumbled as the door began to close. "Please. Tell him Elder Waern has come."

The door slammed shut.

"Load of good that did," Thirl muttered.

They turned to leave when the door was cast open. The same man stepped into the alley and gestured them to enter. Waern felt relieved but remained on guard. Nothing in Fent felt right. A dark energy was settled over the duchy. One making him uneasy. He stepped into the safehouse, the door closing behind.

"Why have you come, now?"

Waern recognized Giles's voice, though it sounded strained. Almost bitter. Armed men shuffled behind him, separating him from the skulking Hask.

"Where else am I to go? Einos's dogs forced me from Palis. He scours the countryside for me, thinking to uncover a plot against his rule," Waern sneered. "You got me into this, Giles. You owe me."

Silence for a moment, then an insane laugh filled the room. "I owe you nothing. Let Einos spend his energy hunting shadows. He is of no consequence to me. You, on the other hand, have become a problem. You should not have come here."

"Where else can I go?" Waern spread his arms. "I have lost everything."

"That is not my problem," Giles insisted. "Get him out of here."

Hands curled around his arms. Waern panicked. "Wait! I am a village elder. I will not be treated so!"

A malevolent glint entered Giles's eye. "Indeed. Who else knows you are here?"

"No one," Waern said, too fast to be believable. "Just these men. Give me safe passage east and you will never hear from me again. I swear."

Giles nodded. His men struck. Hask tried to flee but had his throat slit for the effort. He died without a sound, leaving Waern trembling in a semi-circle of enemies. The prick of steel bit into his back.

"Easy lads. I don't want him dead. Not yet at any rate," Giles told his men. "You return at a perilous time, Elder. That man would have betrayed you, sold you out as soon as it became profitable. I did you a favor. Where is the other one?"

"But, but he helped me," Waern stared at the spreading pool of blood at his feet.

Giles advanced, waving off the concern. "It makes no difference. We will find him and take care of him in time. You owe me now. Funny how life turns, isn't it?"

There was a different air about the merchant. He'd lost weight, grown pale. Thick blue veins spread across his exposed flesh. His right hand trembled ever so slightly. Waern was too afraid to notice. Watching the ease with which his man was killed rattled him, forcing him to reevaluate his thinking.

"Giles, I just want to leave Fent," he said, his voice quiet. "I won't say what you've done. No one will ever know I was here or that we are associated."

"That's the problem, isn't it?" Giles asked. Torchlight flickered over his dark tunic. "See, I don't believe you, Waern. In fact, I think you will sell me out at the first chance you get, just to save your miserable neck."

"No, Giles. I would never."

Giles broke into a wicked grin. "If only I could believe you. Take him and throw him in a cell. Kill him if he protests."

"Damn you, Giles! We had a deal!" Waern shouted.

"Deals change. The price of doing business. Get him out of my sight and clean up this mess. I don't want the city watch snooping around," Giles ordered.

He watched as men dragged Waern away. One problem solved.

Einos watched the setting sun with casual interest. His mind raced through recent events, replaying his slow fall from grace as the once dead man continued to have his way. Fent was no longer the peaceful duchy it had been since inception. Panic and fear gripped the land and there was nothing in his power to prevent it from worsening. Every move he'd made to counter Brogon Lord had failed. His position degraded daily.

When a captain reported that they'd encountered a strange creature offering to help, Einos barely bat an eye. Depression threatened to grab him. He wanted to return to Aneth and hold her tight. Life was always better when she was in his arms. None of the troubles of the day could harm him. No worry was too great to overcome. She offered warmth and reason when he failed to find either.

Reluctant to turn away from the dying day, Einos tucked his hands up into the sleeves of his heavy jacket to avoid the chill and entered the command tent. There'd been no word from Kastus or any sign of their quarry since capturing Bartus and his thugs for hire. All appearances suggested Waern had escaped, disappearing into a lesser known world.

What he saw standing before his field chair was almost unimaginable. Short, barely coming up to his chest, and pale green skin, the sclarem regarded him with calculating eyes. Einos, like most, grew up listening to tales of the elder race. Also like most, he never expected to see one, much less stand in the presence of one. Wonder aside, Einos realized the true danger his duchy was in as more myths continued to surface.

"Baron, Dalem has come with word on the once dead man," the captain announced.

Einos dismissed him with a wave, eyes never leaving the sclarem. "Thank you, Captain. See that no one disturbs us."

"Baron."

Einos waited until he was alone with the sclarem. "I would offer you better food and drink if we were in the village. Regardless, welcome to Fent."

"Human customs are lost on me, Einos of Fent," Dalem said. His voice was broken, as if it hurt his throat to speak the same language. "I am Dalem and I come to you in your hour of greatest need."

"You know of Brogon Lord?" Einos asked.

The sclarem nodded. His black top knot slipping over his chest. "I do. We fought. Outside of one of your villages. He should not be walking this earth."

No, he shouldn't. But what more can I do? Everything I've tried has ended in failure. "Can you help us?"

Dalem cocked his head. "Perhaps. My magic is strong. Ancient, as only my kind have. The F'talle is imbued with equal magic, though from what, I do not know. It will take much to defeat him."

"I have a war priest here," Einos divulged. He'd asked Quinlan to remain outside. A necessary precaution.

Dalem's eyes widened. "Ah, yes. I know them."

Einos wasn't about to try and guess how to take that, for the sclarem proved enigmatic in his answers. "I will not lie when I say that my hopes are now doubled by your presence, Dalem. I believe that between you and Brother Quinlan, we will find a way to raise the miasma consuming Fent."

"Perhaps. We shall see."

The words, meant to be inspiring, filled Einos with ominous portent. A battle was coming. One he wasn't sure he could win. It was all he could do to cling to hope. Einos summoned his attendant. The time to return to the castle and consolidate his forces had come.

THIRTY-THREE

Fent

Soldiers and deputized citizens patrolled the streets, seeking the renegade village elder. Houses were searched. Shops scoured. Kastus had returned and ordered no structure left unchecked. His trail led him into the heart of Fent, where it went cold. No one they spoke to had seen or heard anything out of the ordinary.

Einos and the main army were still in the field, leaving the city to Kastus. He had yet to return to the castle, for the prize remained at large. Fent wasn't as large as many of the capitals in the land, but it was big enough to occupy his entire force and still leave room for more. His first action was to seal off all roads leading out. Outposts were established in a perimeter in the event Waern eluded notice. Not that Kastus thought the old man was going to keep running. He'd gone to ground and would need to be dug out. The end was here.

Kastus occupied his offices in the center of town, using it as a command post where all communications and efforts would be coordinated. Thep and his squad became the command element. It was a foreign situation for the soldiers, and especially Sava. The sergeant begged to get into the streets. His talents were wasted trapped behind a desk. Thep said no.

When pressed, Thep argued that the squad was meant to be the reaction force, on standby for whenever Waern or Lord was spotted. Far from acceptable, Sava took the answer and settled into his new position. Grumbling, he snatched a chair and took up watch outside the door, spitting red streams of kaappa juice as he hoped for a fight.

Nils and Alfar cringed each time they heard his chair creak as the sergeant rocked back and forth. They wanted the mission over. To be away from their increasingly agitated sergeant and the stress compounding daily. A string of defeats left them in low morale. Despite that, Alfar remained optimistic. After all, how bad could duty indoors be? There was food, drink—even if it was just water, and warmth from the fireplace.

"You should stop worrying," he told Nils. "This is the best job I've had since joining the army."

"Don't get used to it. We're not made for this life," Nils countered.

The chair creaked.

"If you say so. I don't want to stay in the army forever. I have plans."

Nils rolled his eyes. As much as he would like nothing better than to punch Alfar between the eyes, he forced himself to listen. "What plans? You just started!"

"I'm going to marry a noble and get my own castle," Alfar said with sincerity.

The chair stopped creaking.

Nils spit the water from his mouth. "A noble! You? Now I know you're crazy. What noble woman would want anything to do with a commoner? You're mad."

Alfar continued smiling and shrugged, as if to say just wait and see. Waving him off, Nils went to the doorway. The office was situated in the center of Fent, providing easy access for every citizen. It did not provide an adequate view. Nils had to strain to see more than the edges of the buildings directly across the street. The thought of going outside meant him standing in Sava's potential line of fire, and that was something he didn't need. Content to stare at drab stone walls, Nils waited for his shift to pass.

Two young men ran up to the porch, where they confronted Sava. Nils listened as they described an impossible scene. He was still trying to comprehend when Sava jumped up and barked for him to follow. Alfar was sent to find Thep and Kastus and told where to meet. They had a lead. Nils barely remembered to grab his sword belt before hurrying out the door.

Murder wasn't common in Fent. The occasional body was found, and the guilty apprehended shortly thereafter. This was different. Two men. Each murdered brutally. Their placement was meant as a message. Kastus knelt, waving flies from the drying blood on the ragged wounds. There was no sign of struggle, nor blood anywhere near the bodies, suggesting they'd been killed elsewhere and dragged here.

"This isn't good," he muttered.

Thep stared at the bodies with casual indifference. He'd been in the army for almost a decade and while attaining a quality rank, hadn't seen any major fighting. The idea of being around corpses was strange enough to force him to pretend. Having the crusty veteran Sava at his side left him with little choice.

"Who do you suppose they are?" he asked. Try as he might, there was no way to keep the strain from his voice.

Kastus used a stick to move one of the dead men's hand. "If I had to guess, I would say they came from Palis with Waern."

"You don't suppose they ran across Lord, do you?" Sava asked. He was genuinely unaffected by the bodies.

"Possible, but I doubt it. There is no reason to believe Lord has taken to killing." He rose. "No. These men stumbled across something they didn't expect. Look at their wounds. The angle of this cut suggests he was killed from behind. It's the same with the stab wound."

"Why dump them here? It's almost as if the killer wants to get caught," Thep asked.

"Or is sending a message for us to back away," Sava countered.

Kastus dropped the stick and wiped his hands out of habit. "I tend to agree with Sergeant Sava. This was meant as a message. Whoever killed these men doesn't want us to dig deeper. This is a warning."

Sava spit and said, "No. It's a challenge. We need to find the killer and settle the whole damned affair."

"How could Waern do this? He's an old man," Thep asked.

"This wasn't Waern."

Thep jerked back as pieces began falling together. "The merchant that old man warned us about."

Kastus nodded. There were only a handful of merchant houses in Fent. Each was required by law to have complete, detailed records for auditing. Anyone who failed, lost their license and was forced to pay heavy fines. To say the least, that happened only on rare occasions. All inspection records were kept with the records keeper. Giving him a place to start.

"Captain Thep detail some men to see to the bodies. They deserve to be cremated but we should afford them the opportunity of a proper burial. We need to send them back to Palis," Kastus said. *If that is indeed where you are from.* "I want details sent to each merchant house with orders to wait. No one leaves or enters. Seal them off. I'm heading to the castle. I'll meet you back at headquarters."

Sava waited until Kastus and Thep were gone before turning back to his few soldiers remaining. "You heard the man. Nils, Alfar, grab that first body. Karis, head back and find a wagon. These bodies are starting to stink."

Nils vomited as he grabbed the body under the arms and lifted. This was not how he envisioned his day going.

Donal struggled to stifle his yawn. It was all he did these days. Yawn. Boredom made him want to pound his forehead into the dusty wooden table. Countless hours were spent buried under Castle Fent as he continued Quinlan's orders. Scrolls and manuscripts filled his dreams. Their dust collected over decades lodged in his hair and clothes. His eyes burned from the strain of reading by candlelight.

It was all for naught. He was trapped in a room without natural light. Time slipped away. The only way he knew what part of the day it was came from the occasional meal brought to him. Donal was unhappy. He hadn't joined the war priests to serve as a scribe. This was a task beneath his talents. Or so he thought.

Still, searching for answers was better than facing the F'talle again. He'd been shown his failures in that moment and it left him stunned. Brogon Lord was formidable in death, easily capable of killing him with little effort. Donal decided spending his time among dusty tomes wasn't that bad after all. Yawning, again, he turned the page of a text listing records of men who'd gone on to take up arms.

Names and deeds scrolled by, each meaning nothing to him. He turned another page. Then another. Donal's index finger was stained black from tracing each line as he read. Halfway down the page he paused. Blinked. Reread the passage. There it was, in fading ink. Brogon Lord. He'd done it. He'd finally found mention of the once dead man. All of Lord's history, from birth to death, was laid bare for prying eyes to see.

The more he read, the more he was sickened. Whatever evil Lord represented in death, was nothing compared to the violence he committed in life. Suddenly, it all made sense. Donal almost ripped the page free before stopping himself. Using a blank sheet of parchment as a marker, he closed the book and hurried out of the records room. Quinlan needed to know what he'd found.

A week had passed since Lord General Rosca granted her permission to assist Quinlan. Arella rode with urgency, sensing that a moment of great portent was approaching. She was one of the best in Andrak. Her skills with a sword were among the top tiered weapons masters. Arella had a quick wit as well, often using it to get her out of trouble. Going to Fent wasn't an option.

She and her novice skirted north around the Indolense Permital and down into the flatlands comprising the central plains. They stopped for food and limited rest, going as far and as fast as their horses allowed. A F'talle. Arella seethed with not being the first assigned to the task. She had seniority and wasn't as damaged as Quinlan. Not that she disliked the man, but he did come to Andrak the bearer of ill news.

The war priests enjoyed a tight bond, regardless of which castle they served in. Quinlan was the only survivor, or so he claimed, of the collapse of Castle Bendris. Not one to judge others without sufficient information, Arella found the notion disgusting. He should have died with the others. Still, there was something to be said for Quinlan refusing to back down or go into exile. That she admired.

Arella was already on the move as dawn broke. Fent wasn't far away, but time grew short. Wind blew her hair in a tangled mess. She didn't care. Never one trapped by looks, Arella was a warrior first, woman second. Her novice struggled to keep up. She wanted to laugh. This was the ultimate freedom. Riding with abandon across the open plain with the wind in her hair and only a destination in mind. Life offered simple luxuries, from time to time.

"Come, Jayon! We are wasting time!" she barked over her shoulder.

"Coming, Sister!" he called back.

Born to the deep deserts in the far west, Jayon's dusty brown skin and black hair were uncommon among the priests. He'd come from a caravan, sneaking away from the wagon master to enlist in the initiate program. Once accepted, the war priests forced the caravan away and began his training in earnest. Jayon advanced without a regret. He was assigned to Arella after attaining the rank of novice and was relieved to find they meshed well. She was both wise and experienced, often letting him find a way out of his own mistakes. Her teaching was invaluable.

What he wasn't was a natural rider. Horses were uncommon in the desert, almost as much as in Castle Andrak. Jayon took to the quest with his usual vigor, all while knowing he was going to be sore for many days once they reached Fent. So fast was their assignment, he failed to find time to get an appropriate briefing. All he knew was that a fellow priest was in peril and they were storming ahead to assist. It was a mission of necessity and glory. Jayon secretly expected promotion from his deeds in Fent. Becoming a war priest was the only thing that mattered to the young man.

Sweat dripped from his hawkish nose and onto his lower lip. It tasted of salt. How he was sweating before the sun was fully in the sky, remained a mystery. Jayon rode with abandon, doing all he could to maintain Arella's pace. As much as the pair appreciated each other, he had no illusions that she would leave him behind if he couldn't keep up.

"Ha!" he shouted and urged his horse on.

THIRTY-FOUR

Fent

Quinlan tugged off his boots, wincing at the smell pulsating off his feet, and leaned back on the bed. He was exhausted, mentally, and physically. The hunt for Brogon Lord had evolved, threatening to take him further away from the goal. Word of the treason of Palis overtook his original purpose, all but consuming Einos.

He empathized with the Baron, but knew if he didn't remain focused, there was little hope of ending the F'talle and finding Lizette. The war priest set thoughts of his closest ally aside and resumed the current battle plan. The main body redeployed inside the main village, leaving a skeleton force combing the countryside for signs of their prey. Quinlan forced that from his mind, knowing there was little effectiveness to be found in pointless searching. They'd already gone over the surrounding area and were left confused.

The longer he stayed in Fent, the more he came to suspect the answers to his questions rested in the dusty, forgotten tomes in the basement. Einos's predecessors were meticulous with their record keeping, making the conditions easy. Producing results was another matter. Quinlan couldn't help but feel he was close. The sudden knocking, almost frantic, was not unexpected, though entirely unwanted. Sleep would have to wait.

"Come," he croaked, voice raw from lack of water.

Donal all but burst into the room. His expression was enough to rouse Quinlan's curiosity. "Brother Quinlan! I've found what we've been looking for."

The war priest was wise enough to understand Donal's true meaning, and the unspoken accusation of having to search alone. Still, his exuberance was almost too much for Quinlan to bear in his current condition. "Calm down, Donal."

The novice struggled but followed instructions. He wanted to shout his findings to the world, but restraint imposed by the rigid discipline of the Order prevented him from doing so.

"Good, now tell me what you have discovered," Quinlan said.

Donal took a breath and began a detailed report. Quinlan sat in stunned silence as his novice explained a sordid and checkered past, revealing who Brogon Lord had been. When he finished, both men were pleased but left without knowing how to utilize the information. One thing was clear.

"We must take this to Einos. Perhaps he or Dalem will know what to do next," Quinlan said. It was the first bit of good news he'd had since arriving in Fent.

"Who's Dalem?" Donal asked as he followed his master down the hall.

Einos hadn't felt this confident in weeks. Not only had unexpected help continued to arrive, but Kastus and his company had returned. The spark of hope flickered, threatening to burst into open flame. Fent stood a chance now. A hint of a smile decorated his face. A face that had been pushed to the point of exhaustion, both mentally and physically.

He listened to Kastus's retelling of the events in Palis, horrified to learn how deep the treachery extended. Both men were soon convinced that the arrival of the Grey Wanderer brought about consequences undreamed of.

"The myths are true," Einos admitted, more for personal gratification than anything else.

Constable and sclarem remained silent. Only one understood his meaning. So much had transpired since Kastus rode north, he felt lost, far behind. Tension thickened the room, leaving all those assembled lethargic.

"What myths?" Kastus asked. His gaze hardly left the impossible creature sitting opposite him. "There appear to be many at work here."

"The Wanderer. Wherever he goes, bad things follow," Einos answered.

"Baron, the Grey Wanderer has not been seen. We have only rumors that he strode the fields the night Brogon Lord was resurrected," Kastus protested. "Hearsay is nothing to go on. Not with the threat from the north."

"At this point, Kastus, I'm not willing to discount anything," Einos defended. "Why else would Dalem have come?"

Kastus had no answer. How could he? He sheepishly admitted to not having believed Sava's recounting of the battle outside of Palis. That a mythical creature was roaming Fent, ready to do battle with a once dead man. "I have no experience fighting the supernatural. My talents are for rooting out crime."

"Which you have done admirably in Palis," Einos applauded. That an entire village under his authority had turned rogue, for what purpose remained hidden, without anyone in the duchy knowing, rattled him. It was another problem he didn't need.

"Thank you, but our work is not yet done," Kastus replied. "We should send a detail back to arrest the other Elders."

The longer he brewed over events, the more convinced he was that all three were complicit. Waern was out of the equation, hiding in the underground. Not that Kastus was worried. It wouldn't be much longer before his agents produced documentation revealing Waern's merchant contact. The conspiracy was ready to collapse. All it needed was a push.

Einos winced. Whatever he did in Palis would have a rippling effect across his domain. Too heavy a hand might push other villages away, while showing reluctance to punish would show Fent his weakness. He was trapped on a narrow ledge and the wind was picking up.

"To what end, Kastus? I cannot have an entire governing body removed without proof. And then what will become of Palis without anyone to lead?" he asked.

That, Kastus had an answer to. "We place the village under martial law until suitable, vetted replacements can be empowered. Ones loyal to the throne. The villagers are already used to a sustained military presence. Having a captain or senior sergeant rule for a limited time poses no threat to their daily lives. It is the only solution."

"Do you realize what that implies? That I am incapable of maintaining order in my duchy. If word of this gets out to other lands, I risk opening Fent up to invasion, or worse. This is a dangerous game we play," he countered.

The Baron drummed his fingertips on his table. Caught between equally poor choices, it was all he could do to keep from going mad. He needed a drink. A lot of drink.

"You already risk losing influence among the larger villages. Decisive action is needed," Kastus insisted. Anger threatened to boil over. He knew he was too close to the situation to provide unbiased opinions, and it mattered not. His love for Fent went almost unmatched.

Dalem blinked, his eyes moving vertically instead of horizontally. "Perhaps he is correct. Many events collide here. It is difficult to see the way ahead with clarity."

"All the more reason for caution," Einos said. *When did I lose my nerve? Was it my inability to protect my people? Or was it watching the ease with which Lord killed my guards, defeated Quinlan, and stole Lizette?*

The sclarem cleared his throat, an awkward gargling sound. Blue tinged mist escaped his mouth. The smell was akin to rotting meat. "Caution has value, but only when used with discretion. You have many enemies, circling like vultures. To defeat them, you must confront them with every weapon in your arsenal. Anything less is injustice to your people."

Quinlan and Donal entered just then. Their excitement obvious. Einos waited for the pair to take their places at the massive oval table. One of his ancestors insisted on the unconventional shape, claiming it helped men feel more equal and valuable in conference. No one in the time since saw the need to replace it.

"Brother Quinlan. Donal. I assume you have something of importance for us?" Einos hoped.

Quinlan clasped his hands together on the table, watching from the corner of his eye as Donal laid out the book containing Lord's history, turning to the correct page. "Donal has made a revelation we believe is pertinent to our task."

Donal openly stared at Dalem, never having seen a sclarem before. Once, it would have been impossible to comprehend sitting among nobles in the presence of alien creatures. The young man from a forgotten village had come far during his time with the war priests. It was a strange sensation, for he'd grown up believing he had no place among the upper crust of society. That he was meant to be seen, not heard. Reality proved a far different creature.

A wry grin twisting his face, Einos made introductions. "Novice Donal, this is Dalem. He has come to offer what aid he might. A more formidable team I cannot imagine. Now, what is it you have discovered?"

Donal cleared his throat, suddenly nervous. He took a calming breath and began. "Baron, my search, while largely unproductive, led me to this volume. It is a compendium of families known to have noble sons in the armed forces. Most of it is dull reading, but I found a passage regarding an interesting turn of events in Brogon Lord's life."

"Continue," Einos said, leaning forward. His heart beat a little faster, eager to learn whatever terrible secrets the once dead man possessed.

Donal's finger traced the lines, stopping where he needed to begin. "Brogon Lord, born the third son of Argal and Wuy Lord. Earned knighthood during his twenty-second year. Unable to procure service in Fent's army, Brogon joined the mercenary company of Kahl Ilunder. He is attributed with seventy-three kills during the Mamlan Campaign. Died from wounds sustained in battle. It is rumored he was murdered by Ilunder. Brogon was interred in the Fent cemetery as afforded by his rank."

"The man was a villain," Kastus uttered.

"It sounds as if he received the end he deserved, though I fail to see how this helps us," Einos added.

"There is more," Quinlan urged Donal to continue.

The novice sipped from the mug of water set before him. "Brogon Lord was considered a familial outcast, often spending his days away from the family compound in Gunn. His childhood was spent along the banks of a small stream. It was here that Ilunder first came to him with the proposition of joining the mercenary ranks."

"Gunn?" Einos balked. He knew the village well, for it was the birthplace of his wife, Aneth. "How have we missed this?"

"The Lord family is, according to official records, all dead. Brogon was the last," Quinlan explained. He avoided telling them his conclusion that Brogon had played a part in their demise.

"If the F'talle remains in this realm, he will roost in a place of familiarity," Dalem offered.

"He will have gone home," Kastus finished.

Stunned silence. Each tried, some failed, to process the information. There was no denying Brogon Lord was a villain, but how deep did his crimes go? None wanted the answers they knew they needed if the once dead man was going to be stopped.

Einos was the first to speak. "Thank you for your efforts, Donal. This may well prove the clue we need. Captain Thep, are your people up for another ride?"

"They are, Baron," Thep affirmed. He bristled at the opportunity to prove his worth after the Palis incident.

"Good. We ride for Gunn. Kastus, keep tightening the noose here. I want Waern found and incarcerated in the next few days."

Quinlan unlocked his hands and flexed his fingers. "What of Lizette? There must be a way to return her."

"This break is much needed, but it leaves us with as many unanswered questions as before," Einos answered. "Quinlan, Dalem, I would ask you come with me. Kastus, bring me my traitors. With a little luck, we can end this nightmare and restore order to Fent."

They rose, shuffling off to prepare. Plans were made and the leaders of the once quiet duchy of Fent prepared for the fight of their lives.

THIRTY-FIVE

Fent

Thep gathered his forces. Those ten soldiers brought south with him from Palis. Far from being a full company, they would suffice. After all, he had Sava at his side. There was no better sergeant in Fent, or any of the surrounding duchies for that matter. Ten would have to do. There was no time or point for briefing. Thep said the name of the target village, putting them on level ground. What happened next remained to be seen.

He cinched his travel bags down on Deana's borrowed horse and found Kastus waiting. Thep walked over and offered his hand. Mud splashed halfway up his black boots. A light rain began overnight and continued until the landscape was coated.

"Take care of yourself, Constable," Thep said warmly. "It sounds like you are about to have more trouble on your hands than you'll know what to do with."

Kastus saw it a different way. The danger was outside of the village, far from the once clogged streets. Still, there was merit in Thep's warning. Desperate men did desperate deeds. Especially ones cornered in unfamiliar territory. Waern and his merchant benefactor threatened to become more than adversaries. They promised to be more trouble than the Constable wanted.

"Sounds like the danger is where you are going. No one has seen the once dead man for some time," Kastus replied. Dirt smudged his cheeks, souring his mood.

"We have a war priest and a sclarem. How much trouble could Lord possibly give us?" Thep asked. His confidence was rising. Forgotten were the miseries endured in Palis. His only wish was that the rest of the company was behind him.

Kastus clasped hands with him. "More than either of us are willing to want. Be safe out there, Thep. You are a good man and a better leader. Fent is fortunate to have you."

"We'll keep the Baron safe. You have my word," Thep understood the message.

A sigh escaped him. Kastus's greatest worry was for Einos. Knowing the Baron was in the field, against dangerous forces, left him on edge. Worse that he wouldn't be there to protect him. The time of rulers leading their armies in the field were past. Einos should remain in his castle, directing all facets of the operation. Kastus had argued it long into the night but the Baron would not hear it. There was a time and place for true rulers to stand at the front.

With a final nod, Kastus left. The time for speeches was ended. It was a day of action. Hundreds of soldiers were already deploying throughout the village as hundreds more formed a cordon to keep Waern and his confederates from escaping. Word had been sent to Palis, ordering the remainder of Thep's company to arrest Mugh and Deana. Everything was coming to fruition.

Thunder rumbled across the sky, prompting Kastus to cast a wary glance up. He didn't foresee any problems unless the rain worsened. A squad of soldiers in boiled leather armor marched up in two files. They halted a few paces away and the sergeant in charge stepped forward to introduce herself.

"Constable Kastus, I am Sergeant Sanice. My squad has been assigned as your personal detachment," she snapped to attention.

Kastus stared into her pale, ice colored eyes and shivered. The slightest hint of blue echoed within them. He wasn't sure if that made her dangerous, or just a simple threat. The pair of short swords attached to her hip made up his mind. "Sergeant, a pleasure. I trust your people are ready?"

Sanice stiffened, if that was possible, "Sir, these are among the best in the duchy. I'd put them up against every other squad you care to bring at me. Captain Thep says you are an honorable man. That is enough for me. And for them. We are ready for everything. Including a dead man."

"You have heard?" he asked, confirming that word had spread throughout the duchy.

"Very few things escape notice from the army," Sanice replied. Her voice was stern, fitting of her position.

Kastus began to wonder if she could give Sava a run. "Good. The rumors are true. A once dead man has been kidnapping children, and now a grown woman. Your orders are to fight him only if he shows up. Our primary objective is the capture of Elder Waern from Palis. A rendition of his likeness is being distributed to the squads."

"Alive, or dead?" she asked.

He was right. She was a dangerous woman and he was glad to have her on his side. "Alive, preferably. At least until we can uncover his network. Fent comes first, Sergeant. Always."

"I'm not hearing anything I disagree with. What are your orders?"

Sanice found no taste for wasting time on small talk. A professional, she was armed and armored. It was time for action. A sliver of jealousy spurred her on. She and Sava were in constant competition, each claiming it made them better leaders. Now, with Sava heading out with the Baron to do who knew what, Fent was hers for the glory. She'd already won in her mind's eye.

"Once all squads are in place, we will begin with the merchant houses. I want private residences, warehouses, and offices raided simultaneously. There will be nowhere in this village to hide. With a little luck, we shall have this mission wrapped up before the end of the day."

Optimism aside, Kastus suspected this was going to prove harder than he expected. Matters of such importance seldom weren't.

She nodded. "You lead. We'll follow."

Thunder rumbled again. Louder. Closer. It was going to be a long day.

"I still don't understand why you have to go," Aneth protested. Her belly was swollen, visibly showing their coming child. "This is a matter for the army."

"This is a matter for the barony," he replied. He had yet to offer validation for his decisions. How could he explain that there were times when a ruler needed to stand before his men, to lead by example?

"Where are you going?" she asked.

A heavy sigh. Another matter he'd neglected to tell her. Lying wasn't an option. Einos summoned his courage and told her. "Gunn. Donal uncovered information that Brogon Lord is originally from there."

"Gunn? But that's …"

"Where you are from," he finished. "Do you remember the name Lord? Records say the bloodline has died out."

Aneth opened and closed her mouth just as fast. A hint of a secret flashed across her eyes before her face returned to calm. "Not that I recall. It has been so long since I was last there."

Einos strapped on his family's ancestral sword, a plain weapon with nothing marking it special. He'd forgotten the story behind it. Some stories weren't worth remembering. He took pride in his relationship to the common man, believing it made him more approachable. A selfish indulgence perhaps, but worthy in his eyes.

"That seems to be the trouble. No one remembers the name. I find it odd that an entire bloodline can be so removed from modern times," Einos admitted. His suspicion that there was a conspiracy around the Lord name deepened the longer he was immersed in this trial.

Aneth slid from their bed to encircle her arms around his waist. She pressed her face against his shoulder and hugged tight. "Find him, love. Bring those children home and let us put this sad affair behind us. For the baby."

His head dipped. The baby. Everything he did was for the baby and he knew there would be no blanket of security for his coming child so long as Brogon Lord roamed the land. He slid around and kissed her. "I'll be back before you know it. We are close, Aneth. I feel it. Whoever this Brogon Lord was, we shall soon root him out and put an end to his reign of terror."

Kissing her again on the forehead, he hurried for the door.

"Einos," she called and fell silent, the words dying on her tongue.

"Yes, my dear?"

She forced a smile. "Nothing. Be safe."

His smile brightened the room. And then he was gone. Aneth leaned back against the bed and sighed. How could she tell him? The secret was eating her from the inside, but she couldn't bring herself to tell him the truth. Not yet.

"Form ranks! The Baron's coming," Sava barked. The whoosh and snap of his favorite stick slapping his trousers followed.

Alfar climbed into the saddle and adjusted himself. "Do you suppose we'll get extra pay for this?"

Unwilling to think about it, Nils tried to ignore him. Some lessons were learned the hard way. Lately, it seemed every time he opened his mouth, Sava was there to rip into him. Nils had performed more unwanted tasks in the past few weeks than his entire time in the army. How Alfar seemed oblivious to the torment was beyond him.

"Focus on the task at hand," he scolded, almost under his breath. Sava was always lurking.

Alfar screwed his eyes up, confused. "I thought I was."

"What are you ladies yapping about?"

Nils winced. "Nothing, Sergeant."

Unconvinced, Sava spit a mouthful of nasty kaappa juice. The red juice left a stain on the dark brown mud. "See that it remains so. We got one job to do and that's protect Baron Einos. I don't need either of you screwing this up. Understood?"

"Sure thing, Sergeant," Alfar replied, far too cheerily for anyone's liking.

Sava fixed him with his most severe glare. "Uh huh. Corporal Ollis!"

"Sergeant?"

"Keep an eye on these two. I'm beginning to not like this one," he commanded.

Ollis fought off her grin, having seen this routine many times before. "You got it, Sergeant Sava."

Einos and Brother Quinlan took their place at the head of the tiny column.

Captain Thep looked back over his shoulder and barked, "Move out!"

The road to Gunn was short, and with it the promise of ending all Fent's miseries.

THIRTY-SIX

The Other Realm

The clock had a face. Luminescent, pale and impossibly large. Lizette stared up at the monstrosity with a feeling of cold dread gnawing her stomach. Numbers were being crafted from an unknown metal and fixed to the face. Soon would come the hands and the foul plan of the Omegri would begin. Ironically, time was the one thing she was running out of. She needed to find Brogon Lord and turn him before it was too late.

Torches glowed, developing winding snakes of light in an otherwise grey world. Children continued hammering and building. Bodies were constantly being added to the pit, despite everything she'd done to prevent it. Whoever the three shadow creatures were, they were little interested in the preservation of their workforce. Lizette knew better than to present the children as living beings. That meant little to a race dedicated to ending all life. So she crafted them into laborers. Each death meant the construction slowed, if but a little. Still they cared not. Work went on and the death toll rose.

She found Brogon standing far from the tower. Stale wind blew his hair across his face. Lizette was revolted by the creature, though she supposed he was once handsome. *Will I become the same once my time expires? Cold, decomposing flesh for the worms*? The thought sickened her, but it was an inevitable fate everyone rushed toward.

He'd continued to deteriorate since bringing her to the Other Realm. There was little left marking him a man. No doubt if he removed his armor he would collapse in a heap of bones. None of that diminished his intensity, however. The once dead man prowled the marshes surrounding the clock tower, except for those rare times he was returned to the world of the living to bring another child.

That hardly happened anymore, suggesting to Lizette that it was almost finished. Soon time would stop and the Omegri would be loosed upon the world. An eternity of nightmares was surging against its bonds. She was the only barrier to ultimate defeat and she wasn't sure she was up to the challenge. Lizette collected her wits and went to Brogon. The only way to succeed was by turning him to her side.

"You should not be here," he said without looking at her.

She came to a stop at his side, folding her arms across her chest. "What's the worst they can do to me? I am already here, in the land of the dead."

Brogon's head turned. He was missing an eye now. The empty hole staring back at her. "You have no idea the suffering they will invoke. It is not safe with me."

She drew a deep breath. "Why do you do it?"

He remained silent.

Lizette took that as a signal. "These monsters treat you horribly. They expect you to kill and kidnap for their cruel needs. Have you ever once been praised for your actions?"

"You are trying to appeal to my humanity. I have none. This is the land of the dead, as you say."

"Were you this way in life?" she pressed.

Something had to work. There must be some trigger to reawaken what he'd lost. If not, all was lost and she had already failed.

"I ... do not remember," came his answer.

Brogon tried remembering his past. Who he was. Where he came from. Was he a man with a stern moral compass? Or did immorality come easier? He wished he knew, all while fearing the answer. The fear of knowing he might have been a bad man was paralyzing.

"Your grave marker suggested you were a knight. That means you had a code of honor," Lizette continued. It was now or never. Her one shot at glory. "Any man worthy of the title could never have accepted this as his final outcome."

"A knight."

"There must be some semblance of your past still within you, Brogon," she said.

His sigh came out a thin rattle. "My name was Brogon Lord. I was a knight."

She nodded. "A man of honor."

"I ... I do not remember." He stiffened, as if old memories resurfaced and quickly moved away.

His face contorted. A tooth fell loose, sliding down his armor to hit the ground. Honor. Integrity. Words knights lived by. He allowed his mind to race. Drifting through space and time in a desperate search for his past. Brogon was blocked at every turn. Frustration settled in. his fists clenched. Not unnoticed by Lizette. She pressed.

"Brogon, listen to me, this is not what you were made for," she said in whispered tones, pleading with his confusion. "A true knight would never allow himself to be used as a puppet for these inhuman creatures. They have corrupted you. Turned you into a monster."

His gaze remained fixed on the clocktower. "I do not remember who I was. Your argument is irrelevant."

She refused to accept that answer. "You don't believe that. How can you? Knights are men of honor. Not kidnappers or … murderers."

He stiffened at the word. Anger flared. "I am no coward."

"No. I don't claim you are, but you have been misused by these monsters," she persisted. "They are using you to commit acts of evil."

Brogon turned on her, fixing her with a hollow glare. "What is it you want of me?"

This was it. Her one chance at getting him to switch sides and rescuing the children. "Help me get these children out of here before it is too late."

A faint wind growled across the endless grey plains. Brogon clenched his jaw and continued to stare.

"We are running out of time."

"Impossible. The Omegri are amassing their armies. Once the clocktower is finished, they will spill through entryways across the face of the world. Time is meaningless, here. Time is endless, until we stop it."

Nonplussed, the first riposted, "Time is the catalyst for all we seek to achieve. What happens when the tower is not finished on schedule? Your faith in the Omegri is misplaced."

"Is it? I do not expect you to understand the true goings on of this endeavor. We have been acquired to perform a task. That task is incomplete until time is stopped," she replied.

"You imply the Omegri are capable of waiting forever," said the third.

The ting-ting of hammers striking up and down the giant tower echoed over the still. Pulleys groaned as hundreds of children struggled to haul the smaller hand up to the clock face. She would have preferred adults, but the levels of sin corrupting most souls rendered them useless for this endeavor. Only innocence powered this realm. The irony of the contradiction was not lost on her, or the others.

She mused on the notion that they were close to ending an event that had occurred since the dawning of the world. The barrier thinned. So close. Armies of the Omegri were forming, ready to assault the unsuspecting nations of the world outside of the Burning Season. She scoffed at the name. Humanity was overly simplistic when assigning names. Pedantic ignorance burrowed deep into their psyches. Soon it would all end.

"They have waited this long. What is time to beings who live outside of it?" she replied.

"They are an impatient species. Incapable of achieving patience," the second countered. "We risk invoking their ire by prolonging this task."

"We risk nothing. The tower will be finished and the Omegri can have their invasion."

"What of the human woman?"

Dust drifted off her desiccated flesh as she craned her head. "Irrelevant."

"She attempts to subsume the F'talle to her cause," the first stated.

"To no avail. Brogon Lord is not what he once was," she snapped. "He is our pawn. A tool to accomplish great ends. No more."

"The possibility of his betrayal is real nonetheless. We must neutralize her, while there is still time," the second added.

Not adverse to killing, the first studied her companions. Neither were as powerful as she, a point she was clear to develop from their inception. The Other Realm was a place of abstract nightmares. Void of compassion. A haven for suffering. She had designs to escape into the realm of the living, knowing that to do so would invite a plague upon humanity that had never been witnessed.

"The woman has not succeeded. She will die when the children are slaughtered," she said, her voice terse with restrained rage.

That was enough to placate the others. They each nodded and slipped away to charcoal colored dust on the stagnant air. *Oh yes. The woman will die, for only innocent souls will open the paths to the living world once time has stopped.* Satisfied that all was happening accordingly, she resumed her watch on the great clocktower, ignorant of the first steps of treason being taken not far away.

THIRTY-SEVEN
Gunn

The village of Gunn was less than half a day's ride east of Fent and quaint. There were no official estimates, but Einos believed it held less than five hundred citizens, most of whom were elderly. Nestled at the base of the southern slopes of the Amrous Mountains and a league from a swath of untamed forests, Gunn was the perfect place to retire. One day, when he was old and grey, Einos hoped to bring his wife back where they might reestablish their household and watch their final years pass by. Given recent events, it was a slender hope.

The column rode into Gunn at midday without fanfare or forewarning. A handful of scouts had ridden ahead to ensure there were no lurking surprises. None returned with reports, prompting Einos to suspect the village was exactly as advertised. A quiet, out-of-the-way place for people to forget the troubles of the day. Mustering as much confidence as he had remaining, the Baron of Fent rode into Gunn as a conqueror.

His only hindrance was the army. Captain Thep insisted they went first. Treason and violence were the commerce of the duchy. They'd witnessed it, in some minor degree, in Palis and refused to allow Einos to ride in without protection. His squad formed in front of the Baron, house guards and his personal retainers, as well as on both flanks. Weapons were drawn and readied—against Einos's wishes. He had no intention of coming to Gunn to attack. These were his people. His wife's family as well.

Thep would have none of it. His primary concern was the Baron's safety. All other considerations paled. He refused to watch another situation like Palis develop. Gunn had no idea what was happening as armed soldiers marched down the single road splitting the village. Those daring few poked heads out doors and windows. Some gawked openly as they spied Einos. Others worried that the duchy's troubles had at last found them. It was with tepid reluctance the village elders organized themselves for presentation.

A brindle colored dog raced across the road, barking at horse and rider. Autumn breeze swayed the red leafed abris trees lining both sides of the road. Golden sunlight turned the southern fields into an ocean of warmth. Einos had always enjoyed this time of year most. When the world was changing. Lush greens were well and fine, but it was the diversity of color that appealed to him. Red, orange, yellow, brown, and a hint of pale blue as leaves turned and began to fall.

A quiet time to sit on the shores of the great lake bordering the northern edge. He recalled with fondness how he and Aneth spent days nestled among the trees and plush grasses there. It was a peace he could only wish to return to. For Baron Einos, the joy of living was fading. Slipping into that awkward space no man willingly dared look. The upcoming birth of his first child—how he'd gone through life without producing any remained a mystery neither he nor Aneth were willing to explore—promised brighter days, but he was unsure if those days were coming. So much had gone wrong in the span of a few short weeks, he lacked confidence.

"Baron, the village is secure," Thep said with a crisp salute.

Einos struggled to nod, broken from his thoughts. Drawing a deep breath, he took a good look at the village. Multi-colored roofs lined the road, adding flavor to an otherwise drab village. He knew he should have felt secure. Gunn was as close to the heart of his kingdom as his castle. There hadn't been any expressed sentiment in opposition. So why was he worried?

"Have the elders been assembled?" he asked.

"They have and are being escorted here as we speak, sir," Thep explained. His defiant look dared Einos to question that decision.

"Not quite the diplomatic entry I expected. Are you sure they will cooperate?"

"They have been *told* what happened in Palis in no uncertain terms. I believe each will behave accordingly, sir." Thep's confidence was inspiring, despite the knowledge that they were all citizens of Fent.

Einos chewed on his inner lip. It was a habit he'd had since childhood, developed from endless hours of waiting for his father to deliver some form of punishment or another. "Captain, I have doubts about the intensity we are attempting to convey here. There is no reason to suspect the citizens are in league with our foes."

"Baron, I understand your concerns and echo them to an extent. My mission is to keep you safe and ensure the duchy is represented. Both tasks are to be conducted by any means necessary," Thep replied dryly.

"He is right," Quinlan interrupted after seeing Einos open and close his mouth too many times for matters to remain calm. "These are dangerous times. Those you think loyal might well be the first waiting for the moment to stab you in the back. Caution is prudent here, at least until we discover what, if anything, Gunn has to do with Brogon Lord."

Einos didn't doubt the authenticity of the statement, nor was he disillusioned to think Dalem had nothing to do with the unwillingness of the people to greet him properly. Not that he blamed them. Having a sclarem ride into your village was as confusing as it was frightening. These were days of walking legends. Fent might never recover.

A commotion halfway down the road drew his attention. Einos swallowed as he saw his father in law head his way, leaning heavily on his cane. Flanking him were the other elders. It was a reunion he wished for under different circumstances. They halted several meters apart, each side sizing up the other's intentions.

"Einos. It has been a long time."

"It has, Hintul. You look well," Einos replied.

The Elder snorted. "I look like shit. Wait until you get this old and others tell you the same lie. How is my daughter?"

"Well, though this matter has put unnecessary strain on her and the baby."

Hintul shifted his weight to the opposite leg. "All care must be taken to ensure the child is born without stress. It is the future of this duchy. I assume you are here because of the once dead man."

It was a statement, not a question. Word had travelled across the duchy, to every village. There were precious few secrets left for Einos to defend. "We are. I think it best we speak indoors. There are prying ears eager for gossip."

"You have no enemies in Gunn, Einos." Hintul's eyes narrowed at the perceived insult. "But you are the Baron. It shall be as you say. You are always welcome in my home."

Einos reserved his comments stating otherwise. Theirs was a tumultuous relationship. Not that he didn't like Aneth's father, but they were of different generations. The span of decades often led to disagreements and the inability for either to see the other's point of view. It was part of the reason Einos seldom visited. The same could be said in opposite, for he had last seen Hintul almost a year before Aneth announced her pregnancy.

Resigned to his course of action, Einos slid from the saddle and walked beside Hintul back to his estate. The mission in Gunn promised to be more stressful than he wished.

Einos yawned, excused himself, and left the dining chamber to stretch. He was sore from a day in the saddle and the near constant grilling of the village elders. One, he noticed, that seemed to go both ways. Exhausted, the Baron of Fent left the elders to the careful interrogation of Brother Quinlan and Dalem. That unlikely combination proved effective enough to throw everyone involved off their defenses. A cough drew his attention.

A slender woman stood atop the staircase, clutching the marble bannister in her right hand. Her long, silver hair flowed past her shoulders, importing a sense of majesty. The lines on her face were superficial, offering little evidence of anything more than age. The alacrity in her eyes whispered much.

"Loreli," Einos said with a polite bow.

Her smile, unlike her husband's greeting, was warm. Genuine. "Einos, it has been too long. Where is my daughter?"

Einos explained, though he suspected she already knew most of it. Her husband was never one for keeping secrets.

Loreli glided down the stairs. The hem of her forest green dress scuffing as she walked. "What is the real reason for your visit? It is my understanding that events are transpiring to the north and west. Why Gunn?"

"We have discovered evidence that the once dead man is from Gunn, Loreli," he said without hesitation. "His name was Brogon Lord." The guarded look she gave inspired fresh confidence and he continued. "I need to find where he lived in the hopes of gaining an advantage over him. Every tactic I have tried thus far has been defeated."

"Brogon Lord."

"You know of him, don't you," he said.

She nodded. The move so slight, he barely noticed. "The Lords were once prominent members of Gunn. I'm surprised Aneth never mentioned them."

"Why would she?" he asked.

Loreli reached out to touch his forearm and answered.

"This doesn't look like a fancy mansion to me," Alfar said with a wry grin.

The ruins were barely a story high with no functioning rooms or chambers. Time and weather combined to bring what might have been a grand home to ruin. Cobwebs decorated corners. Vermin scurried out of sight as the soldiers spread out. Vegetation had returned to claim this part of the land, transforming the building into a miniature ecosystem.

Nils grimaced, refraining from telling his peer to shut up. "We shouldn't be here. There's nothing to see."

"You two geniuses figured that out for yourselves, eh?"

Nils winced as Sergeant Sava slid between them. "No, Sergeant."

"Captain thinks otherwise. You and farm boy here go in and reconnoiter. I want to know every detail of this place before I send in the leadership. Understood?" Sava instructed.

"Sure thing, Sarge!" Alfar replied too enthusiastically.

He and Nils hurried away. Neither wanted to get Sava after them, again.

Once they were deep within the heart of the building, Nils grabbed Alfar by the neck and spun him around. "I swear, the next time you do that, I am going to kill you. Damn the consequences."

He shoved the younger Alfar away.

Stunned, the young soldier brushed the wrinkles from his uniform. "What did I do? I was just trying to lighten the mood. No harm in being friendly."

"You're impossible," Nils snorted and continued on.

They returned with nothing to report, leaving Thep with the feeling that they'd arrived at a dead end. Once again it seemed the once dead man was a step ahead of them. He and Sava had the company comb every inch of the ruins. Aside from random family heirlooms that were meaningless to anyone other than the deceased Lords, they found nothing. Disappointment threatened to lower morale.

"We need to report back to the Baron. This expedition provided nothing of significance," he said to Sava.

The sergeant spit a rope of kaappa juice in agreement. "Sir, we've got to be missing something. The whole damned Lord clan lived right here, even the once dead man. If I were a loyal son, I'd be looking for a way to come back here."

"To what end? They are all dead," Thep countered. He gestured with his right arm. "There is no reason for him to return. Not unless …"

"Unless what?" Sava asked.

"Unless this is where he moves between realms," Thep concluded.

An odd smell clung to the air. One Quinlan couldn't quite place. His stomach soured, suggesting death was nearby. Arms crossed, he and

Donal stood on the bank of a wide stream. They watched as the sclarem hunted through the reeds and dormant grasses that hadn't fallen yet. Silver fish circled at their feet, as if eager to see what food might drop in. The war priest dipped his boot in the water, amused by their aggressive reaction.

Dalem moved through the mud and water with familiarity, prompting Quinlan to wonder where his species originally came from. He'd never encountered a sclarem before and had no knowledge of their past. He suspected the power of the green skinned man was far greater than his own and was glad they were allies. Stopping Brogon Lord was going to prove difficult and he had already been found lacking.

They'd searched a handful of small caves with no results. Daylight was fading as were their hopes. Reporting failure back to Baron Einos wasn't in their best interests. The duchy was on the brink of chaos. He felt it ride the air. All it needed was a spark before the conflagration spread from village to village. Mired in his fears, Quinlan failed to see Dalem disappear.

"Where did he go?" he asked, unfolding his arms to reach for his sword.

Donal pointed. "There. He must have found another cave."

Tense moments dragged by. Quinlan felt helpless, even while knowing this was part of the task. Each time Dalem entered a cave heightened the chances of making contact. Thus far, Quinlan was too large to follow, frustrating him to great lengths. He began to pace. Quinlan lacked patience, or perhaps it had eroded since arriving in Fent.

"Look!" Donal refrained from shouting.

Dalem scurried back up the bank, where he brushed clumps of mud and dead grass from his body. He accepted the water skin and after drinking deeply, broke into a feral grin. "We have found the passage between realms."

Quinlan wanted to clap. At last! They had a starting place.

THIRTY-EIGHT
Gunn

"Absolutely not!"

Einos, having appropriated his father in law's study, sank down into the high backed chair and pinched the bridge of his nose. He couldn't believe what he'd just been asked. As if enough life wasn't already at risk! His respect for the war priests, combined with a healthy dose of suspicion many in the lands shared, failed to translate into a willingness to allow Quinlan to have his way unchecked.

"There is no other way," Quinlan offered.

Einos winced. "Do you have any idea what you are asking?"

"We do."

Dalem stood at his left, the sclarem failing to come up to his shoulders. Donal stood a pace behind, befitting his station and lack of experience. The trio had returned to Einos with renewed enthusiasm, knowing the end of their hunt was near. Finding hesitance bordering on denial left them stunned.

"There is no other way," Dalem added. His voice cracked at awkward syllables.

Shaking his head, Einos finally opened his eyes. "You expect me to believe that? When has anyone successfully returned from the Other Realm?"

They remained silent, allowing Einos to work through the issue on his own. Some questions didn't need to be asked, nor were there appropriate answers for many more. Their proposal was simplistic, yet laden with inherent dangers. The Other Realm was an enigma. No amount of lore collected across the duchies offered enough insight for Quinlan to make an accurate decision. By offering to traverse the boundaries, Quinlan was resigning his life.

"This is an unexpected opportunity we cannot afford to pass up," Quinlan insisted. His eyes burned from the lack of sleep.

Einos threw out his arms. "We could not stop Brogon Lord in this duchy, what makes you think you can do so in his realm?"

Boots shuffling down the hall stopped before carrying on, forcing Einos to lower his voice. Recent circumstances in the capital left him rattled. Trust had become a rare commodity and he wasn't willing to return to old habits, at least not until this situation was resolved.

Quinlan slid into the chair beside Einos, pausing to cast his glance at the others in the room. Only Thep remained unreadable. "Einos, we may not have another opportunity. All signs point to a culminating moment approaching. I fear should we not act now, decisively, we will lose. There is more at stake than the future of Fent."

Einos closed his mouth, abruptly changing what he was going to say. "What do you mean?"

"There are powers gathering. A storm approaches, threatening us all," Dalem answered.

Quinlan deferred, allowing the elder sclarem's wisdom to shine. Emboldened, Dalem continued, "The powers of good and evil have been in opposition for countless millennia. An epoch of humanity is nothing to the great game being played. Should our enemies break through here, in Fent, they will gain a toehold in this realm. Pushing them back will be next to impossible, especially with all but one of the war priest fortresses destroyed. What we do next might well effect the fates of everyone in this world."

"Those aren't encouraging words," Einos groaned. "You leave me with no choices."

"An unenviable position for any ruler, but one we all must accept," Quinlan said with a grim nod.

Silence fell. A curtain of impenetrable discomfort. Einos closed his eyes and prayed for guidance. So many choices had proven wrong, he was unwilling to risk more. Too many lives had already been lost without results. Could he resign more to death with the utterance of a single sentence?

There was nothing in his authority preventing Quinlan or Dalem from enacting their plan. Neither were his citizens, nor could he blame them for wanting to try. The chance to kill the once dead man and end the Omegri's interference in Fent was alluring. The Council of Dukes might demand an inquiry should word of his decision to waste the life of a war priest come to light, but that was a rare occurrence and not an immediate issue. Knowing the Lord General would come down with his full authority was another matter.

"Can you succeed?" Einos asked after some time passed. Despite his lack of optimism, the Baron of Fent saw a sliver of opportunity. He'd live with the consequences.

"I do not know," Dalem answered before the others could.

"If that is the best we can do," Einos added. "I will not say that I like this plan. It is foolish and offers no balance of reward, but I cannot see another way ahead. What do you need from me?"

Nils burst into the room, which was supposed to be private, out of breath and red faced. Heads turned his way, daring him to interrupt further.

"This had better be damned important, soldier," Thep growled.

"Sir, Sergeant Sava sent me. There's a large body of armed men heading this way," Nils reported.

Einos' fist made a fleshy thump as he smacked the desk. "Damnation. How many?"

"Forty to fifty. The scouts weren't sure," Nils said.

"It appears our position grows dire," Einos told them. He struggled to comprehend what was happening, though there could be but one viable reason. His enemies aimed to remove him and take control of Fent. "Brother Quinlan, Dalem, you have my full endorsement. Do what you feel is necessary. Our hands will be full here for the immediate future. Good fortune to you both."

They clasped forearms. Each man stared deep into the other's eyes, searching for signs of reassurance. Of hope. There was precious little of either. It would have to be enough.

Einos turned to his captain as the war priest and sclarem left. "Captain, we must make Gunn defensible. Can your people handle so many?"

"That or we shall all die trying, Baron," Thep sounded confident, giving Einos hope. "Your permission?"

Einos nodded. "Go. The time has come to make these bastards pay for their indiscretion."

"I've never been in a real battle," Alfar admitted under cover of darkness.

It was a common superstition among soldiers. No one wanted to admit to being raw, not when lives to their left and right depended on them. His voice was low so as not to alarm those nearby, though he would have been surprised to learn a great many of them felt the same. Fent was a quiet duchy out of the main trade lanes. There weren't many who remembered the last time an army took to the field.

Sava sat on a tree stump nearby, concealed in the night as he sharpened his sword. He tried to think back to his first battle. All the fear, adrenalin, and anxiety as he slashed into his first opponent. Years had gone by, fled like so many empty seasons. He was older now. Grey of hair and long in the tooth. A veteran. A wall. The anchor his soldiers needed.

"Quiet, fool. You don't want everyone to know," Nils replied. He'd returned as the sun set and took his place in the defensive line.

Taken back, Alfar snuffed his nose. "I'm just scared, is all."

"Me, too," Nils admitted and fell silent.

Sava perked up, interested in their exchange. He'd come to almost enjoy their banter, for it reminded him of his younger days when the world wasn't quite so small. Those had been the days, he mused. Riding and marching across the face of the world in the name of honor and a healthy purse. This was different.

He wasn't fighting for anyone but the men and women around him. Einos and the others in Gunn were fine, but they didn't matter when steel started swinging. There was a time and place for royalty and this wasn't it. Sava expected Nils to snap a quick retort. The man was young, compared to Sava, but had talent and was doing a fine job of molding Alfar into a proper soldier. If only the others in his company did the same, they might just survive the coming fight.

Setting the stone to blade, he continued. There was no such thing as having too sharp of a sword on the eve of battle.

"You all should get some sleep. You're going to need it come morning," he said loud enough that those up and down the line could hear. Every other person hit the sack. Sleep in shifts. I don't want any surprises tonight."

"What about you, Sergeant?" Alfar whispered.

Sounds of soldiers burrowing down to find a few hours of restless sleep echoed up and down the line. Sava knew from experience, no one would sleep well. "Me? I have work to do."

Alone at last, the Baron of Fent clasped his hands behind his back and stared out the window facing his faraway castle and the woman he loved. Thoughts of failure prevented him from relaxing. How he'd failed Aneth and their unborn child. Failed his people. Failed so many parents. Failed Lizette. The list felt endless. He began to wonder if he was meant to rule after all, or if he was to be the last baron of his bloodline.

The word made him cringe. So much rested on where a man came from and he was only now coming to understand that. Einos would trade all of this for the opportunity to escape with Aneth and live a quiet life. But what legacy would that produce? The leader who abandoned his people in their hour of greatest need. He'd be hunted to the ends of the world for such a crime. An outlaw with an entire duchy seeking his blood.

In the end, there was no choice. He would meet the coming force and do his best to emerge victorious. Death held no fear for him. Einos pushed self-centered thoughts aside, knowing they would only serve to crimp his will when bodies started to fall. The time had come to think forward, abandoning the mire that had slowed his movements for so long. The approaching enemy presented new, unanticipated challenges.

"Kastus must have dug too deep," he mused to his reflection.

Einos moved to turn away but his reflection caught his attention. Aged. Weathered. He looked, and felt, much older than his years. There'd been a time when ruling Fent was joyous, ripe with challenges and adventures. Studying the lines edging his eyes closer, he feared those moments lost to darkening memories. Young compared to many of his peers, Einos had grown sluggish and weak with the threat of the once dead man.

Compounding his misery was the imminent arrival of Merchant Giles's mercenary force. No doubt they'd come for his head, thinking him sorely protected. He snorted. What surprise lay in wait for them. Leadership taught him one valuable lesson, if nothing else, never underestimate your opponent. Those men barreling toward Gunn were in for a shock once the sun rose.

Einos knew Kastus would never let him live it down if he got hurt. Fighting was a young man's trade, not the ruler of a duchy. Sword sitting on the end of his bed, carefully sheathed just as it had been for too many years, Einos turned from the failings of his reflection. There'd come a time for lament later. For now, the rule of a land was at stake. And more.

He still couldn't come to terms with what Quinlan and the sclarem suggested. The Other Realm! What madness! How anyone could survive the horrors trapped beyond the veil was beyond his ability to comprehend. Why they decided upon this course of action made little sense, despite his acceptance. At this point, he was willing to do whatever it took to defeat Brogon Lord and bring the missing children home.

That battle was out of his control, however. Einos bent his focus on the approaching mercenaries. Come the morning, there would be bloodshed and mayhem. More than enough for any leader. The night, he decided, was not long enough.

THIRTY-NINE
Castle Fent

"It's not much to look at," Jayon said with slumped shoulders. His body ached from his neck to his ankles. Endless days trapped on horseback didn't suit him.

Arella scratched a bug bite on her jaw. She agreed. "They seldom are. It is important to remember that aesthetics don't make a duchy. These people are plagued by a nightmare if Brother Quinlan's report is accurate. We must not frown upon their way of life."

"Yes, ma'am," he said.

Rebuked, he fell silent and rode beside her. The main village of Fent was dominated by Einos's family castle. An ugly building of grey stone rising up into the sky. Countless rows of thatch roofed houses stretched away like fingers, marred only by multi-level structures of wood and stone. Fent was unremarkable. Arella had grown up in a similar village. The idea of returning left an ill taste in her mouth.

They reached the outskirts of Fent and were halted by a half squad of armored soldiers. Her instincts were correct. Much had gone wrong in this duchy for soldiers to patrol their own streets. Arella unlaced her riding cloak, allowing the proud emblem of her Order to show. Quinlan's influence was known, for the soldiers showed little reaction.

"Go and get the sergeant," the head guard ordered before addressing her. "Ma'am, mind if I ask what business you have here? We weren't informed any additional aid was coming from Andrak."

"Brother Quinlan requested my presence. I am here to assist with the F'talle," Arella announced. Guards shuffled, unnerved by the mention.

Swallowing his discomfort, the guard gestured for the barricade to be moved. "Constable Kastus will be pleased to see you. He's up at the castle."

"Where is Brother Quinlan?" she asked. Arella was under the impression he would be there to greet her.

"Gone off with the Baron. They should be coming back in a few days."

A stern looking woman with as much beauty as brawn stormed toward them. Arella was taken aback by the haunting ice colored eyes.

"I am Sergeant Sanice. If it pleases you, I will take you to the Constable."

Left with little alternative, Arella slid from the saddle and gestured for Sanice to lead on. Empty streets greeted her. Arella supposed martial law was in place, a fact confirmed by the wary glint in Sanice's eye.

"What happened here?" Arella asked. A shutter moved, rattling against the cold stone of the second story window.

Sanice stiffened, composing her thoughts. "They say the Grey Wanderer started it. He came around weeks ago, bringing the dead with him. We've been hunting that bastard since but have failed each time. The Baron is off to find the truth of this Brogon Lord. Folks are scared enough, what with the missing children, but now we have a battle on our hands."

Arella ignored the way Sanice glossed over the missing children comment. Of course, this had all been in Quinlan's message. The sole purpose for her arrival was to assist with defeating the F'talle. With Quinlan gone, she failed to understand what battle the people of Fent were expecting. Surely not against the Grey Wanderer. To do so would be death on widespread levels.

"Who are you fighting?" she asked.

Sanice kept walking. They were past the houses and crossing the open training grounds separating the two sides of the village. "Some of the merchants are engaged in a conspiracy to usurp the crown. Baron Einos has entrusted the task of clearing them out to Constable Kastus, and the army. You will be more than appreciated in this endeavor."

She and Jayon exchanged wary looks. They hadn't come to fight a civil action. War priest mandate said they were to disengage from political infighting. Violating the Order's laws was punishable by banishment. She needed to walk carefully, and for good reason. Generations ago, the war priests were embroiled in a civil dispute to the north. The damage done left the Order weakened and distrusted by much of the population. Those with power were often frowned upon, for it was only natural to assume the desire to gather more power was inescapable.

"The war priests do not fight internal battles. We must not be seen to take sides," she said.

If Sanice was bothered by that, she didn't show it. They crossed the street and found Kastus waiting outside with a trio of soldiers. "Constable, this is Sister Arella, from Andrak."

Kastus glanced up, arms folded. He studied the priest, wondering if she was what they needed. "Sister. I was unaware that Quinlan summoned additional help. You are most welcome, regardless. Thank you, Sergeant. If you will gather your squads. I want this done before nightfall."

Sanice saluted and stormed off, giving Arella the distinct impression she was far more dangerous than she let on.

"What is happening here, Constable? I came to fight the F'talle, not an insurrection," Arella said after following Kastus inside.

Empty weapons racks lined the far wall. A table stacked with charts and reports dominated the center of the single room. Faint autumn light poured in through a pair of windows, accented by three oil lamps. Kastus dropped into a rickety chair and offered the other to her. Jayon went back outside to tend to their horses, leaving the pair to discuss matters.

"Where do I begin?" he said with a rueful look. "I assume Quinlan explained our once dead man problem."

"He did," she confirmed. "What he did not tell us was the potential for usurpation. I need a valid reason to get involved. Otherwise, I return to Castle Andrak."

Kastus frowned, though he'd expected such resistance. Quinlan was obstinate at best, giving him no other expectation for other war priests. "It is my belief, as well as that of the Baron's, that this plot is related to the once dead man."

He went on to explain his findings in Palis and the subsequent hunt for Elder Waern. Kastus laid out a plan leading him to the merchants. Giles in particular. "Tender Cannandal's death was too convenient to be coincident."

"You suspect this merchant is in league with the F'talle?" she guessed.

"I do."

His confidence inspired her. Arella shifted, the aged wood uncomfortable. "If what you say is true, that would mean the Omegri have found agents in Fent and are using your duchy to exploit a weakness in the veil."

"Does this mean you will help?" Kastus asked, hopeful he'd said enough to convince her. Having companies of the army at hand was more than enough to suit his needs, but a war priest would end Giles's fight with little bloodshed. Enough citizens had already paid the full price. He didn't want more on his conscience.

Tugging off her riding gloves, Arella extended her hand. "Yes, Constable, I believe your plight is in the best interests of the land. When do we begin?"

Unable to conceal his childish grin, Kastus rose and showed her one of the more detailed charts. "All signs point to Merchant Giles as the epicenter of this mess. We believe he is responsible for turning Waern and the other Elders from Palis, using the pretense of extra payment for services. I doubt any of the three understood the full implications against them."

"The Other Realm constantly seeks ways into our world. That Fent should fall victim is not significant," Arella said.

"Giles is in league with the Omegri, which leads me back to the once dead man and the missing children," Kastus continued. "If we stop Giles, we cut off the Other Realm's hold on this land and end all of our problems."

"You are positive he is the one?" she asked.

At this, Kastus paused. "Actually, no. There are a handful of large merchants in Fent. Any of them could be guilty. If I were a gambler, I would place my coin on Giles. He is the most powerful and influential merchant in the surrounding duchies. Even if he isn't the one, his capture will be the spark needed."

That was enough for her. Arella rose and donned her fighting gloves. "When do we begin?"

Kastus blinked twice. "Now."

The armored column marched down the empty street. Swords were bare. Spears sharp. Kastus and Arella walked at their front. One resplendent in Fent's colors. The other authoritative in the pale blue of the war priests. Where she strode, fear spread. Unopposed, the company speared toward Giles's main warehouse complex. They were given explicit instructions. Giles was to remain unharmed. Everyone else foolish enough to get in their way was expendable.

Waern watched them come, fear building in his old heart. Death was all he saw. "Damn you, Giles! You told me I was safe."

Head down, hair dangling over a cup of liquor, Giles snorted his reply. He'd had enough of Waern's endless whining, regretting the decision to bring him in. Giles threw back another drink. Flashes of

Cannandal, murdered by his deeds, taunted him. Right now, he regretted everything. If only he had been strong enough to fend off the Omegri, none of this would be happening. If only.

"Shut your face, old man," he growled. "I've enough troubles without you getting underfoot."

Waern, nonplussed, wheeled on his benefactor with a crooked finger. "Get us out of this mess! We can't fight the entire army."

"Who said I was dumb enough to try?"

"What?" Waern asked, his eyes crossing briefly.

"Think. Kastus has hundreds of soldiers in the village right now," Giles explained. "What good would it do me to send my guards out?"

"What are you going to do?" Waern asked.

Giles drained his cup and cast a feral grin. "Offer them a sacrifice."

The elder paled as realization dawned. His hands, cramped and liver spotted, trembled. "You can't! This was all your doing. I would not be here if not for you."

"I can and I will. You are nothing. It would serve you well to remember that."

Darkness flashed and in that moment Giles became dangerous. Days of faceless whispers twisted his mind. Pushed to the breaking point, Giles felt stretched. Thin. Pain had become a constant reminder of his weakness. He'd given in to fell powers and now suffered without end. Each day the noose drew tighter. Kastus was coming to pinch him. Of that, there was no doubt. The end of his nightmare fast approaching. He was almost relieved.

Waern forced him to think otherwise. The man had become a liability. No doubt he would sell Giles out to save his own neck. Giles wanted to laugh. If the old man thought he was going to sell him out, he was about to discover differently. Giles had built a small empire across the southern duchies, amassing wealth and power a small village elder couldn't dream of. People of authority owed him many favors, Einos included. Mind settled, there was naught to do but act.

"Lads," he growled. "Grab our esteemed elder. He's got a destiny to fulfill."

Waern struggled as rough hands clamped onto his arms. They squeezed and bruised. "Stop this at once, Giles. This is madness! We are partners."

Giles crossed the room in the blink of an eye, dagger pointing at Waern's heart. His hand trembled as the rage threatened to take over.

"We were never partners. Understand that. This is my world. My time. After today, no one will remember your name. Get him out of here. Our esteemed Constable will enjoy his gift."

"You can't do this! I am a …"

"You are a nobody. Your time is over, old man. Gag him if you have but do not harm him. I want him to enjoy every delicious moment of suffering he has coming," Giles ordered.

FORTY

The Other Realm

Pain, but not. An odd crawling sensation danced across his flesh, irritating him with a flash of fire that quickly cooled. Quinlan emerged from the haze and slumped to his knees. Strength had left him. He felt sluggish, unable to respond. The weight of his bones threatened to drag him down into the ash and leave him. A forgotten reminder of what should not be done. Dust poured from his mouth when he tried to speak. The urge to collapse, to succumb, strengthened.

A steadying hand on his shoulder helped shrug off the effects of the transition. Quinlan wiped the grey crud from the corners of his eyes and looked at the long, green fingers on his shoulder. Creased with countless lines, each ended in a gnarled nail, broken and covered in grime. Whatever else, Dalem had lived a long, hard life.

"Donal?" Quinlan asked as his wits recovered.

"Here," came Donal's reply from behind.

Quinlan found his novice doubled over, hands on his knees. A pool of liquid was absorbing into the ash and dirt. The sclarem crossed the distance and performed the same on Donal. Soon, both war priests were able to stand without their vision swimming. Strength returned. It was then Quinlan looked at the desolate surroundings. A colorless world of gentle slopes and vast plains stretched out in every direction. There was no sun, only a haunting glow in shades of grey.

"How can life be sustained in such a place?" he asked.

Dalem used his staff to support his weight as he hobbled over. "This realm is ancient, older than our own. Legend says it was not always so. Perhaps it was once as verdant as ours. I do not know."

"The Omegri did this?" Quinlan asked. "How?"

"Much is unknown about their origin, though they are the harbingers of doom. An evil as old and ancient as the Purifying Flame," Dalem explained. "One cannot exist without the other. Nor should one be more powerful than the other. They must strike a balance if any of the realms are to find harmony."

Donal wiped the bile from his lips. "Will they do this to our realm?"

"Assuredly."

The single word answer chilled him. Donal struggled with the urge to return to Fent, to a world that made sense. A quick glance over his shoulder told him such was impossible. The way was shut. They were trapped with but one way forward.

"How long can we stay here before we become trapped?" Quinlan asked after catching Donal's despair.

Dalem twisted his lower jaw. Elongated tusks rubbed against his lips. "Provided we can find the way home? Not long. We must find the F'talle and end this."

"I hope you have an idea where to begin?" Quinlan stared at the expanse of nothingness, unable to comprehend what he saw.

Dalem answered by walking. His wide feet easily traversed the loose ash, kicking up small dust clouds with each step. Quinlan got the impression the sclarem was at ease here, almost as if he had been here before. Was there possibility for betrayal? The prospect frightened him, for he had already been found wanting against Lord.

He looked at the black of his clothing and armor, grateful for leaving his traditional priest armor behind. The less attention he drew, the better. Quinlan had spent years defending the world from the Omegri and here he was, trapped in their realm without any way home. The Order was hard pressed to fend them off in Castle Andrak. Fighting the Omegri in this realm wasn't his first option.

How long they walked, he didn't know. Time seemed to lack meaning. The Other Realm was an abyss, void of all life. It didn't take much imagination to see why the Omegri wanted out. Wanted another realm to conquer. A war was coming. Quinlan forced those thoughts aside and bent his focus toward finding Brogon Lord, and Lizette.

The march continued.

Every time she glanced up brought the completion of the great clock tower nearer. Both hands were now fixed. Numbers were placed. Construction on the exterior was all but complete, leaving only the internal mechanism to start the clock. Time was almost up and she was no closer to stopping Brogon's masters. Desperation crept into her thoughts. Lizette had failed to find a way to turn the once dead man and save the children. Once the clock was finished, so too, was her time in this realm.

The promise of a quick death awaited. She and all the children, whom she tried so hard to protect, were trapped for the rest of their days, however short they may be. For she could not find a way that any of them would be allowed to live. The masters, in all their wicked glory, were seductive and invective in their treatment. What their final goal was remained a mystery, though she began to suspect something far more nefarious than what they explained.

Lizette tore her gaze from the tower, knowing it held her doom. That desperation spurred her to move faster. She knew Brogon clung to a measure of humanity. That his fight against the masters wasn't finished. Appealing to that hidden wellspring was another matter. Her efforts ended in failure, but she was determined to continue trying. Something had to work. Otherwise…

She found him along the rise to the east. It was a familiar place he returned to, as if it reminded him of warmer times. The gloom of the Other Realm permeated everything, robbing her of heat necessary to thrive. Lizette knew none of that mattered to the once dead man. He was a creature of death. An impossibility of nature. She needed to remind him of who he had been.

"You waste your time," he said without looking at her.

Lizette forced a smile, tight lipped and fleeting. "I do not believe so. We are both trapped, Brogon." He flinched at his name. "I know there is good in you. Buried perhaps, but enough to know that this is wrong."

"Right or wrong. These words mean nothing here. You are all going to die."

"Not if you help us," she replied in a pleading tone.

He turned. Parts of his cheekbone were visible through his face. "I do what the masters command. My life is forfeit."

She reached out, touching his forearm. "You were a man once. You had a family. Honor. How much is it going to take to get you to remember?"

"You do not understand. I remember everything," he said.

She recoiled, witnessing the abject depression in his eyes. *How could I have been so wrong? This man's pain isn't from being resurrected. It's that he isn't allowed to forget!* The realization left her stunned. Brogon Lord. The terror of Fent. His mind locked in a decomposing corpse, forced to perform reprehensible tasks in the name of evil. She knew what to do at last.

"The tower is almost complete. It is time to summon the Omegri. The conquest of the living world must begin."

Dust flaked from her desiccated flesh, she stared up at the clock face and wondered if their scheme was going to work. The Omegri were unforgiving. "Have we enough souls to power the machine?"

The third added, "With the addition of the woman, yes. Many of the children perished during the labor. Her unexpected arrival should prove beneficial."

"Good. The moment the tower is complete, I want all prisoners taken to the sacrificial chamber. The Omegri must return. The hour of their reign is upon us."

Subtle winds blew a dusting of ash across their robes. Hammers continued pounding up and down the tower. Less than before, for the work was almost finished. She had accomplished her task. The future no longer held promise of suffering. She, along with her two companions, would be allowed to return to nothing. No more toil. No languishing between realms. Soon oblivion would claim them all.

"We are close. Do you smell that?" Dalem declared after the trio crested a small rise.

They'd marched until they were sore. Blisters formed in their boots. Ash coated them. The Other Realm was one of desolation. Quinlan felt weaker, as if his connection with the Purifying Flame was strained, diluted.

"Coming here was wrong," he told Donal. "We do not have our full power."

"Inconsequential. There is power here. Latent. Waiting for the right ones to use it. The Omegri are powerful but lack control. Given to indulgences and whim." Dalem interrupted.

"You are certain you can access this power?" Quinlan asked.

The sclarem chuckled and kept walking. Quinlan was left with mixed emotions. This was not the time for withholding. Not in the face of their greatest enemy. He toyed with the idea of stopping Dalem and demanding answers. Doing so would not prove conducive to their quest. Instead, Quinlan turned his focus toward finding Lizette and killing the F'talle. All else was secondary.

Slowly, a shape emerged from the grey mist. A tower. Glowing at the top with strained light, as if sickened. Quinlan resisted the urge to take up his sword. They were still too far away, though his instincts screamed that this was the epicenter of their destination. Mind racing through possibilities, the war priest pressed on.

"What is that?" Donal whispered. Since entering the Other Realm, he'd grown convinced they were being watched, followed.

Dalem remained quiet, for he too lacked knowledge. At least until they were close enough to witness the monstrosity rising over a hundred feet. The lines were twisted, uneven. Walkways and scaffoldings dominated the lower reaches. Numerous torches could be seen, their light haunting in the quasi-light.

"A clock," Quinlan said in shock. "Dalem, have you any idea what it is for?"

"Perhaps," was all the sclarem said.

He crouched, setting his weight on the balls of his feet. Orange flecked eyes took in the sight before them. His neck muscles bulged as he began to understand what he was seeing.

Quinlan crouched beside him, poorly concealed behind a pair of dead bushes. "You know something."

The sclarem was slow to answer. "There is a legend. A tale. The Omegri constantly seek ways into our world but can only do so for one hundred days each year. What then do they do in the remainder? An old dream suggested that if they could stop time, they would be able to conduct a relentless assault on us."

"That would be the end of the world," Donal uttered. His eyes widened as the clock face shifted into view.

Quinlan ignored the dread building in his stomach. "We must hurry."

Donal stared at the monstrosity looming over them. Squinting, he could barely make out tiny figures climbing up and down. The children! Any shock he might have felt was nulled by the sensory overload they'd experienced since arriving. It wasn't until he tracked two adult figures atop the edge of a small rise that his excitement overtook him and he grabbed Quinlan's arm.

"Brother Quinlan, look! To the left of the tower," he exclaimed.

"Lizette," Quinlan said, following the pointing finger. She appeared unharmed, and she was with the F'talle. "Dalem, can we get down there unseen?"

"Perhaps. I believe there is nothing but to try," the sclarem said with a nod.

The trio crossed the final stretch of the Other Realm separating them from completing their mission. Each was filled with doubts and fears. Private matters that couldn't be shared lest they be strengthened beyond imagination. Bad things lurked in unseen places. Quinlan summoned his training to maintain control. The hope of defeating the F'talle and stopping the Omegri rested on his shoulders. His following actions. Countless lives in the balance and they knew it not. Strained under the pressure, Quinlan kept moving.

All they had to do was reach Lizette.

FORTY-ONE

The Other Realm

"The tower is finished. We can charge the machine now."

The words tugged at what little humanity Brogon Lord clung to. He regarded the three shadowy figures with disdain, for they were the antithesis of all he once stood for, or so Lizette had convinced him. The masters, he concluded, were wicked beings best forgotten by creation.

Their leader beckoned him with crooked finger. "Go. Bring me the children. The time has come."

"What of the woman?" he asked.

The master grinned, wicked and cunning. "Kill her and bring the corpse to me. I wish to wear her as a trophy. Now go."

Brogon obeyed, for he had no choice. The children. He was already responsible for their abductions, now he would be their executioner. How low he had fallen. The shame heaped upon his name would last generations. The F'talle stomped off. Each step leaden, almost reluctant.

"Go with him. There can be no error in this," he heard from behind.

So, it was to be a watchdog. Brogon ignored the wisp of rustled clothing as the second monster caught up with him. His every action would be monitored, for his masters bore little trust. This, he decided, complicated matters.

"Quiet, children. This will all pass soon enough."

The words, spoken with sincerity, felt hollow even as she said them. Lizette took in the small, round faces covered in grime and fear and felt her heart melt. Any of them could have been her Tabith. But no. Her daughter was gone. The children amassed before her served as painful reminders of the fact. All looked to her for salvation. A forlorn dream of better times. She wished she could have done more, but that was not hers to decide.

Lizette looked to Quinlan, silently begging him to intervene. To tell the children she was truthful. The war priest remained stoic. Taciturn. He'd barely spoken since finding her. Nor had Donal or the sclarem. Once a plan was developed, the three scurried into hidden corners to await the proper time. She still wasn't clear on what they intended, or how they planned on making it happen. Only that they were reluctantly confident of success. It was more than she'd had since arriving here.

"Will this work?" she knew better than to ask. Quinlan had never been free with information. The war priest kept his own counsel while serving the Baron. Expecting him to do otherwise now was foolish at best. "Quinlan, answer me. Please."

Sword bare, the war priest cocked his head and blew out the breath he'd been holding. "I do not know, but we must try."

"There is no other way," Dalem added. "Can we trust this F'talle? He has tried to kill each of us, in his own right. I should not like to find betrayal in the Other Realm."

She shrugged. "What else is there in this wretched place? No one living should ever come here. We must be away, and soon, for I fear the masters are ready to enact their plan."

Approaching footsteps drew their attention. Quinlan placed a gloved finger to his lips and gestured for silence. It was time. The door to the massive hall opened with a groan. Haunting light flooded in, abolishing the darkness. Tiny faces blinked and covered their eyes as a desiccated figure filled the opening. Shadows swirled on his right.

"Come children. The masters have need of you," Brogon Lord announced. "We must all go into the tower."

No one moved. He turned to Lizette, imploring her to help. She swallowed her rising fear. "Do as he says. It will be all right."

Dissatisfied with the pace, the master puffed out his robes, increasing to twice his normal size. "Now! Move before it is too late! All of you. The last one to the tower with die a miserable death."

Brogon stood aside as Lizette led the children out. The master, ignorant of all else, watched with greed. The desire to kill strengthened. Perhaps a child or two would not be missed. He swept across the floor, inching closer to the shadows. A mistake. Brogon slammed the door shut behind the last child just as Quinlan and the others emerged from hiding.

"The time for reckoning has arrived," Dalem announced.

The master recoiled, for it had been long since he last laid eyes on his ancient nemesis. "Your kind is extinct!"

Dalem responded with a bolt of bright orange energy from his staff. The robed figure cringed, rocking back as he was engulfed. Flames swept upward, spreading across the ceiling as the sclarem's full fury was diverted away. A scream erupted from the burning figure and the flames were extinguished. Weakened by the unexpected assault, he dropped to a knee. Shadows swirled around him, drawing across his flesh in preparation of attack.

Quinlan and Donal burst into action. The war priest crossed the space of the floor in three steps and brought his blade down on the back of the robed figure's neck. Steel bit deep, sweeping through bone and fabric. Droplets of black ichor splashed across the ash strewn floorboards. The withered head followed, bouncing to a stop at Donal's feet. The novice scowled with disgust and kicked the head away. Puffs of ash and dust kicked up with each roll.

Head cocked, Dalem bent down to retrieve the head.

"What was that thing?" Quinlan asked.

"A monster," Brogon Lord answered.

Quinlan spun, sword steady before him. Though an accord had been reached, solely at Lizette's behest after she pleaded her cause, the war priest remained cautious toward the F'talle. Nothing was as it appeared in the Other Realm and he wasn't willing to risk having his throat slit from behind.

Dalem placed both palms on the top of his staff and rested his elongated jaw on them. "The F'talle speaks true. This was a demon of the old world. Once, long ago, our two races fought a war of genocide. Those few who remained were banished here, while my kind was destined to roam the world as nomads. How many more are there?"

Brogon met the sclarem's glare with determination. He knew they were destined to battle one another when this ended and if Dalem was true to his word, Brogon would at last find solace. It was a dream. "Two. This was the weakest, I believe."

"The others will not be taken unawares," Quinlan surmised. "And they will come looking for this one when he doesn't show up."

"Our moment of opportunity shrinks," Dalem agreed.

Knowing what must be done, Quinlan walked up to Donal and placed a hand on his shoulder. "Donal, it is time. You must escort Lizette and children home while we finish the task."

Donal bowed, though he was reluctant to leave his master's side. The argument was hard fought and he lost. The world of life was more important than either of their lives. "I will do what I can, Brother."

Protecting the children shouldn't prove an issue, though finding a way back to their realm was another matter. Brogon promised them a way home, for the F'talle was versed in the secrets of passage. Despite that, trust was limited. Neither man was willing to place their lives in his hands, lest he betray them. Neither man had a choice. Even should they destroy the three creatures in control, there was no other way to return home. Brogon Lord had become indispensable.

"See that no harm befalls him," Quinlan demanded of Brogon.

"I will do so," the once dead man confirmed.

Quinlan's stomach rebelled at the sight of Brogon's missing eye. It was an unnatural thing, this living dead man. "Do so and your reward shall be delivered."

Brogon followed Donal out the same door Lizette used. They found her and the children waiting under the cover of a ramshackle building about to collapse. Quinlan watched through the cracked door until the last of them were out of sight. He'd done all he could. Their paths split, Quinlan turned his attention to his own task.

"Do you have the power to defeat both of them?" he asked.

Dalem blinked several times, as if contemplating his answer. That alone was uninspiring. "Perhaps, though I will need your assistance, war priest."

"I cannot feel the connection with the Flame," Quinlan admitted. It was as he feared. Since arriving in the Other Realm, he was cutoff from the strength of the Purifying Flame, forced to rely on his wits and skills with a sword. Fortunately, Master Sergeant Cron was one of the premier swordmasters in the world.

"It is there. Buried. Hidden in the face of this nightmare. Summon it when you need it most and the heart of the Flame will spring forth," Dalem replied. "We have waited long enough. Let us find our hosts and make our presence known."

Quinlan tightened his grip on his sword and slinked outside.

The area was quiet. No guards patrolled. No watchers ensured compliance with the labor force. It reminded Quinlan of those quiet moments when one begins to die. Serenity, if not for the abhorrent nature of the realm. He wasn't sure what to expect, thus was not disappointed. The Omegri were an unseen presence, looming, yet just out of reach. He aimed to keep it that way, for there was no way he could hope to defeat them here.

Dalem appeared unconcerned. The sclarem moved with assurance and purpose, as if he had been born for this event. Whatever dark past Dalem endured was private. Quinlan didn't bother asking. Each bore their guilt and pain. They crossed the rows of buildings used to house the children and came upon an open area leading up to the base of the clocktower. Quinlan still had no idea what purpose the tower served, only that it meant doom for untold millions.

Inside, he expected to find the other two creatures. It was too late to ask Dalem what they were and Brogon's assignation of masters felt wrong on his tongue. Whatever they were, the war priest knew them as abominations. The F'talle's warning of them stopping time and ending creation was dire and spurred Quinlan's actions. He prayed to the Flame for strength and guidance. Only his grasp of undying devotion might sustain him against the dark machinations of the Omegri.

"We cannot enter through the front. Surely they will expect an attack," Quinlan whispered.

Dalem kept moving. His footsteps so soft, they produced no sound. "Surprise is yet ours. We must move faster if there is hope of catching them unawares. They will not ignore their missing companion for long."

Quinlan remained unconvinced but failed to arrive at a different conclusion. They crossed the open ground in a matter of heartbeats. Still there was no sign of their enemy. Nerves played on his mind, tickling his innermost thoughts with dark temptations. Lifetimes were born and ended in the blink of an eye. Strength threatened to abandon him. Shaking his head, Quinlan forced one foot in front of the other until they crept along either side of the massive entryway.

Small skulls edged the opening, mouths agape with eternal torment. Quinlan saw rows of bones rising on either side. A macabre demonstration of the unholy. It sickened him. Chanting rose from the darkness. The ground vibrated as words of power laced the air.

"It has begun," he hissed.

Dalem raised his staff, green light glowing with power, and slipped inside. The war priest cursed and followed. Whatever destiny awaited, Quinlan was going to find it in the bowels of the monstrous clocktower. Here, at the border between realms, all things began and ended. The tunnel slopped down at awkward angles. A haunting glow bathed the lower reaches, beckoning him. This was the place where he claimed his fate.

His breath came in ragged gasps. His muscles threatened to abandon him. Only the gentle slapping of his boots on wood accompanied the pounding in his head. Quinlan had known fear before, though never on levels this severe. His mind screamed to turn back. To escape the nightmares stewing in the deep. It took every measure of will to keep going. Quinlan caught up with the sclarem, who appeared oddly unaffected. Then he heard it.

"Bring the children. The slaughter must begin!"

Time was up.

FORTY-TWO

Gunn

"You figured right, Captain," Sergeant Sava said, as he slumped down against the stone wall.

Two squads of house guards flanked them. Sava considered them briefly, for they'd come to be fair travel companions. Not to mention they bulked the meager ten soldier force up to nearly thrice its size. *Nothing like strength in numbers*. Being undermanned left a sour feeling in his stomach, but there was nothing for it. He was forced to make due with what he had. His one hope was that the castle boys lived up to their reputation. Otherwise it was going to be a short lived fight.

Thep glanced down at the five sword belts Sava dropped beside him. Wet blood spattered several. "How long?"

"Maybe an hour. Not much longer," Sava said after inserting a pinch of kaappa leaves in his cheek. "They're coming right down the main road. I counted at least fifty. Well, forty-five."

Satisfied, Thep said, "Get some rest, Sergeant. I'm going to need you."

Sava spat. "I'll be fine, sir. Besides, who else is going to make sure you don't do anything foolish?"

"Let's finish this," Thep was emboldened. People like Sava were the guts on which the army thrived.

Time passed and the sun rose over the horizon. The chill of night was lifting, though not by much, as winter was edging closer. Thep yawned. His eyes were sore from lack of sleep. He felt old. A common theme among the others. Campaigns were brutal on both mind and body. Thep was amazed that people like Sava etched out a career in the army, for this was not the life he wanted to lead. It was all he could do to focus.

Sava ignored his commander's influences. This was his world. A lifetime spent with sword in hand. There was little point in worrying over matters outside of his control. Satisfied that he'd done what he could, Sava moved down to his soldiers. The castle boys had their own chain of command, though they'd been augmented to Thep's command.

The enemy arrived before he finished. Waves of horsemen charged into Gunn with impunity, neither expecting a defensive force, nor a pitched battle. They got both. Arrows struck their boiled leather armor. Some penetrated flesh, both horse and rider. Man and beast collapsed in screams. Dust kicked up, choking the air.

"Now, you bastards! Block the road before they figure out what's happening," Sava barked.

Nils and Alfar lit torches and threw them over the wall. Flames spread across the road as the shallow line filled with pitch caught fire. The inferno forced the bandits deeper into Gunn. As Sava planned. A quick look confirmed a second wall of fire was burning on the far end of the street. "Time for part two. Spears!"

The men and women under his command obeyed instantly. The castle boys were slower and over ten bandits escaped the trap. Growling his contempt, Sava snatched his own weapon from the ground and moved to the center of the line. The bandits slashed at the longer weapons, but the combination of confusion and fear rising from the horses left them at a disadvantage. The bandits were forced back, taking wounds when soldiers found opportunity.

A handful of bodies fell from their saddles. Some were old men, others boys. All had come with the promise of gold. Sava didn't blame them, nor could he justify given them quarter. They'd come to kill the Baron. Treason. He aimed to put every last one in the ground. Anger blazing as hot as the fire, Sava broke ranks and charged into the bandits.

Three converged on him, encircling him as the greater mass of riders fell back. Sava stabbed with all his strength and was rewarded with his spear plunging deep into the first man's exposed belly from the side. Blood and gore splashed as the spearpoint ripped free. A horse whinnied. Men shouted. Sava was blinded. A jerk on the spear told him the weapon was gone. He let go of the blood slickened shaft and drew his sword.

Sava swiped, cutting a gash across the nearest thigh. Steam drifted from the wound as hot blood spread. Engrossed in his actions, Sava failed to see the bandit behind him. The veteran growled in rage and pain, a throaty combination more feral than human, as the sword point drove through his shoulder armor and into his flesh.

"Sergeant Sava!"

The words, though shouted, came in a daze as his pain level intensified. Vision darkening, Sava let the force of impact propel him forward, oblivious to the pair of soldiers rushing the third bandit from both sides. A wild spear thrust took the bandit low in the throat, pitching him from the saddle. The sword blow to his unprotected heart killed him. Horses scattered and Sava was pulled back to safety.

Sword removed in the road, he slumped down behind the stone wall and in protest, allowed his men to treat his wound. "Damned fools! You could have been killed."

Alfar grinned, as if being scolded by a brother. "We wasn't going to let you die."

Nils, a half step behind and panting, agreed. "He's right. You're the best of us, Sergeant."

"Ahh!" Sava roared as Alfar pushed a wad of gauze into the entry wound. "Careful, you, or I'll have you flogged. You don't leave your men. Ever. Understand?"

Neither man bothered pointing out the obvious. Each took his tirade in stride, knowing that they'd saved the man responsible for molding them into the soldiers they were. Alfar finished dressing the wound, covering it in a wide bandage, and the two went back to the fight. Bandits, and one soldier, lay dead in the road. Horses roamed lost. The stench of blood and iron choked the air.

Sava popped his head up to survey the scene. The battle had moved on, between houses and heading for the far side of Gunn. *Exactly where the Baron and those castle boys are. We might make it out of this after all.* Sava's gaze went to Nils and Alfar, proud to see them getting fresh weapons for the next part of the plan. They were among the best he had. A fact he would never admit aloud. Grunting from the effort of getting back on his feet, Sava refused to give in to the pain. There'd be time enough for that later.

"Let's go, people! We've got a battle to win," he growled and led them on the hunt.

Thep drew back and took aim. The bandit leader was twenty meters away and riding as hard as he could. Confirmation that Sava's delaying action had worked. Castle guards crouched on either flank, each with short throwing spears. Thep prayed they stood in the line of fire, else his plan ended in failure and everyone died. Ten meters.

He inhaled a deep breath, exhaling slowly. His fingers slipped from the string. The arrow flew. Wood whistled. The bandit pitched back as the arrow took him in the lower chest. His armor protected him, to an extent, but the impact was enough to drive him to the ground. Unaware of what was happening, the others continued riding for the Baron's location. They trampled the lead rider.

"Now," Thep whistled.

As one, the castle guards of Fent rose, took aim, and let loose their spears. Horse and rider were slaughtered.

"Advance!" Thep roared above the din.

The guards leapt the wall and quickly formed ranks. Thep took his place in the center and they advanced on the enemy. His heart pounded. The sound like thunder in his ears. He'd never been in close combat this intense and thought of dying crept in. Knowing such was a death sentence for soldiers, Thep forced the thoughts aside and doubled the grip on his spear. They made contact moments later.

Blocked on either side by buildings, the bandits were unable to recover and spin around. Those at the front saw the approaching threat but couldn't react in time, for those at the rear continued to push forward — unaware of what was happening. The result was violence on an unprecedented scale. Blood spilled in waves. Men died screaming. Arms were hacked off. Legs pierced through.

Thep stabbed for all he was worth. His steel bit deep on several bandits. Others fended him off, only to be caught by another. Chaos ruled the streets of Gunn. Chaos that worsened when Sava and his soldiers closed the exit. Faith renewed, Thep ordered his guards to continue the attack.

Baron Einos stood on the second story balcony of his in-law's home. He was alone and watching the battle unfold. That he'd been prevented from participating, and for good reason, sat ill with him. Leaders were meant to be at the front of every action, not skulking far from danger while others fought and died in his name. It was a grave insult.

The footsteps coming up the stairs behind him were distinct enough to prompt a cringe. Einos stiffened as the door opened and he was no longer alone.

"You shouldn't have brought this to our doorstep."

Einos was thankful his father in law was unable to see the wince he couldn't conceal. "You say that as if I had a choice."

"All men have choices. Especially ones in charge of their own duchies," Hintul snorted.

"This is not the time," Einos warned. "My people are dying. Good men and women whose only crime is their loyalty to the duchy. Do not begrudge them that."

"I've lived longer than you. Enough to know the truth of men. Greed is a powerful tool when weaponized," his father in law replied.

"Gunn doesn't need this foolishness. You should leave as soon as you can."

"I rule this village, Hintul," Einos reminded. His tone was gentle yet growing sterner as the conversation progressed.

The sounds of battle dulled and faded altogether.

Hintul rapped his knuckles on the banister. "Do you?"

"Considering your involvement with the Lord family's fall from power. If I were not married to your daughter, I'd have you all exiled," Einos gave in to his anger. "Mind your tongue when you speak with me from here on. I am a forgiving man, but to an extent only."

The threat robbed most of the ferocity Hintul exhibited. "My daughter …"

"Will know nothing of this. Leastwise not from me," Einos assured. That his wife's family played a role in the downfall of a rival family of power, forcing Brogon out into the life as a sell sword, sickened him. The thought that had they not gotten involved, for the unspoken promise of power, might have changed the fate of all Fent was almost too much to bear. Fortunately, he wasn't given opportunity to stew over it.

"Excuse me, I go to meet with my Captain," Einos brushed past a stunned Hintul. There were more pressing matters at hand.

He spied Loreli standing off by the kitchens, pretending not to notice or care. Einos knew better. She was one of the sharpest people he'd met. Family matters aside, the Baron of Fent strode outside where he received Thep's salute and report.

"It's over, Baron," the blood-stained soldier said. "The bandits have been routed. A handful escaped, but the majority are dead or wounded. Gunn is secure."

"Very good, Thep. Very good, indeed. Are any available for questioning?" He desperately wanted to know the truth. That the Merchant Giles was responsible for the uprising and that it was all connected with Brogon Lord rising from the grave. Nothing else was satisfying.

"One or two. Most of the wounded are a bit … disgruntled by recent events," Thep said with a grin. "We have them rounded up and detained away from the others."

Einos clapped him on the shoulder. "Well done. Take me to them. I will question them myself."

"Yes, Baron," Thep said with a bow.

It was all Einos could do to maintain dignity as he stormed across the ruined street.

FORTY-THREE
Castle Fent

"Wait. No one move!" Kastus called as he held up his right hand.

He watched as Waern wobbled into the street. Whatever had befallen the Elder was unexpected, perhaps worse. Two ruffians prodded him on, only backing away when they were sure Waern was in the middle of the street. Wary looks, prompted by eyes flitting from side to side, took in the scene. Kastus spied the hopelessness in them. The advantage was his.

Arella, the war priest, was unconvinced. "You suspect a trap?"

"After all we've been through? Anything is possible," he confirmed.

"Let me go in. None can withstand the power of the Purifying Flame," she said. Her demeanor was stern, overbearing.

Kastus wondered where the Order found their recruits. He was impressed with Quinlan, and now Arella, but neither were the sort he wanted to share a mug of ale and conversation with. People like that didn't belong in Fent, and he hoped to never see another once this affair ended.

"This does not feel right," he reiterated.

Those suspicions were confirmed a heartbeat later when three arrows were fired down from nearby second story windows. All three struck Waern in the back. The old man cried out and fell to the ground. Dead before he hit.

"Back! Get out of range!" Kastus shouted.

Soldiers hurried to escape the potential slaughter from unseen enemies. Frustrated, Kastus scanned rooftops and windows for potential hiding spots. No further arrows were fired. No signs of Giles's men preparing to attack.

Arella was at his side, sword drawn and cloak cast aside. "They will not come out in the face of this force. Perhaps it is best to burn them out."

"And risk burning half the village?" Kastus exclaimed. "There must be a better way."

"There is. Let my novice and I do what we came here to do," Arella insisted. "We are warriors. The best in the land."

"If I do that, and he escapes, I risk turning the entire village into a combat zone. Every civilian will be in jeopardy," he told her, reasoning through his thought process as he did.

"An acceptable risk provided all works out in our favor. Constable, we are wasting time."

Kastus decided he did not like the war priests, necessary as they may be. Not only was Arella unexpected, she was forcing an issue that might result in countless innocent deaths. It was his worst nightmare. "No, there is a better way. Let me do this my way. If that fails, burn the place to the ground."

She stepped back and sheathed her sword without comment.

One battle won. Emboldened, Kastus puffed out three quick breaths and took charge. "I want that building surrounded. Bring up the ram. Shields for everyone getting close. I don't want any undue risks. Our primary objective is to capture Merchant Giles and subdue his men. The less violence, the better. These are still citizens of Fent."

Sergeant Sanice left him to relay the orders. Her place, as assigned by Captain Thep, was at Kastus's side, no matter how much he protested otherwise. Not that Kastus took solace in such, for she was every bit as hostile as the war priest. Soon after, he was ready to enact the second part of his plan.

She returned almost too easily. Despite his misgivings, Kastus took comfort in her presence. "Ready?"

"Enough. We must strike now," she said.

He clenched a fist and stormed into the middle of the street. "Merchant Giles! This is Constable Kastus. Under the Baron's authority, I am placing you under arrest for treason against Fent and the suspected murder of Tender Cannandal. Throw down your arms and come outside. This is your one opportunity."

Silence replied in mocking severity. A pair of black winged pigeons burst from their perch to his right, startling him. Kastus frowned despite predicting this outcome. He had nominal command of half the army and all his police forces, to include a war priest, and his presence of force wasn't enough to inspire dread in the accused.

"Giles!" he bellowed.

A shutter cracked open. Gloved hands shoved a bucket out and dumped the contents in the street. A chamber pot. Kastus had his answer. Infuriated, the Constable turned back to his force. Choice was gone. Giles dared him with the insult, forcing him into a corner.

"Break the doors down!" he shouted.

Men and women rushed to the building. Flanking ranks of shield bearers protected them from arrow fire. Kastus flinched at the sound of the wooden ram striking the door repeatedly. Each impact fractured and splintered the old pine until the door burst inward. More liquid poured from the second story windows, drenching some of his men. Kastus and the others watched in horror as a flaming brand was cast down and those covered in liquid caught alight.

"Inside, now! Kill the bastards," growled a female voice to his right.

In shock, Kastus watched as Sergeant Sanice drew her short sword and led the follow up element to clear the building. Butchers work. Soldiers roared. Some in rage. Others in fury. The sprint across the street went unmolested and he soon lost sight of her. Mere moments had passed from the dropping torch to her assault. A heartbeat, possibly two. Kastus hadn't moved.

A gentle hand grabbed his forearm. "Constable, order your people to help those on fire. There is yet time."

Arella was right. Good citizens of Fent were dying, roasting to char while he stood mouth agape. Embarrassed, Kastus did as instructed. Four men and two women died from their wounds. Several more would be horribly scarred for the rest of their lives, painful reminders of the lure of greed and the consequences of treason. His heart wept, for he knew a handful would not survive the night. Their burns were grievous. Heart heavy, he hardly heard the furious sounds of combat coming from the warehouse.

A rage came upon him. Alien. Unfamiliar as it insinuated through his veins. He stormed to where Waern lay and began kicking the corpse. Bones crunched with a sickening sound. Kastus screamed, a pitiless cry lost among the men and women being extinguished nearby. Weeks of pent up frustration burst free. Each kick moved the body. He only stopped when Jayon pulled him away.

Madness turned his visage into blind hatred. Kastus jerked free. "Leave me alone! I want that man dead."

"Constable, this outburst is pointless. Others are looking to you for guidance," Arella said, after slipping beside him. "You must show composure and strength."

He clenched his fists. "Not now. I've had enough of playing the good guy. It is time to make our enemies pay."

Arella addressed her novice. "Do not let him enter that building. Detain him by force, if necessary."

"Yes, Sister Arella," Jayon said with a bow. The shriek of steel being drawn echoed across the street.

Satisfied she'd done what she could to keep Kastus from succumbing to a creature less than what he hoped to be, Arella collected ten of the nearest soldiers and led them around to the rear of the building. They skirted past the charcoaled bodies, the smell of burnt flesh rancid. Most of the flames were extinguished, though a small part of the building was starting to burn. If they didn't stop it in time, there was the potential of losing half of the village.

Such concerns weren't her issue, so she kept moving. Others were taking care of the flames. As was proper, all things considered. Finding the merchant and ending his collusion with the Omegri was paramount. All else was relegated to secondary interests. Arella moved with grace and confidence in her pale blue armor, replete with a silver cross emblazoned in the middle. She'd decided against her helmet. Urban warfare was unlike combat on the open plain. She couldn't risk having her vision impaired.

"We breach here," she said after leading them to a seemingly ignored side door. Her calculations suggested they would enter nearest the stairwell. Arella had no illusions that her prey was hidden away in the upper recesses of his private fortress. "I go first. Follow two steps behind. I will have need of room to swing should we meet contact. We make for the stairs and do not stop until this Giles is in custody. Understood?"

Heads bobbed and nodded.

Not the disciplined soldiers who came to Andrak for the Burning Season, but they would do. "Good. Go forth and fear no darkness."

Rather than barge in and face a similar incident as the initial assault, Arella placed her gloved hand on the knob, twisted, and pushed. That the door swung open in a quiet groan surprised her. Arella suspected a trap but it was too late. With Sanice engaging the brigands from the front, she was betting on no one watching the back.

She wasn't disappointed. Arella slipped into the building and found she was alone. The others followed behind; some eager to watch the war priest in action, others too nervous to stay outside alone. They were in a small chamber with a small window. Gloomy and filled with distorted shadows. An empty barrel lay on its side, lid askew. Two chairs lacking the same layer of dust coating everything else were on opposite sides of the barrel. A guard room. She gestured for the soldiers to hang back.

Arella shifted her balance and raised her sword as she forged ahead. Two steps later a shadow displaced and she was faced with one of the defenders. The man attacked without sound, whether from training or malevolence, was unclear. The war priest barely managed to block the thrust, shoving it aside as her attacker crashed into her. They stumbled back and forth until Arella threw an elbow into his face.

Roars of pain as cartilage shattered filled the small room. Arella moved with grace and speed. The lethal combination won through his meager defense. Her sword plunged into his exposed chest. She twisted, enlarging the wound and ensuring his demise, and jerked the blade free. He slumped to the floor, still clutching his ruined nose.

"The stairs are ahead of us. Follow me," she grated.

They filed up, into the unknown. Once, so long ago she barely recalled, Arella had been afraid of such circumstances. That was before fighting the Omegri for the first time. Her encounter with the Great Enemy stripped away the innocence of youth, reforging her into a weapon of war. It was with this confidence she emerged on the second story.

The floor was wide open, half filled with crates, barrels, and boxes. Giles had to have known they were coming and was moving his stock before Kastus arrested him. Sounds of battle increased below. Her confidence buoyed and she suspected all of Giles's henchmen were engaged. Arella knew better than to trust to hope. Matters found a way to spiral out of control the moment one let their guard down.

Giles didn't disappoint. Five men were huddled on the far end of the building. Four waggled swords at her. They were unimportant. It was the fifth that drew her attention. Merchant Giles. Arella closed her eyes, brought her sword to her lips, and blew softly. The cross on her chest began to glow. The power of the Purifying Flame flowed through her. She was a weapon. An extension of the guiding power of the world.

Arella locked eyes with Giles and addressed her soldiers. "Remove the swordsmen. The merchant is mine."

Opposing forces rushed into a collision of steel, straining muscles, and exertion.

FORTY-FOUR
The Other Realm

Quinlan picked himself up, unsteadily getting back on his hands and knees. The blast of energy, while mostly contained by his magically enhanced armor, threw him across the chamber. Steam billowed off him. He felt a dull ache deep in his chest. Sparks danced in his head and it was all he could do to blink them away. The enemy was stronger than he anticipated.

"Brother Quinlan!" Donal shouted.

The novice came from the murk and raced to his side before their attacker cast a second blast. Donal helped Quinlan to his feet and they narrowly avoided being skewered by raw energy. The war priests took refuge behind a series of wooden walls partitioning the lower floor. Four stairwells dominated the center, merging into one before rising. Iron railings provided an imposing scene. A dark pit lay beneath the central stair. How deep it went and for what purpose were unknown, though Quinlan suspected the worst.

"Are you injured?" Donal asked in concern. He'd watched Quinlan take the full brunt of the initial attack moments after entering the tower.

Quinlan waved him off. "Fine. What are you doing here? Is Lizette safe?"

Donal helped him up. "She and the children are safe. Brogon Lord is watching over them. I…I felt an urging whisper you were in danger and had to return. I am sorry, Brother."

"Where is Dalem?" Quinlan asked after processing the information.

He didn't say it, but they both knew there was no chance of victory without the sclarem's power. The minions of the Omegri were ruthless and immensely powerful, regardless of how easy killing the first had been. Quinlan suspected the other two were going to prove most difficult. And they knew he was coming. Advantage was lost.

"He was on the opposite side of the stairs when I saw him last."

"We must find him. It will take all of our strength to defeat these creatures."

"War priest! Your hour dwindles. Your castles are destroyed. Your ranks depleted. The time of the Omegri rises. Come. Come and die, so you may be the first to witness their ascent."

The voice felt like nails dragging down his back. Words echoed in the deepest recesses of his mind. Quinlan felt violated. Soiled. He remembered his training and uttered a prayer. The debilitating assault faded and his strength returned.

"Ignore them, Donal. They mean to beguile us. Trick us into submission while they launch treacherous attack," he said, after seeing the haze in Donal's eyes.

Explosions rocked the far side of the chamber. Smoke and flames erupted in green, blue, and pink. Quinlan knew them for what they were. Witchcraft. Slapping Donal's shoulder, he beckoned the novice follow. They crept along the wall, circling the battleground until he had a clear vantage point. What he saw sickened him. Twin shadowed figures lashed out with bolts of power. Their energy poured from beneath the hoods of their cloaks. Vitric light seeking to devour all semblance of goodness.

He searched for any sign of weakness. Watching them, Quinlan felt the pieces of the puzzle slide into place. The Omegri used these fell creatures to facilitate their takeover of the world. He knew the Grey Wanderer took no sides but walked a wobbling line. No doubt these monsters took advantage of Brogon Lord's resurrection to enslave him. What part the children played after building the tower, remained to be seen.

"There must be a way," he whispered.

It dawned on him that the only attacks were coming from their heads. Neither bore physical weapons, nor were their hands in use. Quinlan didn't pretend to understand the workings of the Other Realm, nor could he fathom the well of power they drew from. Or how removed from it they were so long as the Omegri were still far away.

The answer became clear. Remove the heads and the enemy died. Knowing this and being able to enact it were vastly different elements. "Donal, this is the hour you must rise above all your doubts and fear. There is a weakness in these monsters and it will take our combined power to stop them. Are you prepared?"

No, but how do I admit such? "Yes, Brother," Donal said.

"Aim for the necks. Sever their heads and this ends. Use the power of the Flame sparingly. There is not much available," Quinlan explained.

A blast of white-gold power splashed over the robed creatures and burned the walls and floor. Dalem emerged from the cloud of power bruised and bleeding from a dozen cuts. Smoke lifted off his body. His hair was wild and tangled. Through it all, the sclarem bore a wild look of supreme confidence as he carried the attack to his ancient foes.

"Do not delay! Strike now," he projected his voice to the war priests.

Quinlan burst from cover. Time, he mused, dominated all. There were no battle cries. No shouted oaths of promised fury. The war priest attacked with professionalism and experience. His charge took the distracted foe unawares. The power of the Flame flared in his armor, funneling into his sword. It was weak, barely noticeable. Quinlan hoped it would be enough. He struck.

Opposite powers collided in a blinding explosion. Quinlan used all his strength and was rewarded by breaking the enemy's resistance. Blade sliced through the barrier of power and into the desiccated flesh and bone, ripping through the other side. The creature exploded. Priest and novice were thrown away in the blast.

The last of the enemy whirled, stunned by the loss of her companion. "No!"

Dalem, having closed the gap, struck. His staff slammed into the creature's face. Unimaginable powers mixed under the hood. A kaleidoscope of colors illuminated the tower. Radiance beyond words. The ground vibrated, tearing in several places. Loose planks fell from above, crashing to the floor in a hail of debris. Dalem, teeth grit, shoved harder and twisted.

The robed creature spasmed and collapsed in on herself until nothing remained but a glowing ball the size of a fist. Satisfied he had lived up to his legacy, the sclarem ground his foot down and didn't stop until naught but ash remained. The death of his final foe, the last of her kind, filled him with vigor though his body was almost broken. More of the clocktower broke apart. It was time to escape.

Dust was rising in great clouds, obscuring vision beyond a handful of meters. Dalem limped through the chamber in search of the war priests. They'd borne more of the assault than he, and for that he was regretful. But their assistance provided the necessary catalyst. His efforts were rewarded when he stumbled upon Quinlan dragging his novice toward the exit. The sclarem slid an arm under the unconscious novice's shoulder and helped carry him away while the tower collapsed.

They didn't stop moving until they were well away from the site. Quinlan slumped to the ground in time to witness the glory of the clocktower crashing down, devoured by its own malevolence. Soon only a pile of rubble remained. The task was finished. Ended like so many lives in its creation. Tears sprang forth, unwanted and uncontrolled. As rewarding as seeing the culmination of their labors was, Quinlan knew they were not yet finished.

"Do you suppose Lizette got the children out?" he asked the sclarem.

Dalem grabbed his lower jaw and shifted it back and forth. The pain radiated up his face and into the back of his skull. "There is one way to find out."

"Do you know the way?"

He did. Dalem knelt beside the fallen novice and placed three green fingertips on his forehead. Jolts of power, what little he had remaining, filled Donal with energy and soon he awakened. Dazed, confused, he had presence of mind to withhold any questions until after he took in the sight of the fallen tower.

They hobbled after Lizette and the children, the war priests trusting in Dalem's reckoning. The sclarem had done well enough for them this far. Quinlan ignored the unending sea of ash dunes. Nothing in the Other Realm was worth salvaging. It was a place of despair. They walked until their legs were sore, stopping only when they spied Brogon Lord standing atop a slow rise in the center of a ring of boulders, each the size of a man. His sword was out, point stabbed into the ground with both hands gripping the hilt. His legs were shoulder width apart and the breeze tousled his unkempt hair.

The F'talle awaited them at the crossing point. Quinlan grew nervous, suddenly fearful that a field of slaughter awaited on the opposite side of the rise. Nothing for it, the war priest climbed to the top and confronted the demon of his nightmares.

"Where are the children?" he demanded.

Maggots fell from Brogon's mouth. "Safe. They are returned to Fent."

"And the woman?"

"Also safe. Are the masters destroyed?"

Quinlan cleared his throat, the act producing new pains. "They are. The tower is in ruins."

Brogon cast a longing look over their shoulders. "I have done as you asked. Now it is yours to follow your word. Send me back to the grave."

Quinlan drew his sword but placed a hand on Brogon's shoulder. "Thank you, Brogon Lord."

The war priest swung his sword in a long arc and took the F'talle's head. The corpse collapsed in a pile of forgotten flesh and bones that dissolved before their eyes.

"It is done," Dalem said, his demeanor stoic.

Quinlan wiped his sword clean and slid it back in the sheath. "The time has come for us to return to Fent. Omegri agents there must be rooted out and removed so that their taint no longer stains the duchy."

"Step through those stones. You'll find the passage instantaneous," Dalem instructed.

Donal started forward, eager to be freed of the horrors of the Other Realm. Quinlan hesitated. "You are not coming?"

Dalem made a show of absorbing the landscape. "No. There is work yet to be done here. This is but a nexus between realms. So long as it remains unprotected, the Omegri will find new purchase in the world of life. Perhaps one day life will return here. Go, Quinlan of Andrak. You have done your kind a great service. May the rest of your days be filled with peace."

There was nothing left to say. He had come to know the sclarem well enough to know that no amount of speech would change his mind. Clenching his teeth, the war priest nodded his goodbye and joined Donal through the portal. Their time in the Other Realm had come to an end. Alone again, Dalem clucked his tongue several times before turning back toward the site of the battle. He had much to do before the war began.

FORTY-FIVE

Home

They arrived under cover of night. A column of armed and armored soldiers with full gear and weapons. The village of Palis was caught unawares, for the few on night watch were rounded up and subdued as the occupation commenced. Those soldiers who'd initially arrived with Captain Thep and had yet to receive recall orders responded quickly. Like wraiths, squads dismounted and spread throughout Palis. The village would never be the same.

Doors were kicked open. Those few servants awake were cast aside and apprehended. Their mouths gagged, hands bound. Houses were searched without regard for intimacy or personal affects. Pots lay shattered, their contents spilled recklessly. The soldiers were gruff, weary from endless days on alert. This one task provided inspiration of purpose. An ending of weeks of stress.

Elder Mugh was the first to be dragged from his bed and into the street. He sputtered and wept. An old man bereft of pride, struggling to comprehend what was happening. The soldiers remained tight lipped, for it was not their place to explain the will of their Baron. Too weak to escape, Mugh stumbled to his knees, where he was allowed to remain until a sergeant barked. Rough hands pulled him up and dragged him away to the waiting jail wagon.

There was no pleasure exhibited by the armored men and women. They performed a task. Nothing more. Elder Deana's home was ransacked next. A show of force was made, for Constable Kastus was assured of her treachery. She was bruised and stripped of dignity even as she strode haughtily through her front door. Deana defied them, begged them to abuse her for the sins of her pride. Chin thrust out, back stiff, she marched to the wagon.

Chains were woven through the door. Locks clasped. The prisoners stared wide-eyed at their captors. Mugh whimpered, realizing the culmination of his life had been reduced to shame. His heart expired before arriving in Kastus's prison. Deana remained defiant, for she was ever a prideful woman.

The captain of soldiers mounted and addressed them, "Elders Mugh and Deana, you are accused of treason against the duchy and sentenced to immediate trial in Fent. All you own has been seized in the name of the Baron."

Her gaze was filled with vitriol, lingering on his back long after the wagon began to trundle away. The scouring of Palis began in earnest. No lead was ignored as the men and women sworn to service confiscated every asset and owning of the former Elders. Martial law was established in Palis. It would remain for the time being. At least until Baron Einos was satisfied it had been cleansed of heresy.

A great feast was ordered. The citizens of Fent celebrated. They celebrated the return of their children and the ending of the once dead man. A host of plagues was ended and the promise of normalcy sprung anew. Autumn was ending. Yet for the rising cold and lack of life in the world surrounding, mirth was rampant across the duchy. Baron Einos ordered a week of celebration, for his tiny band of heroes had succeeded far beyond the limits of imagination.

Many of the stolen children were returned to their homes. Lizette ensured those who were from other duchies received care until loved ones could come to claim them. Yet for each reunion there was a bitter finality for other families. Their children were gone, never to return. Rather than wallow in grief, Lizette mourned Tabith and resolved to never allow such to happen to anyone ever again.

All was not without concern. There had been no sign of the war priest or the strange sclarem. Einos began to fear the worst. He sat upon his throne, absorbed in doubt. Life was many things, but it was seldom fair. The Baron wasn't especially fond of Quinlan. The war priest lacked humanity, rendering him distant on the best of occasion. There was an aura of mortality surrounding the man. One Einos failed to penetrate. None of that absolved the Baron from his feelings of guilt for allowing Quinlan to enter the Other Realm.

Violent images flashed each time he closed his eyes, tired as they were. Men and beast slaughtered in the streets of Gunn. Lives lost at his command. Fent had not been to war during his lifetime and the notion that so many people ended, gnawed heavily on his conscience. The true price of a leader revealed at last. Einos was no warrior and despite having fighters like Sava to carry his banner, lacked the stomach for combat.

His army continued to train. They lacked a foe but retained a newfound sense of urgency. Wounds began to heal. Weapons were reforged. Orders came down from the castle that a new battalion was to be raised. Fent would no longer be caught unawares by dark powers. Einos vowed to protect his people, by any means necessary.

Mind disturbed by a hundred opposing thoughts, Einos pinched his nose and winced. He couldn't help but feel responsible for all that had transpired. A negligent ruler mired in ignorance as the world schemed around him. That his family was somehow involved soured his stomach. How could his in-laws prove so deceptive, subversive against the crown, without outright betrayal? They weren't inherently bad people. But greed was a powerful tempter. He hoped the price of destroying a noble family was worth the suffering they risked.

Einos knew his hands were tied, however. Arresting them would not only spark revolt among the larger noble houses but sunder his marriage and destabilize the throne. Fent would unravel despite his best intentions. It was a guilt he refused to suffer, even while knowing there was a time for confrontation with Aneth. He must address the issue with his wife, and pray she was ignorant of the situation or that she saw matters in similar light.

That was for another time. Now he was needed to provide inspiration to the people. The feast was approaching and with it the pomp of celebration. Soldiers who'd exhibited extreme bravery were to be honored. Sergeant Sava, Nils, Alfar, and others were presented Fent's highest medal for bravery. Thep was promoted to Commander for his actions and given responsibility for raising the new units. Likewise, Sergeant Sanice was appointed his counterpart.

Arella disturbed his solitude. The war priest's boots echoed as she marched to the base of his throne. She didn't wait for him to look up. "Baron, the time has come for me to return to Castle Andrak. There is no more I can do here."

"What of Quinlan?" he asked, eyes closed.

"His loss is regrettable, but such is the way of life. We are not the masters of external forces," she replied. "His name will be recorded in our annals and he will be hailed a hero. There is little more that can be done."

She turned to leave.

"Thank you," he called to her back. "Your assistance rooting out the treason of Giles was most appreciated."

"I did what was necessary, Baron."

There was no pride in her actions that day. Merely duty. Arella captured Giles and forced confessions—through manners Einos was unwilling to discover. Mind broken by arcane power, Giles admitted to the murder of Tender Cannandal, the turning of the Elders of Palis, and establishing a quiet empire to usurp the rightful rule of Dukes. His admission of being a servant of the Omegri, lured by their whispered promises of untold wealth. Giles played no part in the resurrection of Brogon Lord but had profited from the once dead man's actions.

For all those crimes, Einos could not see fit to execute him. Giles had been a puppet, nothing more. Whatever magics Arella used ruined his mind, rendering him into a drooling mess. Kastus, taking unusual pity, locked him away with explicit instructions for care. Giles languished in his cell for a brief time before passing on the last day of the year. His crimes at last atoned for. He was buried in an unmarked grave.

Einos watched the war priest disappear and decided his solitude was pointless. No leader worth his salt remained hidden from the people who risked their lives for him. His stride lacked conviction, however, for he had not yet come to terms with his loss. A commotion in the main hallway stole his attention away from those miserable thoughts. Servants and menials clapped and cheered. No, not for him, it was for another. Curious, he lingered in the doorway so as to catch a glimpse. His surprise was immediate.

Lizette stood in the center of the throng, tightly hugging a weary man in ash covered clothes. Quinlan! The war priest had survived and returned home. Perhaps there was hope for a peaceful future after all. Curious, but unwilling to disturb the moment, Einos craned his neck and listened.

"I thought you lost," Lizette said through mumbled weeps. Her grip around Quinlan tightened. Not from love or misplaced affection, but from gratitude.

Quinlan struggled not to smile. "It was a dangerous path, but we succeeded. The tower is destroyed and the passage between realms guarded."

He went on to explain how the shadow masters were destroyed and their terrible work with them. How Brogon Lord met his final demise and the refusal of Dalem to leave. Donal stayed back, unwilling to accept the adulation of the crowd. A tear sprang to Lizette's eye, for she had come to learn Brogon was not entirely evil. A shred of decency remained in his corpse. That was the only way she convinced him to lead the children to safety. Knowing he was at peace lightened her heart.

"Thank you, Quinlan. For everything," she whispered, so that only he heard.

To his surprise, he hugged her back. There were no words to express his emotions. Numerous children had been rescued, but nothing he did would bring her daughter back. Lizette understood that better than anyone. It was personal burden she would use to give meaning to her life. Accepting a full-time position in the Baron's employ, Lizette went on to become one of the most influential women in Fent history. She found fame during the Northern War, returning home to found an orphanage that specialized in caring for the children of fallen soldiers. She never remarried nor had another child.

They unembraced, each going separate ways. Quinlan spied Einos and made his report. The Baron's shoulders slumped with the news of what happened in the Other Realm. His nightmare was over. The duchy was at peace again. Einos remained in power for another thirty years, surviving wars and plague. Fent prospered, eventually becoming one of the most powerful of the duchies. His bloodline continued to rule.

"What will you do now?" Einos asked.

Quinlan's eyes softened. "Return to Andrak. My work is finished and there is much I must discuss with the Lord General. It has been an honor to serve you, Baron Einos."

"The honor has been mine, Brother Quinlan," Einos returned. "Fent owes your Order a debt of unpayable gratitude."

"The Burning Season approaches. Repay it by sending quality knights to stand the walls," Quinlan replied. He made his excuses and left the duchy of Fent behind.

The road back to Andrak was serene compared to both the ride west and his trials in Fent. The Majj remained hidden in the Indolense Permital, no doubt preparing their clans for the coming war that was prophesized. He caught up to Arella less than a day's ride east and the two shared experiences. Each was envious of the other, secretly wishing they'd traded places.

Halfway back to Andrak, they made camp for the night. Dinner was eaten and bed rolls laid out. Quinlan swallowed the last of his water and gave Donal an appraising look. "Donal, you did well in Fent. Your actions reflect the highest traditions of the Order."

"Thank you, Brother Quinlan," Donal was embarrassed. He seldom received praise for a job well done. That Quinlan recognized him now spoke volumes.

"When we return to Andrak I am going to recommend you be tested for promotion. It has become time for you to wear the colors of a war priest," Quinlan finished.

Shocked and pleased, Donal Sawq bobbed his head with thinly restrained joy. Years of dedication and training were about to pay off. He didn't remember the rest of the ride home.

Christian Warren Freed

OTHER BOOKS BY CHRISTIAN WARREN FREED

WHERE HAVE ALL
THE ELVES
GONE?

CHRISTIAN WARREN FREED

Everyone knows Elves don't exist. Or do they? Daniel Thomas spent years making a career of turning his imagination into the reality of bestselling fantasy novels. But times are tough. No one wants to read about elves and dragons anymore. Daniel learns this firsthand when his agent flatly says no to his latest and, what he deems, to be greatest novel yet. Dissatisfied with the turn to zombies and vampire lovers, he takes his manuscript and heads out to confront his agent.

His world changes when he finds his agent dying on the floor of her office. Too late to help, he watches as her dead body disintegrates into a pile of ash and dust. Daniel doesn't have time to ponder what just happened as a band of assassins breaks in, forcing him to flee to the Citadel and the home of the king of the high elves in order to survive. Daniel soon discovers that all of the creatures he once thought he imagined actually exist and are living among us. His revelation comes at a price however, as he is drawn into a murder-mystery that will push him to the edge of sanity and show him things no human has witnessed in centuries.

Everyone knows Elves don't exist. Or do they? Daniel Thomas spent years making a career of turning his imagination into the reality of best selling fantasy novels. But times are tough. No one wants to read about elves and dragons anymore. Daniel learns this firsthand when his agent flatly says no to his latest and, what he deems, to be greatest novel yet. Dissatisfied with the turn to zombies and vampire lovers, he takes his manuscript and heads out to confront his agent.

His world changes when he finds his agent dying on the floor of her office. Too late to help, he watches as her dead body disintegrates into a pile of ash and dust. Daniel doesn't have time to ponder what just happened as a band of assassins breaks in, forcing him to flee to the Citadel and the home of the king of the high elves to survive. Daniel soon discovers that all of the creatures he once thought he imagined actually exist and are living among us. His revelation comes at a price however, as he is drawn into a murder-mystery that will push him to the edge of sanity and show him things no human has witnessed in centuries.

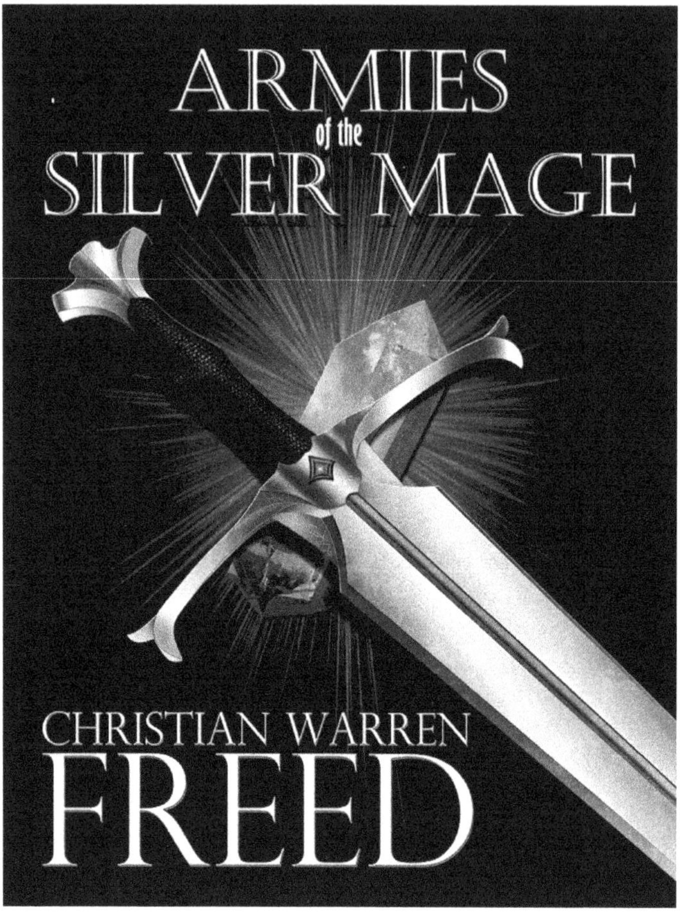
ARMIES
of the
SILVER MAGE
CHRISTIAN WARREN
FREED

Malweir was once governed by the order of Mages, bringers of peace and light. Centuries past and the lands prospered. But all was not well. Unknown to most, one mage desired power above all else. He turned his will to the banished Dark Gods and brought war to the free lands. Only a handful of mages survived the betrayal and the Silver Mage was left free to twist the darker races to his bidding. The only thing he needs to complete his plan and rule the world forever are the four shards of the crystal of Tol Shere.

Having spent most of their lives dreaming about leaving their sleepy village and travelling the world, Delin Kerny and Fennic Attleford never thought that one day they would be forced to flee their town to save their lives. Everything changes when they discover the fabled Star Silver sword and learn that there are some who want the weapon for themselves. Hunted by a ruthless mercenary, the boys run from Fel Darrins and are forced into the adventure they only dreamed about.

Ever ashamed of the horrors his kind let loose on the world the last mage, Dakeb, lives his life in shadows. The only thing keeping him alive is his quest to stop the Silver Mage from reassembling the crystal. His chance finally comes through the hearts and wills of Delin and Fennic. Dakeb bestows upon them the crystal shard, entrusting them with the one thing capable of restoring peace to Malweir.

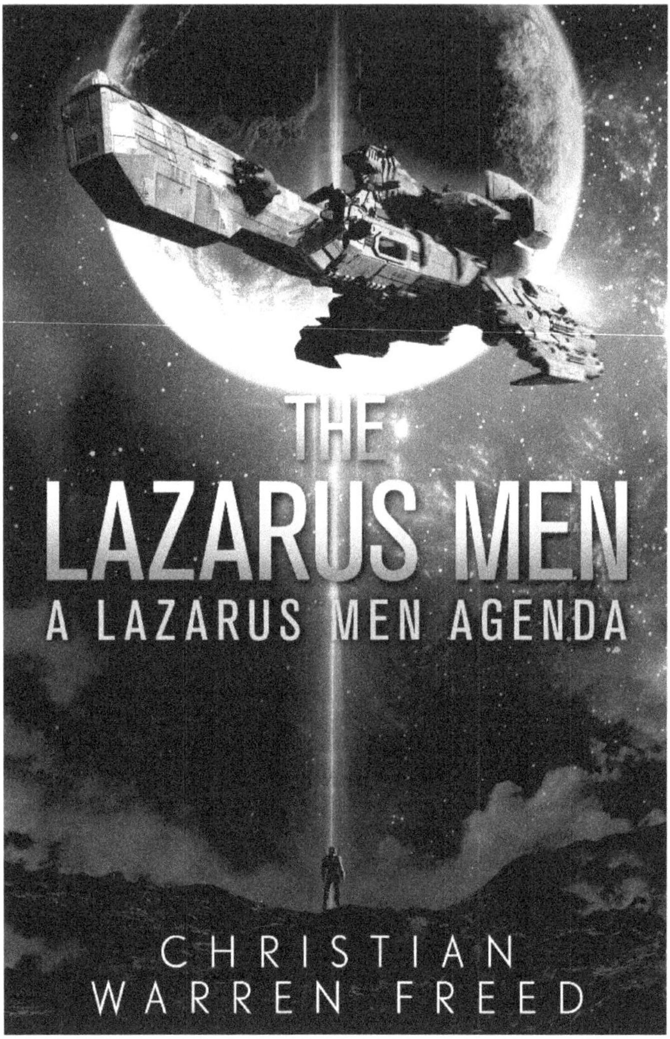
THE
LAZARUS MEN
A LAZARUS MEN AGENDA
CHRISTIAN
WARREN FREED

It is the 23rd century. Humankind has reached the stars, building a tentative empire across a score of worlds. Earth's central government rules weakly as several worlds continue their efforts toward independence. Shadow organizations hide in the midst of the political infighting. Their manifestations of power and influence are beholden only to the highest bidder. The most powerful/insidious/secret of these, The Lazarus Men, has existed for decades, always working outside of morality's constraints. Led by the enigmatic Mr. Shine, their agents are hand selected from the worst humanity has to offer and available for the right price.

Gerald LaPlant lives an ordinary life on Old Earth. That life is thrown into turmoil on the night he stumbles upon the murder of what appears to be a street thief. Fleeing into the night, Gerald finds himself hunted by agents of Roland McMasters, an extremely powerful man dissatisfied with the current regime and with designs on ruling his own empire. To do so, McMasters needs the fabled Eye of Karakzaheim, a map leading to immeasurable wealth. Unknown to either man, Mr. Shine has deployed agents in search of the same artifact and will stop at nothing to obtain it.

Running for his life, Gerald quickly becomes embroiled in a conspiracy reaching deep into levels of government that he never imagined existed. His every move is hounded by McMasters' agents and the Lazarus Men. His adventures take him away from the relative safety of Old Earth across the stars and into the heart of McMasters' fledgling empire. The future of the Earth Alliance at stake. If Gerald has any hope of surviving and helping save the alliance he must rely on his wits and awakened instincts while foregoing the one thing that could get him killed more quickly than the rest: trust.

The Children of Never

BIO

Christian W. Freed was born in Buffalo, N.Y. more years ago than he would like to remember. After spending more than 20 years in the active duty US Army he has turned his talents to writing. Since retiring, he has gone on to publish more than 20 science fiction and fantasy novels as well as his combat memoirs from his time in Iraq and Afghanistan. His first book, Hammers in the Wind, has been the #1 free book on Kindle 4 times and he holds a fancy certificate from the L Ron Hubbard Writers of the Future Contest.

Passionate about history, he combines his knowledge of the past with modern military tactics to create an engaging, quasi-realistic world for the readers. He graduated from Campbell University with a degree in history and a Masters of Arts degree in Digital Communications from the University of North Carolina at Chapel Hill. He currently lives outside of Raleigh, N.C. and devotes his time to writing, his family, and their two Bernese Mountain Dogs. If you drive by you might just find him on the porch with a cigar in one hand and a pen in the other. You can find out more about his work by clicking on any one of the social media icons listed below. You can find out more about his work by following him on:

Facebook: @https://www.facebook.com/ChristianFreed
Twitter: @ChristianWFreed
Instagram: @ christianwarrenfreed

Like what you read? Let him know with an email or review.

warfighterbooks@gmail.com

CPSIA information can be obtained
at www.ICGtesting.com
Printed in the USA
JSHW032337270323
39464JS00009BA/190

9 781734 907513